P9-CFQ-692

THE BOOK OF
BEASTS

John May & Michael Marten

THE VIKING PRESS NEW YORK

Published in 1983 by The Viking Press
625 Madison Avenue, New York, N.Y. 10022

Published simultaneously in Canada by
Penguin Books Canada Limited

Library of Congress Catalog Card Number: 82–40374

ISBN: 0-670-17915-9

Filmset in England by JH Graphics Ltd., Reading
Printed in Spain by Mateu Cromo, Madrid
Set in Baskerville

Contents

The Book of Beasts is illustrated by Philip Hood,
Norman Weaver, Stephen Lings, John Woodcock,
Terry Oakes, Robert Morton, Elizabeth Goss, Sarah De'Ath
Linda Garland, David Webb, Ray Winder, Peter Jones
John Rignall, Roger Garland, Catherine Bradbury,
Tim Hayward, Peter Boman, John Chesterman,
Richard Sparks, Milne Stebbing Illustration
and Stuart Bodek.
Text arranged by John Chesterman.

Introduction

In the beginning was the word, and the word was most probably the name of an animal.

That is only speculation, of course, but one of the first books to be written, and one of the earliest extant works in Sanskrit (which itself is one of the first languages) was *The Panchatantra*, and that was certainly about animals. In fact, it consisted of the five collections of animal fables that formed the basis of most Hindu mythology. It was also the forerunner of a unique form of literature, which included the Book of Revelations and eventually led to Beatrix Potter and science fiction and this book.

Animals were the first metaphors and there is no question that they shaped the common culture from which we all come. Many of these origins were lost in thousands of years of oral culture, but from the invention of writing onwards they were kept alive in books of animal stories.

The Greeks and Romans gave the bestiary its classic form of a catalogue of wild beasts and curious animals from the frontiers of the empires, and beyond. Most of it was based on rumours, intended to be as sensational as possible, and was very popular.

The first transformation occurred in the Middle Ages, when the Christians had a monopoly of all the media and decided to use bestiaries as propaganda against the ancient animal cults that still flourished over most of Europe. They did this by inventing a kind of religious sci-fi, full of monsters and chimeras from Revelations, with some lurid embellishments of their own and a heavy moral caption to every picture.

The myths looked a little thin when the world was gradually explored in the fifteenth and sixteenth centuries and people discovered there really were monsters in distant countries, and some of them, like elephants and polar bears and giraffes, were actually brought back home and put on show.

The recording of the exotic animals and plants became a serious profession during the seventeenth century, and by the eighteenth it was as accurate and important as map-making. The bestiary had suddenly become a textbook.

But by then it had branched out in a new direction. When printing was invented, the church's monopoly was broken and publishers wanted something lighter for the general public than religious tomes. The first thing they turned to was the bestiary – but with a difference. Monsters were no longer in fashion (and were considered rather vulgar, because the entertainment industry had taken them over as exhibitions and freak shows). Instead they returned to the ancient folk tales (a part of the old animistic cults that the Church never quite suppressed) and brought them up to date. The stories were cleaned up, where necessary, and the characters were based on familiar animals – foxes and geese, ants and grasshoppers – who spoke and behaved like human beings. The morals were reduced to a few commonsense clichés – and the traditional children's stories were born.

However, the reprinting of *Aesop's Fables* and La Fontaine's new stories was originally designed for adults, and it was not until much later that they were relegated to the nursery, along with Hans Andersen and the Brothers Grimm.

The tradition of children's bestiaries continued through Victorian times, until they were given a new and exciting form by the realism of Rudyard Kipling, in his *Just So Stories*, and the surrealism of H. G. Wells who brilliantly translated the mythical monsters into science fiction. Sci-fi still contains this element of mythical beasts, both organic and mechanical (though they are all based on sadly earth-bound models of animals and technology).

Since then the two elements have remained separate. They both started out as short stories, which was in keeping with the idea of the bestiary as an anthology, but it was not long before there were full-length novels about animals (from Jack London, through *Animal Farm* to *Watership Down*) and machine monsters (*War of the Worlds* to *Star Wars*).

When they were turned into films, the nature of the medium separated the two still further. The monster myths were an irresistible challenge to studio effects men, whilst exotic animals were so naturally photogenic that documentary teams were sent out on safari to film them in the wild. So while the monsters became tamer and more predictable, the images of wildlife became increasingly fantastic and surprising.

Real life had finally proved, beyond any doubt, that it was stranger than fiction.

But what had happened to the traditional bestiary? The only place where animal fables still flourished was, curiously enough, in cartoons. In fact, cartoon films have depended on the children's stories of talking animals, with a few sanitized dragons thrown in, ever since they began. But they miss the essential ingredient of bestiaries – that the animals are (or might be) real. King Kong could be straight from the pages of a bestiary; Bambi and Dumbo are certainly not.

The only places where a sense of awe survived were the 'Amazing Facts' columns in corners of newspapers, and in meaningless books of statistics about the Longest, the Shortest and the Tallest, where it is only the dimensions that matter, not the mystery of the living animal.

So we have attempted to write a bestiary in the traditional sense. To reawaken a feeling of wonder and imagination by cataloguing the rare and curious animals from forgotten corners of the world where cameras cannot go, species that no one is sure actually exist, and by describing in words the things that can only be described in words, the odd facts that give you a new perspective on what you *thought* was a familiar animal, or astonishing new phenomena that have recently been discovered.

There is no need to spell out any morals. It is obvious that natural laws have nothing to do with 'moral values', and the disastrous results of confusing them is reflected on every page. It is why we see ourselves as 'different', why we think of animals as 'ours', and why nobody has ever included *himself* in a bestiary.

It is a delusion we can no longer afford, because the unavoidable fact is that we are the strangest monster of them all.

How could we ignore the existence of an animal that, by the turn of the century, will be eliminating the other fauna on earth at the rate of a species an hour? A species that has already managed to by-pass the system, take over evolution, destroy a third of the natural ecology without any idea of the consequences, and is on the point of creating its own life-forms?

One way or another it affects every creature on earth, and its influence on other species – the relationship between them and us – is a theme that appears and reappears throughout these stories.

So the moral is there, and apart from the blessing (or curse) of hindsight, there is only one difference between *The Book of Beasts* and its predecessors. We did not have to invent a single thing.

J.M. M.M.
London, 1982

A

Aardvark

PHILIP HOOD

A is for Animals

'The possibilities of existence run so deeply into the extravagant that there is scarcely any concept too extraordinary for Nature to realize.'

– Louis Agassiz

There are 31 kinds of animals. Or, rather, scientists have devised 31 categories, or *phyla*, to help them keep track of the teeming variety of species. But it is an untidy fit. Like overstuffed drawers that will not close properly, animals keep falling out of one group into another and there are always one or two left over.

This is hardly surprising when you consider the numbers involved. The basic phyla range from sponges (with 10,000 species) to mammals (with 4,500), but they include, for instance, a whole universe of worms. Tongue worms, hair worms, tape worms, thread worms, ribbon worms, acorn worms.

Then there are the tardigrades, rotifers, slugs, starfish, moss animals, and the whole teeming world of micro-organisms on which the rest of life depends.

We seldom see these 'lower' forms of life because they are so small (though the longest animal in the world happens to be a worm) and they usually live underground, underwater, or inside other plants and animals (including ourselves).

The creatures we usually think of as 'animals' come from just three phyla: the molluscs (*mollusca*) which include the oyster and the octopus; the arthropods (*arthropoda*), an enormous group which includes scorpions, spiders and insects; and organisms with a central nervous system (*chordata*) which include everything else – birds, fish, bats, rats, pigs, porcupines and ourselves.

The chordata are divided into two groups, according to whether or not they have a backbone. Those that do, the *vertebrates*, are subdivided into eight classes: *agnaths* (jawless fishes), *placoderms* (extinct armoured fishes), *chrondrichthyes* (sharks and rays), *osteichthyes* (bony fishes, i.e. most other fish), *amphibia* (frogs, toads and salamanders), *reptiles* (snakes, lizards and dinosaurs), *aves* (birds), and *mammals* (ourselves).

However you divide them up, and whatever labels you give them, it is this profusion of beasts whose marvellous differences and similarities we celebrate.

But first we need to adjust our focus to the widest possible angle in order to get our bearings and a sense of perspective. What are the dimensions of this amazing zoo?

The Earth

The habitable surface of the earth consists of 317 million cubic miles of ocean and 57½ million square miles of land. The terrain is so varied – with mountains, deserts, oceans, plains, rivers, lakes, forests and wetlands, glaciers and fertile valleys, long coasts and shorelines (which are steadily lengthening as the continents drift apart), hot, humid tropics and bleak, oxygen-poor uplands – that it provides for most, if not all, the potential forms of carbohydrate life.

Life

Life on earth is made up of a network or organic systems which has been called the *Scala Naturae* or 'great chain of being'. No part of it is independent. It is one thing; and, as far as our experience goes, it is unique. We may speculate about other forms of life, but this is the only example of a planetary bio-mass we have yet discovered.

Since we have nothing to compare it with (except itself) and since we are part of it, any attempt to understand it is a voyage of self-discovery.

Life on Earth

After 3,500 million years of evolution, it is estimated that there are now 3×10^{33}, or 3,000 quintillion (or 3,000,000,000,000,000,000,000, 000,000,000,000) living things on earth.

Of these, 75 per cent are bacteria, and 0.000,000, 000,000,000,000,00013 per cent are human beings.

The Species

It has been estimated that there are between 5 and 10 million different species of plants, animals and other life-forms on earth. Only a small percentage of these have so far been identified, but they include 1,300,000 species of animals and 300,000 species of plants.

Only a third of the estimated three million species of insects have been given a name.

Incredible though it seems, human beings are now destroying species at a faster rate than they can be identified.

The Most Successful Species

The most successful form of animal life are undoubtedly insects. They have a head start of 1,000 million years of evolution, occupy a wider range of habitat, and outnumber us by twelve million to one.

A column of air one mile square, beginning 50 feet above the ground and extending up to 14,000 feet, contains an average of 25 million insects – as well as large quantities of seeds, bacteria and pollen known as 'aerial plankton'. Most of these are light-bodied insects such as small flies, wasps and lice; but wingless insects, mites and spiders travelling on carpets of gossamer have been found at high altitude.

The most successful life-form of any kind are bacteria. They can withstand 6.5 million roentgens of radiation (ten thousand times the fatal dose for humans); they can survive boiling acids, and the immense pressures in deep oceans and, as NASA reported in 1967, they have been found in the rarefied atmosphere on the edge of space, at a height of 135,000 feet.

The Largest Animal

The smallest animal is a single cell. The largest living animal (and probably the largest there ever has been) is the blue whale. The record is presently held by a female blue whale measuring 113 feet 6 inches. Blue whales (along with rorquals and some other species) average out at approximately 1½ tons per foot in length, so this creature must have weighed over 170 tons. In terms of other animals it is equivalent to 35 elephants, or 2,380 human beings, or 136 million pygmy shrews (the smallest living mammals).

The Fastest Animal

The slowest are species, such as the tardigrade, that are capable of suspended animation. The fastest are more difficult to define, because few of the claims are properly timed or substantiated. The fastest physical action of any organism yet recorded is the wing-beat of a common midge (*Forcipomyia*). It normally beats its wings 57,000 times a minute, but is capable of increasing to a rate of 133,000 times a minute, which represents a muscular cycle of contraction and expansion in 0.00045, or 1/2218th of a second.

The fastest muscular cycle in human beings is the blink of an eye, which takes about 1/25th second.

The Human Biomass

At the moment, there are about 4,250,000,000 people on earth. They occupy a volume of 10 billion cubic feet, and weigh about 115 million tons, with an annual turnover (by births and deaths) of two million tons, and a net annual increase of one million tons.

This is nothing, compared to the rest of the bio-mass. The insects still outweigh us by three to one.

These are just a few of the parameters of animal life, but they give no idea of the variety, ingenuity, beauty, eccentricity, complexity, mystery, intelligence, drama and downright oddness of what lies between.

This is a personal anthology, arranged in roughly alphabetical order (which should not be taken too seriously), of examples that we found surprising, unnerving, unusual or funny. They range from group portraits of a whole species, to some interesting detail of biological engineering. But along the way we have chosen some of the individual animals we would include in our own private collection. A hypothetical zoo of creatures that for some reason have been overlooked, underrated or misunderstood, and deserve a better hearing. There are stories, anecdotes, an elegy or two for animals we will never see again. We have made no distinction between wild animals and domestic ones, large or small, friend or enemy, for they are all animals, and each one has a story. It is, in other words, a book of beasts.

PHILIP HOOD

Aardwolf

Aardvark and Aardwolf

The beginning of the alphabet is rich in possibilities like the avahi and angwantibo, aate and agouti*. But when you open a dictionary, the very first page is dominated by a group of animals discovered by the nineteenth-century Dutch settlers in South Africa – the aardvark (or earth-pig), the aardwolf (or earth-wolf), and the vulture they called an aasvogel (carrion-bird). The names are irresistible and the aardvark, in particular, has earned a place in any bestiary as an evolutionary one-off. A creature that, in the words of the zoologist Ivan Sanderson, 'stands quite alone in the mammalian tree of life, like a single green leaf caught adventitiously in a spider's web'.

It's a large, solitary animal, up to 6 foot long, which is found throughout Africa south of the Sahara, from the bare mountains of Abyssinia to the tropical savannah. It lives on termites, and its hearing is so sharp it can tell whether a mound is occupied by listening for the sound of insects beneath the earth.

Aardvarks are nocturnal burrowers and when they are overtaken by daylight in the open they dig themselves into the ground with powerful claws. Alternatively, as they are immune to termite bites, they often curl up inside the mound itself, with insects running all over them.

They are not related to any living species. The trombone-like snout resembles that of an anteater, but in the important details like toes and teeth they are quite different. There again, most animals can be traced back to an ancestral form, say five or ten million years ago. But before aardvarks there were just more aardvarks.

** A woolly Madagascan lemur; a kind of African bushbaby; the small crustaceans eaten by Atlantic whales; and a nervous South American guinea-pig that can leap 20 feet from a sitting start.*

Their fossilized remains have been found in rocks sixty million years old, and they could be even older. Recent discoveries in Wyoming suggest that they originally evolved when the continents were still joined. It is not the only animal to retain its identity down the years, but the aardvark may prove to be a descendant of one of the early mammals which first took over from the dinosaurs.

The aardwolf is an entirely different animal and only finds itself alongside the aardvark by an alphabetical accident. Yet, by some fluke, its behaviour is so similar it could be a mirror image.

Like the aardvark, it is a nocturnal termite eater, though it is less fussy about its diet and also eats eggs. It inhabits the same areas of southern Africa – and even sleeps in old aardvark holes – and it has an equally mysterious ancestry. Though it looks like a hyena there are basic anatomical differences, and the aardwolf seems to be an indeterminate species which is evolving (backwards, as it happens) into a form of civet cat.

Addra and Addax

A is definitely for Africa, and a little way down the list is this pair of beautiful and rare Saharan antelopes. The addra is a white, long-legged gazelle with elegantly curved horns. The addax, or screw-horn, is a grey animal whose horns, which can grow to three or four feet long, corkscrew up from a curious black hood over its head.

They are true desert animals and (unlike camels) can last indefinitely without water. They obtain all the moisture they need from vegetation, though they will drink gallons when they get the chance.

Herds of addax once roamed from the Nile to the Atlantic, but Italian soldiers machine-gunned vast numbers in World War II and they are now reduced to about 5000 animals, wandering in scattered groups in Mauritania and Mali.

Addax

Aestivation and Hibernation

There's more to hibernation than bears in caves and the family hamster disappearing into the back of its cage. When the going gets tough, many animals instinctively curl up and go to sleep till things get better. It is a basic escape mechanism that can mean the difference between life and death when you are suffocating in solid ice or being baked alive in dried mud.

When this happens in winter, to avoid the cold, it is *hibernation*; when it occurs in summer, because of the heat or lack of water, it is called *aestivation*. In both cases the animal's temperature approaches the ambient temperature, to conserve as much energy as possible.

The Hibernating Bird

One of the few birds known to hibernate is the whippoorwill. Its body temperature drops from the normal 102°F to 65°F, its breathing stops, and its digestive processes cease. The American Indians have known about this phenomenon for centuries, but it was not accepted by modern science until the 1940s.

The Long Sleep

Snails can aestivate for a year or more, if it is too dry. One African snail that had been on exhibition in the British Museum came to life and began crawling around when the humidity rose, and a record aestivation of twenty years has been claimed.

Fish out of Water

Burrowing fish often find themselves stranded when lakes and streams dry up, and the only way they can avoid death by dehydration is to seal themselves in a capsule, like an astronaut, and reduce their life-support system to the minimum.

The goby of the Ganges sleeps so soundly it can even be handled without waking it up, and the fish fits so tightly into its mud burrow there is no room for its waste, which has to be stored internally. The South American lungfish chooses a specially impervious clay that sticks to its body and helps to reduce the moisture loss – and the African species go one better by packing themselves in temporary skins of wax paper.

Freshwater fish also hibernate, and since their bodies freeze several degrees below the freezing point of water, they can be encased in ice and still survive.

Carp and certain other species may spend months dormant, buried at the bottom of ponds where they live on stored energy. Their oxygen requirements are provided by a curious property of water. When the temperature drops below 39°F, water is at its heaviest and the oxygen-rich layer sinks to the bottom, providing the hibernating fish with enough to keep them alive.

Frogs, like fish, burrow in mud to hibernate and absorb oxygen directly through their skins. As long as the ice does not reach their hearts, they can survive.

Snakes and Lizards

Snakes sometimes hibernate together in large groups. In America, northern species of rattle snakes often return to the same site, or *hibernaculum*, each winter. Prairie rattlesnakes have been observed in groups of 200–300, and in one case over 1000. They will share their hibernaculum peaceably with non-venomous snakes, and even with burrowing owls and prairie dogs (one of their favourite prey when they are not narcotized by the cold).

Other hibernating American snakes include the garter snake, black snake and copperhead. Many tropical snakes, including boas and anacondas, cannot tolerate severe heat. Anacondas bury themselves in river mud and aestivate.

The chuckwalla, an American lizard, crawls into a crevice and inflates itself with air until it is firmly lodged, before hibernating. Unfortunately, certain Indians regard it as a delicacy, especially when game is scarce in winter. They merely push a sharp stick into the chuckwalla's hole, deflate it, and drag it out for roasting.

The Automatic Thermostat

Zoologists now agree that there is no physiological difference between aestivating and hibernating. Each animal responds to a different temperature, but the mechanism seems the same, and there is no clear demarcation between the two states.

The Mohave ground squirrel, for instance, is completely dormant when its body temperature is as high as 80.6°F, whereas most hibernators do not become torpid until their body temperature falls below 50–55°F. The higher their temperature during aestivation, the more easily animals are aroused. Hibernating bears, for example, sleep quite lightly, and are liable to suddenly wake up and charge an intruder. Many small rodents, on the other hand, sleep so deeply that they can be picked up, and even tossed about, without being disturbed.

The Ai

The ai, or three-fingered sloth (*Bradypus*) has an unusually shaggy coat which not only supports a population of cockroach-like moths, scuttling around in the dense hair, but carries some of the oddest markings of any animal.

The individual hairs have pits in them that support an algal growth which can turn the animal bright green; while between its shoulder-blades are two black, kidney-shaped marks, surrounded by a white and yellow sun-burst – said to resemble the clusters of flowers on the wild paw-paw tree, on which it feeds.

The Albatross

At length did cross an Albatross,
Through the fog it came,
As if it had been a Christian soul,
We hailed it in God's name.

It ate the food it ne'er did eat
And round and round it flew.
The ice did split with thunderfit,
The helmsman steered us through.

In mist or cloud, on mast or shroud,
It perched for vespers nine;
While all the night, through fog smoke white,
Glimmered the white Moon-shine.

– Samuel Taylor Coleridge,
'Rhyme of the Ancient Mariner'

When a fledgling albatross leaves its nest on the shores of the Arctic, it launches itself on a flight that can last up to two years. The whole world is its environment and, together with the whale, it is free to roam from pole to pole. So it is not surprising that sailors, who came upon the giant bird a thousand miles from land, regarded it with awe as some kind of sea spirit.

The wandering albatross begins life as a massive 21 ounce (588g) egg, and takes up to three months to hatch – longer than any other bird. The adults have the largest wingspan (almost 12 feet) and more wing feathers (88 compared to an average of 66) than any other living species.

They can glide for six days without beating their wings, and can even sleep in mid-air while gliding at speeds of 19–35 mph.

Their huge size and weight (over 26 lb) demands a constant diet of fish, squid and crustaceans. There is even a documented case, during a naval battle off the Falkland Islands in World War I, when albatrosses attacked men in the water with their 8-inch (20-cm) beaks.

Young albatross taking off

The Ambrosia Beetle

Ambrosia was the food of the classical Greek gods, which was supposed to give them eternal youth and beauty. It is difficult to trace the myth to an actual substance, but it is believed to be based on a kind of fungus (also called bee-bread) which is cultivated by the bark beetle, *Scolytidae*.

Ancestors

It is surprising how little we know about the most familiar animals. Where do cats and mice come from, for instance? Or chickens? Or budgerigars? What were their ancestors like, and how close are they to wild animals?

In some cases, this is a complete mystery (which itself is interesting) and exploring their family tree can produce unexpected discoveries. For instance, most of us assume that camels come from the Sahara, and that horses were first introduced to America by the Spanish. But neither supposition is correct (or, at least, not the full story) and their true origins are far more interesting.

Camels

The camel is descended from a range of experimental mammals which evolved about a million years ago (including one of the oddest animals of all time: a creature called the macrauchenia which combined a giraffe's neck with an elephant's trunk).

The ancestors of today's camels and dromedaries evolved on the plains of north America. Most of those which stayed in the New World were wiped out by the first human tribes that invaded the continent at the end of the ice age, about ten thousand years ago.

Fortunately, several herds had escaped in the reverse direction, across the Bering Straits into Asia, and had settled down to a new life in Siberia.

Over the centuries, these animals gradually spread down into China and central Asia, until they reached the Middle East at about the time the first human settlements were being founded there. It was here that these animals, which resembled the two-humped Bactrian species of today, were first domesticated.

The single-humped species was developed by selective breeding, and the first record of its existence is on ancient Egyptian pottery of the sixth dynasty, about 3500 BC. It was still a rarity at the time, and the animals were not introduced into the Nile valley until three thousand years later.

It was only with the rise of the Islamic empire, later still, that they became associated with the caravan routes of the Sahara.

A further stage in their worldwide journey took place in the nineteenth century, when camels were imported to Australia to help with the construction of the railways. Over the years, some of these animals escaped and found conditions so much to their liking that there are now herds of them roaming the outback.

These are feral animals, rather than a truly wild species (surprisingly there is a similar herd in Italy, on the sandy plains outside Pisa), and it was long believed that the original animals had died out. However, in 1945 a Russian zoologist, A. G. Bannikov, discovered a herd of two-humped camels, closely resembling the ancestral stock, living in a remote part of the Gobi Desert.

Horses

The horse, like the camel, originally evolved in north America. It was the first animal whose history was reconstructed from fossil remains; and every stage of its evolution, from a small fox-terrier-like animal sixty million years ago, is thoroughly documented.

These ancestral horses were also killed off by the human invaders who swept down the continent massacring all the great ice-age fauna such as the plains cat (*Felis asterox*) and the giant sloth. But, like the camels, some had escaped into Russia and they spread across the Old World in much the same pattern.

It is ironic that the Spanish conquistadors should have used horses to conquer the Aztecs, for when they landed in central America, these animals had circled the globe, and in a sense they were going home.

Cats

The first domestic cat was the genet (*Genetta*), a north African animal which one writer has described as 'a miniature dinosaur in a leopard-skin coat'. The ancient Egyptians who adopted it called it 'Basta' and trained it to catch mice. However, they later discovered that the Abyssinian tabby cat (*Felis lybica*) which they called 'Mu', as well as being a good mouser could also be trained to retrieve wild-fowl. From then on the genet appears to have been given a vaguely religious status and forgotten.

Incidentally, the 'cat' of ancient Greece was neither of these animals but the polecat (*Putorius*).

The European wild-cat (*Felis sylvestris*) played

little part in the development of our present domestic breeds. Most modern cats are descended from Mu, although zoologists believe there was once a European wild-cat with a blotchy coat pattern, which produced the tortoiseshell and calico types by cross-breeding.

Mice

The ancient mice (*Cricetidae*) originally evolved in Asia about forty million years ago. The murids, or modern mice (including rats and house-mice) later drove them out as they spread across the Old World. Like pigs, horses and venereal disease, they were introduced into America by the Spanish.

Pigs

Swine first evolved about thirty-nine million years ago, and along with goats and sheep were the first animals to be domesticated in permanent settlements. Pigs are reluctant to be herded anywhere and would not have been any use to nomadic tribes.

The wild boar and the domestic pig flourished side by side for centuries. At first they were remarkably similar in appearance, though different in temperament; but the domestic animal gradually changed by selective breeding.

According to legend, pigs colonized America just ahead of the white man, because Columbus is supposed to have left eight of them behind on the island of Haiti, when he headed home to Europe during his first voyage. The original stock were transplanted from island to island through the West Indies, and were eventually introduced into the southern United States.

Along the way, a number of them escaped and reverted to the wild, so America was simultaneously stocked with both wild and domestic species. The speed with which they regressed in the wild was remarkable, and their appearance changed dramatically. Within a few generations they had turned back into a smaller version of the European wild boar – a dark, lean aggressive animal with razor-sharp teeth and many ancestral features such as flattened heads and long guard hairs.

The descendants of these animals have been living and breeding in the wild for four hundred years on an island off Savannah, Georgia.

Talking Birds

Parrots were the favourite talking birds of the Romans. One writer mentions a course to teach parrots to talk, and anyone who could afford such a bird usually had a special servant to look after it.

The Emperor Augustus favoured ravens, and it is said that he once bought a bird, from a cobbler, whose preferred expression was '*Opera et impensa periit*' – It's a hopeless case!

The story of the first talking budgerigar is known with some accuracy. In the late eighteenth century, one of the convicts transported from Britain to the penal colonies in New South Wales, Australia, was Thomas Watling, an accomplice in a counterfeiting ring. He was employed there as assistant to Dr White, the physician. Watling noticed that budgerigars were easily tamed, and one day when the physician entered his hut, the bird promptly said: 'How do you do, Dr White?'

Hens

Hens were probably pecking around prehistoric settlements long before anyone thought of domesticating cows and pigs and goats. The domestic fowl is the oldest, most reliable, most universal of all farm animals – or so we think. In fact, it is barely domesticated at all. The traditional barnyard hen (*Gallus domesticus*) still resembles the jungle fowl (*Gallus gallus*) from which it is descended, in almost every respect. There was simply no need to change, because its natural habits happily coincided with our requirements, and it had no fear of man. It just continued laying the same eggs, brooded on its clutch and reared its chicks as it had always done.

It is one of the few natural and utterly blameless relationships we have had with any animal on earth. Unfortunately it may soon come to an end, because new breeds are being developed to meet the disciplines of factory farming, and *Gallus domesticus* will rejoin its cousins in the wild. If it goes the way of the tarpan and the aurochs, it will be a pity. As Daniel G. Kozlovsky points out in *An Ecological and Evolutionary Ethic*, we shall be losing something more valuable than free-range eggs.

'A cock crows under my bedroom window, a wild jungle call that we never bred out, probably because it doesn't affect laying capacity or meatiness. That crowing seems as wild and free and primitive as that of the northern Indian jungle fowl from which our chickens are derived.

'For a thousand generations men woke to a crowing cock, had interjected into their subconscious lives that small part of the jungle wildness. In a couple of generations we have excluded these cocks from town and barnyard, and even the farmer now wakes to an alarm clock. The human world is the poorer for it, but does not know that, *cannot* know that.

'Can you regain what you do not know you should have?'

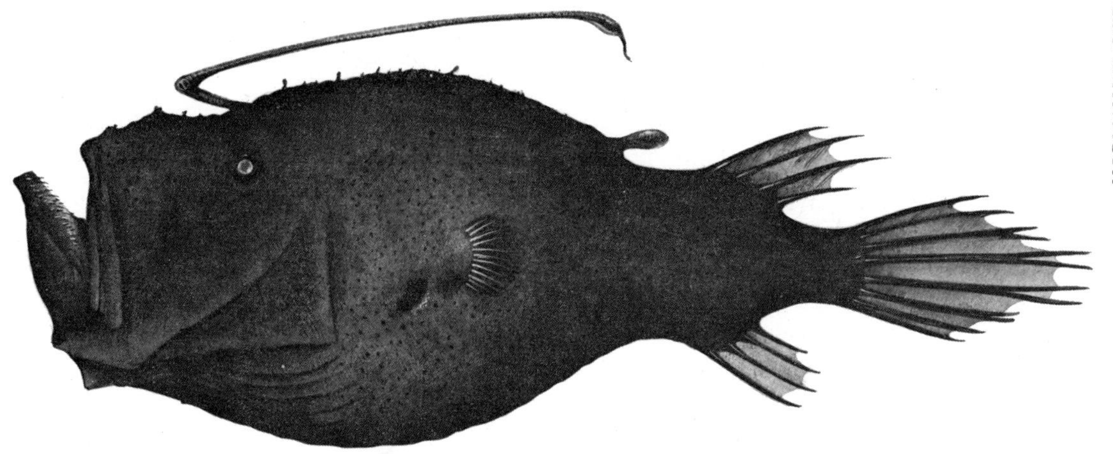

The Angler Fish

The oceans contain a number of species which are fishers of fish. The bait of the angler fish is a fleshy knot which dangles from its upper lip directly in front of its open mouth, and wriggles in the current while the angler itself remains motionless. As soon as another fish takes the bait, the angler swallows fast, ingesting its victim along with a huge quantity of water which washes the meal straight into its stomach. The baits of deep-sea anglers are luminous, the light being provided by bacteria which live symbiotically inside the bait.

Other fishing fish include the reddish frogfish, whose bait resembles a grey-white wriggling worm, and the Phynelox whose pink bait coils and uncoils itself like a worm on a hook.

Animal Sounds

' "*Of the musics you have ever got,*" *asked Conan,* "*which have you found the sweetest?*"

"*I incline to like pig-grunting in Magh Eithne, the bellowing of the stag of Ceara, the whinging of fauns in Derrynish. The low warble of water-owls in Loch Barra also, sweeter than life that. I am fond of wing-beating in dark belfries, cow-cries in pregnancy, trout-spurt in a lake-top. Also the whining of small otters in nettle-beds at evening, the croaking of small jays behind a wall, these are heart pleasing.*" '

– Flann O'Brien, *At Swim-two-birds*.

On the face of it, a grunt is not the most promising means of communication, but pigs have developed it into an extensive and expressive language – questioning, challenging, ordering, summoning and announcing their presence with different intonations.

Grunts are an intimate, personal form of talk, which certainly cannot be said of a pig's squeal. Pigs only squeal when they are distressed (there is no such thing as 'squealing for joy') and when they let rip, the sound can be loud enough to exceed official noise-pollution levels.

If you think that is an exaggeration, Dr Stanley Curtis of the University of Illinois has measured the average pig squeal at between 100 and 115 decibels. The supersonic Concorde was originally banned from New York's Kennedy Airport because the noise of its engines exceeded 112 decibels at take-off.

Big is Bass

Small animals squeak and large ones rumble because the smaller the animal's head, the higher the frequency of sounds it can receive and transmit.

The theory goes like this. In order to determine which direction a sound is coming from (which, after all, is the main reason for hearing it), the brain must distinguish which ear it reaches first, and the time difference between them.

This means that the closer the animal's ears are together, the shorter the wavelength, and therefore the higher the frequency, will be necessary for good discrimination.

In tests, bats top the scale of hearing at 115 kilohertz, followed by rats at up to 72 khz, dogs up to 44 khz, and humans up to 19 khz. A test on an elephant at the University of Kansas seems to confirm the rule. A young Indian elephant was trained to press a button with its trunk in response to brief sounds, and the highest frequency it registered was 17 khz. The bigger the head, the lower the frequency.

The theory is fine as far as it goes, but there must be more to it, because it has recently been discovered that certain birds, with relatively small skulls, can communicate with ultra-low sounds.

Elephant Talk

Elephants in the wild usually communicate by a series of rumbling noises they make in their throats and trunks. An elephant cow calls to her young, on the other hand, by simply slapping her ears against the sides of her head. Trumpeting is restricted to times of excitement or danger. When an elephant threatens, it may also beat its trunk against the ground, producing a sound which has been described as 'like automobile tyres striking against a hard surface'.

Garrulous Geckos

We tend to think of reptiles as relatively silent animals, but the gecko is a startling exception. The females produce no more than a soft hissing sound, but the males can be one of the noisiest tropical animals – hence their name *garrulus*, or talkative.

The African gecko (*Ptenopus garrulus*), for instance, inhabits holes in the Kalahari and Namib deserts, and as the sun declines in late afternoon, it begins to make occasional chirping calls. These gradually build up to a deafening crescendo as thousands of geckos poke their heads up above the sand, squeaking and barking at each other.

As soon as the sun sets and it grows dark, the noise stops all at once, and the geckos leave their burrows for the night's business of insect hunting.

The house-dwelling tokay (*Gecko gecko*) of south-east Asia makes a sudden loud barking noise, variously described as 'to-keh' or 'geck-oh', which is said to awaken sleeping people at night. It is regarded as a sign of good luck to hear the noise while inside a house.

The Dialogue of Frogs

Aside from the humming of insects, the first creature voice to be heard on land was that of the amphibians. Frogs and toads have developed singing to a fine art, using bags of air as resonators. These are usually in the mouth or throat, but in the case of the edible frog they project like pale balloons on either side of its head.

Each has its own distinctive call, ranging from clicks and groans to mewing, wailing, sharp cries and long-drawn whinnies. One of the strangest is produced by the American tree frog (*Eleutherodactylus coqui*), which is named after its call – 'co-qui'. Although humans can hear the whole sound, the males of the species only hear the first part, 'co', which warns them of another male in the area, while the females only hear the 'qui', which informs them of a potential mate.

The difference is not simply a matter of interpretation on the part of the frogs; scientists at Cornell University have shown that the ears of the two sexes are actually tuned differently.

Howls

There has never been any solid evidence that wolves howl at the moon. Their howls consist of twelve related harmonics, and when a pack howls together, they harmonize.

Newts

Even newts make a noise. In the case of the European newt, it sounds like a finger squeaking on wet glass.

It is not even necessary to have lungs. The lungless salamanders of California produce mouse-like squeaks by contracting their throats and expelling the air through their nostrils.

Knock on Wood

Animals which live in a denser medium – like solid wood – are forced to pass on information in a digital form, using the equivalent of Morse code. The death-watch beetle telegraphs to its mate by banging its head on the roof of its tunnel; while nocturnal fiddler crabs, who live amongst dense vegetation and have much the same problem, tap out a rhythmic, species-specific signal on the ground, which the females receive by their sense of vibration.

Whale Song

The largest animal in the world happens to have the ideal medium for communication. Sound travels much further through water than it does through air, and the song of the whale can be heard for hundreds of miles.

It is estimated that one whale could communicate with another across the width of the Atlantic – provided that there was another, halfway across, to relay the message. This procedure would take about two hours.

However, it would have some difficulty separating the signal from the background, because the ocean is a very noisy place. In the upper layers especially, there is a cacophony of sound, from the booming and whistling of larger creatures to the clicking of cuttlefish and the crackling static of shrimps. Whales are thought to overcome this problem by using the quieter, deeper layers, and bouncing their songs off the thermoclines.

Ants and Antagonists

'Discovering that I could speak the language of ants, I approached one and enquired, "What is God like? Does He resemble an ant?"

"God? Resemble an ant?" he replied in astonishment. "Of course not! We only have one sting. God has two."'

– Central Asian folk tale

The most surprising thing about ants is the mind-numbing size of their population (about 10^{15} individual insects), and our almost complete ignorance about any of them.

When O. E. Wilson published his famous work on Sociobiology in 1975, he pointed out that of the 12,000 species of ants that have been identified, less than a hundred, or 1 per cent, had been studied with any care – and only ten have been examined thoroughly.

Those we know about are fascinating. A column of army (or soldier) ants, for instance, is one of the few organisms without any territorial instinct. Their environment is movement itself, in any direction, at whatever cost.

Army Ants

The army ants which inhabit parts of Africa and South America are permanently at war. Aggressive nomads with no permanent nest, they advance in a destructive swarm, building living bridges across streams (their limbs are designed to interlock like Lego), and surviving floods by rolling into balls that float (the ones at the bottom get drowned for the good of the others).

The only time that the juggernaut stops rolling is for the queen to give birth to the next generation. For about three weeks they set up a permanent camp and the whole column gathers in a massive swarm, with the queen in the middle.

The queen then lays 100,000 new eggs, and a few days later the previous generation of larvae, which have been transported around in their cocoons, hatch out, more or less simultaneously. This sudden increase in population generates a new cycle of activity, and the swarm moves on again.

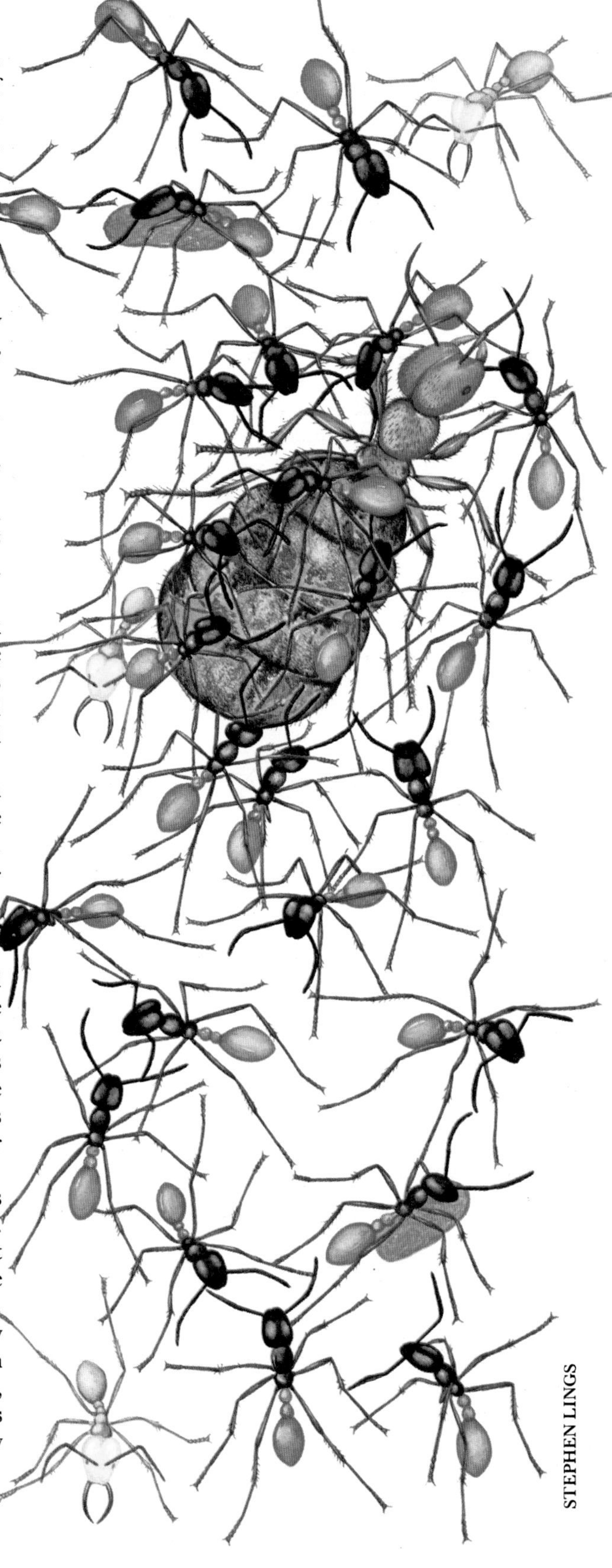

STEPHEN LINGS

Giant anteater

The Giant Anteater

When it stands still, the giant South American anteater has a certain majesty about it, growing up to seven feet (2m) long, with distinctive diagonal stripes along its body, and a long plumed tail.

But as soon as it moves, the animal sheds all dignity, because it staggers along with an ungainly pigeon-toed gait. This is because it walks on its knuckles rather than the pad of its foot, to protect its long digging claws from being blunted.

These claws are so formidable that even large predators, like the jaguar, will leave it alone; but their main use is for disinterring the nests of ants, termites and other grubs.

The anteater, which is toothless, then probes around inside the nest with its 10-inch-long tongue, coated with sticky, insect-adhering saliva.

There are two smaller species: the two-toed or silky anteater, and the tamandua. Both are tree-climbing forest-dwellers with prehensile tails.

All three species are solitary creatures. The females only bear one offspring, which is carried on the mother's back until it is almost half her size.

The Tiger Beetle

The tiger beetle is the only insect which stalks and attacks it prey like a carnivorous cat, and ounce for ounce, it is every bit as fierce as a real tiger. When moving in for a kill, it crouches down, then makes a blinding dash, seizes its prey, snips off its head with razor sharp mandibles, and devours the body whole.

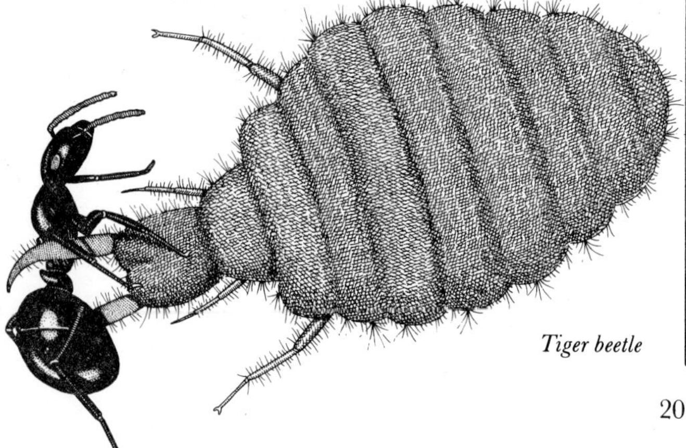

Tiger beetle

One beetle biologist watched in awe as a pair of tiger beetles fed on an ant-hill. They sat down opposite each other with the main trail leading to the ant-hill between them – like gentlemen at a banquet – and the ants came marching by, with conveyor-belt persistence, into the jaws of death. The beetles took turns in picking off and wolfing down each passing morsel. Not one ant was overlooked, and after half an hour of continuous eating, the flow of ants dried up.

The two tiger beetles then attacked the ant-hill itself, digging away at it as if they had not eaten for months, with dirt flying in every direction, devouring every ant they found.

The biologist later uncovered what was left of the ant-hill with a small shovel. He could not find a single ant left in the entire colony.

Armadillos

Armadillos cross rivers by walking underwater across the bottom. Reports of such behaviour were first regarded as 'one of those myths', but they gained credence when it was found that the animals were able to hold their breath for up to six minutes.

This ability also explains how they are able to dig into the ground with their noses jammed in the earth, usually in search of insect food. They have an excellent sense of smell but are almost blind and completely dumb, and they have no vocal chords.

Adult armadillos are such solitary creatures that no one has ever observed two of them together, except when mating. When they do so, it is a brief affair, and biologists are mystified by the fact that the offspring are always quadruplets, which are identical right down to the number of hairs on their bodies.

Another unusual aspect of their metabolism is that they are the only animals, apart from human beings, who can contract leprosy. Numbers of them are now being bred in laboratories for the manufacture of leprosy vaccine.

They come in a variety of sizes, including the giant species up to four or five feet (1.5m) long, but the rarest, and shyest, is the pichiciego or pink fairy armadillo.

This animal, which lives on the grasslands of South America, looks for all the world like an armour-plated rabbit. Its body is covered with fine hair, except for a strip of soft pinkish-grey scales down its back and over the tail. Like a rabbit, it

Pink fairy armadillo

dives into a bolt-hole at the first sign of danger, but instead of burrowing underground it remains in the entrance, with its pink, reinforced butt blocking the hole.

In the United States, the armadillo's chief enemy is the automobile. Every evening the animals hobble out on to the long, straight Texas highways and sit there, presumably soaking up the heat from the roadway. And every evening the slaughter begins again.

Fewer would undoubtedly be killed if only they would lie still and let the monstrous machines hurtle over them. But, when startled, the animals spring straight up, three feet into the air, and become dramatically impaled on the chrome grill-work of the cars.

The Aye-Aye

Many strange animals have evolved on the island of Madagascar, and at first glance the aye-aye looks no odder than the rest. In fact, apart from its claw-like fingers and large eyes, it looks rather like a domestic cat. But what fascinated zoologists about *Daubentonia madagascariensis* is that it has somehow managed to combine two impossibly different lines of evolution.

When the first aye-aye was discovered on Madagascar by a French explorer in 1780, the shape of its teeth left him in no doubt that it was a rodent – possibly a large new species of squirrel. But later, when its anatomy came to be examined in more detail, scientists were forced to change their minds and reclassify it as a distant relative of monkeys and human beings, because it possessed one of the most advanced characteristics of primates – an opposable thumb.

Not surprisingly, it became the subject of intense curiosity, because the rodents are known to have parted company from other mammals at a very early stage in evolution, and this shy, nervous creature was the only living animal to combine the key features of both.

Unfortunately, the aye-ayes are difficult to study because they have now retreated to the remote forests and mangrove swamps to escape the expanding cultivation and coconut plantations on the island. As they are nocturnal animals, which spend the day asleep in the treetops, they are seldom seen; and the only sign of their presence are their occasional cries (described – rather unkindly – as sounding like 'two pieces of metal being scraped together').

However, patient observation has shown how it makes the most of its mixed heritage, by combining the lifestyles of both rat and monkey. The rodent-like incisors are ideal for gnawing wood, and it lives off the grubs and larvae beneath the bark of trees; while the primate grasp and its other distinctive feature – a very long middle finger – come into play at night when it goes in search of food.

They enable it to creep so silently along a branch that it can actually hear the tell-tale sound of a grub chewing. The aye-aye's hearing is so acute that, if it fails to detect anything, it delicately taps along the branch with its long middle finger until it gets a hollow rap, indicating the presence of a bore-hole underneath. It is then a matter of seconds to strip away the bark and hook its finger into any available hole and grab the grub.

Its ancestry, however, remains a mystery. It has no close relatives, not even among the numerous species of Madagascan lemurs (which are unique to the island and themselves include some very odd animals). It seems to be an evolutionary freak, the survivor of a small group of species – or even a single animal – that preserved its own solitary line of descent for millions of years. A defiant exception which proves the rule.

Aye-aye

B

The Banana Alarm

Colonies of insects often have ingenious built-in alarm systems to warn their inhabitants of danger. Ants and bees use chemical systems which call up reinforcements and send the colony to action-stations when they are under attack. The guards in a termite mound will even mark out special emergency routes, clearing the traffic from busy corridors so that 'civilians' can be evacuated and convoys of soldiers rushed to the front line.

The alarm signals consist of a variety of highly volatile chemicals which are usually dispersed by the colony's own air-conditioning system. This allows the insects to control how far the message spreads and what it says, so that there is no unnecessary panic.

The formic ant (*Acanthomyops claviger*), for instance, was found to release a mixture of two alarm pheremones from reservoirs in its mandibles and Dufours gland. A single ant could apparently raise the alarm for a distance of about 4 inches (10cm) and the signal was reinforced by others, according to how serious the problem turned out to be.

Bees have some of the most sophisticated systems, and this is where bananas, or rather the smell of them comes in. The alarm scent of the honey-bee has been analysed in detail and the main ingredient turns out to be isoamyl acetate, which smells strongly of that fruit.

When a beehive is attacked by other bees or wasps, the guards produce the pheremone from a gland beside their sting. When an enemy is stung, the barbs catch in the victim's skin and the whole assembly breaks off. The sac of alarm scent which is attached to it bursts, so that although the bee is out of action its sting continues to act as a marker, enabling reinforcements to zero in where the banana-flavoured clouds are thickest.

Bandicoots

Kangaroos and wallabies are not the only Australian marsupials. Nearly all the mammals on the continent have followed the same pattern of evolution; and, though they were isolated from the rest of the world, they developed along parallel lines, so that there are now pouched equivalents of shrews, mice, rats, rabbits and goats, not to mention predators like cats, dogs and foxes.

One of the largest groups are the bandicoots, or *Peramelidae*, which come between the carnivorous *Phascogales* and the herbivorous *Phalangers* and kangaroos. Among these are the bilbies, long-eared bushy-tailed bandicoots that kill rats and mice (and sleep sitting up); and a bandicoot which occupies the same ecological niche as an antelope.

This is the rarest of the *Chaeropus* family, also known as the pig-footed bandicoot, which is the only marsupial in the world with trotters. It is a nocturnal animal that looks and stands like a tiny deer, and makes its nest in tall grass during the day.

Barnacle Glue

Thomas Henry Huxley once described the barnacle as 'a crustacean standing on its head and kicking food into its mouth with its feet'. His somewhat jaundiced view is explained by the fact that the great Charles Darwin spent eight years of his life studying them instead of writing *Origin of Species*. In fact they are quite endearing creatures, and they have one unique feature that still fascinates scientists.

Whilst feeding under water, the barnacle lies on its back in the shell with six pairs of legs beating the water to trap minute particles of food – hence Huxley's description. But when the tide goes out, it flattens itself to a rock, trapping a small bubble of air which enables it to go on breathing, and seals itself off from the outside world.

The glue which it uses to anchor itself is twice as strong as epoxy resin, and appears to be resistant to all known chemicals.

In test conditions a mere 3/10,000 of an inch of barnacle cement provided a sheer strength of more than three tons. At 662°F the glue only softens slightly; while at –383°F it does not even crack or peel.

It seems that the barnacle produces two glandular secretions: one a milky-white fluid for building the shell; the other a thick, pale brown fluid which may be the basic cement.

If barnacle glue could be made synthetically, it would have many applications, one of which could be in dentistry, as no one has yet devised a glue that will keep a filling permanently in place.

The Basilisk

In medieval bestiaries, the basilisk was described as a fabulous creature, about a foot long, with fiery, death-dealing eyes and breath. According to Pliny, it acquired its name from a crown-like crest and, as with the Gorgon, the mere sight of it was supposed to be fatal.

That could hardly be more different from the shy little iguana in central America that now bears its name. But the modern basilisk does have one magic talent, which has earned it the name of the Jesus Christo lizard. It walks on water.

Basilisks always live near water, usually in overhanging trees or bushes, from which they can dive in at the first sign of danger. In most cases the animal sinks to the bottom and stays there till it is safe to come out. But occasionally it will take off, skimming across the water at high speed, with its body erect and the long, finned tailed curving upwards.

No one is quite sure how it achieves this feat. The usual explanation (which is somehow satisfying, though hardly scientific) is that it runs so fast it does not have time to sink. It seems to be assisted by large, long-fringed toes and, provided these do not break the surface tension, it appears to remain afloat. However, as its speed slackens, it tends to sink in the water and is reduced to swimming.

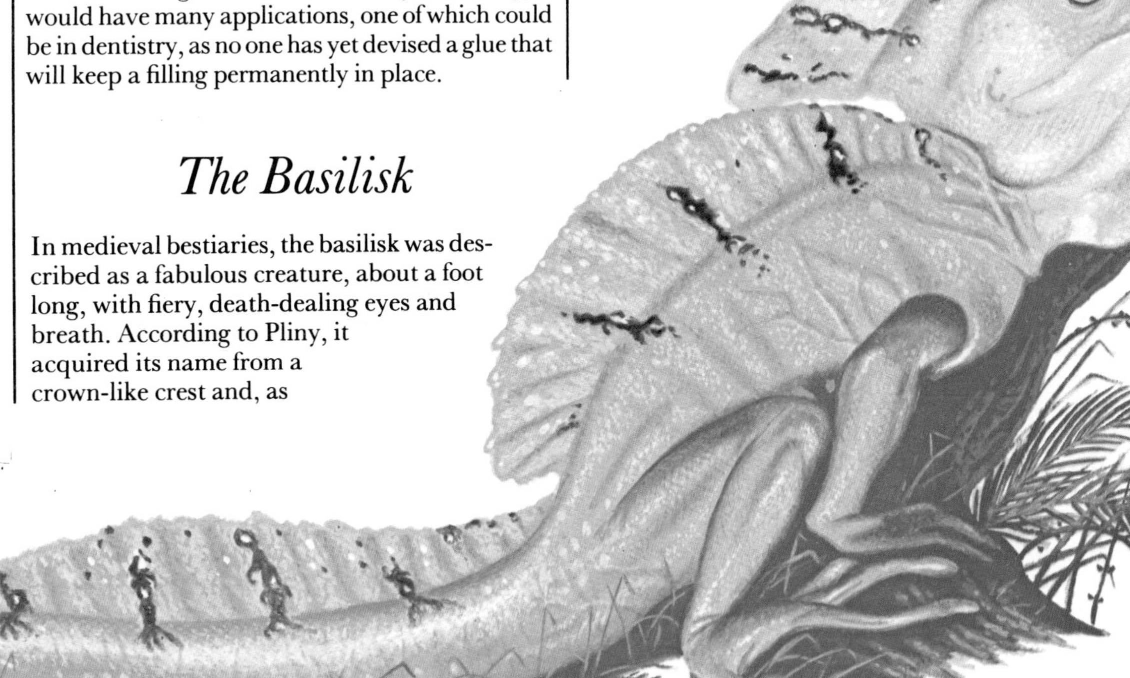

TERRY OAKES

TERRY OAKES

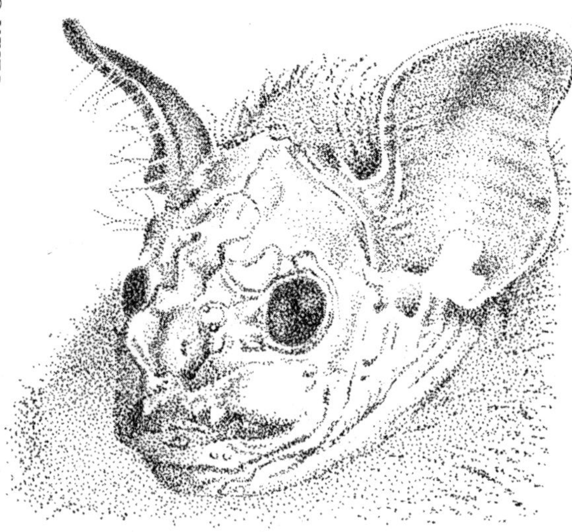

Vampire bat

Bats

Bats are the only mammals that have learnt to fly; and with little natural competition they have evolved into a bewildering variety of species. Hairy-lipped, leaf-nosed, mastiff and mouse-tailed; the common fruit bat, and the tiny British pipistrelle which weighs only a fifth of an ounce. There are naked bats, painted bats and tomb bats; and the horse-shoe bat whose high-frequency sonar is so sophisticated it can detect the fall of a moth a hundred yards away. But there is one species, above all, which seems to have a fearful fascination for us.

The Vampire

The vampire bat of the American tropics (*Desmodus rotundus*) feeds exclusively on the blood of other animals, mainly cattle but also humans.

It is a nocturnal predator which spends the day suspended in clusters in the darkness of caves, and swarms out at night in search of prey. When it senses the presence of a hot-blooded victim, it alights nearby and approaches on tip-toe. The bite of its needlesharp teeth rarely awakens the sleeper, but its saliva is laced with an anti-coagulant which causes the small incision to continue bleeding for hours. The vampire bat then licks the blood rather than sucking it. The meal may last twenty-five minutes, until the bat is almost spherical (hence the name *rotundus*).

'We slept so soundly,' wrote one Amazon explorer, 'it was not until morning we discovered we had been raided during the night by vampire bats and the whole party was covered with bloodstains from the many bites. It may seem unreasonable that we could have thus been bitten and not disturbed in our sleep but the fact remains that there is no pain produced at the time of the bite, nor for several hours afterwards.'

Bats and Birds

Bats have adapted completely to night life, filling the ecological niche left empty by daylight-feeding birds. At night insect food is abundant and predatory birds are rare, though both the bat falcon and the bat hawk have specialized in preying on bats as they emerge from caves or buildings at dusk. The bat hawk catches them in its claws and swallows them whole in flight. Most bat species are insect-eaters, but there are exceptions. The fisherman bat swoops down to catch small fish that swim too close to the surface; while the long-tongued bat eats nectar and pollen. The 'flying foxes' of northern India, which have a wingspan of up to three feet and move in flocks of thousands, live exclusively on fruit. They are a local delicacy, and their flesh is said to resemble that of chicken.

Fisherman bat

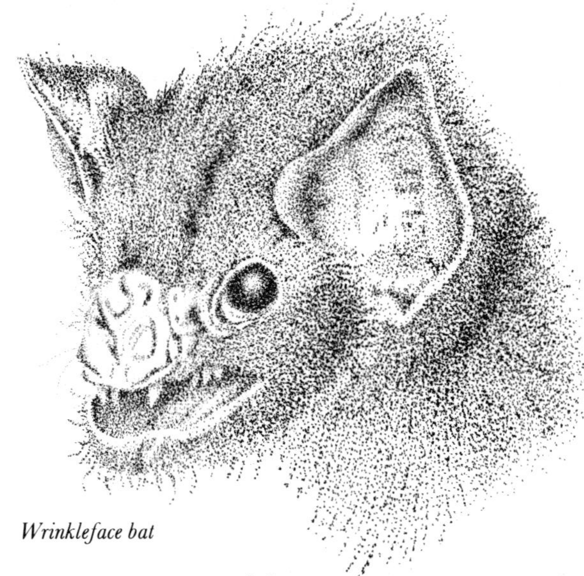

Wrinkleface bat

Upside-Down

Why do bats sleep hanging upside down? The traditional answer was that the position made for rapid and easy take-off: the animals just dropped into immediate flight. Recent research, however, suggests another reason. The bones of bats' legs are considerably longer and thinner – per pound of body weight – than those of other mammals. Such light legs are useful to flying animals, but they are also much more prone to fracture, so bats hang upside down to minimize the chance of breakages. The vampire bat is the exception to the rule. Its thicker leg bones allow it to sneak up to its victims along the ground.

The Carlsbad Freetails

There are over 980 species of bats collected in 17 families around the world, but perhaps none is quite as strange as the freetail bat colony in the Carlsbad Caverns of south-east New Mexico. They have lived in the great domed caves for centuries. Their earliest recorded contact with humans was with the Aztecs, who slaughtered thousands of them to make regal cloaks from their grey, velvety skins.

When the colony leaves the Caverns each evening, it is like the eruption of a volcano. One of the first detailed observations was made in 1936 when Dr Vernon C. Allison, on the night of 16 June, recorded over nine million bats leaving at once.

'They pour from the cave opening,' he wrote, 'in such a dense black stream that they can be seen from a distance of two miles. They will fill the shaft so closely that they can be caught in the hands as they pass out, while the noise of their beating wings is plainly apparent at quite a distance.'

The freetail is equipped with sharp teeth to crush the hard shells of insects. Small prey is chewed and swallowed whole on the wing, but larger moths and beetles are stuffed into a membrane between the bat's hind legs. During a big catch the bat will wrap this membrane around its stomach to hold the prey, and curl its head into this pouch to take bites as it flies along.

When a bat returns from the hunt, it drops into the cave in a dramatic power-dive from maximum altitude, attaining speeds in excess of 35 mph, and streaking inside with a ghastly tearing noise. Once inside, the bats sleep all day, so closely packed on the Caverns' ceilings that there may be up to three hundred of them per square foot.

Because the Carlsbad freetails all tend to breed at the same time, mothers returning from the hunt cannot tell which of the millions of squealing young on the ceilings are their own. So the mother bats will suckle any infant – a rare practice for any mammal.

When a young bat reaches the right age it learns to fly the hard way. There are no test flights. One evening, as the whole community begins to mill around in the Caverns before the mass exit, the youngster loosens its toehold and drops from the ceiling. If it can learn to fly before it hits the floor, it departs into the night with the rest of the colony. If not, it impacts at high speed on the mountain of guano, or bat dung, which covers the Caverns' floors.

Guano can be used as a fertilizing manure, and between 1902 and 1923 miners at the Carlsbad Caverns dug out more than 100,000 tons from a single pile the depth of a five-storey building!

Swordnose bat

Beavers

One summer in the Colorado Rockies, scientists at a local research station fought for weeks to destroy a beaver dam that was flooding the only road into town. They tore it down each day; the beavers rebuilt it each night. And as the days passed the dam grew larger and more complicated. One night the beavers incorporated whole trees into the dam, fixing them together so tightly that it took the scientists three hours to break the dam. By now the demolition duty had turned into a research project. The scientists' next step was to try and trap the beavers, but when they returned in the morning their traps had been sprung with twigs and used in the building work. The scientists finally conceded defeat and a new road was cut around the edge of the beavers' pond.

It was estimated that at the beginning of the seventeenth century the beaver population of North America was close to one hundred million. By the late nineteenth century, it was close to extinction. For more than two hundred years, beaver skins were one of the main exports from the North American continent. The French began the trade in 1603, and the Hudson Bay Company joined the slaughter in 1669.

The beaver was once common in Britain, too, becoming extinct in the thirteenth century. It is believed that the English fens may have been created by beavers destroying the natural drainage. They are also claimed to be responsible for the destruction of the Pennine woodlands and the formation of peat mosses in Lancashire.

Beavers build dams primarily to create a depth of water sufficient to transport food supplies and to retreat when necessary. The dams also serve to control floodwaters.

Some astonishing beaver dams have been discovered. Several are one thousand years old, maintained by succeeding generations. One dam discovered in 1899 in North Dakota was made entirely of coal. As the species declined, however, it was noticed that, in smaller groups, the beavers seemed to lose their dam-building ability.

Incidentally, 'busy as a beaver' is a misnomer. As David Hancock puts it, 'Like all other animals, beavers work only when necessary.'

ROBERT MORTON

The Love of Bees

Much has been written about their industry and ingenuity, the way a swarm can live and die as if it was a single organism, about their extraordinary means of communication and their uncanny direction-finding. Their complex life-cycle has probably been studied more than that of any other insect. But bees, which were one of our first domestic animals, have a social as well as a scientific importance, and it might be interesting to look at them from this point of view for a change. To record, as it were, their 'cultural' history and to celebrate the long love affair between our species.

'The Lord spake by inspiration unto the bee, saying provide thee houses in the mountains, and in the trees, and of those materials wherewith men build hives for thee. Then eat every kind of fruit, and fly the beaten paths of the Lord.'

– The Koran.

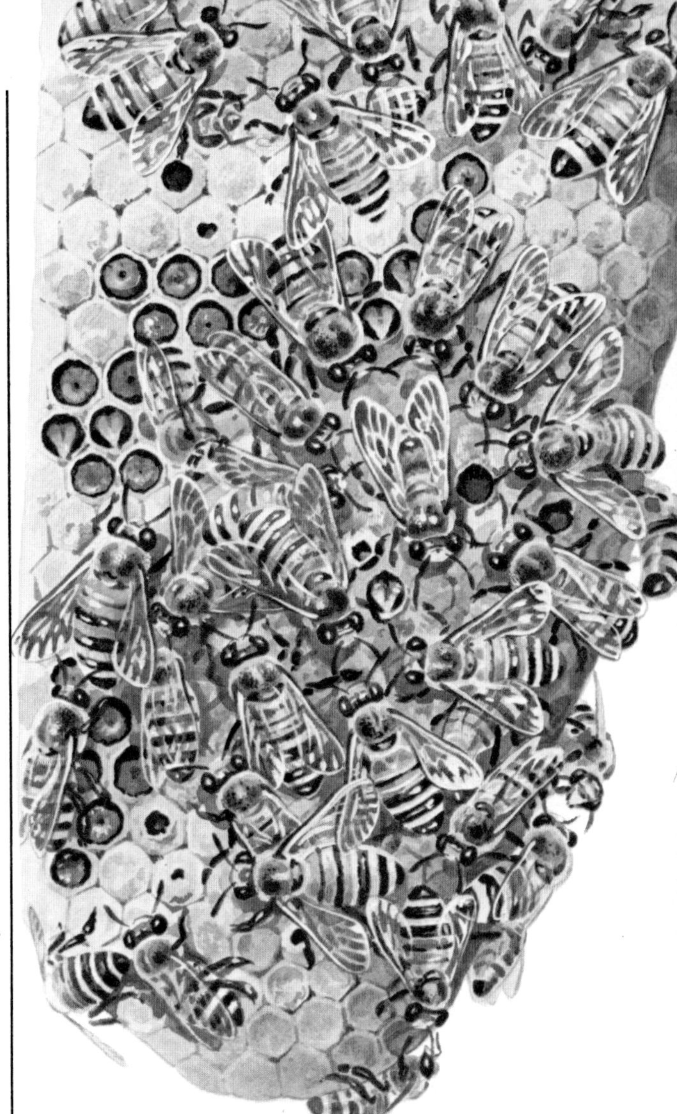

Sugar, as a common household product, is little more than two hundred years old, and up to the middle of the eighteenth century the only sweetening agent available was honey.

There is a prehistoric cave painting, more than ten thousand years old, at the Cueva de la Arana, in Spain, which shows a human figure gathering wild honeycombs, surrounded by a furious swarm of bees. But the first step in the domestication of the honey-bee – the provision of an artificial hive – had probably been taken five to six thousand years ago; and an Egyptian bas-relief from 2600 BC shows honey being collected from a man-made hive.

The Egyptians favoured cylindrical hives placed horizontally (modelled on hollow tree branches) and made of clay. In the more sophisticated version, smoke could be driven in at one end to force the bees to leave from the other. The Romans made beehives from wicker, bark and other materials and added a coat of cow-dung for weatherproofing. In northern Europe, hives were built around a willow basket, packed with wool and moss for insulation, and with the exterior daubed with clay – the same method of construction they used for their own homes. As Dorothy Hartley pointed out in *The Land of England*: 'Throughout the centuries mankind – with the exception of those who built stone houses – has housed his bees much as he housed himself.'

The introduction of beekeeping in ancient societies carried the same kind of political and economic clout as the introduction of a railway in the nineteenth century, or a social security system today. When the governor of Sukhi, on the middle Euphrates in Mesopotamia, introduced beekeeping in 1100 BC, he made sure his people did not forget it:

'I, Shamash-resh-ussur, governor of Sukhi and Ma'er, have brought from the mountains of the people of Khabkha into the land Sukhi the bees that collect honey and which since the days of my ancestors nobody has seen. I settled them in the gardens of the city of Gabbarini, so that they should collect honey and wax. The manufacture of honey and wax I understand, and the gardeners understand it also. Whosoever wishes to raise his voice, may he ask the elders of this country: Is it the truth that Shamash-resh-ussur, Governor of Sukhi, introduced the honey-bees into the land of Sukhi?'

Honey was one of the luxuries of a settled life. What tempted the Hebrew tribes to give up their nomadic life was the promise of a 'land flowing with milk and honey'; and in Greek myth, Zeus himself was raised on the same combination.

The Romans drank a mixture of honey and wine called *mulsum* and, in its fermented form, it became one of the most popular drinks throughout the Middle Ages. In fact, the word 'honeymoon' comes from the tradition, once common in central Europe, of drinking mead for thirty days after a wedding.

And while honey provided the loving-cup, the bee's wax soon became a vital ingredient of everyday life. It was used in the metal-casting process known as *cire perdue* which revolutionized Bronze Age technology. The ancient Egyptians covered their writing tablets with it, since the letters could then be rubbed out and the tablet reused. Beeswax candles provided light. It was a major ingredient in medicines throughout history. Greeks used it in painting and sculpture. Their athletes made their muscles supple by rubbing in a mixture of wax, oil and earth. Roman women used it in cosmetic preparations. Unwashed beeswax was the earliest form of chewing-gum. It was used to make moulds, metal casts, and as a furniture polish.

Sailors used it to wax thread, as tailors and leather workers still do today. Eggs were preserved with a coating of melted wax. And cloth which had been soaked in it even provided a form of greaseproof paper, which formed an airtight casing for bottles and jars when it set hard.

Wax was so important to the Romans that, in 181 BC, they were demanding a tribute of 100,000 pounds of it annually from the island of Corsica. And two years later the tribute was doubled!

Another useful product was propolis, a type of resin that bees gather from trees, which is still used in dyes and medicines. Bees have even been used as military weapons, by catapulting whole hives (complete with bees) into the enemy ranks – a form of biological warfare that was particularly useful in seiges, and remained in use as late as the Thirty Years' War (1618–1648).

Unfortunately, our understanding of the bees themselves did not keep pace with the ingenious use of their products, and strange misconceptions took root. The Roman writer Pliny, for instance, thought that the honey fell from heaven, and collected on leaves like dew, while others thought it was the sweat from trees. The Romans were also convinced that the queen bee was a male, as befits the 'ruler' or 'king' of the hive.

But the most curious, and persistent, belief, which was solemnly discussed in a treatise by an Englishman called Carew as late as 1842, was that bees could be generated, not just from other bees, but from the bodies of dead animals – especially lions and oxen. Some even took the Bible as evidence. 'Out of the strong,' they were fond of quoting, 'shall come forth sweetness'.

Anyone who has ever kept bees, from ancient Egypt onwards, knows otherwise; but craftsmen keep their secrets to themselves. They would probably agree, though, that the rhymed instructions of the English beekeeper Thomas Tusser (1524–1580) are altogether more reasonable.

Set hive on plank, not too low by the ground,
where herb with flowers may compass it round;
And boards to defend it from north and north-east,
from showers and rubbish, from vermin and beast.

How to Eat a Bee

There is a colourful species of bird, found mainly in the tropics, called the bee-eater, which has evolved an ingenious technique for eating the insects without being stung. The process requires considerable agility, and goes something like this.

They first catch the bee in mid-air, by grasping its narrow waist in the tip of a long curved beak. They then bang its head several times against their perch or the nearest hard object, shifting their grip in the process to the edge of its abdomen, just behind the sting.

They then rub the sting vigorously against the perch until it is torn out, or the venom squeezed from it. Finally, they juggle the bee back to its original position in their beak, bang its head a few times to make sure it is dead – and swallow it.

The Bird-Eating Spider

People who are afraid of spiders may think of the black widow or the tarantula as the ultimate horror, but the bird-eating spider leaves those standing. With its muscular, hairy body and 10-inch (25cm) leg-span, it is like a figure from a nightmare.

The creature was first described by Maria Sibilla Merian in 1705, in her book *Metamorphosis Insectorum Surinamensium*, but the description seemed so grotesque that scientists refused to believe her. She was accused of lying, and denounced in print; and it was not until 1863, when the naturalist H. W. Bates watched spiders killing finches in the Amazon jungles, that they were accepted as fact.

The bird-eating spider is one of the most aggressive creatures known. Their usual prey are large insects or humming-birds, but they will attack almost anything that moves, including members of their own species, which makes courtship a risky business. When mating, the male actually has to grasp the female's fangs to avoid being eaten.

They are nocturnal insects that hide during the day, but when they emerge from their holes and crevices at night, they hunt in the same way as other predators, by running down their prey, seizing small mammals with a sudden silent dash, or dragging birds from the nests and sinking their fangs into them.

A single meal can last them a long time and they have been known to fast for up to two years.

Surprisingly, they are not the only spiders which eat birds. Trapdoor spiders occasionally kill small birds, and the genus *Nephila* spins a web that is so strong that birds are sometimes accidentally trapped in it and eaten. But the bird-eating species (*Theraphosidae*), apart from being the largest, is uniquely adapted to its role as a hunter.

It has four lungs instead of two, four spinnerets instead of six (because it does not need to spin webs) and instead of working its jaws sideways, like other spiders, it moves them vertically, which gives it an even more clearly carnivorous appearance.

However, spiders do not chew their prey; they drink it. Like most insects, they have to digest their food *outside* their bodies, and the stabbing motion of their fangs, which looks as if they are tearing the victim apart, is in fact a way of injecting protein-dissolving enzymes into its body.

In the case of the bird-eating spider, this poison is not fatal to humans, but it can cause a painful reaction; and it is advisable not to handle them, since their reddish brown hairs are charged with a powerful irritant.

This battery of defences, together with their size, makes them almost invulnerable. In fact, the only enemy they are thought to have is the hunting wasp, whose sting can immobilize any prey, and against which the spiders have no defence.

This offers little comfort for the arachniphobe, because the bird-eaters are so successful they live for up to thirty years.

ELIZABETH GOSS

Bird Kill

All the birds of the air fell a sighing and a sobbin'
When they heard of the death of poor Cock Robin.

During the last half of the nineteenth century, while their menfolk were destroying the big game of the world, the women of Europe and North America were eliminating the birds, by supporting one of the bloodiest massacres of wildlife in history.

They wore feathers on their clothes; they stuffed pillows and mattresses with them. They decorated their fans with the bodies of dead birds; they pinned them to their hats, used them in flower arrangements, and had glass cases full of them in their living rooms. The demand was insatiable.

In 1885 the London market handled 750,000 bird skins in three months. A single delivery to just one dealer included 80,000 sea birds, 800,000 assorted wings, and 32,000 humming-birds.

At the height of the craze, the feather trade in Paris employed ten thousand people. In 1900 *ten tons* of willow-grouse wings were imported from Russia for dyeing; and an entire colony of herring-gulls off Cape Cod was destroyed to meet an order for 40,000 wings from just one fashion house.

Heronries were pillaged, and the egret colonies of South America and southern Europe were wiped out. Three hundred thousand albatross were killed by Japanese plumage hunters in Hawaii. Eagle skins were exported from China, lyre-birds from Australia, guinea-fowl and weaver birds from Africa. From eiderdown to the silver wing coverts of condors and the royal tail-feathers of the South American quetzal, it was big business.

In 1907, seven million dollars' worth of skins and plumage were sold in New York. Pelican skins fetched as much as one dollar each, and egret plumes were worth twice their weight in gold.

Like all big business, the feather trade could afford to buy political support. 'I really want to know,' said Senator Reed of Missouri during the debate on the protection of egrets, 'Why there should be any sympathy or sentiment about a long-legged, long-beaked, long-necked bird that lives in swamps and eats tadpole, fish and things of that kind. Why should we worry ourselves into a frenzy because some lady adorns her hat with one of its feathers, which appears to be the only use it has?'

The American government finally banned the import of bird products in 1913, but the trade lingered on in Europe until World War I, when people turned to the more serious business of slaughtering each other.

Although commercial interests were responsible for the most concentrated and purposeful assault on avian species, they were by no means the only ones. Birds were killed as pests, for sport, for stuffing as trophies, for their eggs, and simply out of vandalism. In terms of sheer numbers, the most astounding extinction of all was that of the passenger-pigeons. But that story deserves to be told in full, not only for their tragic end but for the astonishing beauty and spectacle of their lives, and is described separately.

Like the Great Auk and the Dodo, we will never see them again.

Who killed Cock Robin?
I, said the sparrow,
With my bow and arrow,
I killed Cock Robin.

SARAH DE'ATH

Bird-Song

'I first heard the melodious whistle of the Himalayan snowcock in the Pandjir Hindukush when the altimeter showed 3,900 metres.'

– Niethammer

The musical skill of songbirds is due to a structure called the syrinx, which takes the place of a voice-box and larynx. The sounds originate entirely from the syrinx, and are not modified in any way by the bird's mouth or tongue. But the bird has such fine control that some species can sing two notes at once. The Gouldian finch can even manage three – two simultaneous songs accompanied by a bass drone like a bagpipe's.

A number of accessories have been added to the syrinx in different species. For instance, the long windpipe of the trumpeter swan and the whooping crane gives them their deep organ tones, while the grouse, whose bizarre sound-system is described elsewhere, has a pair of inflatable throat pouches that act as resonators for its 'popping' call.

'They're Playing Our Song . . .'

Bird-song is more than just a form of self-advertisement. Sound is as vital a sex-stimulant for birds as scent is for mammals. In fact, a deaf songbird simply cannot breed.

The males start to sing at the beginning of the breeding season, when their testes become active and start pumping out hormones, and their singing literally 'turns on' the female by triggering her ovulation.

A female canary, for instance, needs a dark nest hole to lay her eggs, but even when she is provided with a suitable nest-box and a suitable mate at the right time of year, her eggs will not develop until she hears the one special melody that will trigger the pituitary gland in her brain, release the hormones, and start her breeding. The more the male canary sings to her, the faster her ovaries ripen and the eggs develop.

The Most Beautiful Song

Warblers, linnets and other songbirds have their admirers. Poems have been written about nightingales, Keats immortalized the skylark, 'The Song of Solomon' celebrates the turtle-dove, and many believe that blackbirds produce the most beautiful song of all. But for the real connoisseur none of these compare with the song of the tinamous.

Tinamous are dowdy creatures, regarded as game birds in South America, where they are referred to as 'the partridge of the pampas'. They are one of the oldest and most primitive species of birds, and can barely fly, but their song is uniquely beautiful.

It is said that their calls, which range from flute-like trills and whistles to rich organ notes, have such purity and softness of tone they can be mistaken for a child's voice.

(birds) Collared sun bird, Cardinal, Blue bird of paradise, Quetzal, Paradise fly-catcher, Ruby-throated humming-bird, Humming-bird

The Most Ugly . . .

Birds also make some uniquely unpleasant noises, and it would be difficult to select the ugliest call from the cacophony of screeching, croaking and hammering they can produce.

Is the scream of a parrot more or less penetrating than the cawing of rooks or the boom of bitterns (which can carry for miles if the wind is in the right direction)? Who knows?

Certainly one of the least attractive noises must be the sound made by grouse as they settle down for the night. When they take up their sleeping perch in a tree, grouse produce a distressing vomiting sound which the Germans call '*Worgen*' and which sounds like someone being violently sick.

Another form of ugliness is monotony, and there are some birds that just do not seem to know when to stop. The song of the whippoorwill, a shy nocturnal bird that lives in North America, is a melancholy refrain that is repeated exactly, and without pause, 150 or 200 times. An American naturalist, John Burroughs, claimed to have once counted 1,058 repetitions.

But even the whippoorwill may not be as terrible as the hawk cuckoo who enjoys displaying its abilities in the hottest weather. Its song consists of an ascending scale of notes, getting increasingly excited, and then suddenly ceases . . . but only to start again at the bottom of the scale a few seconds later. It is reported to suggest the words 'brain fever', the bird's popular name, though according to one affected source, it may be intended to induce that condition.

SARAH DE'ATH

. . . And the Most Unusual

The Australian whipbird has a call that begins on a single pure note, rises in volume, and ends with a loud sharp crack, like a whip. The male of another Australian species, the so-called rifle bird of paradise, emits a two-note sound which is said to be identical to the acoustic doppler effect of a passing bullet.

Emperor penguins have a whole range of calls, including a courtship song, a fright cry, a cry of anger, and one of satisfaction which has been described as 'a sort of "con-con" frequently made by the birds when bathing'. There is also their trumpet call, an extraordinarily piercing noise which can be heard over a kilometre away and which has been variously compared to a concertina abruptly starting and just as abruptly ending, and a klaxon.

Several species of birds have evolved songs that mimic other sounds: they may disguise themselves as other birds, or as mammals. There are birds which sound like the whine of a circular saw, the hoot of a car horn, or the whistle of a railway engine. The wonderfully named naked-throated bellbird makes a resounding 'clonk' like a falling bell, while the bell miner is reported to sound just like the tinkling of a small silver bell. The jackass penguin gets its name from its distinctive braying call, like a donkey's.

The Sound of Wings

Several larger species of birds use the sound of their wing-beats to communicate with other members of a flock when they are in the air. No one who has heard a flock of mute swans pass overhead will forget the eerie sound they make. Some species of duck have specially modified wing feathers, with a saw-tooth profile along the leading edge, to produce particular notes. The Indian whistling duck produces, as one would expect, a distinct whistle; and the golden-eye and common scooter make a clear ringing noise in flight. The European snipe has special feathers that vibrate in the slipstream, producing a whistling and bleating sound when they dive. The slipstreams of birds flying in formation amplify such sounds, so that they can be heard over great distances, and on long, migratory journeys they probably play an important role in keeping the flock together, especially in bad weather or poor visibility.

The male ruffed grouse attracts its females by apparently 'drumming' on a rock or log. In fact the bird simply uses the rock or log as a perch; the drumming noise is produced by rapidly beating its wings in the air.

Perhaps the strangest wingbeat is the sound reported by German researcher Oskar Heinroth from New Guinea: 'As I stood in the bush forest at Simpang, I suddenly thought I was hearing the approach of a train from the distance. It was not long before I saw the hornbill fly past and land in a tree. The noise ceased at the same moment. Only when more and more birds flew past, each again accompanied by the train noise, were my doubts stilled.'

The Bird that Roars

The ostrich is the only bird that makes a noise comparable to the roar of a mammal. It does this by taking a deep breath and forcing the air down its gullet, rather than the windpipe. The entrance to the stomach is closed, so its whole neck balloons out, and when the pressure is released it produces a kind of dull, booming belch that can be heard over a considerable distance.

Bird Strikes

The relationship between birds and the giant metal species that now share their airspace is not a happy one. One of the major, and potentially disastrous, problems is that birds are often attracted to airports, where they can get sucked into the turbines of jet engines – the phenomenon known laconically as 'bird strikes'.

Alarm systems, poisons, smells, firearms, flame-throwers and bombs are just some of the devices used to scare the birds away. But in 1960 an Electra taking off from Boston airport crashed when its jet engines were clogged by starlings, and sixty-two people died. And on one October day in 1972 at London's Heathrow airport, more than ten aircraft suffered bird strikes; hundreds of gulls were killed, two British Airways Jumbos had to land to have engine turbine blades replaced, and a Vanguard was dented.

Modern jet engines are designed to absorb the shock of swallowing birds, and are even tested with a cannon which fires carcasses into them at flying speed.

Until 1978 the US Air Force bases in Britain used falcons as a deterrent to other birds, but as this cost £72,000 per year they have adopted the cheaper methods of broadcasting distress calls.

Airports in other parts of the world face different problems. At Collagatta airport, 450 miles north of Sydney, pelicans invaded the runways after their breeding grounds on Lake Eyre began drying up in a drought. Twenty bird-catchers had to be hired to try and round them up.

Perhaps the most ingenious bird-trapping method was developed at Toronto airport, which was troubled by snowy owls. The birds liked to warm themselves by the landing lights, and found the runways useful open spaces where they could catch their prey.

Ordinary traps were set, but many of the captured owls died because there were not enough people to inspect the traps sufficiently frequently. The solution that was devised involved installing a homing pigeon in the owl-trap to act as bait. The trap was so designed that the pigeon was released as soon as the owl was caught. The pigeon then flew back to the roost where it was identified and someone was immediately sent to rescue the owl.

Ironically enough, there is actually a reservation for burrowing owls between the main runways at Miami Airport, in Florida, which must be one of the oddest wildlife sanctuaries in the world.

The Bombardier and Blister Beetles

Beetles have many enemies, and as they are usually too small to fight back they have evolved a variety of chemical defences.

One of the most sophisticated experts in chemical warfare is the blister beetle (*Lytta vesicatoria*). Its whole body, particularly the wing cases, is impregnated with cantharidin, a potent blood and stomach poison. Just touching the creature produces large, burning blisters on the skin, and a dose of two-thousandths of an ounce is fatal to humans. (Incidentally, blister beetle larvae feed on bee eggs and, when first discovered, were dubbed bee-lice.)

Other beetles produce strong-smelling digestive juices which are spat at the enemy. But the master of them all is the bombardier beetle, which defends itself with its own chemical bomb, a mixture of a cohesive fluid and a liquid which evaporates extremely fast on contact with air. The result is a gas that explodes with a small bang or pop, leaving behind a yellowish precipitate. The bombardier can fire off twenty-nine of these bombs in quick succession before it has to rest and refuel. If still under attack, however, it fires faeces from its digestive tract.

Camouflage

From the snow-white Arctic hare to the leopard's spots and the tiger's stripes (which have been adopted by armies around the world), the art of blending into your surroundings is vital. It happens at all levels of evolution, but some species have taken it to surreal extremes.

Insects, especially in their larval form, come together in groups that are carefully choreographed to represent a single object. The young caterpillars of a certain moth (*Triloqua obliquissima*) huddle together in a pile that looks exactly like bird droppings – about the only thing a bird would never eat.

Camouflaged examples (if you can find them) of the dry leaf butterfly, inchworm, cryptic caterpillar, and dung spider

Another moth, discovered in Panama but as yet unnamed, is even more subtle. Instead of disguising itself, it sits in the light in such a way that it casts a shadow like a thorn. When these moths are scattered strategically in a perfectly harmless tree, with their pale bodies almost invisible against the leaves, the branches appear studded with sharp black thorns.

Many animals imitate flowers, but there is a species of bug that impersonates lupins in a way that reminds one of a Busby Berkeley musical. The insects come in two colours, yellow and green, which are usually mixed together; but when they are disturbed they separate, and hundreds of them arrange themselves in bands which exactly match the part of the lupin where the green bud at the tip of the flower joins the yellow petals below.

Leaves and Raindrops

The pupa of the crane-fly, which lives in tropical rain forests, actually disguises itself as a drop of water. It gets away with this unlikely subterfuge by hanging from the edge of a palm leaf and smothering its body in a transparent mucus, technically known as hydroscopic mucoprotein. This defracts the light in such a way that the animal's body is almost invisible, and all one can see is a drop of moisture about to drip from the leaf.

Stick and leaf insects, whose names come from the objects they resemble, are amongst the best-known camouflage artists. They belong to the order *Phasmida*, which is Greek for 'apparition'.

Resembling a twig or stick is not sufficient on its own; the insect must also be able to remain completely motionless. Many species, indeed, only move at night, and stay absolutely rigid throughout the day.

Decoy Spiders

Many spiders use their nets as camouflage netting. The argiope spider of Brazil's Matto Grosso, for instance, has silvery zig-zag markings on its back which would instantly draw the eye but for the dazzling geometric patterns of its web.

The orb spider of the Adaman Islands in the Pacific has adopted a quite different method. It arranges the bodies of the insects it has sucked dry in two small piles, which exactly match the shape and colour of its own body. These are strategically placed on the web as decoys, so that an enemy only has one chance in three of catching the spider first time.

Bits and Pieces

Masking crabs camouflage themselves by sticking bits of seaweed and other debris all over themselves, and one species has struck up a symbiotic relationship with sponges. Using their pincers, they cut a piece from a living sponge, chew it in their mouths to make it sticky, and then implant it on tiny bristles that grow from their shells. The crab benefits by appearing sponge-like, the sponge benefits by being transported to new sources of food. A different technique has been adopted by the sponge crab (*Dromia vulgaris*) which uses its specially adapted rear legs to hold pieces of live sponge over its back.

A similar means of camouflage is employed by a large leaf-eating weevil in the mountains of New Guinea. It carries an entire garden on its back, planted with minute algae, fungi, moss and liverwort. As many as nineteen different varieties of plant have been found on the back of a single inch-long creature. Even more astonishing, the plants in turn provide the environment for a whole population of microscopic mites, rotifers and nematodes.

Infra-red and the Fake Chipmunk

Many jungle creatures, notably frogs, have evolved green colouring as a camouflage among the leaves. But this defence is useless against snakes and birds which can see in infra-red. So some tree frogs have developed a skin pigment that matches the leaves, not only in the visible part of the spectrum, but in the infra-red as well.

Finally, mention should be made of the extraordinary trick of the female green-tailed towhee, the bird that imitates a mammal. When a hawk swoops over her nest, she drops to the ground like an animal that has lost its footing, throws up her tail and goes scurrying off just like a chipmunk, even imitating the mammal's bounces and darts.

LINDA GARLAND

The Courtship of the Carpenter Bee

The carpenter bee has a strong but somewhat short-sighted sexual instinct. In fact, it will attempt to mate with anything that flies – literally anything. Moths, birds, dandelion seeds, scraps of paper, provided it is airborne the carpenter bee will have a go at it. They have even been seen in desperate pursuit of aircraft.

But this is not the only example of courtship with inanimate objects. Tortoises have difficulty distinguishing each other from the surrounding landscape at the best of times, and the garden (or common) species will butt against sundials and garden furniture, or even try to mount people's shoes, if it cannot find a female.

The Cat-Bird

On the face of it, the bird-dog and the dog-fish are improbable animals, but the cat-bird sounds even stranger. In fact, there are two kinds of them. 'Cat-bird' is the common name for a type of American thrush that mews like a cat, and this name is also applied to the Australian bower bird.

Cats

The history of cat breeds is virtually unknown, but the evidence seems to suggest that the main ancestor was a wild north African striped tabby. It was this animal which proved more efficient than genets, ichneumons (the north African mongoose), weasels or ferrets at destroying the vermin which threatened the grain stores of the early agricultural settlements.

Most of the names for the cat have a Middle-Eastern or African origin. 'Puss' and 'pussy', for instance, are derived from the name of an Egyptian goddess – Pasht, Bastet or Bubastis. 'Tabby' is of Turkish origin, a word used to describe striped or watered silk taffeta before it became associated with cats with a striped coat.

'Cat' itself is thought to come from north Africa. In Ethiopia princes were named after animals and one was called *Schaba-Ko* (Cat Lord). The Arabic word is *quttah.*

Throughout Europe the word in different languages sounds very similar, derived from the Romanic forms *cattus* and *catta.* There is *chat* (French), *gatto* (Italian), *gato* (Spanish), *katti* (Finnish), *cat* (Gaelic), and *kot* (Russian).

Cats reached China from Egypt around 3000 BC and were given the name *mao* or *miu.*

In some societies cats were worshipped, in others condemned as a symbol of Satan. In Egypt it was a crime to kill them, and they were mummified and buried in consecrated cemeteries, a fact exploited in recent times by an entrepreneur from Manchester, England, who unearthed large quantities of their remains and sold them as manure.

In Turkey a unique breed of swimming cats, which still survives, was considered sacred because of the auburn mark on the back – the 'thumbprint of Allah'. These cats have only one coat (others have two), which allows them to swim for long periods without getting waterlogged.

In pre-Christian Scandinavia the cat was sacred to the mother goddess Freyja. But by the Middle Ages a neat about-turn had taken place, with the black cat becoming the symbol of Satan and the constant companion of witches. In 1484, Pope Innocent VIII ordained that when a witch was burnt at the stake, her cat should be cast into the fire with her.

Despite this change in fortunes, the cat has remained a valuable domestic companion. As one author put it: 'It is remarkable that neither the invention of the mousetrap nor any of the refinements of chemical warfare now practised against rats and mice have succeeded in putting the cat out of business.'

The cat's influence on our language remains in innumerable phrases and sayings. Back in 393 BC, Aristophanes wrote: 'If a cat crosses your path, it's a sign of bad luck.'

In Japan it is said: 'The borrowed cat catches no mice.' In other words, no one is going to lend his best mouser. In Arabia the saying goes: 'The cat that is always crying catches nothing.'

The phrase 'A cat may look at a king' has an uncertain origin but, in its German form, is said to have originated with a remark of the Emperor Maximilian I in 1517 when he visited the shop of one Hieronymus Resch, who made wood-cuts. Resch's cat lay at ease on a table and stared suspiciously at the Emperor throughout the interview.

'To be a cat's paw' dates from an ancient fable about a monkey who seized hold of a cat and used one of its paws to take roast chestnuts from a fire. The same story is told in Arabia, except that roast crab is substituted for the chestnuts.

'To live under the sign of the cat's foot' is to be henpecked. 'To let the cat out of the bag' refers to a common trick whereby a cat was put in a bag and sold as a suckling pig. If you were stupid enough to buy it unseen, you had acquired a 'pig in a poke'.

The term 'cat's cradle' is a debased version of 'catch cradle' – the manger of Jesus.

Chinchilla

Chinchilla, the small burrowing animal with fur so fine you cannot feel it with your fingertips, was hunted almost to extinction fifty years ago. Its last refuge was along the remote frontier of Chile and Peru, but the pelts were so valuable that the Indians used to hunt them with trained weasels, in the same way that Europeans use ferrets to catch rabbits.

However, in 1922 an American engineer called M. F. Chapman, after a five-year search, managed to bring fourteen live specimens down from the mountains of Chile and transported them to America in a refrigerated cage. There are now about seventy thousand of them, being bred in captivity on fur farms.

Choir Birds

Like other Russians, the citizens of Kharkov have enjoyed concerts of classical music by their local choir for some thirty years. But the difference in their case is that the choir consists entirely of canaries.

Now, there is nothing new about animal 'musicians'. Circus seals have been trained to play horns, and a chorus of barking dogs from Chicago has even released a hit record. But these are crude efforts based on trickery and carefully edited tape-recordings. The Kharkov canaries are in an altogether different league.

Under their conductor, Fyodor Fomenko, the birds have given more than two thousand performances from a repertoire of eighty works which include Beethoven's 'Moonlight' sonata, Strauss waltzes, Russian folksongs, and pieces by Schubert and Shostakovich. In fact, their only limitation has been that the choir was restricted to works which do not require a bass voice. But even that problem now seems to have been solved. As *The Times* reported on 7 May 1980: 'Local ornithologists, who have been trying for years to induce some of the leading soloists to sing the lower parts, have succeeded at last, with careful crossing and good breeding, in deepening the vocal range of some of the performers.'

The Water Civet

Some animals are so rare that they have only been seen in the wild on one occasion. Civets, for instance, are a group of cat-like animals which includes linsangs and musangs, and in 1916 the Lang-Chapin Expedition to the Congo noted another species. While in the Iturbi region, they obtained a specimen of an entirely new civet of considerable beauty.

Unlike the other species, it was a semi-aquatic creature, about 18 inches (45cm) long with a 14-inch (35-cm) tail, webbed feet and markings like a racoon.

The animal was called *Osbornictis* after the American zoologist, Dr Henry Fairfield Osborne, but has never been collected since, and nothing is known about its life in the wild.

Cloth of Gold

The meeting between Henry VIII of England and the King of France was a great historical pageant, which became known as 'The Field of the Cloth of Gold' because of the glittering cloaks and tunics of the noblemen. However, this had nothing to do with gold. The shimmering fabric called the 'cloth of gold' was actually woven from the beards of mussels.

The byssus threads (or 'beard') which acnhor mussels to their rocks have been made into cloth for centuries, and were used for such things as gloves up to Victorian times.

Cockroaches

Fossil remains confirm that the cockroach has been around, virtually unchanged, for 275 million years. Of the 3,500–4,000 species, only 5 per cent have been studied in detail, and only about half a dozen have adapted to life in human dwellings, but these few are a major pest which a multi-million pound exterminator industry has yet to bring under control.

Adult cockroaches are designed for feeding and reproduction, and little else. They spread around the world on slave shops, Phoenician vessels, Spanish galleons (and Jumbo jets), and can survive practically any conditions.

When a supermarket in East Osaka, Japan, offered a bounty for each cockroach caught, it was inundated with 98,499 within a week. Two women collected 1,351 in just one apartment house.

Various methods of control have been tried. After twenty-four years of research a Dutch chemist succeeded in isolating the sex hormone from 75,000 virgin cockroaches – a mere 200 millionths of a gramme of periplanone-B. After analysing its chemistry and synthesizing it, he found that one hundredth of a gramme was sufficient to excite 100 million males. Sex control may be the key to dealing with cockroaches in the future.

Cockroaches have many unusual attributes. For example, they can live for up to seven days after having their heads cut off – due apparently to clusters of nerve cells in their bodies. Even more curious, they learn faster without their heads than with them.

The cockroach's body also contains 'giant fibres' which are even larger in diameter than human nerve fibres. Impulses can travel along them at a staggering 15 feet per second, ten times faster than impulses travel along our nerves. This may account for the cockroach's quick reactions.

The German cockroach, the biggest household pest in the United States, has the unique distinction of being 'born' twice. The female first lays the eggs, only to draw them back inside her body until they emerge as young cockroaches.

Cockroaches are closely related to termites, and there is some evidence to suggest that termites are in fact little more than 'socialized' cockroaches. In Australia there is a cockroach-like termite, in America a termite-like cockroach.

The Song of the Cricket

Did you know that crickets sing with their right wing over their left, while katydids rub their left over the right? There is no answer to this kind of conversation-stopper, but there's more to these cheerful little insects than meets the ear. Did you know, for instance, that they hear through their knees – and can be used as thermometers?

Crickets and grasshoppers produce their sounds in the same way, by rubbing a 'file' (a row of toughened pegs attached to one of the veins in the wing) over a 'scraper' (another toughened vein, at the edge of the wing). The amplification is provided by an almost circular wing membrane stretched as taut as a drumhead.

Their remarkable hearing organs are located near the knees of their front legs, and are so sensitive they can hear ultrasonic tones at a frequency of 90,000 cycles a second – two octaves higher than the human auditory threshold.

But there is something even stranger. In most animals, the eyes, ears (and other sense organs, like whiskers) are arranged in pairs, so that the animal can use them as directional range-finders. Humans locate a sound by subconsciously comparing the time it takes to reach each ear, and it is only possible to measure this split-second difference because the distance between our ears is fixed. But the distance between the cricket's front legs is constantly changing, so each of them must act independently as a highly directional microphone.

If we had ears like this, we would probably use them by moving them around until the sound was loudest, and then noting in which direction they were pointing. For some reason, the crickets do exactly the opposite. They move their legs around until the sound is weakest, and then move in the opposite direction!

What makes this so strange is the fact that the other crickets have so many different signature tunes, they need to hear every detail to identify them. No two species of crickets, katydids or grasshoppers have the same song. In most of the four thousand species of crickets, it is only the male that chirps; and members of the same species in a field may synchronize their chirping to keep in time with each other.

The songs are inherited and play a vital part in their life-style. Courtship songs lure the females. Rivalry songs ward off other males. The 'staying together' song ensures that during the mating the female does not leave before the male's sperm has entered her. Mole crickets even produce 'recognition chirps' to keep in touch with each other underground.

In 1897 a professor of physics named Dolbear worked out how to tell the temperature by cricket chirps, and explained the technique in an article entitled 'The Cricket as Thermometer'. All you had to do was to time the chirrups and apply the formula:

$$T = \frac{50N - 40}{4}$$

where T is the temperature and N the number of chirps per minute. If you have the patience, you might like to try it out.

Incidentally, crickets are not the loudest insects. This accolade goes to the male cicada, which produces a sound that can be heard a quarter of a mile away, and which is officially described by the US Department of Agriculture as 'Tsh-ee-EE-e-ou'.

D

Devil's Flowers

One usually thinks of a mantis as being a green insect, but there are a number of species that imitate the colouring of flowers. (It is astonishing how many insects imitate flowers, and how few flowers imitate insects.)

The most beautiful is probably the Malayan species which looks like a delicate pink orchid. But the name 'Devil's Flower' was originally applied to an African mantis with brilliant red and white legs.

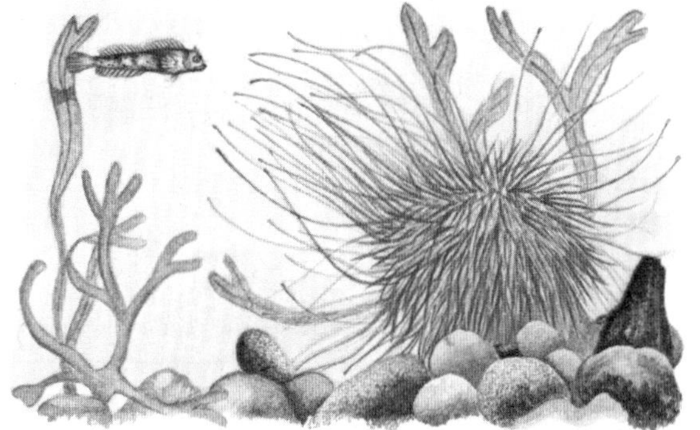

DAVID WEBB

The Diadem

There are many plants and animals which protect themselves with spikes. Provided they are sharp enough and stick out in all directions, it is an effective way of making themselves inedible. These have to stick out in all directions because they never know where the attack may come from. But suppose they could. Suppose they had some kind of early warning system, think what an advantage it would be to concentrate their defences by pointing them all in the same direction.

Only one creature seems to have evolved this technique, and it happens to be one of the simplest – the Diadem sea-urchin.

To a sea-urchin, anything which swims (and therefore casts a shadow) is potential danger, When a fish swims by and the shadow falls on it, an automatic control system takes over; the Diadem's spikes swing towards the intruder and track its movements as it passes overhead.

How to Tell the Difference

Latin names are all very well, but most of us have a more basic problem in identifying animals. What's the difference, for instance, between alligators and crocodiles? Or camels and dromedaries? The question is so obvious, it is almost embarrassing to ask.

But do not despair, because you are not alone. After much research, we came to the surprising conclusion that most scientists do not know either. One authority after another gives different answers, qualified by endless 'ifs' and 'buts' and 'on the other hand's'.

However, we have tried to sort out a few of the more common confusions and here, for the first time, is a list of Everything You Wanted To Know But Never Dared Ask. Now what exactly is the difference between, for instance . . .

Alligators and Crocodiles

In habits and appearance, alligators (which include the animal called a caiman) and crocodiles are almost identical. The main difference between them lies in their teeth. When a crocodile has its mouth closed you can see a pair of fangs sticking up from the lower jaw. Alligators also have fangs (they're actually the fourth tooth on either side), but you cannot see them because their lower jaw is smaller than the upper, and their fangs fit into a socket in the gums above. With their mouths open it is difficult to tell them apart, except that the alligators' heads are wider and shorter, and they usually have a blunter snout. The best way to identify them is geographically. In China or North America it is probably an alligator. Anywhere else, especially in Africa, it is almost certainly a crocodile.

Camels and Dromedaries

This one makes a good trick question, because there is no difference. Dromedaries *are* camels. The difference lies between two types of camel, the dromedaries with one hump, and the bactrians with two. There is an easy way to remember: if you lay a capital D (for dromedary) on its side, it has one hump, and a capital B (for bactrian) has two.

Dolphins and Porpoises

Dolphins have often been called porpoises and they are both intelligent, warm-blooded mammals with similar habits. The bottle-nosed dolphin is actually referred to as the common porpoise in many textbooks. It is no good checking an atlas this time, because they both live just about everywhere (including freshwater lakes and streams). There are so many different species it is difficult to be precise, but porpoises are generally smaller, with pronounced beak-like snouts and laterally-compressed spade-like teeth. Incidentally, they belong to the order of cetacea – in other words, both dolphins and porpoises are a form of whale.

Frogs and Toads

In the temperate areas of the world it is easy to recognize a toad, because it is much larger than frogs, with a drier, warty skin. In the tropics, things are more confusing because there are some very bizarre kinds of frog, and a number of species which are anatomically part-frog and part-toad.

Tortoises, Turtles and Terrapins

The main difference here is between the American and English language use. In America, a tortoise is one of the forty species of land-living chelonians of the Testudinidae (including the garden tortoise). A terrapin means just one species, the diamond-back (*Malaclemys terrapin*) – and everything else is a turtle.

In England, however, the terms are used more loosely. Tortoises include water-living species such as the pond tortoise, terrapins are any of the freshwater testudinidae, especially those kept in aquaria – and 'turtles' is applied only to the deep-sea ocean-going chelonians.

Kangaroos and Wallabies

Scientists have failed to find the slightest difference – anatomically, biochemically or in any other way – between kangaroos and wallabies. So they took the only course open to them, and invented one. As a result we can state with complete confidence that if its hind feet are more than 10 inches (25.4cm) long, it it a kangaroo; and if they are less, it is a wallaby.

This rule only applies to 'proper' kangaroos. As practically everything in Australia hops, there are also ten species of 'rat-kangaroos', two species of 'tree-kangaroos', and the rock-climbing species, too.

Snakes and Lizards

It may seem unnecessary to include these creatures as the differences would appear so obvious – but they are not. Snakes originally evolved from lizards, and several species got stuck halfway between. Many of teiid lizards, for instance, only have rudimentary legs and look remarkably like snakes. But the classic example is the slow-worm (or blind-worm) which has lost its legs entirely and is often assumed to be a snake. Yet it possesses all the other distinctive characteristics of lizards: it has eyelids (which snakes do not), it does not have a forked tongue (which snakes do), and the two halves of its lower jaw (which are separated in snakes) are still joined together at the front.

Sheep and Goats

Once again, you may wonder why people make such a fuss about 'separating the sheep from the goats', because they are so obviously different. But this is only so in the domestic varieties. In the wild they are indistinguishable. The only characteristic unique to one group, and not possessed by the other, appears to be the transverse slot across the pad of goat's hooves. But even here there is an exception, because there is a breed of sheep in India with slotted hooves. Zoologists classify all these wild varieties as goats, with the exception of three vaguely sheep-like species – the aoud, the bharal and the 'true sheep' (*Ovis*) which includes a wild Mediterranean animal called the mouflon.

Panthers and Leopards

It sounds rather over-emotional, but eminent naturalists once challenged each other to duels over whether panthers and leopards were different animals. In fact, it was the same confusion as that which arose between camels and dromedaries, because they are the same thing. All of the 'great cats' that can roar – including lions, leopards and tigers – are varieties of panther (as is reflected in their Latin names, *panthera leo*, *panthera pardus* and *panthera tigris*).

Pumas and Cougars

Pumas, cougars, mountain lions, catamounts, and scores of other Spanish and Indian names, all refer to the same single species (*Profelis concolor*), now generally called the puma.

Moths and Butterflies

Moths and butterflies are both lepidoptera, but it is easy to tell the difference between them. Apart from the fact that moths are usually smaller and duller, and have fatter bodies, there are two clear distinctions. A moth's antennae are not clubbed, and it cannot fold its wings together vertically in the way that butterflies do.

You can also tell their larvae apart, though you will need a magnifying glass to spot the difference. If you look closely at the rear legs of their caterpillars, the butterfly's are smooth but the moth's have rows of small hooks down them.

The Dik-Dik

The dik-dik is a species of pygmy antelope with the prodigious jumping power of rodents (in fact, their colouring is almost identical to an American rodent, the agouti). They are the most acrobatic of all four-legged animals. Not even the kangaroo can equal their mastery of the hop as a means of locomotion, and when a herd of dik-dik takes off, bouncing up and down like ping-pong balls, flying in all directions oblivious of trees and rocks, it is one of the most spectacular and elegant sights in nature.

Dingleberries and Discus Fish

Dingleberries are not fruit but fish. To be more precise, they are the pale, globular young of the American trunk fish, which are often found lurking under patches of seaweed along tropical coastlines.

The adult form is a slow-moving, ungainly animal with a rigid, box-like body. It is so rectangular it actually has corners and, the bony structure on the outside of its body prevents it swimming in the usual way of fish, so it floats slowly through the water like a small suitcase.

Fortunately it is so heavily armoured that rapid movement is not necessary, and it has a very efficient defence system based on nerve poison. When a trunk fish is placed in an aquarium, the other inhabitants immediately show signs of distress and rise to the surface gasping for air, and eventually die. How it emits the poison and what it consists of is still a mystery.

If the trunk fish is the squarest animal, the discus fish is the nearest thing to a plate – perfectly flat, perfectly round and about 8 inches (20cm) in diameter. They are species of Pompadour fish from the Amazon and come in three colours: green, blue and brown. Amongst their usual habits, the parents hang their new-born by a thread from a

Trunk fish

JOHN WOODCOCK

convenient leaf or plant stem, and fan them for sixty hours. They also – which is very strange for a fish – appear to suckle their young. When the babies hatch, the only food they will accept is a 'milk' or white mucus exuded from their parents' bodies.

Distraction Displays

Many reptiles and birds – and some mammals – have the ability to feign death as a means of defence, but in some creatures the trick is carried even further.

Ladybird beetles, for instance, will fall over as if dead when attacked, and then squeeze drops of blood from their knee joints. Since their blood is extremely poisonous, this ploy can prove even more effective.

Several species of crickets of the *katydid* family, known as long-horned grasshoppers, also have this ability to cause blood to flow from their joints. The master of the technique is a north African species, *Eugaster guyoni*, which is able to squirt well-aimed streams of its blood directly at an attacker.

But the most curious example of the bleeding trick was published by W. E. Bartlett in *Nature* magazine in 1920:

'On Sunday morning, 30 May, about 10 o'clock, I noticed a common western hog-nosed viper, about 20 inches (50cm) in length, basking on the lawn in the warm sunshine. I approached the serpent in company with a friend to make some investigation of it, and only to interfere with it enough to keep it from crawling away. The creature went through the usual feint of being a dangerous snake that is peculiar to this species, and quickly began to coil and recoil and to hide its head under its body. After it had done this a short time it turned on its back, but continued to writhe as though injured severely. Gradually it assumed a position simulating that of a dead snake lying on its back, with its mouth completely inverted and bleeding. This was done in such a way that the head appeared to be completely mashed or severed. The exudate of blood from the entire surface of the mouth was perfect. It was the most complete and well-carried-out feint of a tragic death that I have ever witnessed, and all without the least torture or stroke of any kind from me. I only detained the snake by placing my foot in front of it and turning it back once at the beginning. We left the creature in this apparently killed condition, only to see that it disappeared in a very short time.'

Dogs

The most surprising thing about dogs is that no one knows where they came from. It is odd, when one thinks of the care lavished on their pedigrees, that they should be the only domestic animal whose ancestry has never been established.

There are nine wild species recognized as canine: wolves, jackals, foxes, fennecs, the Arctic fox, grey foxes, the South America jackals, the maned wolf and the racoon dog. But none of them, with the possible exception of wolves, bear any relationship to domestic breeds.

Are they all descended from wolves? Or from some other animal, now extinct? (In which case, where are the fossilized remains?) Or are the different breeds descended from different ancestors? There is simply no evidence to say for sure.

Dogs produce new breeds so rapidly that it is impossible to trace their ancestry from historical records. From that moment the first animal strayed into a prehistoric camp-site, there have evolved many thousands of different kinds which have

'False' canines include (left to right) the maned wolf, Indian dhole, Columbian bush dog, and Cape hunting dog

appeared, and disappeared, with the cultures that produced them.

The ancient Egyptians, for instance, had hunting dogs and animals which resembled both the greyhound and dachshund, but none of them were related to their modern equivalents. In fact, most of our domestic breeds go back no further than a few centuries. The older ones, like spaniels and terriers, were first recorded in fifteenth-century Dutch breeding books. Poodles made their appearance about two hundred years ago, and many breeds have only emerged since Victorian times.

False Dogs

There are three species with the curious name of 'False Canines', because they differ in some respect from the basic dog model.

The Dholes of Tibet and Mongolia look like dogs but they have different teeth, fourteen nipples instead of ten, and upturned muzzles (all other dogs have convex noses). African hunting dogs have a different number of toes, the colouring of a tortoiseshell cat, and wide bell-shaped ears. And the Bush Dogs of South America are like fat little dachshunds with bushy tails, and make a distinctive chirruping and clicking sound.

The African species are ruthlessly efficient hunters who tackle any kind of big game, including lions. They show contempt for domestic dogs, which they hunt and kill.

Rare Dogs

Among the wild canines of South America are the only endangered species of dog, the xoloitzcuintlis, and a coastal species called the crab-eating dog, which dives for shellfish in shallow water.

Domestic Dogs

The idea that domestic dogs are somehow more intelligent than their counterparts in the wild is nonsense. What we have done is to take these adaptable, go-anywhere, eat-anything, all-purpose animals and turn them into rather stupid specialists.

Greyhounds, for instance, have developed better eyesight, but they are so weak and neurotic that they could never survive on their own. Without the pressures and tensions of life in the wild, many of their senses seem to atrophy. The sense of smell of the most highly trained tracker dog cannot compete with that of a wolf.

Perhaps the most telling difference is that the brain of a domestic dog is, on average, about 30 per cent smaller than those of wild species.

Shaggy Dogs

From wolf-pack to poodle parlour, it has been a long and often bizarre relationship.

In eleventh-century Norway, a deposed king gave his subjects a choice of being ruled by a slave or a dog. They chose the dog, which was crowned King Saur I and successfully occupied the throne for some time, until the royal bodyguards allowed a wolf to devour it.

The last independent ruler of the Indian state of Gujarat was His Highness Sir Mahabat Khan Babi Pathan, Nawab of Junagadh. Each of his eight hundred pedigree dogs of various breeds had its own room, electric light and uniformed servant. Their upkeep cost the Nawab £32,000 a year, not including the cost of the ceremonial state canine weddings and funerals, which were conducted with enormous pomp, including dog clothes covered with precious jewels, and processions of elephants. When India became independent, the Nawab, a Muslim, retired to Pakistan.

The Greek historian Xenophon wrote the first manual on dogs. Aristotle was the first person to note that dogs have dreams.

The Romans had as many as 180 names for their

PHILIP HOOD

dogs. Bitches were called Alce, Margarita, Myia, Patrice, Pasa, Phile, Theia and Therippe. Watchdogs were named Aello (listener), Cerberus (watcher), Hylactor (barker). Hunting dogs were dubbed Lailaps (tempest), Agriodus (sharptooth), Cainon (killer). Incidentally, there were so many dogs in the larger cities of the Roman Empire that every piece of property guarded by a dog had to be marked *cave canem* (Beware of the dog!) to warn potential thieves that this was not just an ordinary street animal.

When Alexander Pope presented the Prince of Wales with a pet dog, he had the collar inscribed with what turned out to be one of his most famous epigrams:

'I am his Highness' dog at Kew,
Pray tell me, sir, whose dog are you?'

Reykjavik, the capital of Iceland, has a population of one hundred thousand but not a single dog. It is against the law to own a dog in Iceland unless it is needed to herd livestock.

In 1978 the French Post Office published a report stating that three thousand postmen had been attacked by dogs in the previous year – a 41 per cent increase over a five-year period. In rural areas, the report said, 66 per cent of dogs attacked the postmen's calves, and 12 per cent their buttocks.

The world's first dog museum opened in July 1979 at Leeds Castle, near Maidstone in Kent. It contains a collection of sixty antique dog collars dating from the early sixteenth century. They range from a spiked collar for wolf-hounds to a velvet-lined silver collar which belonged to the Prince Archbishop of Salzburg's dog.

The first solar-heated doghouse – the 'Solar Rover' – was marketed by Solar 1 Manufacturing Inc. of Virginia in 1979. A large cedar structure, it came complete with solar panels, complete insulation and a flexible plastic door flap that magnetically sealed itself after the dog entered or departed. The inside temperature remained 20–40 degrees warmer than the outside even during the night. In summer, the solar panels could be covered, a company spokesperson explained, 'so Rover doesn't turn into a hotdog'.

Anders Hallgren opened the world's first school for dog psychiatrists in Arboga, Sweden, in June 1979, although he admitted that his graduates might have problems getting jobs. Hallgren himself owned a cat. He did not have a dog, he explained, because 'I just don't have enough time'.

Domestic Animals

There are so many domestic animals that it is difficult to imagine they have any physical characteristic in common, apart from their dependence on human beings. Yet they do have something in common: they literally *look alike*. In every case the domestic species has developed smaller brow ridges and smaller, flatter faces than the same species in the wild!

If one compares cats, dogs, pigs, horses and cows, the wild form always has a larger face with heavy muscular ridges. Human beings, who after all are *the* most domesticated of animals, share the same anatomical trait. The skull of *Homo sapiens* bears the same relationship to that of Neanderthal hominids as the skull structure of a tame rat bears to a wild one's.

The reasons for this are a 'chicken-and-egg' problem. Curt P. Richter of Johns Hopkins University has shown that domestic animals, which have been chosen over generations for their docile nature, have relatively small adrenal glands. But which came first – appearance or temperament – is anyone's guess.

It may be that the chemical balance is linked to bone growth, or that less aggressive animals do not need such muscular jaws – or a combination of both reasons. It is even possible that the protected environment encourages neoteny (retention of juvenile features in adult animals), and that domestic animals are 'fixed' at an immature stage. Passivity, like curiosity and the ability to learn, is a characteristic of the very young. People have often remarked on the affinity we have with flat-faced animals – koala bears, rabbits, cats and so on. We feel much closer to chimps and gorillas, for instance, than we do to baboons; and children, in particular, have a marked preference for flat-faced cuddly toys. Are we responding to their physical appearance, the passivity and sociable nature that goes with it, or to the fact that, like us, they are a form of adult 'children'?

Here is a miscellany of some of the stranger animals we have selected, and shaped, to share our lives, from sea-sheep and aquatic cows to edible dogs and guard-rabbits.

The North Ronaldsay sheep of the Orkneys are the only animals that live exclusively on seaweed, mainly kelp. Local rumour has it that they are alerted to the turning of the tide by a worm that tickles their feet.

In western and north-western South America the guinea-pig has for several centuries played an important role as a domestic animal, providing one of the only sources of meat for the Indians of that region. Thousands of guinea-pigs were kept in every Indian settlement, and in some houses flocks of up to one hundred shared the accommodation with their human hosts.

One of the most startling facts about dogs is that they have frequently been bred for their protein rather than their loyalty. Dogs are still sold as foodstuff in the streetmarkets of China and south-east Asia. By all accounts they make excellent eating, usually in stews, and taste rather like rabbit. The Aztecs of Central America considered them a delicacy and raised a special breed of edible dog for the table. It is long extinct, but we know exactly what it looked like from the stone carvings and paintings they left behind, which show a plump, cuddly little animal the size of a hare or small terrier.

In many ancient societies, cattle were the earliest currency. In pre-Christian Ireland, for instance, three cows were the price of a maidservant, and one white cow was worth six women slaves. In Rome cattle were called *pecus* and a herd *pecunia*. As the Romans generally had to pay for cattle in cash, *pecunia* became the word for money in general – hence 'pecuniary'. *Fee* originally meant cattle in Old English; while in Hindi a herd of zebu is called *rupa*, from which Indians get the word 'rupee'.

The Christmas turkey originated in Mexico and Central America, where it was domesticated by pre-Columbian Indians. It was introduced into Europe in 1523–24 and rapidly became popular. In 1560 a hundred and fifty turkeys were eaten at a wedding feast at Arnstadt in Germany. The turkey first became part of the traditional English Christmas feast in 1585.

The humpless Kuri cattle which live on the shores of Lake Chad in central Africa have unique inflated, spongy horns. They often swim from one of the lake's islands to another in search of forage, with their heads tilted back and horns resting on the surface to give them extra buoyancy.

The tent-dwellers of the Nejd, in present-day Saudi Arabia, were an example of a whole culture based around the camel. His coarse wool was used to make sleeping mats and light coats. The hides were used for tents and shoes, and the dung was collected for fuel. Camel milk was drunk thinned with water, made into sour-tasting cheese, or used in a cosmetic preparation as face cream.

The Belted Galloway, a rare British breed of cattle, has a coat well adapted to protect it from cold, moist winds. An inner layer of hair carries a positive electrical charge, which retains heat, while an outer coat has a negative charge. When the wind blows over the beast, the charges are strengthened and the hairs cling closer together so as to provide better weatherproofing.

The Aztec's 'edible' dog, thought to be the ancestor of today's dwarf chihuahua

RAY WINDER

Oraculum ex tripudio was a Roman form of future forecasting in which hens in a cage were given food and observed to see if they would eat fast (a good omen), slowly (a bad sign), or not at all (disaster). The method was popular with the army since it was portable and, in emergencies, edible. Knowing generals were careful to starve the hens beforehand so that they would immediately set to and assure the troops of victory. During the First Punic War (264–241 BC), the consul P. Claudius Pulcher lost his temper when his hens disdained the meal he offered them. He had them thrown into the sea, saying, 'May they drink if they won't eat.' But the drowned hens had the last laugh – Pulcher went on to lose the sea battle of Drepana (249 BC).

Keeping sheep for their milk was common in medieval England, and there was a thriving sheep dairy industry in the fourteenth century. The old English word for this kind of dairy, *wich*, survives in the names of such towns as Norwich and Ipswich.

In 1788 the first twenty-nine Merino sheep reached Sydney after being shipped from South Africa. Just twenty-two years later, Australia had 290,000 of them.

Certain North American Indian tribes used to keep eagles as captive, semi-domesticated animals. Amongst the Shoshone, for instance, eagle aeries in the mountains were owned by particular braves –

one of the few types of property recognized by the tribe. The owner had to scale the cliffs to take the fledgling eagles from their nests. They were then reared in cages or tied to rocks and fed with pocket gophers or young groundhogs. When full grown, their feathers were plucked for arrows, decoration, or religious ceremonies. The eagles were then released at the top of a cliff, though it is doubtful if they could have survived in their denuded state.

The smallest domestic creatures are probably insects. Domestic insects? Put like that it seems unlikely, but there are several species of insect that are bred and nurtured in different parts of the world. The silk worm and the cochineal insect (whose crushed body provides the common food dye) are two of them. But in terms of sheer numbers, and the care lavished on them, the most common domestic insect is the fruit fly.

Because of the fruit fly's phenomenal breeding rate, it has become the favourite subject for the study of genetics and scientists raise millions of them in laboratories around the world. Every detail of their biology and behaviour has been studied, and more is known about them than any other creature (and certainly any insect) in the world.

At the annual rooster-crowing contest in Rogue River, Oregon, in 1978, White Lightning became the champion by sounding a record 112 cock-a-doodle-doos in half an hour. The previous record had been held by Beetle Baum for a quarter of a century.

In 1979, at the annual International Chicken Flying Meet in Rio Grande, Ohio, a 15-ounce barnyard bantam called Lola B. established a new record with a flight of 302 feet 8 inches, beating the previous record by some five feet.

A publican in Bristol, England, kept an aggressive guard-rabbit called Lollyplugs to protect his premises. It went about its duties with some enthusiasm until, sadly, it was kicked to death by intruders. Fortunately its offspring, Lollyplugs Jr, inherited his father's aggression – and his job. Aggressive rabbits are not as rare as the cuddly image of the 'bunny' suggests. In the United States, a rabbit called Harvey bit sixteen people during its brief but spectacular career. Adopted by the ASPCA as a victim of mistreatment, it became the focus for a national campaign against animal abuse, before succumbing to an ear infection in April 1978, at the age of three.

'Said my mother, "What is all this story about?"
"A cock and a bull," said Yorick.'
– Laurence Sterne, *Tristram Shandy*.

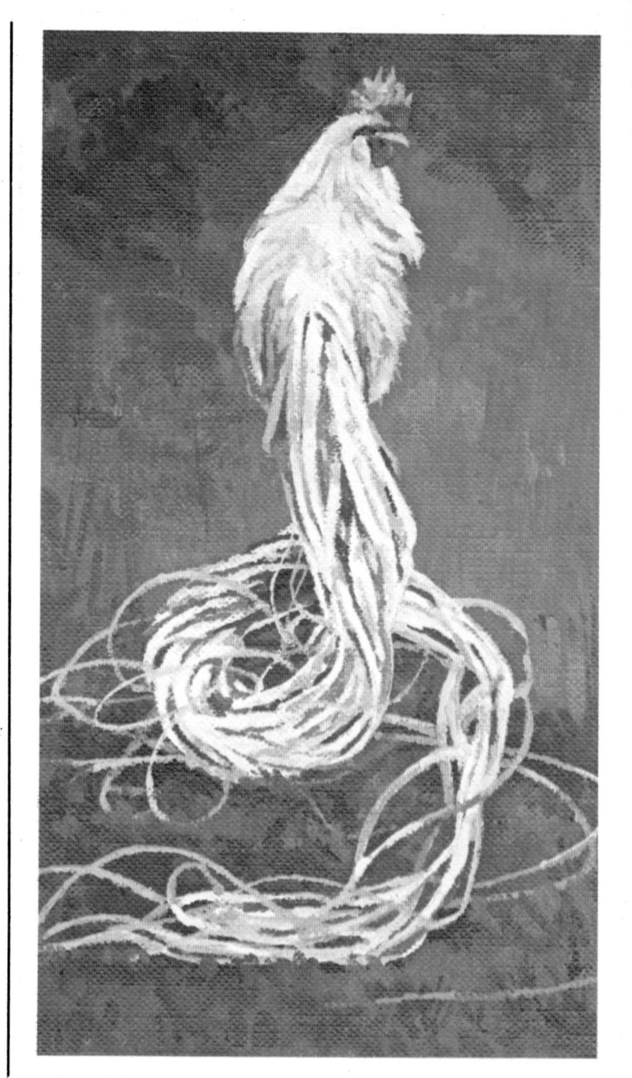

One of the most exotic (and impractical) of domestic animals, the Yokohama cockerel is bred for its 15-foot-long tail feathers.

The Doodlebug Trap

The doodlebug is one of those species, like army worms, which are named after their larvae because the adult form is so inconspicuous. In this case the adult is an insect like a dragon-fly with a 2-inch (5-cm) wing-span, which is rarely seen because it only flies at dusk, feeding on flies and the honeydew of aphids.

The larva, on the other hand, is a bristling, aggressive little creature with disproportionately large jaws, which lives off ants; and the resourceful way that it deals with its prey has earned it the alternative name of 'ant lion'. The ants may be just as big as it, and a great deal faster, but they are no match for the 'doodlebug trap'.

The larva lives in a burrow in dry sand, with a steep-sided, cone-shaped opening. It lies buried at the bottom of this pit until a passing ant disturbs the sand, and a few grains trickle down the side. It then rises from its lair, scoops a jawful of sand on to its head, and literally throws it at the intruder. It does this again and again, jerking its head backwards and forwards, and directing a stream of sand with remarkable force and accuracy. At the same time it is frantically digging away at the bottom of the pit.

The ant, caught off balance and half suffocated, finds the ground giving way underneath it, and eventually slides down to the waiting jaws below.

If the doodlebug cannot get a suitable grip on it, it may toss the ant in the air or bang it against the sides of the pit. It may even let it go, and if it shows signs of escaping, throw more sand at it as it tries to climb out.

Eventually, when the ant is exhausted, the doodlebug drags it down into the burrow, where it uses its secondary mouthparts to inject a paralysing fluid. It then eats the ant and disposes of the remains by putting them on its head and catapulting them out of the burrow.

Dry Crabs

Thirst is one of our most basic instincts, and the problem of maintaining the right amount of water in their bodies is common to all animals. If the water content falls, the chemicals in the body become dangerously concentrated: acids become more acidic, salts crystallize, and toxins build up with potentially fatal results.

Human beings, for instance, will become seriously ill with a loss of about 10 per cent of their body fluid, and death occurs when dehydration reaches 25–30 per cent. Even a desert locust can tolerate no more than a 30–35 per cent water loss. But there is one animal which can survive up to 50 per cent dehydration, literally doubling the ionic concentration of its body fluids – the Australian crab (*Holthusiana transversa*), commonly known as the side-walker.

Very few crustaceans have taken to dry land, let alone to the Australian outback where the average rainfall is only 6 inches (15cm) per year, but the side-walker can survive years of drought, thanks to its metabolism and a battery of survival techniques. Amongst these is the habit of sitting in the draught at the entrance of its burrow in the evenings until its shell is chilled, and then scuttling down into the warm earth so that condensation will form on it. The shell has even been specially modified for the job, so that every drop of moisture on it drains along small channels to the side-walker's mouth.

The Duckmole

If the camel looks as if it was designed by a committee, the duckmole appears to have been assembled from a random kit of parts. It has the brain of a reptile, and spurs on its ankles that inject a venomous poison. It has the fur of a mammal, the beak of a bird, and it lays eggs – though the beak is as soft as doeskin and the eggs do not have shells, but a leathery sheath like those of reptiles.

It spends most of its time underground or underwater, where it trawls for small larvae or crustaceans. The larger morsels of food are crushed between horny ridges, and stored in cheek pouches, as with a squirrel. Its young, however, are born with a full, and quite useless, set of teeth.

It has webbed claws, like those of a duck. But on dry land the webbing is drawn back, in a way no duck can do, to reveal the digging talons of a mole.

The animal combines so many different evolutionary lines that not surprisingly one scientist named it *Paradoxicus*, the paradox. Today we know it better as *Ornithorhynchus anatinus*, the duck-billed platypus.

The duckmole, or watermole or duckbill (call it what you will) is still regarded as one of the oddities of nature, but its original discovery caused a sensation. When the first complete skin to reach Europe was examined by naturalists at the British Museum, in 1798, they unanimously declared it a hoax. It was only when a complete carcass reached them four years later that they could bring themselves to accept the animal as genuine.

But arguments about it continued for nearly a century. It is now known that there are two species of egg-laying mammals (the other is the spiny ant-eater), but such behaviour was unheard of at the time. It seemed so unlikely that many authorities refused to accept the idea.

Finally, in 1884, the zoologist H. W. Caldwell set out for Australia to settle the matter once and for all. After dissecting several specimens, he had positive proof, and sent this laconic telegram to the British Association for the Advancement of Science, then meeting in Montreal: 'Monotremes oviparous, ovum meroblastic.' (Mono-tremes egg-laying, egg only partly divides). When this was read out, it is said that the delegates stood and cheered.

It is easiest to think of the duckmole as an example of convergent evolution, a reptile which has adopted the same environment and many of the adaptations of beavers.

Its pelt, and the broad tail it uses for swimming, are similar to a beaver's, and they have the same obsession with building tunnels. However, the duck mole burrows them into earth banks, so it does not need the gnawing teeth of a beaver to cut down vegetation. Another difference is the poor eyesight inherited from its reptile ancestors. Unlike beavers and otters, it cannot see underwater. It simply floats on the surface until something tempting comes along, closes its eyes, and dives for it.

Since duckmoles have no external ears (another reptilian drawback), they are deaf as well as blind underwater and have to rely on touch. They can stay under for up to five minutes at a time, and are silent swimmers, though according to one source they occasionally emit soft humming sounds.

Blindness is no disadvantage underground, and here the animal comes into its own. The tunnels are marvellous constructions up to 60 feet (18m) long, with an arched roof and a flat floor. Unlike most burrowing animals, they do not eject the earth, but compress it on either side to form a hard smooth lining to the tunnel. This not only keeps the burrow clean, but absorbs the water from their coats as they run along it. The technique is so effective that an animal can enter a tunnel dripping wet and emerge at the other end, a few minutes later, bone dry.

Duckmoles are not reptiles, of course, any more than birds are. But both are descended from them, and one of the most telling signs of their ancestry is their giant appetite.

Mammals are much better at extracting energy from food, and their superior metabolism gives them a huge advantage. In order to compete with them on equal terms, reptiles have to stoke up their metabolic rate by eating more.

It is not unknown for a duckmole weighing less than 3.5 lb to consume 540 earthworms, 200 meal-worms, 20–30 shrimps, plus a few small frogs and a couple of eggs each day. When two young animals were flown to New York from Brisbane, they were provided with a supply of 10,000 earthworms, 2,500 mealworms and 550 shrimps – and when the plane was delayed for two days en route, an urgent telegram had to be dispatched for fresh supplies.

Curiously enough, their main enemies are not human beings but that alien creature that has ravaged so much of the Australian environment – the rabbit.

In this case it takes the form of a competition between two burrowing species. The duckmole is very particular about its tunnels. A new one must be dug each year for each new brood, and it must be dug in virgin soil. Unfortunately, an average cross-section of Australia is riddled with rabbit holes, and whenever they run into one of these, the duckmoles abandon their territory in disgust.

PHILIP HOOD

Earwigs

Earwigs are those long-bodied insects, with a pair of calipers at one end, which you find scurrying around garden sheds. They appear flightless, but they do possess rudimentary wings and occasionally take to the air on summer evenings.

However, the strangest aspect of their lives is their intensely emotional approach to motherhood. Earwigs are the closest thing to mammals in the insect world, and one species even gives birth to live young.

The eggs of earwigs are not communal property, like those of ants. On the contrary, a mother earwig knows exactly which are hers, and defends them aggressively. During the breeding season in March, the female's behaviour changes. She starts acting like a broody hen, constantly fussing over her eggs, picking them up in her mouth and rearranging them, and licking them repeatedly. In the four weeks it takes them to hatch, she never leaves the nest, and has nothing to eat except the occasional egg that has gone bad.

The species that takes this behaviour to extremes is the Himinerus, which retains the eggs inside its body, where they are nourished by a kind of placenta, and whose young are born alive.

Why 'earwig'? Do they have a special affinity to ears? The notion is certainly widespread, as these insects have the same name in German (*Ohrwurm*) and French (*Perceoreille*). And there are certainly cases on record of them crawling into people's ears (one victim described it graphically as sounding like 'thunder in the ear'). But no zoologist would confirm that they prefer ears to any other nook or crevice.

Echo-Location

A wide range of animals employ a form of natural sonar called 'echo-location' – detecting and interpreting changes in the echoes of emitted sounds. Bats and dolphins are the best known users of this system, but it is a technique also employed by whales, certain seals, hippos, several species of birds, and possibly by penguins, rats and shrews.

The first insight into the phenomenon came at the end of the eighteenth century when Lazzaro Spallanzi began a series of experiments to try to determine how nocturnal animals could 'see' in the dark. He blinded bats but found it made no difference to their navigational abilities. Only when he plugged up their ears did they fly helplessly into objects. This left him, at the time, with an insoluble problem since it was believed that bats were mute.

The conundrum was solved in chance fashion one afternoon in 1938 in the laboratory of Harvard physicist G. W. Pierce, who had recently developed an apparatus for detecting ultrasonic sounds. A graduate student, Donald Griffin, came into the laboratory with a cage of bats and passed in front of Pierce's equipment, and there, for the first time, the ultrasonic chatter of bats was revealed.

Griffin went on to study how bats fly and feed using echo-location. The precise mechanisms and methods employed vary between species, but all are astonishingly accurate. The little brown bat, for instance, can detect fruit flies from 20 inches (50cm) away. The force of the sound it emits is twenty times more powerful than a pneumatic drill's (60 dynes per cm^3 compared to 3 dynes per cm^3).

While the military has devised many radar and

sonar systems since World War II, none can match the bat's equipment at close range. In military laboratories, bats have successfully dodged wires only a few times thicker than a human hair . . . which is not to say that bats never have accidents. There is considerable evidence that bats occasionally fly straight into walls and break their necks, and that such collisions occur more frequently than we are led to believe.

While cruising for food, the bat's sonar system operates on a 'scan mode', sending out about 10 signals, or bleeps, per second. But when it is tracking insect prey, the bat can emit bleeps at up to 200 a second, improving its accuracy as it zeroes in on the target. But how does one bat in a swarm recognize its own return echo?

One answer might be that bats modulate the frequency of their broadcast like an FM radio station. In the course of each broadcast in the scanning mode, a bat begins at a frequency close to 100,000 cycles per second, and then slides down to about 40,000 cps; each bat modulates its broadcast differently to give it its own distinctive signature. Similarly, when tracking, the bat starts at 30,000 cps and slides down to 20,000 cps.

One of the handful of bird species to use echo-location is the guacharo or oil-bird, whose best-known habitat is a vast subterranean cave, over half a mile long and 100 feet high, in Venezuela's Humboldt National Park. Like bats, the guacharos are nocturnal animals. They emit a series of 'clicks' at a frequency of about 7,000 cps.

The frequency range of dolphins, in contrast, extends up to 175,000 cycles per second. The first person to suspect the dolphin's echo-location capabilities was Arthur McBride, first curator of marine studies in Florida. He wanted to capture some bottle-nosed dolphins for display but was foiled by their apparent ability to sense the presence of his fine-mesh net. Only when he used a larger mesh did he succeed in capturing them.

He concluded from this that air bubbles trapped in the fine-mesh net must have reflected sound. To the dolphins, the densely-packed bubbles must have appeared like a solid wall, but with the larger mesh the sound echoes became scattered and diffuse.

His insight was not rediscovered until several years after his death, when detailed studies of dolphins' abilities were conducted.

Dolphins and whales live in a sea of sound. They have a large vocabulary of clicks, grunts, chuckles, squeaks and whistles. They can change frequencies at will, vary the energy peak, produce broad-band clicks or narrow-beam signals, and can flatten, heighten or shorten the sound beam.

They use a large pocket of fat in the forehead, called a 'melon', to focus the sound beam in much the same way that a lens is used to focus light waves. The melon emits a stream of clicks which are produced inside the animals' heads by a mechanism that is still not understood. The returning echoes are sensed through the jawbone, which is connected by a number of major nerve bundles to the inner ear.

By constantly turning its head as it listens, the dolphin is able not only to get an accurate fix on its target but also to determine the frequency of the returning sound, which provides vital clues as to the nature of the object. The system is astonishingly sophisticated, as this example quoted by Robert McNally indicates:

'After training a captive dolphin named Doris to recognize a copper plate while blindfolded and thus earn a reward, William Evans presented her with glass, plastic and aluminium substitutes of the same dimensions as the copper one. Doris recognized them immediately as counterfeits. Evans then tried an aluminium plate of a thickness calculated to have the exact same sonic reflectivity as the copper original. Doris still picked out the copper correctly. To do so, she had to perceive not only the basic features of the echo, but also their precise frequency composition, an analysis humans can make only with sophisticated engineering instruments.

'A feat like Doris's requires much more than keen ears. She had to remember the frequency mix in the copper echo, analyse the sound from the aluminium, then compare the memory with the sound for subtle, proportional differences. In addition, she performed the assay quickly, in a matter of seconds. Behaviour of this sort indicated cerebral activity of a very high order.'

The cetacean sonar system is not, however, a foolproof method for navigating the oceans, as the occasional strandings of whales indicate. It is now believed that whales become stranded when a gradually shelving coastline confuses their sonar apparatus. The most tragic of these occurrences occurred in 1974 when seventy-five sperm whales, including many pregnant females, were stranded on Muriwari Sands near Auckland, New Zealand. Because they have no sweat glands, and with insufficient water to cool their blood, the whales died of suffocation through overheating.

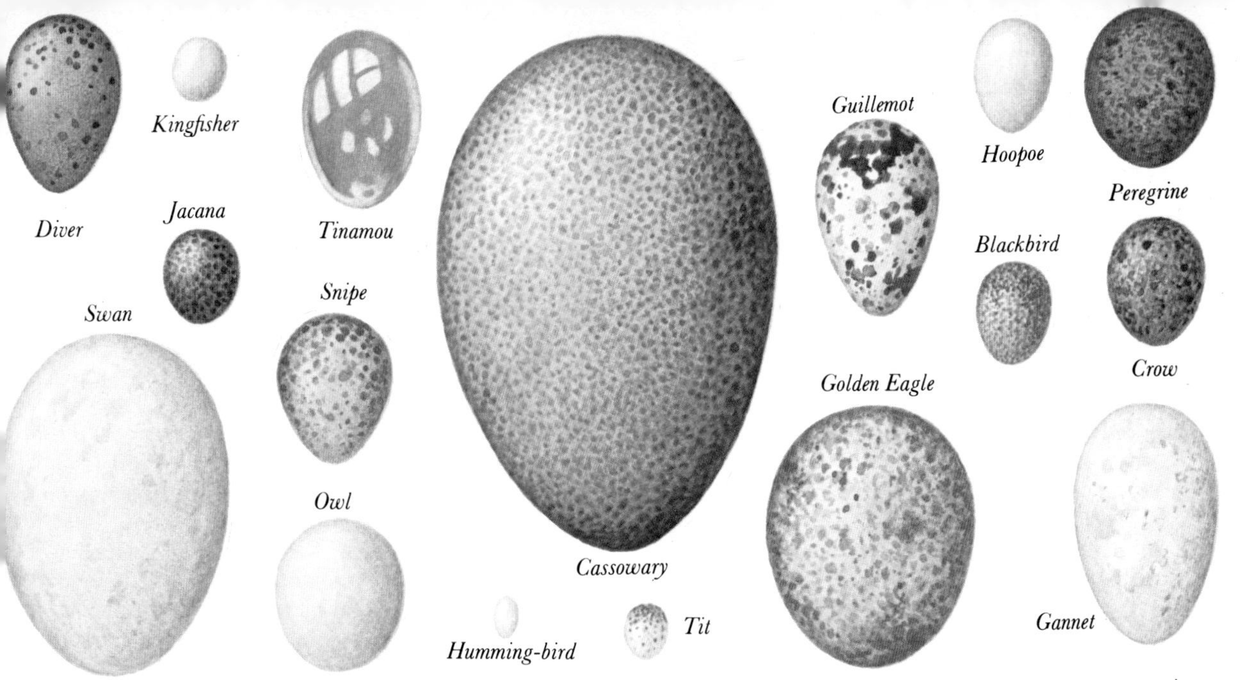

ROBERT MORTON

Eggs

Eggs can be spherical, elliptical or conical, but they are mostly egg-shaped – pointed at one end and blunt at the other. Aristotle believed that pointed hen's eggs produced male chickens and less pointed ones females, a myth that survived for many centuries. Another theory was that the shape of the egg is directly related to the form of the animal it contains.

In *Gulliver's Travels* the Lilliputians went to war over which end of their boiled eggs should be cracked first. That is a matter of preference, but it is interesting to note that all bird's eggs emerge from them *narrow end* first – though in 20–30 per cent of cases, they are reversed just before being laid.

Harvey's classic book *On the Generation of Animals* has a frontispiece showing the deity holding a large egg from which various animals are spilling. On it is inscribed the words EX OVO OMNIA, 'Everything from the egg'. It is the almost universal form of reproduction in the animal world.

Fish, insects, reptiles, amphibians and birds lay eggs in a bewildering variety of shapes, colours and sizes, and each species has developed its own method of protection. Mammals, of course, keep their eggs protected inside their bodies. Snails, grasshoppers, marine turtles and many other animals bury theirs underground. Pythons, butrefish and newts envelop them in their bodies. Komodo dragons place theirs high up in trees; centipedes roll them in sand to disguise them from predators.

Egg camouflage is a widespread phenomenon. The cassowary's eggs may be bright green, but they blend in perfectly with moss and other vegetation. Penguins carry their eggs on their feet to protect them from the freezing antarctic ice. Spiders spin a cocoon of silk around their eggs; while mosquitoes lay rafts of eggs with such tough shells that they can withstand drought and temperatures above boiling and below freezing point.

The Pipa toad extrudes her eggs from her body, which the male then fertilizes and spreads over her back with his webbed hind feet. When the female's back is covered with a hundred or more eggs, the skin slowly envelops them so that within thirty hours they have disappeared completely from view. Two weeks later, however, her back is vibrating as the tadpoles move about underneath, and after twenty-four days the young break out and swim away.

Female cockroaches keep their eggs in orderly rows in a hardened capsule called an *ootheca*. This has been described as a 'dainty lady's handbag' which opens at the upper edge when the nymphs hatch out. In some species, the female carries the bag about with her, sticking out of her genitalia; others drop it on the ground and camouflage it.

During the spring tides a fish called the grunion rides the Californian surf, along with the beach boys, to complete its unusual life-cycle. In their thousands, the females catch the largest breakers and head for the sand. There, as the surf ebbs away, they speedily drill a hole in the sand with their tails, deposit their eggs, cover them over and, sixty seconds later, ride the next wave out to sea. For two weeks the fry develop untouched by water and then emerge, ready to catch the next big tide out to the ocean.

Some species of birds lay an egg only once every two or three years. House sparrows and pigeons raise as many as five broods a year, but the hen is the only bird that can lay more than one egg a day.

It is now known that eggs are formed within that elastic, muscular tube, the oviduct. It is the pressure of waves moving down this which shapes the fluid egg. Different shapes are the result of different-sized oviducts and, in some cases, of stronger muscles.

Environment also has a part to play. Seabirds' eggs, for instance, tend to have an extreme oval shape, so that they roll in an arc of very small radius and are therefore less likely to fall over cliffs.

Giant Eggs

The bird which lays the largest egg in proportion to its size is the kiwi, which is about the size of a chicken but lays an egg ten times as big. It is difficult to know what advantage this gives kiwis, though, because there are numerous reports of them being found dead in their burrows with fully developed (but unlayable) eggs inside them.

The largest in terms of sheer size is the massive 30-lb ostrich egg – the biggest single cell in the world, and quite capable of supporting the weight of a 252-lb human being.

Ostrich eggs are supposed to be good to eat, and have been part of the human diet since prehistoric times, but since they contain the equivalent volume of several dozen hen's eggs, it takes about four hours to hard-boil them. It may also be advisable to have a saw or chisel handy to open them, because the shells are rock hard and more than ¾ in (2cm) thick.

Because they are so tough, they make an excellent substitute for china, and in certain parts of Africa the shells are carefully trimmed and decorated for use as water vessels.

It is a wonder that the baby ostrich ever gets out of its shell, but it has two advantages on its side. Firstly, the egg is a monococque structure, designed to withstand external compression, and it is much easier to break out than break in. Secondly, the embryo chick s equipped with a reinforced horn on its beak, which it uses as a miniature pick-axe.

The largest egg of all time belonged to the elephant bird (*Aepyornis maximus*), the giant prehistoric creature which gave rise to the legend of the Roc. It was 33 inches (84cm) long, 28½ inches (72cm) in circumference and held more than 2 gallons of liquid – about the largest size possible without requiring a shell so thick that no young could possibly get out.

The Numbers Game

The ostrich has a reasonable chance of survival in its armoured capsule, but the eggs layed by fish are so small and vulnerable they are almost certain to be destroyed.

The odds of a sturgeon's egg surviving to maturity are about two million to one (roughly the same odds of a person being struck by lightning). It does happen from time to time, but requires something like a miracle. In order to beat the odds and ensure that the miracle does happen, the fish have to lay seven or eight million eggs at a time.

Most fish have been forced to adopt this technique and rely on 'safety in numbers'. The salmon lays 1000 eggs to every pound weight of the fish, the herring lays 50,000 at a time, the sole 134,000, the perch 280,000, and the turbot an astonishing 14,311,000.

Electric Fish

Towards the end of 1941, a curious accident occurred at a remote hacienda in the state of Amazonas in Brazil. Two native workmen were crossing a plank stretched over a large cement pool, when they slipped and fell in. The pool was not deep, and was full of water, which would have softened their fall, but they both died instantly in violent convulsions the moment their bodies hit the surface.

Their deaths (and that of another worker who later met the same fate) were the result of a strange, undercover exercise in biological warfare, which occurred during World War II.

Throughout the war, the Allies were deeply concerned that Hitler might resort to the chemical weapons, especially the devastating nerve gases developed by German scientists in the 1930s. So the US Army Chemical Corps began an urgent research programme, led by Dr Christopher W. Coates and Dr David Manson, to find the antidotes.

Their work on neurotoxins eventually led to one particular animal, which was essential for their research but, unfortunately, only available in South America. So a covert operation was set up to smuggle in some of the oddest contraband to cross a frontier in wartime – electric eels.

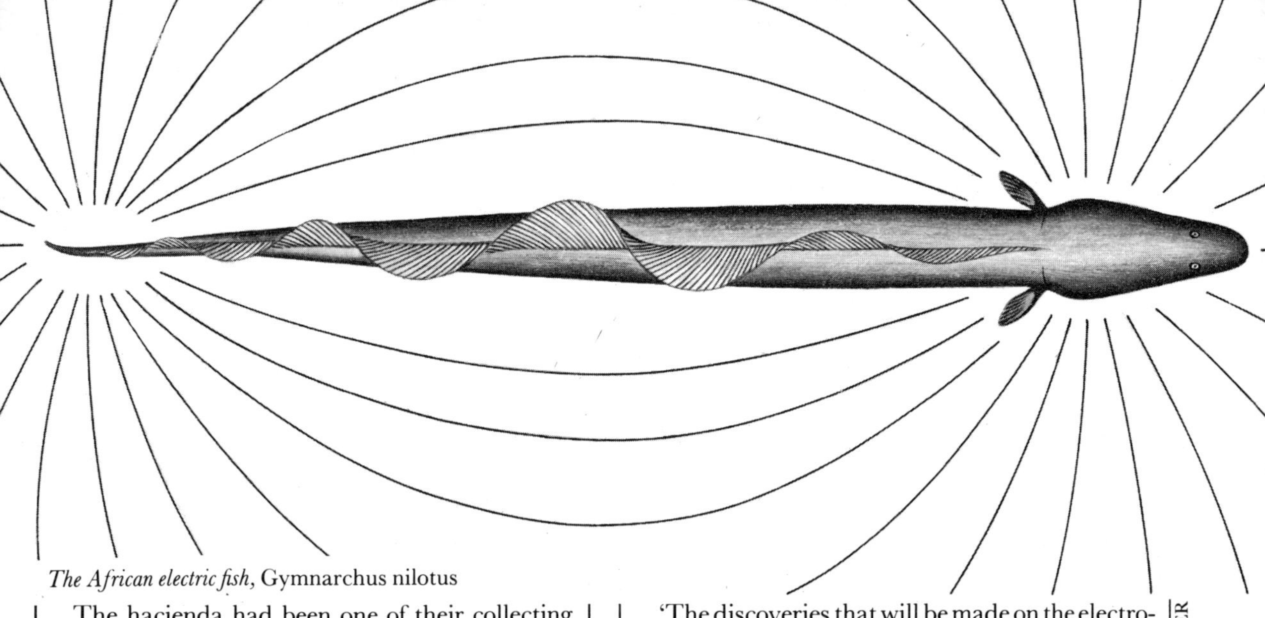

The African electric fish, Gymnarchus nilotus

The hacienda had been one of their collecting stations, and the pool into which the workmen had fallen was full of them. It is unusual, if not unique, to find electric eels concentrated in such numbers in one place, but it demonstrates the extraordinary power that biological organisms can generate.

However, in a sense this is the middle of the story, because eels were not the first electric animals to be used by science, and some of the more recent discoveries are even stranger.

Baron Humboldt and the Muscle Battery

The first electric fish was one the ancient Egyptians were familiar with, a creature they described in hieroglyphics as 'he who releases many' because its shocks made the fishermen drop their catch. More surprisingly, both the Egyptians and the eleventh-century Arabs used the fish (now identified as the electric catfish, *Malapterurus electricus*) for medical purposes, by applying it to their patients as a primitive form of electric shock therapy.

It was not until nineteenth-century physicists were trying to harness electricity for themselves that they began to take an interest in the electric eel. It seemed to offer a model for electric cells, and it is said that the idea of linking batteries in series, to increase the voltage, first came from the eel's anatomy.

One of these pioneers, Baron Friedrich von Humboldt, made a journey to South America to study electric fish and, apart from being stung (which left him with crippling after-effects for the rest of his life), he had the foresight to recognize that this new force was an essential part of biology, common to all animals.

'The discoveries that will be made on the electromotive apparatus of these fishes,' he wrote, 'will extend to all the muscular motion subject to volition. It will perhaps be found that in most animals, every contraction of muscle is preceded by a "discharge" from the nerve.'

The prediction was remarkably accurate because the electricity is created by a mechanism very similar to the interface of muscles and nerves. It is now known to depend on a chemical called acetyl choline (ACH) which allows electrically-charged particles to cross a cell's membrane, and so build up a potential. In other words, electric animals run on batteries.

The power-supply varies from the thorn-back ray, which can manage a mere 5 volts, to the Egyptian's catfish which could generate a respectable 350 volts. But none of them can match the power of the eel, whose batteries consist of half a million plates (in a kind of jelly), capable of discharging 550 volts, at a frequency of 400 Hz, with enough punch to knock out a horse at twenty paces or kill a human being who touched it. And it can keep this up, two or three times a minute, for days on end. It is not surprising that *Electrophorus electricus* has no dangerous enemies.

However, an animal which is too successful stops evolving; and the eel's powerful shocks were so effective as a weapon that it has never bothered to put them to any other use. This eel may be the most powerful of its kind, but it was the fish with the *weakest* power-supply which have put it to the most ingenious use. If the eel resembles the equipment used by nineteenth-century physicists, the *mormyrid* and *sternopygus* are like space-age elecronics.

The Feel of Electricity

The strange electrical 'environment' in which these creatures live was stumbled upon almost by accident in 1958, when H. W. Lissman of Cambridge University discovered that two mormoryd fish could detect each other's presence on either side of a cloth barrier, by means of an electric field.

His investigations showed that they were creating this counter-density field by means of very high-frequency pulses; and though the current was fairly weak (about one or two volts), the fish were so sensitive to anything within it, they could detect an almost invisible ¾ in (2cm) glass rod underwater.

The technical terms are difficult to avoid – but this was quite unlike the bolt of electricty spat out by eels, or a passive awareness of electrical phenomena, such as our sense of sight, or magnetism. Nor was it a high-frequency transmission like radio waves. It was more like a sense of touch.

The fish were actually projecting themselves into their environment and feeling the water around them *as if it was part of their own body*. The knife fish, for instance, seems to enjoy 'massaging' itself by swimming between two reeds, which 'squeeze' in the field on either side.

A number of other species, including skate, elephant fish, Nile fish and most of the rays possess this sense, and put it to a variety of uses. At short range, it is an efficient form of 'echo-location' (and more reliable than sound in turbulent water) and a way of identifying different species. They can feel each other's shape at a distance, turn the sense off to 'listen' for other signals, and warn off intruders by stepping up the frequency.

For instance, when two eigermannia fish meet, they carefully adjust their signals up or down to avoid jamming each other's frequencies – for all the world like CB radio users.

It may be a more sophisticated means of communication than we yet understand, because the fish have been found to have a group of neurons in the mid-brain, analogous to our own 'language centres', which can analyse variations of frequency. What scientists find so remarkable about this is that the discharges are not pure tones (i.e. sinusoidal waves), but are rich in harmonics – which makes them even more like 'speech'.

The study of this fascinating world has only just begun, but Carl Hopkins of Rockefeller University has already recorded what he describes as the 'love song' of a fish called the sternopygus, which lives in Guyana.

It appears that, when a female sternopygus swims past an adult male, she literally 'turns him on', so that his signal breaks up with excitement and turns into a kind of electronic chant. On the other hand, according to Hopkins, when two males pass each other, they keep up a steady drone which resembles 'a bassoon stuck on a low-register note'.

Words like 'echo-location', and the comparison with music, are useful analogies, but it is important to realize that this sense does not involve *sounds*. What we are dealing with is something far more exciting – a new (and previous unknown) physical sense. An electric sense, as different from the others as taste or sight. The tiny organs in these fish are performing *electronic* functions that Humboldt never dreamt of, like setting up permanent fields, generating carrier waves and modulating frequencies, not to mention monitoring their own feedback. And they do it without a single wire or transistor.

In spite of our micro-chip and computers, that is something to wonder at. In fact, some of their systems are so sophisticated that it is only when our technology catches up with theirs, that we will be able to detect them.

Elephants

Everyone knows something about elephants. Their phenomenal memory, their fear of mice, the legend of the 'elephants' graveyard' – few animals are surrounded by so much folklore, and so many myths. But the truth is, as ever, far stranger than the fictions. Did you know that elephants are the only animals with four knees (and the only ones which cannot jump), that they purr like cats, can detect water underground, and make pillows to rest their heads on when they go to sleep.

The African elephant, which can weigh over 6 tons and grow 11 feet tall, is the largest of the four-footed land animals. Its average body temperature is 103.8°F. It breathes twelve times a

minute, and its heart, which weighs 26½ lb, beats forty times a minute. Its life expectancy is roughly the same as a human being, about 30–40 years in the wild (where it is subjected to numerous parasites, diseases and enemies), and about 65 years in captivity.

Adult elephants sleep for about five hours a night. They can doze in an upright position, sometimes leaning on their tusks, but they lie down, like a horse, for a deep sleep. In this condition their heart speed drops to half, and they have been observed to gather vegetation beforehand to make a pillow for their heads.

Elephants have frequent colds, but sneeze rarely. An elephant's sneeze has been compared to 'the bursting of a boiler of considerable size'.

The trunk of the elephant is a muscular, delicate extension of the animal's upper lip and nose combined. It contains some 40,000 muscles, and can tear a tree up by its roots. It is a highly developed olfactory sensor which can detect the direction, and perhaps the distance, of all kinds of odours. Elephants can sniff water three miles away, and other elephants two miles away. The tip of the trunk ends in one (Asian elephants) or two (African elephants) finger-like projections which the elephant can use with almost as much delicacy as humans can their own fingers. Using these 'fingers', elephants can pick a pin off the ground, unbolt a gate, pull the trigger of a gun, untie a slip knot or, as in the case of an elephant kept by the Duke of Devonshire in the 1880s, uncork a bottle of wine.

When an elephant drinks, it sucks about a bucketful of water a little way up its trunk, partially covers the trunk tip with its 'fingers', and then blows so as to squirt the water into its mouth.

Elephant skin is ¾–1½ in (2–4cm) thick, but is extremely sensitive. Few other animals spend as much time in skin care as elephants, bathing it, massaging it, and even powdering it with dust.

Elephants can make a deep rumbling noise from the pit of their stomach. In the past it was assumed to be no more than a noisy digestion, but recent tests have shown that it is a controlled phenomenon, like the purr of a cat. When they are browsing contentedly, they purr continuously, but this stops the moment they are approached or alarmed.

It is an old myth that elephants are afraid of mice. One of the earliest records of it is in Lupton's book *A Thousand Notable Things*, published in 1595, in which the author wrote: 'Elephants of all other beasts do chiefly hate the mouse.' But the idea has been disproved by numerous experiments. In 1938 the American zoologists Francis Benedict and Robert Lee introduced a number of rats and mice of differ-

JOHN RIGNALL

ent colours into the elephant enclosure at a zoo. The pachyderms showed no concern whatever as they ran over their feet and even climbed up their trunks. However the German zoologist, Bernhard Grzimek, who carried out the same experiment (with the same result) at the Berlin Zoo, claims that they are afraid of rabbits and dachshunds. When he put these animals in with the elephants, they retreated in some alarm, using their feet to kick sand and stones at them.

Elephants need to drink about 20 gallons of water a day, and in times of drought they can detect it underground. In fact, they are the only animals, apart from baboons, who will dig into dry river beds at exactly the right spot to find it, often excavating holes up to 10 feet (3m) deep with their tusks.

Feeding is an elephant's primary activity, and occupies it for 18–20 hours a day.

Another myth is that elephants flee in panic at the first sign of danger. In a herd, the lead cow flaps her ears as a signal to the others to assemble in a defensive position. If any of the cows tries to break out of this group in panic, the matriarch puts a quick stop to this by grabbing a bundle of grass in her trunk and forcibly shoving it into the frightened cow's mouth. The lead cow checks out the danger, and if she decides it is real leads an orderly retreat.

Elephants have very small eyes only in relation to the size of their heads, and experiments have shown that their vision is at least as good as a horse's. Smell and hearing, however, are their primary senses. Their hearing is very acute, and there is evidence that elephants can recognize each other individually just by their voices, even in large herds. They can also learn simple melodies or rhythms and recognize them when they are played on instruments as different as violin, piano and xylophone.

When they fight, which is rarely, two bull elephants raise their heads, swing their trunks back over their foreheads, spread their ears and charge at each other so that the bases of their trunks meet. The impact is tremendous, but the bulls will continue to charge until one of them is pushed back, and thus defeated. Sometimes a tusk pierces one of the elephants, seriously injuring or even killing him.

The gestation period of elephants is 20–22 months. When her time approaches, the pregnant female approaches the so-called 'kindergarten group' of cows. When labour begins, these cows surround the expectant mother and help her as she gives birth, then remove the newborn baby from its fetal membrane and help it stand on its legs. Such 'midwife' behaviour has been observed on many occasions. The baby is about 3–4 feet tall at birth and weighs 180–250 lb. It can stand on its own after five minutes, and walk after an hour. Young elephants sleep much more than adults and are extremely playful, chasing each other or other animals.

Forest-dwelling elephants clear and regularly use specific 'roads' through the jungle. Some of these roads are used by generations of elephants, and are so wide and flat that they can accommodate trucks. The animals build them to suit the terrain, so that they follow the contour of a hill without losing altitude. These roads are often used by other animals, including rhinos, tigers, deer, buffalo and humans. In Sri Lanka and Assam, people have built their own roads on top of elephant roads, since the way has already been cleared for them.

For centuries it has been believed in both Africa and India that there are secret elephant cemeteries where the giant beasts go when they are ready to die. As one writer fancifully put it: 'It has been an interminable procession of the doomed since time began. To the stricken old elephant, the coming of death brings an irresistible nostalgia which draws his faltering feet homeward to this mist-shrouded valley piled high with the white bones of his ancestors.'

The legend of the elephant graveyard valley is incorporated in the story of Sinbad the Sailor being transported to one after he is knocked unconscious when an enormous elephant uproots the tree in which he is hiding. The search for such mass graveyards has attracted adventurers for many years, since they would clearly be incredible treasure-houses of ivory.

The evidence for their existence, however, is thin. In the first place, the carcasses of elephants can be seen both on the plains and in the forest, though they are very quickly devoured by animals large and small. Secondly, the occasional mass collections of elephant bones that have been found can be explained in terms of large herds dying together as a result of drought, bush fires, or mass poisonings by early elephant hunters.

The Emu War

Farmers have long assumed the right to destroy any wildlife they regard as a nuisance, by any means available. In the case of the Australian emu, they even called in the artillery.

In just over a century, the large emu (*Dromaius*

novaehollandiae) has been exterminated from Tasmania and all the populated areas of Australia. The birds were originally hunted for the same reason as whales – for their oil. In a world without electricity, lamp oil was a domestic product for which there was an insatiable demand, and it was possible to extract four gallons of it from each full-grown emu.

When they no longer had an intrinsic value, they were hunted as pests. Farmers disliked them because they grazed on the grass and vegetation intended for sheep (as do most of the animals of the outback), and they were blamed for drinking water put out for stock, leaping over boundary fences and trampling down crops.

So the emus were steadily eradicated, state by state, until, by the 1930s, the survivors were confined to a few hundred square miles in the south-west tip of the huge state of Western Australia.

In 1932 the citizens of Campion and Walgoolan called in the Army to implement the final solution to the emu problem. A company of the Royal Australian Artillery, under the command of a major and assisted by the local farmers, went into action with two machine-guns and ten thousand shells.

They set out to drive the birds along the boundary fences into the range of the guns, a tactic which had been particularly effective in New South Wales. But the exercise was not a success, because the emus proved to be more skilful at fieldcraft than the soldiers. Of the estimated 20,000 emus in the area, they managed to kill exactly twelve.

ROGER GARLAND

Unfortunately, the emus may have won one battle but they eventually lost the war. Throughout the 1930s, up till as late as 1964, the state authorities paid out a bounty for each bird destroyed. In 1937, 37,000 emus were killed in the Northampton district alone.

Nowadays the birds have some measure of protection, and one or two herds in the northern area are even multiplying – but they came very near to extinction.

Excretion

Human beings use four times as much water to remove their excreta as they use for all other purposes, including drinking, cooking and washing. Is it pure, disinterested hygiene, or are we somehow washing away our sins? Although we take an obsessive interest in one activity and pretend the other does not exist, it is a fundamental equation that if you eat, you excrete . . .

Most foods consists of carbohydrates, fats and proteins, and they are digested by a process of oxidation, which produces wastes. The oxidation of carbohydrates and fats produces only carbon-dioxide and water. The former is disposed of by gas exchange (breathing), while the latter is a valuable addition to the body.

But the oxidation of proteins produces large quantities of ammonia, which is highly toxic and must be got rid of as quickly as possible. Rabbits, for instance, will die if the concentration of ammonia in their blood rises above 5 mg per millilitre.

Animals have various mechanisms for turning ammonia into less toxic nitrogenous products. Most mammals produce urea, which is excreted in solution as urine. Insects and birds, on the other hand, need to conserve their body liquids, so they produce uric acid, an insoluble substance commonly known as bird lime.

Spiders probably make the most creative use of their toxic wastes by turning them into guanine, which they excrete in crystalline form as the thread for their webs.

The larvae of the Cassida beetle are also highly ingenious. They pack all their excrement, plus the dried skin from the moultings, into a lumpy bag which they throw down when attacked by their chief predator, the ant. This excrement bomb presumably puts the ant off its meal.

Most animals excrete a mixture of nitrogenous wastes and any food material they have been unable to digest. The simpler the organism, the more it has to dispose of. Earthworms, who virtually flush their food straight through their bodies, produce eight times their weight in solid material and 60 per cent of their weight in urine every day. By comparison, a frog produces 25 per cent of its own weight in urine daily, while a human being produces less than two per cent.

The Tarpory bird excretes more or less continuously when it is feeding. As it spends most of its day pecking around on the ground, it has an extraordinary ribbon of dung trailing for up to 25 feet behind it.

But this is an exception. Most animals excrete in a more orderly fashion dictated by the internal rhythm of their metabolism. In certain cases, however, it becomes advantageous not to excrete at all. For instance, the bear plugs its rectum in autumn by eating dry pine needles, which are digested very slowly and finally stop the exit altogether. This enables the bear to retain inside itself any food it eats afterwards, so that its nutritive value is exploited to the maximum during hibernation.

Finally, mention should be made of the oldest dung in the world. It is the fossilized turd, or *coprolite*, of a dinosaur, and is in the British Museum. About 11 inches (28cm) long, it is not known which species it came from, though it must have been a large one. It is dated at 80–100 million years old.

Extinction!

'If all the beasts were gone, men would die from great loneliness of spirit, for whatever happens to the beast, happens to man. All things are connected. Whatever befalls the earth befalls the sons of the earth.'

– Chief Seathl

This is the story of just three of the species we will never see again. A number of other extinct animals appear from time to time in this book, but these are the classic cases – the ones that everyone has heard of, though probably a little hazy about the details. In fact, many of the details have only recently come to light, and they deserve to be told in full, for the first time, side by side, because they show how easy it is to wipe a species off the face of the earth – casually, almost by accident, and for ever.

The Dodo

The dodo, poor thing, is the ultimate cliché. Other birds have lived on as symbols – the dove of peace and the owl of wisdom – but this tame, bewildered, comical creature, whose absence has reverberated down the years, is immortal for being extinct. There is nothing as dead as a dodo. It is the essence of non-existence.

Dididae, to give the official name, lived on the island of Mauritius, in the Indian Ocean – the kind of remote, evolutionary cul-de-sac where the pressures of life are suspended. With no predators to weed them out, miniature species, like dwarf elephants, can thrive, birds no longer need to fly, and animals can develop into the most eccentric forms.

The dodos were one of these evolutionary experiments: fat, flightless birds about the size of turkeys, whose only protection was a bulbous, black beak.

They waddled around on spindly legs, lived mainly on fruit, and made their 'nests' by scraping shallow depressions in the ground.

The early explorers who visited the islands found them easy to catch, but Jacob Corneiszoon van Neck, the Dutchman who first discovered them, called them *walghvogels* – 'nauseous birds' – because he disliked their taste.

An Englishman who was with him described them as: 'Great fowles, having great heads and upon their heads a skin, as if they had a cap upon their heads. They have no wings at all, but in the place of wings they have four or five small curled feathers, and their colour is greyish. They sat still and could not fly down from us, so that we with our hands might easily take them.'

And take them they did. Within a generation of being discovered, the dodo was extinct. In 1634, a visitor to the islands reported seeing numerous birds there, but by 1681 the last one was dead.

A few were brought to Europe, so we have a good idea of what they looked like from drawings and engravings, but they soon died out. The only specimen to be preserved mouldered away in the Ashmolean Museum at Oxford until it became so moth-eaten that it finally had to be burnt in 1775.

And that, for the next two hundred years, was that – except that a postscript has recently been added to the story.

In 1977 an American ecologist, Dr Temple, suggested that the dodo might be the first known example of the extinction of an animal resulting in the decline of a plant species.

The birds were known to feed on the fruit of the Calvaria Major tree, and no new Calvaria trees have grown since 1681. In 1973 only thirteen of them were still alive on the islands, none of them younger than 300 years.

The theory is that the bird and the tree evolved together, and the tree's seeds had a coating strong enough to survive the powerful juices of the dodo's stomach. At the same time, however, these tough shells needed to be weakened by the dodos before the infant plants could escape.

Dr Temple tested the theory by feeding the seeds to turkeys and planting them after they had been digested and defecated. Three of the ten seeds germinated – the first in 300 years!

It is unthinkable that anyone would deliberately kill the very last member of a species. In many ways it is a crime worse than murder, or even genocide. But it has been done, and in two cases – that of the Great Auk and Steller's sea cow – we even know who was responsible.

The Man who Killed the Last Great Auk

One of the most obvious gaps in the distribution of the world's wildlife is that there are no penguins in the Arctic. It is a glaring anomaly. Vast numbers of them thrive on the Antarctic iceshelf, but there is no longer any equivalent in the northern hemisphere. The ecological niche is vacant and the seas are empty, for this was the role once played by the Great Auk.

Like the penguin, it was a black and white, flightless bird two or three feet high. Defenceless on land but superb underwater swimmers, they used their stubby wings as hydroplanes. They thrived in the rich waters of the north Atlantic and, like the penguins, lived a sociable life in large colonies. No one will ever know their full numbers, but at one time their colonies stretched along the edge of the Arctic pack-ice from Canada to Norway.

RAY WINDER

Unfortunately, unlike the penguins, they were within easy reach of humans and, from the earliest days, explorers found them a useful source of meat and eggs.

The largest colony was on Funk Island, off Newfoundland, and Jacques Cartier, a French captain who landed there in 1534, reported that his crew filled two longboats with them, and killed thousands more which they had to leave behind. Many sailors followed this example, and it became a regular means of restocking ships on long voyages.

With the increase in sea trade and the growth of settlements in America, the number of Great Auk steadily dropped. Local fishermen raided the colonies, and when times were hard whole communities would live off them, boiling down the bodies for oil, making needles out of their bones, and preserving the meat for the long winter months.

As the auks only laid one egg each season, the colonies were unable to make up for this toll. By the beginning of the nineteenth century there were no longer any birds on Funk Island, and the auks had retreated to their last breeding colony on the island of Geirfuglasker, off the coast of Iceland. Their association with the place was so strong that the popular name for the birds used to be 'gare-fowl' or 'geir-fowl'.

The Icelanders continued to treat them as a natural resource. Catching birds was easier than fishing, and in fine weather boats would go out from Reykjavik to 'harvest' them by the thousands.

Under pressure from man, and with their numbers dwindling, the auks were now struck by a natural disaster. Iceland sits astride a geological fault called the Mid-Atlantic Ridge and is very prone to earthquakes and volcanic eruptions. In 1830 there was a particularly violent upheaval, and the whole island of Geirfuglasker vanished beneath the icy waters – taking most of the auks with it.

The survivors sought refuge on a nearby speck of rock called Eldey, but it offered them little safety. They were no longer hunted for food, but they were now so rare that collectors would pay high prices for an auk skin, and boatmen would still risk a landing to catch them.

In 1844, when it was widely believed that they were extinct, a Reykjavik merchant offered a cash bounty to anyone who could bring him the last specimens. A local fisherman called Vilhjalmur Hakonarsson thought that there might still be a few birds on Eldey, and set sail for the island with a small crew.

It was a rough landing, but when Hakonarsson climbed the rock he discovered that there were indeed two birds left, a male and a female guarding a nest. They were the only ones. The last two Great Auks in the world. But they were what he had come for, so he killed – and in the excitement of the 'hunt' someone accidentally trod on their last remaining egg.

Steller's Sea Cow

Giant of the Sirenian family, growing up to 30 feet (9m) in length, Steller's Sea Cow was first discovered and scientifically described in 1741. Twenty-seven years later, in 1768, a Russian fur trader called Ivan Popov harpooned the last specimen and rendered the species extinct.

The creature is named after Georg Wilhelm Steller (1709–1746), ship's physician and naturalist on the Bering Expedition, which was seeking a north-east passage between the Pacific and Atlantic.

He was touched by the animals' devotion to each other when one of them was harpooned. 'Several of them formed a circle about their wounded comrade,' he wrote, 'and attempted to keep it away from the shore, while others tried to capsize the boat. Still other sea cows lay on their sides and attempted to strike the harpoon and knock it out of the wounded sea cow's body, an attempt that succeeded many times. We also looked in amazement as the male returned to his dead female on the beach two days in a row, as if he were inquiring about her.' Thirty men had been needed just to haul one of the harpooned sea cows onto land.

The Bering Expedition returned to Kamchatka in the spring of 1742. Its winter on the ice had made little difference to the numbers of Steller's Sea Cows. It was in the next twenty years that the bulk

of the population was slaughtered. Between 1743 and 1763 about nineteen groups of fur hunters, each numbering 20–50 men, wintered on Bering Island. They were out to catch sea otters, seals and arctic foxes, and they killed off the giant sea cows almost as a sideline – for their meat and oil, and for their elastic skin which they used instead of scarce wood for the keel, ribs, sternpost and after-deck of their boats.

Boats made in this way with sea cow hide were not only cheaper, but also faster, lighter and less subject to fires than their purely wooden counterparts. Sea cow skin was also used to make shoes, especially the soles.

It has been estimated that the species cannot have numbered more than 1,500–2,000 animals at the time of its discovery, and was restricted to the waters around Bering Island, so it may have been hovering on the verge of extinction anyway. But the fact that it was wiped out just twenty-seven years after its discovery remains a striking example of human vandalism.

Is it the End of the World?

All this happened a long time ago, before anyone knew what 'extinction' really meant. But the threat to the world's wildlife is now such an emotional issue that it has become a buzz-word (like the 'environment'), which has taken on the strongest moral and political overtones. So it is worth trying to sort out the jargon from the reality.

Firstly, there can be no doubt about the scale of the problem. The Red Data Book of the IUCN (International Union for Conservation of Nature and Natural Resources) is the only authoritative source of information on the world's endangered animals. It lists over one thousand species and subspecies now on the brink of extinction, including 305 mammals, 400 birds, 138 amphibians and reptiles, and 193 species of fish.

But this only applies to the larger animals. It takes no account of the hundreds of thousands of invertebrates, such as crabs, snails, butterflies, shrimps, spiders, ants, worms of all kinds, and the teeming millions of micro-organisms, from krill to bacteria. On this scale, the destruction is horrific.

Human activities, like the clearing of the Amazon rain forest, now account for the disappearance of one or two species each day *– and if we continue at the same rate, this will have risen to several species an hour!*

Many people believe we are heading for a catastrophe, an alteration to the biosphere so drastic that it can only be compared to prehistoric disasters, like that which overtook the world of the dinosaurs.

We obviously need to stop this process, or at least try to slow it down and try to preserve every single animal we can. Or should we? Do we now regard extinction as a kind of 'disease' to be cured? Or a natural – and necessary – part of the process?

The question puts things in a very different perspective, because extinction – even mass extinction – is perfectly natural, and the history of life on earth is punctuated by such events. For instance, air-breathing plants and animals could not have evolved without the build-up of toxic gas (called oxygen) which destroyed their predecessors. The death of the dinosaurs was not the only crisis of this kind. There was a similar disaster to marine life in the Cambrian period, which wiped out the great families of trilobites; and, later on, the dramatic changes of climate during the Permian period killed off nearly two-thirds of all the species on earth.

Whether it happens slowly or abruptly, evolution proceeds by the elimination of the many and the survival and diversification of the few. For instance, there were about as many species on earth 100 million years ago as there are today, but no more than half a dozen *of them have any living descendants. In fact, 98 per cent of all modern vertebrates come from* just eight *Mesozoic species.*

In other words, the natural (and overwhelmingly probable) future of any species, including our own, is extinction. There is nothing good or bad about it. It is the way things are.

RAY WINDER

F

(*falconry*)

Falconry

Falconry has been a sport since the first millennium BC, originating in the plains of Mongolia, India and China. The favoured hunting bird then was the golden eagle, which was carried on a 'crutch' fastened by leather loops to the horse's saddle.

Marco Polo claimed that the Khan of Shiva had an army of ten thousand falconers, and that the bags from their hunting was at times sufficient to feed his whole country.

In the twelfth century, stealing a trained hawk was punishable in England by a fine of 45 shillings. If the thief was unable to pay, the bird was allowed to peck six inches of flesh from his thighs or buttocks.

Falconry reached a peak in Europe in the thirteenth century, when it became a symbol of the age. The Chief Falconer of the Holy Roman Empire held one of the most important positions at court.

Today, falconry is said to be experiencing a new boom in the United States, with several thousand enthusiasts nationwide. In the Middle East it is still a traditional pastime of princes and sheikhs, though some of the trappings have been updated. In July 1980 it was reported that King Khaled of Saudi Arabia had ordered from a Swiss company a £75,000 car specially designed for falconry. It was fitted with six wheels for negotiating desert terrain and two storage tanks, one holding 80 gallons of petrol, the other 35 gallons of water. The most unusual feature, however, was the special seat with a hydraulic lift that would raise the king through an opening in the roof so that he could release his falcon and then descend again into the air-conditioned interior.

ELIZABETH GOSS

The Farmers

The search for food can dominate an animal's existence, and for some species it is an unremitting task simply to stay alive. So there are obvious advantages (as human beings discovered about ten thousand years ago) in being able to control your own supply, and a number of species have experimented with 'farming' techniques.

Some of these are so obvious that we tend to overlook them. It depends how you define the term, but there is even a sense in which predators have the same relationship to their prey as farmers do to their animals. For instance, there is evidence that wolves practise a kind of conservation (like 'fallow-field' farming) by allowing deer to recover their numbers before hunting them again.

But the most ingenious, sophisticated – and famous – example are ants and aphids.

Ants and Aphids

It is well known that ants 'keep' aphids, much as we keep goats or cattle, and that they 'milk' the minute drops of honeydew aphids secrete by stroking them with their antennae. What is even more surprising, is the amount of care they lavish on them.

The small black lawn ant is one of the most successful aphid herders, keeping colonies of them on nearby plants, and even building shelters for them out of earth and saliva. Weaver ants actually spin little tents for their herds.

In some cases aphids are kept in underground chambers, where they are allowed to feed by sucking the juices from the roots of plants. Certain species of ants collect the eggs of flying aphids during the autumn, store them in their nests during the winter, and then take them out in the spring and place them on the kinds of plant the aphids like to eat.

One aphid, the pineapple mealy bug of Hawaii, has become so dependent on ants that it dies unless it is milked regularly.

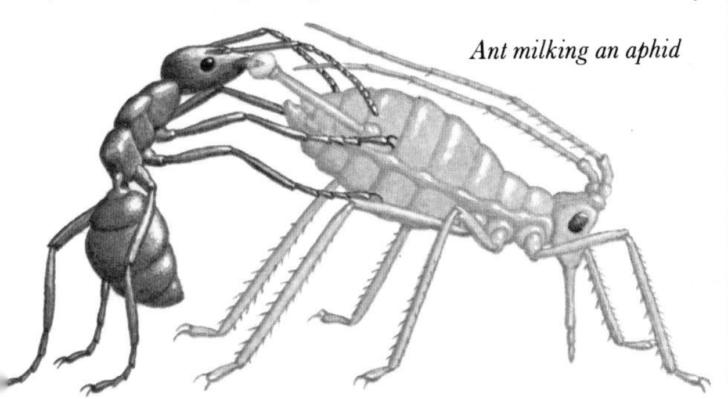

Ant milking an aphid

Green turtles

The Turtle Herds of Nicaragua

Many herbivores browse like cattle, but it is rare to find a species that behaves like this under the sea. The Caribbean green turtle, whose cartilages form the raw material for turtle soup, is one of them.

Large numbers of them are known to gather off the coast of Nicaragua, where there are abundant pastures of so-called turtle grass. Far from grazing at random, the turtles deliberately exploit the food supply in the most efficient way, by consistently grazing certain strands while they leave others untouched, in order to maximize the availability of the more digestible, and more nutritious, young shoots.

The Internal Garden

We all have a symbiotic relationship with our food, but some species have taken it to extremes by growing it inside their own bodies.

The giant 5-foot (1.5m) clams which live on Australia's Great Barrier Reef have learned to cultivate gardens of microscopic plants inside their shells. The plants are a family of algae (*Zooanthellae*) and they live as parasites in the blood vessels under the mantle. The mantle is equipped with a structure which looks like an eye, but which is, in fact, a lens-like window admitting light (and therefore life) to the algae.

The clam controls this internal farm by eating it: as the algae population grows, the surplus is simply carried by the bloodstream to the digestive organs.

STEPHEN LINGS

The Feast of Life

'It cannot be overemphasized that the whole concept of flesh – or plant – eating is old fashioned and invalid. With surprisingly few exceptions, almost any animal will eat anything and everything that is digestible as occasion arises or shortages demand.'

– Maurice and Robert Burton, *The Animal Kingdom.*

The cockroach is officially classified as vegetarian, but according to the German naturalist Kemper it has been known to eat 'cooked potatoes, vegetables, flour pudding, dough and the like, dead and sick members of its own species, chocolate, honey, butter, vaseline, bread, flour, sugar, leather, wool items, rayon, shoe polish, book bindings, fruit and other items according to season.' Cockroaches spread around the world on sailing ships. It is said that on Spanish galleons they would emerge each night, crawl on to the sleeping sailors, and begin to eat the rims of white skin at the roots of their fingernails.

An adult African bull elephant consumes 300–600 lb of fodder per day, and eats its own weight in food each month. Lions and cheetahs consume their own weight every 7–10 days. A large lizard like the Komodo dragon consumes its own weight every 60 days. Puffins, because of their active life, must eat their own weight in fish every 24 hours in order to survive.

The renowned voracity of dragonflies led Dr Phillip P. Calvert of the University of Pennsylvania to pose this question: 'How many mosquito larvae and pupae are required to make one dragonfly?' To find out, he reared a dragonfly for a year, during which time it ate 3,037 mosquito larvae and 164 pupae, plus 17 larvae of damselflies and other dragonflies. Calvert's subsequent paper was simply titled with his original question.

The common toad has an astonishing appetite. One specimen from the island of Jersey, in the English Channel, swallowed so many earthworms, one after the other, that after a time they were being excreted alive. Another was found to have thirty-two undigested honey-bees in its stomach. Toads not only eat insects, but are eaten by them. One of their most dangerous enemies is the Greenbottle fly, which lays a single cluster of eggs on the toad's thigh. Within minutes the larvae hatch out, wriggle up the toad's body, crawl into its nostrils, and block them so that it cannot breathe. The toad dies within a few days, and the larvae then eat its entire body except the bones.

A turkey can grind in its gizzard twenty-four walnuts in the shell. It can deal with steel needles, and surgical lancets; and, after being in a turkey's muscular stomach, a piece of sheet-iron tubing was found flattened and partly rolled up.

Shrikes have acquired the name of 'butcher birds' from their habit of impaling their victims on thorn trees or barbed wire. They stock their larder with large insects, lizards, rodents and even other birds. In parts of Germany they are known as 'ninekiller' because they reputedly kill nine song-birds every day.

The robber crab, *Birgus latro*, is the only animal that can open a coconut unaided. Measuring up to 12 inches (30.5cm) across its shell, the robber grasps the trunk of a palm tree between its outstretched limbs, climbs rapidly to the top, cuts young coconuts down with its pincers, then descends to feast on its harvest. The robber, by the way, is a land crab that has evolved true lungs – it drowns if submerged for more than five hours.

The walrus's diet consists mainly of clams, whose meat it apparently sucks out through cracks in the shell. Since no one has managed to photograph a walrus in the act, however, there is some disagreement among experts as to how this feat is accomplished. A peculiar walrus trick, often demonstrated in captivity, is the animal's ability to suck the skin and meat clean off a mackerel, leaving the human attendant holding the fish's tail and backbone. Clams have often been found whole inside a freshly killed walrus, however, suggesting some other technique. But no one has ever reported finding the clam's shell inside a walrus stomach. It may be that the animal uses pebbles and small stones, which it is known to swallow, to crush and grind the shell in its intestines. In any event, Eskimo hunters consider it a supreme delicacy to eat clams while they are still warm from a freshly killed walrus's stomach.

Newts are equipped with a muscular tongue which can be shot out, carrying the whole floor of the mouth with it. Having no appreciation of size, however, newts often choke on prey too large for them. One of their favoured foods is snails, which are swallowed whole, the body being digested and the shell excreted unbroken.

There are no vegetarian snakes. They all eat other animals, or their eggs. King cobras and kraits are specialists who feed almost exclusively on other snakes. If two cobras seize the same prey, the larger may sometimes devour the smaller.

Being limbless, snakes cannot tear their prey

apart and must swallow it whole. Large pythons have been known to swallow domestic pigs, antelopes, leopards and even humans. 'The body of a 45-year-old man was found in the stomach of a six-yard-long python killed by villagers in Indonesia when it was found attacking another man' (*Observer*, 20 November 1977).

In spite of such feats, snakes are extremely ascetic, and most of them require little more than their own body weight in food per year. The ability to go for long periods without any food at all is one of the keys to their success. An Indian python in a zoo fasted for 149 days and lost only 10 per cent of its body weight, while a reticulate python at Frankfurt Zoo ate nothing for over a year and a half without apparent ill effects.

Snakes can regurgitate food after swallowing it, especially if startled or attacked. Pythons have been observed regurgitating goats and antelopes because of the discomfort of their horns. In the case of non-venomous snakes, the regurgitated animal may still be alive – frogs have been seen hopping away after being spat out by ringed snakes.

Eating your Mother – and other last resorts

A number of female insects are able to reproduce without the assistance of males, by 'virgin birth' or parthenogenesis. It can be a very effective system, although it sometimes leads to bizarre forms of recycling.

One type of beetle, *Micromalthus debilis*, gives birth, by itself, to single male offspring. For four or five days this larva attaches itself to the mother's skin, but it then puts its head into her genital opening and eats her alive from the inside.

In many species of nematodes, or threadworms, the female can delay her egg-laying so that the larvae actually hatch inside her body and then emerge, in a process similar to mammalian live birth. In some species, however, when times are hard, the larvae remain in the mother's body after hatching, and parasitize her organs until they have completely consumed her.

If children can eat their parent, then parents can eat their children – a process known as faganism. It is often found among deep-water scavenging fish and other species living in a harsh environment where food supplies are unpredictable. It obviously tends to upset the population balance – some of the ecosystems which have been studied had almost no juveniles at all – so it is assumed to be a temporary phenomenon.

Every day between three and four o'clock in the afternoon, the baby koala eats its main meal of the day. It is still in the pouch and a month away from being able to eat the adult koala's diet of eucalyptus leaves. Instead it feeds straight from its mother's anus. This practice, known as coprophagy, serves both to nourish it and to stock it with intestinal flora and fauna.

The Atlantic species of sea-cow, the manatee, is another animal which can feed on its own faeces, or those of other animals. According to one source, manatees 'smash the faecal balls as they close their mouth, dispersing the material and forming a cloud around them as they eat'. Their preferred diet, however, is aquatic plants.

Many simpler forms of animals, when faced with starvation, simply absorb part of themselves as food. Both planarian worms and nemertean worms, also known as ribbonworms, have this ability. In one case a ribbonworm consumed all but one twentieth of itself over a period of a few months, but grew back to its former size when food again became available. Octopuses sometimes go even further and actually make meals of parts of themselves, a practice known as autophagy (self-eating).

ELIZABETH GOSS

A fish-eating spider drags its catch from the water

CATHERINE BRADBURY

Fighting Animals

Bullfighting began as a bloodless sport with the Minoan civilization in Crete around 3000 BC. The killing began when it was adopted by the Greeks and Romans, and has not stopped since. As a symbolic link between past and present, matadors still wear short pigtails, usually false, into the ring – the caste-mark of the Roman gladiator.

The father of modern bullfighting was a Spaniard, Pedro Romero. Credited with introducing the matador's red cloak, he killed 5,600 bulls between 1771 and 1779 without suffering a single injury. He died peacefully in bed aged eighty-four.

Since 1850 more than 520 people have died in Spanish bullrings. The rate dropped, however, after the introduction of penicillin, a fact commemorated by a statue to Sir Alexander Fleming at the entrance of the Madrid Plaza.

A favourite sport in northern Thailand is beetle-fighting. The animals used are male Hercules beetles (*Dynastes gideon*), known locally as 'kwang'. Professional trainers select beetles with strong bodies, short narrow necks and large horns. They keep them on peeled sticks of sugar-cane, with long pieces of string attached to their horns to stop them flying off.

A beetle is trained by bathing in early morning dew, swimming in tepid rainwater, and flying. When strong enough, it is wrapped in the soft moist bark of a banana tree and taken to a special stadium in the village.

The beetles flight on a wooden pole about 6 feet (2m) long and 6 inches (15cm) wide. A female beetle is used to encourage the two males to fight over her. Most fights consist of twelve rounds, with a win occurring when one of the beetles runs away. A round finishes when the two insects clamp their horns together, a situation known as 'pa-ta-krarm'. If neither beetle has run away by the end of the twelfth round, the fight is a draw.

Camel fighting was first started by the Greeks thousands of years ago, but survives today only in Turkey. In the province of Aydin, contests are staged every weekend during the rutting season (January and February).

Fighting camels are aggressive hybrids specially bred from a female Arabian (with one hump) and a male Bactrian (with two humps), usually from the Russian steppes. Known as 'tulu', they start fighting at the age of five, reach their peak at fifteen and live for about forty years. In summer they are fed a special diet of wheat, barley and oats to build their weight up to a massive 2,640 lb (1,200kg), three times the weight of a normal camel.

They become increasingly irritable during the winter and will fight to the death for the attention of a female placed nearby. The winner tries to suffocate his opponent by knocking him down and lying on his head, but with champions now priced at a minimum of £4,000, this is rarely allowed to happen.

Reporter Jeremy Hunter of the *Guardian* joined a crowd of ten thousand people who had come to witness forty-eight camels fighting for the Grand Championship of Kusadasi. 'Five referees categorized each fight into ayak (foot), orta (middle), basalti (lower head), or bas (head); and animals were matched who were known to fight in a particular style – 'the left-hander', 'the camel who hooks the hooves of his opponent', and 'the one who crushes his opponent's head under his two front hooves'. The bouts lasted on average fifteen minutes. After seven hours the climax of the championship was reached when a camel called Crazy One challenged Ipci, the undefeated champion. Ipci won.

Cricket fighting became a Chinese passion during the Sung dynasty (960-1278 AD), with large sums wagered on contests, and champion crickets fetching as much as a good horse. In southern China champion crickets were called *shou lip*, 'conquering, or victorious, cricket', and were solemnly buried in small silver caskets when they died.

According to Berthole Laufer, in his essay 'Insect-Musicians and Cricket Champions of China', the tournaments took place in a public square or in a special house known as 'Autumn Amusements'. The insects were classified as heavyweight, middleweight and lightweight, and were matched according to size, weight and colour. Usually the two adversaries tried to flee, but were prevented from doing so by the glass walls of the bowl or jar in which they were placed.

'Now the referee . . . intercedes, announcing the contestants and reciting the history of their past performances, and spurs the two parties on to combat. For this purpose he avails himself of the tickler (a special instrument consisting of rat whiskers inserted into a bone or ivory handle) and first stirs their heads and the end of their tails . . . The two opponents thus excited stretch out their antennae . . . and jump at each other's heads . . . One of the belligerents will soon lose one of its [antennae], while it may retort by tearing off one of the enemy's legs. The two combatants become more and more exasperated and fight each other mercilessly. The struggle usually ends in the death of one of them.'

Coon-baiting is an American version of the old English sport of badger-baiting. A dog has to draw out a tethered racoon, then engaging it in battle. The fastest dog of the day wins the money, while the racoon usually winds up dead. The sport is still legal in the USA, where a number of variations have been developed:

Coon-in-a-hole has the racoon chained at the bottom of a pit.

Coon-in-a-barrel, where the barrel swings from a rope so that it is more difficult for the dog to get at the racoon.

Coon-on-a-pole, in which the dog tries to drag the racoon down from the top of a six-foot pole.

Coon-on-a-log, a Texan favourite, in which the racoon is chained to a log in a river and the dog has to swim out and pull the animal into the water.

Cooning occurs in most southern states of the USA, and prize money can go as high as $12,000.

Ratting was a popular English pastime in the nineteenth century. A Staffordshire bull terrier was put in a pit with a number of rats, and bets were placed on how quickly the dog would kill them, or how many it would kill in a given period of time. In 1848 a black-and-tan terrier called Tiny, who wore a woman's bracelet as a collar, killed 300 rats in fifty-four minutes. In 1862 Jacko killed 1,000 rats in one hundred minutes. '*Ratting! Ratting!! Ratting !!! There will be an extraordinary number of rats destroyed on Monday evening at J. Ferriman's Graham Arms, Graham Street, City Road*,' ran one advertisement in the sporting journal *Bell's Life*. Sometimes a man, his hands tied behind his back and biting terrier-style with his teeth, would compete with the dog.

Cockfighting is the oldest and most universal of pit sports. It probably originated in religious ceremonies in Asia, and was established in Greece in 479 BC, after Themistocles had employed a pair of fighting cocks to inspire his troops to victory over the Persians. The Romans took the sport over from the Greeks, and added iron spurs to make it a lethal and bloody business.

In the later Middle Ages cockfighting was so popular that London boasted a large number of permanent cockpits. Birds were specially imported from India and Asia. Pepys, the great English diarist, noted in 1663: 'I did go to Shoe Lane to see a cocke-fighting at a new pit there, a sport I was never at in my life; but Lord! to see the strange variety of people, from Parliament men . . . to the poorest 'prentices, bakers, brewers, butchers, draymen and what not; and all these fellows one with another in swearing, cursing and betting.'

Though illegal, cockfighting is still a major sport in parts of the United States. Birds cost $100–$1,000, and hundreds of thousands are killed each year. There are three nationally-distributed cockfighting magazines, offering such paraphernalia as

hand-forged gaffs at $60 a pair, carrying-boxes at $270 a gross, and patent medicines with such names as 'Blitz Drops' and 'No Bleed'. In New York, according to enthusiasts, up to one thousand cockfighting 'mains' occur each weekend; and there are an estimated half a million practising cockfighters nationwide.

In May 1976 a deputy sheriff and twenty state troopers raided a cockpit at Inglecress Farm, near Charlottesville, Virginia, and arrested eleven of the eighty participants. The judge dismissed the case, however, when the police could produce no evidence of gambling money changing hands. The deputy sheriff was placed on six months' probation by his superiors.

Mrs 'Mamma' Jones, owner of Inglecress Farm, later said: 'My father did it, and my grandfather before him. My son fought chickens. My husband fought chickens. We've been fighting chickens since the Civil War! And we *never* got in trouble in our lives before! This is an animal farm; always has been.'

Cockfights are usually continued to the death, and may last an hour or more. Birds who can no longer stand, or who have had one or both eyes pecked out, or whose neck muscles have been torn so that they can no longer hold their heads up, are still brought repeatedly up to scratch in the hope that they will nonetheless win with a lucky, last-moment blow.

When the cockfight is over, it is time for a stiff drink. Or rather a 'cocktail' – the toast which is traditionally drunk to the winning bird (or the one with the most tail feathers left).

The Fire-Belly Toad

The fire-belly toad (*Bombina variegata*) sounds as if it is brimming over with machismo, but its name is the only aggressive thing about it. When threatened, the animal throws itself on its back to expose a bright yellow belly, covers its eyes with its paws, and holds its breath until the danger is past. When pushed to extremes, it gives off a mildly corrosive white fluid.

Big Fleas and Little Fleas

Fleas look as if they have been caught and squashed in a vice, since they are taller than they are wide.

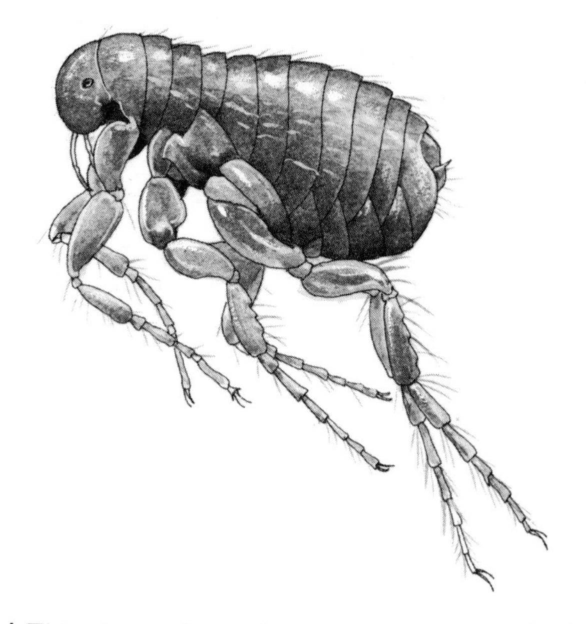

This shape allows them to move more easily through the dense undergrowth of their host's feathers or fur. They have hook-like spines on their backs to prevent them falling off their host, and helmet-like heads comparable to the streamlined prow of a ship for forcing a way through their microscopic jungle. Their faces have been described as 'striking rather than beautiful, resembling a Red Indian chief with long whiskers and old-fashioned motor goggles.'

Since they evolved as wingless, blood-sucking insects, fleas have remained virtually unchanged. Specimens preserved in amber millions of years old look just like their modern descendants. The two thousand or so species live on birds and all types of furry mammals, with the exception of monkeys. Why monkeys should be immune is not known. There's even an Antarctic flea which spends nine months of the year frozen, but alive, within the ice.

If you have a problem with domestic fleas it is rarely caused by the so-called human flea (*Pulex irritans*). Not only is that almost extinct, it also prefers to feed on badgers, foxes or hedgehogs, attacking humans only when its favoured hosts are not available. The vast majority of domestic fleas are either cat fleas (*Ctenocephalides felis*) or dog fleas (*Ctenocephalides canis*), or species living on rats and mice. Fleas can survive many months without any food at all, but when they do find a source of suitable blood, they gorge themselves several times a day.

In the great plague years of 1347–1350 an estimated 25 million people died in Europe, a quarter of the total population of the continent. The rat flea (*Xenopsylla cheopis rothschild*) was in large part responsible, since it acted as intermediary, carrying the fatal bacteria from rat to man. Bubonic plague still exists today, and about seven hundred cases are reported to the World Health Organization each year, including a number in the United States. Other fleas also transmit diseases, including murine typhus and myxamatosis.

It was the great English diarist and poet Jonathan Swift (1667–1745) who wrote the famous lines:

> *So naturalists observe, a flea*
> *Hath smaller fleas that on him prey;*
> *And these have smaller fleas to bite 'em,*
> *And so proceed ad infinitum.*

Swift, or his naturalist friends, were zoologically inaccurate, however. Fleas never parasitize other fleas, only birds and mammals.

The Fluorescent Scorpion

One of the most surprising discoveries of recent years is the simple fact that the carapace of certain species of desert scorpions can fluoresce under ultra-violet light. This may not sound like a miraculous breakthrough, but zoologists go suddenly quiet at the implications, because it undermines one of their basic assumptions about life on earth – that plants are the only organisms to evolve photosynthesis.

According to the textbooks, every creature on earth (except bacteria) eats organic food. Whether they eat plants, or the animals which eat them, or the animals which eat the animals which do, sooner or later at the bottom of every food chain is vegetation of some sort. The plants alone can live on fresh air, by sunlight and photosynthesis. No animal (it is believed) has evolved this ability to turn light into chemical energy.

Many species can reverse the process, i.e. turn chemical energy into light, by bioluminescence. Many species have markings that show up under ultra-violet light, or eyes that are sensitive to it – but they do not fluoresce. Fluorescence is different; it is a chemical process directly triggered by radiation.

How the scorpions make use of it is still not known. The light-sensitive chemicals may be a waste product or side effect, but they may, just may, be on the first step towards photosynthesis.

Food for Thought

Opinions as to what is acceptable as food, and what is taboo, have varied throughout history and from one culture to another. It is all a matter of taste. For instance, human society was in existence for fifteen thousand years before the first wheat or rice was planted, or domestic animals were tamed. In the early days there were mammoths, and later on we developed the technology for fishing and catching birds, but for most of that time our diet consisted of roasted horsemeat, supplemented by eggs and shellfish when times were hard.

In fact, it is arguable that the boiled egg was the first form of cooking, closely followed by the discovery that fermented fruit juice got you drunk. The basic foodstuffs we take for granted, such as milk, salt and flour, came much later. Since then we have experimented with eating almost everything, including ourselves.

An Eskimo cookbook, published in 1952, gave recipes for pickled seal liver, stewed polar bear paws, puddings made from the stomach contents of caribou and wapiti, and ice-cream made from seal oil, wild berries and reindeer fat.

The Yakut people of Siberia eat their reindeer meat raw because they believe the cooking process destroys the soul of food.

Czimer Food, based 25 miles outside Chicago, is the most unusual meat store in the United States, catering for a nationwide gourmet clientele anxious to taste exotic meats and game.

Run by the three Czimer brothers, the store has been selling strange meats since 1914. You can buy hippo roast, buffalo steak, bear, wild hare and snapping turtle. If you get tired of that, there's always peacock, elk sirloin or a llama T-bone steak.

Meat is ordered by phone and mail. Hippos are delivered in 400–600 lb slabs. Czimer's customers include a Chicago allergist who drives out in his Mercedes to pick up exotic meat for his patients, and an electrical supply company in Michigan, which once ordered 300 lb of reindeer roast and 150 lb of hippo stew for a company dinner.

Arthur Czimer commented: 'The big problem is supply. We haven't been able to get elephant for five years. There's a scarcity of alligator and bear because of tightened conservation rules. But we're expecting ten lions in a few months. Lions we need badly.'

In parts of Asia and the East Indies dragonflies form part of the diet. On Bali, they are fried in coconut oil with vegetables and spices. In Thailand, they are roasted and are said to taste like crayfish.

Humans eat more sharks than sharks eat humans. The porbeagle, for instance, is fished commercially off Norway, most of the catch being exported to Italy where it is a delicacy. In Britain the spurdog is eaten under the euphemistic name of 'rock salmon', since people would be unlikely to buy it if they realized that it was in fact a kind of shark.

Shark meat spoils rapidly, releasing ammonia. The flesh of the Greenland or sleeper shark – the only member of the family that lives the year round in Arctic waters – has even stranger properties. Unless it is boiled in several changes of water, and dried after each boiling, it produces symptoms of drunkenness which the Eskimos call 'shark sickness'. Their legends claim that an old woman was washing her hair with urine and then dried it with a cloth that blew out to sea and turned into the Greenland shark.

In January 1980 the Nugget Casino in Sparks, Nevada, held a Safari Game Feed. The menu included Roast Tom Ostrich with Campfire Dressing, fillet of white shark, sturgeon in Veronique sauce, stingray with caper butter, soaked and roasted salmon, baby squid vinaigrette, braised sirloin tip of lion, sesame guinea-pig, oven-braised Chinese rabbit in Ng-Ka-Pi sauce, hippopotamus Salisbury style, broiled elk steak, grilled quail with grapes, roast loin of boar with cinnamon apple, and pheasant in Perigordine sauce.

Dick Roraback of the *Los Angeles Times* reported: 'For the record, the lion was an excellent dish with a pleasant and lingering aftertaste of the wild. The ostrich was totally unlike fowl, resembling roast beef. Tough roast beef. The hippo meat was ground and slightly spiced and tasted like meat-loaf with muscles, though dissenters discerned overtones of corned beef.'

The Insect Eaters

In many parts of the world, insects form a vital part of the everyday diet. Crickets, for instance, are 50 per cent protein, compared to 17 per cent for beef. Entomophagy, the word for insect eating, was coined by the Athenians, who used it to insult barbarians – though they themselves happily munched on grilled cicadas.

In Ethiopia some people live almost exclusively on grasshoppers, while others are partial to giant mosquitoes. Some Chinese eat the chrysalis of the silkworm. in Colombia, soft fat ants fried in butter are considered a delicacy. In Mexico, sweet fat worms are fried and sold on street corners like hot chestnuts.

Termites are a favourite of many African tribes. In *The People's Cookbook*, author Huguette Couffignal describes how one society harvests termites by what she calls the 'simulated rain' method.

'The termite hunters, having noted that termites leave their nests in great numbers when it rains hard, fool the insects by imitating the noise of rain. To do this they station themselves around the termite hill, which may be as tall as a man, and beat on pots. The patter must be gentle. Termites expecting a downpour stream out of their holes and are drawn to lamps held by the hunters. The hunters grill the insects with straw torches as they come out, or knock them into tubs of water with great beaters. Grilled, crushed, shaped into sausages and rolled up in banana leaves to be poached, these insects form "termite sausage".'

Locusts are also nutritious. Tuaregs eat them raw or crushed into a fine powder. Arabs boil them in salted water and dry them in the sun. Chinese, Vietnamese and Japanese roast them, fry them or make them into pancakes.

In 1875, at a time when locusts were plaguing the United States, entomologist Valentine Riley delivered a paper to the American Association for the Advancement of Science suggesting that they should be used as a food. He described the night he had prepared a locust supper at a hotel. The chef had refused to touch them, but he was aided by a 'brother naturalist and two intelligent ladies'.

'The soup vanished and banished silly prejudice,' he explained. 'Then cakes with batter enough to hold the locusts together disappeared and were pronounced good; then baked locusts with or without condiments; and when the meal was completed with dessert of baked locusts and honey à la John the Baptist, the opinion was unanimous that the distinguished prophet no longer deserved our sympathy, and that he had not fared badly on his diet in the wilderness.'

The Gourmet

The story is almost certainly apocryphal, but it is said that the heart of Louis XIV was plundered from his tomb after the French Revolution and was eventually consumed at a dinner party in Victorian London. 'I have eaten many strange things in my lifetime,' the host is reputed to have said, gazing at

CATHERINE BRADBURY

the royal offal on his plate, 'but never before have I eaten the heart of a king.'

True or not, the incident made a fitting climax to the career of Dr Frank Buckland, surgeon, naturalist, omnivore and exhibitionist, the man who claimed to eat anything.

He first discovered the publicity value of a hardened stomach at Oxford University, when he would invite his fellow students to meals consisting of such delicacies as boiled elephant trunk and rhinoceros pie. The whole roast ostrich he shared with Sir Richard Owen is said to have given the eminent zoologist indigestion, but Buckland went on to make a career as what he called a 'gourmet extraordinaire'.

His recipes were frequently published in newspapers and magazines, and in the 1860s he helped to found the Society for the Acclimatization of Animals in the United Kingdom. The official aim of the Society was to widen the diet of the general public by breeding kangaroos and bison in the English countryside, but it was mainly an excuse for Buckland to organize bizarre annual dinners, when almost anything might appear on the menu.

Not all his experiments were a success. It was a pity, he said, that cockroaches tasted so 'horribly bitter', and he frequently complained that there was no way to cook porpoise heads without them tasting of oil-lamp wick. Neither he nor his guests were able to face the south-east Asian trepang sea-slug he served at one of his dinners; and he drew the line at stewed mole and bluebottles (though his unfortunate cook still had to prepare them for him).

But, by and large, he lived up to his self-appointed reputation, and among the culinary traumas he survived were mouse on toast, slug soup, and the dish he especially recommended for breakfast – crocodile à l'orange.

Folklore

In every country in the world, farmers have developed a body of knowledge, myth and customs concerning their animals. The following examples are a random selection from the English countryside – the result of three thousand years of slow, uninterrupted evolution. This folklore carries traces of Saxon and Celtic words, and symbolism that goes back beyond the Roman occupation.

* Pigs have an ability to 'see the wind'. When high winds or storms are coming, they get restless and move quickly around their pens, often squealing.

* Counting sheep. Shepherds have their own traditional ways of counting their flock. In different parts of the country, 1-2-3-4-5 becomes:

> *Hant, tant, tethery, futhery, fant.*
> *Sarny, darny, dorny, downy, dick.*
> *Ina, tina, tether, wether, pink.*
> *Yahn, tayn, tether, mether, mumph.*

* A tup is an uncastrated male sheep; a teg is a ewe having its first lambs.
* Feed a sheep parsley to prevent foot-rot.
* Cows love dried nettles, but not fresh ones.
* In wet weather a cow has five mouths, because each foot destroys as much sodden grass as the animal can eat.
* The gat and the wattle are two kinds of sheep-hurdle. The first is made of ash wood, like a six-barred gate, and is used with bales of straw against it in lambing time. The latter is made of woven wattle.
* Horse brasses are good luck charms fixed to the animal's harness. They often include gypsy (Romany) or classical (Roman) symbols. The shape of the crescent moon is the sign of the Roman goddess Diana, who was associated with horses. The sun represents a wheel derived from its rays. A heart was used by the ancient Egyptians to protect the horse's owner.
* When milking a cow, the last half pint contains twelve times as much butter as the rest. But the richest milk, called 'beestings', comes from a cow which has just calved.
* Very small eggs which contain no yolk are called 'cock's eggs', and it is unlucky to bring them into the house.
* Ducks will not lay until they have drunk lide (March) water.
* One goose will eat as much grass as a sheep.
* This is a bee 'wassailing' song from medieval times, when bees were considered religious symbols:

> *Bees, oh bees of Paradise,*
> *Does the work of Jesus Christ,*
> *Does the work which no man can.*
> *God made bees and bees made honey,*
> *God made man and man makes money.*

* Propolis, or 'bee-glue', is gathered by bees from the sticky buds of poplar or chestnut trees, and is a natural antiseptic which will cure a sore throat.
* It will be fine if swallows and skylarks fly high, and the sheep lie down peacefully. Signs of coming rain include: short, broken spiders' webs; bees staying close to their hive; cattle lying down together and facing the wind; horses acting restless and shaking their heads; sheep bleating for no reason.

A Turrible Lot o' Lambs

'An old Essex shepherd was very successful, his ewes dropping twins (or even occasional triplets) with seasonal regularity. When very old and bedridden, he confided his secret to his boss's young son: "Because you be young, as tis that it would die with me, so I give it to you to keep.

"In the spring, get you a goat, a male. You know what lewd little beasts they *be! And kill it, and put it warm into a bottle and cork it and bury it in a dung-heap . . . where it's same warm as he be. No – you can't put it to stove, old woman she'll let stove out, or heat it up. No – the dung heap stays a nice even temperature all winter and right through summer. Then, come late autumn (when breeding starts) take you up the bottle, and ther'll be some-like water in it . . . and squeeze out what's left of him and take that water and mix it with some nice war mash of soft bread, and give it to tup before he sets to ewes – and you'll get a turrible lot o' lambs, Mas' John, a turrible lot o' lambs." '*

– Dorothy Hartley, *The Land of England.*

The Frog-Fish

The frog-fish, also known as the monk-fish or goose-fish, belongs to the same family as the angler-fish. Like its relatives, it is a bottom-dweller and propels itself along by digging its pectoral fins into the sand. An unusual feature is that its fins have elbows, which allow it to make long, lazy jumps remarkably like a frog.

Frogs and Toads

Like the other amphibians, frogs differ from reptiles, birds and mammals in several important ways.

Like fish, they have no necks. Having no ribs, they cannot expand and contract their chests to pump air into and out of their lungs. Instead, the floor of the mouth pulses rhythmically, forcing air through the nostrils. They can also draw air into their lungs by lowering the throat and contracting its muscles.

Their skin, which is only fixed to the body at certain points, also helps in respiration – notably when they are hibernating. As amphibians do not drink, the skin also absorbs water, as well as secreting moisture and, in some cases, poison.

Frogs and toads blink frequently for two reasons. First, to lubricate their eyes which, being similar to those of fish, need to be kept clean and moist when out of water. Secondly, to help swallow their food. Their eyes are not fixed, like ours, in bony cavities; and when they blink, the eyeballs sink down inside their heads and help to squeeze food down their throats.

Their formidable tongues are attached to the front, not the back, of the mouth, which is why they can be stuck out so far to seize an insect or worm. When a toad seizes an earthworm, it cleans the grains of soil off with its front feet before swallowing it.

West African hairy frog

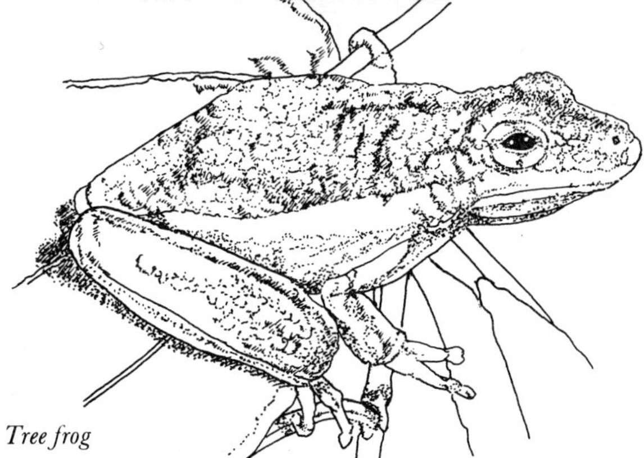
Tree frog

Another unusual attribute of amphibians is that their sperm, after leaving the testes, passes through the kidneys.

The common toad (*Bufo bufo*) mates in the spring. There are usually many more males than females, and intense competition is the result. Successful males clamber on to the backs of females and clasp them fiercely. They may be carried about by the female for several days before the eggs are laid. During this time they often have to resist attempts by other males to dislodge them. If a male is dislodged, others frantically climb on to the female, forming clusters of up to twelve individuals. The female often suffocates under the weight, though the males may hang on for several days while her body decomposes beneath them.

If the males cannot find any females, they will make frenzied clasping motions and attempt to mate with anything in sight – sticks, water-lilies, even goldfish. In the spring of 1977 there was such a shortage of females in southern England that thousands of goldfish were reported to have been attacked in this way by toads, who suffocated them by closing their gills. In another case, seven males were removed from the head of a dead rat.

Frogs only appear to be green. Their skin is in fact translucent, but only the green rays of light escape absorption. Scotland is noted for the number of its red frogs.

The horned frog, Bell's *ceratophrys*, which lives in Argentina, has small horns growing out of its upper eyelids. It is equipped with large, pointed teeth which it uses to attack and kill other frogs, which it then eats.

The European green tree frog changes colour from bright green to grey when frightened or when the sky becomes overcast. As a result it was often kept to forecast rain.

The 'flying' tree frogs have webs of skin between their toes. When they leap from the branch of a tree, they spread these webs out so that each foot forms a kind of parachute, allowing them to glide up to 45 feet (13.7m) to another branch.

CATHERINE BRADBURY

PETER BOMAN

G

The Armoured Gar

The gar is an armoured fish, one of a class of animals now almost extinct, although they once dominated the world's oceans. This survivor from the age of dinosaurs is a 5-foot (1.5-m) silver javelin, with the profile of Concorde and jaws like scissors, which lives in the shallow waters of the Caribbean and along the Mississippi.

Its remarkable armour-plating takes the form of tough, diamond-shaped scales, which fit side-by-side instead of overlapping in the usual way. They are made of an enamelled substance, rather like teeth, and are so strong that native tribes once used them as arrow-heads, and wore the skins as breast-plates. It is even said that the early settlers in America used to reinforce the blades of their wooden ploughs with gar-skin.

The Gecko

Geckos are among the most common lizards found in warm countries around the world. There are fifty species in Australia, for instance, and another fifty in Madagascar alone. Some are nocturnal, some diurnal, they range in size from just over an inch (2.5cm) to the 14-inch (35-cm) long animal called a tokay, and they come in all shapes and colours.

Among the more bizarre examples of gecko anatomy is the swollen appendage of the 'turnip-tail' lizard, and an African species which is one of the few animals you can literally see through.

But their best known feature is something all geckos have in common – the device which makes them the only four-legged animal able to run effortlessly, upside-down, across a ceiling.

The secret lies in the soles of their feet, which at first sight appear to be covered with folds of skin. On closer inspection the pads turn out to be thousands of fine bristles. If you had a microscope handy, you would find that these bristles are covered with still finer hairs; but it is only if you put them under a giant electron microscope, as scientists have recently done, would you discover that these hairs are themselves covered with still smaller ones which end in millions of Velcro-like hooks.

The hairs are so dense they act as suction pads, while the hooks can get a grip on the smallest irregularity in a surface. The gecko must be careful how it puts its foot down – toe first, with a rolling motion, followed by a contraction – and still more careful how it picks it up, if it is not to become permanently stuck.

However, the technique is so effective that the animal can support several times its own weight hanging upside down from a sheet of glass.

The see-through gecko is a web-footed species that lives in the sand dunes of south-west Africa. Apart from its golden eyes and a pale lemon line down its side, the skin is almost completely transparent and one can see the pinkish-brown organs at work within the body.

The naturalist G. K. Brain, in his book *African Wild Life*, has described how the creature's ears go so deep into its head that they almost connect, and if one looks through one ear-hole, one can see the light coming through the other.

As one of the first daytime animals on land, lizards were forced to develop eyelids and other ways of coping with bright light. The geckos incorporate many examples of these early evolutionary experiments.

One of the most popular models works on the principle of the roller shutter in a camera. The eyelids are permanently joined, but the lower lid has a small transparent window which can be rolled across the iris like a blind. The nocturnal species have vertical slits, like cat's eyes, but the daytime species have developed round pupils, like ours. However, they often have irregular shapes. In one species, the edges of the pupils are notched, so that when they contract they leave four pin-hole apertures, each of which focuses a different image on the retina.

It is not known how the creature copes with this abrupt change in what it sees, but it must have some evolutionary advantage – probably as a range-finding device.

The Genet

The rare, nocturnal genet, a catlike carnivore that inhabits forest and dense brush in Africa, is considered a pest because of its appetite for chickens. Yet by physicians it is considered a biological wonder because of its unique body chemistry.

'If the genet were human, it would have kidney stones the size of grapefruits,' says Clyde Hill, curator of the San Diego Zoo, which specializes in breeding rare species. 'But somehow, the animal's system has a way of eliminating toxins before they form into stones, and its kidneys remain disease-free in spite of constant danger signals in the blood. If this were better understood, it might be possible to eliminate kidney disease in humans.'

The Giant Squid

The giant squid inhabits the shadowy area between myth and reality, but unlike other legendary monsters, the truth may turn out to be stranger than fiction. It all depends on what you consider a 'giant'.

The animal which figured in so many sea-shanties and travellers' tales is now recognized as a legitimate species, and the specimens examined by zoologists have produced some remarkable statistics.

* They have the thickest nerve fibres of any animal, one thousand times thicker than our own.
* They are the heaviest of all invertebrates, weighing up to 1.78 tons, as much as an adult hippopotamus.
* They have the largest eyes of any living animal, up to 15 inches (38cm) in diameter, or about the size of a human head.

These figures represent only the squids which have been caught in offshore waters, which are typically about 20 feet (6m) across with 1 inch (2.5cm) diameter suckers on their tentacles (the size of the suckers is important, as we shall see).

However, larger ones have turned up from time to time. A 32-foot squid was caught off Newfoundland in 1871, for instance, and more recently a 36-foot specimen was found in the stomach of a whale caught off the Azores in 1955.

But these are small fry compared to the real monsters which could be lurking in the deep oceans. In 1888 a squid was found stranded at Lyall Bay, New Zealand, that measured a full 62 feet across, but unfortunately the body decomposed before it could be examined. But whales have been caught in the Atlantic (again off the Azores) which

had sucker marks on their sides that measured 3½–4 inches in diameter.

These must have been very large animals to take on a full-grown whale in the first place, and if the sucker marks were in proportion to the rest of the body, they must have been over 70 feet across – large enough to wrap their arms around a double-decker bus.

The evidence is slight and no one has seen one alive, but Tennyson may have been right when he wrote:

Below the thunders of the upper deep,
Far, far beneath in the abysmal sea
His ancient, dreamless, uninvaded sleep
The Kraken sleepeth.

The Gila

Of the three thousand or so kinds of lizards in the world, only two species are poisonous – the gila monster and the beaded lizard. Curiously enough, these two animals not only resemble each other, but live side by side in the same desert areas of Mexico and the south-western United States.

The gila (pronounced 'heela') is an ugly animal with a reputation for spitting poison and possessing of magical powers. The first scientists to give it a name called it *Heloderma suspectum* (because they suspected it was venomous), while the beaded lizard (about which they were quite sure) was simply described as *H. horridum*.

It is now known that it does not spit venom, but injects it through rather clumsy fangs; and the poison – a neurotoxin which causes vomiting and dizziness – is not especially powerful. There are only eight recorded cases of people dying after a gila bite, and most of them were in poor health anyway.

Nevertheless, it is hardly an attractive trait, especially when combined with the animal's obese, slug-like appearance, and makes it even more surprising that people should want to domesticate them. But over the last fifty years there has been an increasing demand for them as domestic pets.

In 1952 they were so popular (and fetching such a price on the US market) that they had to be protected by law to save them from extinction. However, illegal gila hunting is still widespread, and may eventually lead to the animal's disappearance from the wild. If this were to happen, it would, paradoxically, become the first poisonous reptile to be fully domesticated by man!

The Giraffe

They used to call it a cameleopard, and everyone agreed that it must be a mutation. Some authorities suggested it came from an unusual liaison between at least three different animals. 'The giraffe', wrote Zakariya al-Qaswini, in his thirteenth-century bestiary *The Marvels of Creation*, 'is produced by the camel mare, the male hyena and the wild cow.' One can see how he came to this conclusion, because the animal certainly combines the spindly legs of a camel with the sloping shoulders and colouring of a hyena, and the hooves of a cow. But these unique, gentle animals have a history (and biology) which is far stranger than Zakariya al-Qaswini could have imagined.

Giraffes were once common throughout the Middle East, and the rock engravings of prehistoric tribes show that they used to roam the plains of the Sahara. They are well adapted to life in semi-arid areas, and can go without water almost as long as an elephant; but as the deserts spread, they were finally driven south and east. By the time of Zakariya, they were rare in North Africa and little more than a legend in Europe.

The last giraffe in Egypt was portrayed on the tomb of Rameses II, about 1250 BC, but the animals survived in Arabia and their fame eventually spread to the Far East. The Arabs gave them to foreign heads of state, in the way the Chinese now distribute pandas. The first giraffe arrived at the Peking Zoo in 1414 AD, where it created such an impression that the Chinese adopted it as their symbol of peace.

With its tiny head perched 18 feet (5.5m) above its spindly ankles, the giraffe is the tallest living animal, and its life is dominated by the huge neck, which takes up most of the intervening space and can weigh almost as much as its body.

The most obvious problem, of course, is how it sits down. One has only to look at the animal to wonder how it can fold up that tottering gantry of a body without collapsing in a heap. And how it ever manages to stand up again.

The secret of this lies in using the top-heavy neck as a counterbalance. The neck is swung back to take the weight off its front legs, while it goes down on its knees; and then it is swung forward to allow the hindquarters to go down.

When it is sitting down, the giraffe has its legs folded underneath and its neck balanced vertically on its shoulders. If it dozed off in this position it could topple over, so when the animal goes to sleep it lays the burden down along its own back.

RAY WINDER

The neck creates a number of other problems, and zoologists have long been intrigued by the mystery of the giraffe's circulation. How does the heart pump blood to its head, 10 feet (3m) above, against the force of gravity? For that an animal would normally need an organ that filled its whole chest, producing enough pressure to burst its blood vessels. There again, how does it avoid a rush of blood to the brain when the head is suddenly lowered to ground level?

The answer, which has only recently been discovered, is that the giraffe's circulation contains a special system of pumping muscles and one-way valves, which is unique in the animal world, and seems to have evolved for this one problem.

If it becomes necessary, giraffes can defend themselves with their sharp hooves, but they have almost no natural enemies. Even the predatory cats leave them alone because their vital organs are so far above the ground, and they can keep watch for miles around from their look-out tower.

The neck plays such a part in their lives, it is hardly surprising that it should be one of the most sensual areas of their body. The males use them to buffet each other in ritual combat, and family groups will stand together entwining or caressing each other's necks.

It is popular myth that giraffes are mute. They are certainly very quiet animals, and many zoo-keepers have never heard them utter a sound. Yet the animals have a large voice-box and they are perfectly capable of using it.

Young giraffes can bleat like a calf, the adults signal to each other with grunts and coughs, and the females have a cry that sound like 'wa-ray'.

The size of their voice-box remains a mystery. If they could make full use of it, the effect would be devastating – but they never do. It seems to be a piece of biological equipment left over from an earlier stage in their history. One may even speculate that once, long ago, when they ranged the prehistoric Sahara, giraffes could roar like lions.'

Grave Fauna

During the nineteenth century, a French scientist, Pierre Megnin, who was on the look out for new methods of criminal investigation, decided to make a study of the insects and larvae found in buried corpses. As a result of this unsavoury research, he claimed it was possible to tell the age of a corpse fairly accurately by the fauna in the grave.

This study was followed up by another in 1898, when M. G. Motter investigated one hundred and fifty disinterred bodies in Washington, DC, and wrote a paper entitled 'A Contribution to the study of the Fauna of the Grave'. Apparently, the most common residents of this unusual environment are springtails, 'rove' beetles, and the aptly named coffin flies. However, Motter disputed Megnin's findings and said it was doubtful that any useful legal evidence could be obtained by studying these insects.

The idea was finally discarded with the introduction of today's hermetically sealed caskets.

Gravity Sensing

It has recently been discovered that certain marine crustaceans, such as shrimps and lobsters, have a unique gravity-sensing device.

On either side of their heads, at the base of the antennae, are small boxes that are open to the sea through minute pores. As the animal moves through the water, sand seeps in through the pores and collects at the bottom of each box. The walls are lined with sensors, and as the creature moves up or down, or varies from the horizontal – and the sand shifts – it can tell how it is aligned to the earth's gravitational field.

In effect, it is an ingenious mechanical substitute for the fluid sloshing around our own inner ear, which keeps us upright and causes sea-sickness when agitated too much.

The Gopher

It looks like a grin, but the cheeky appearanc of the pocket gopher stems from the fact that its mouth is *behind* its teeth. The huge incisors have moved out along the projecting upper jaw, the skin has sealed over behind them and the mouth itself is a small, round hole barely visible in the fur above its lower jaw.

The reason is that the gopher is a *fossorial* or subterranean species, specially adapted to life underground. The teeth make ideal picks and, by using its claws as rakes and its flat paws as spades, it is a formidable burrowing machine. The tightly pursed lips simply ensure that it doesn't get a mouthful of earth at the same time.

What gophers prefer to eat are roots, which they tear off in chunks and turn in their paws, like a lathe, until their juddering incisors have reduced them to splinters. Piles of these mouth-sized chips are then stored in their underground larders.

If you live in tunnels, your rear end is as important as the front and, in the case of the gophers, is just as odd. The tail is a loose bag several sizes too big, so that the vertebrae can move around inside it. The exact purpose is not clear, but it makes such a sensitive feeler that they can run down a tunnel backwards as fast as they can forwards.

The tunnels are rather haphazard but their excavations are carried out on such a massive scale that gophers are a major ecological factor in the western half of North America.

Gray's Paradox

There is a whole branch of science, called bionics, based on the fact that biological engineering is far more sophisticated than anything human technology has yet produced. The student of bionics sets out to explain how they work and, if possible, to plagiarize them. Stealing nature's patents and copying them can be a profitable business. Sonar research began with animal models, for instance; and the early heat-seeking missiles were based on the infra-red detection of the pit viper.

The story of Gray's Paradox is an example of what can happen when a scientist notices that an animal is behaving in a way that, on the face of it, is impossible – and wants to know how it does it. The paradox is named after Professor James Gray of Cambridge University who in 1936 first discussed the problem of how dolphins swim as fast as they do.

Dolphins can swim at up to 25 miles an hour, but tests with rigid models of a dolphin showed that the energy theoretically necessary to produce this speed would be ten times the amount that the dolphin's muscles could produce.

There were two possible answers. Either the dolphin's muscles were able to develop a far greater energy output than those of other mammals – which was considered unlikely – or they possessed some unique way of reducing the friction drag of sea water, a secret which the navys and air forces of the world were eager to know.

Gray suggested that the rear part of the dolphin's body, and its tail, helped to reduce the turbulence in the water, but he remained mystified. As he put it, 'Nature's design for a dolphin is much more efficient than any submarine or torpedo yet produced by man'.

The story of how the real truth was revealed is a fascinating one.

TIM HAYWARD

In 1938 Max O. Kramer of the German Research Institute for Aeronautics in Berlin, was granted a patent entitled 'Device for the Reduction of Friction Drag'. His system suggested a method to reduce the turbulence of fluids passing over a rigid object, such as that of water over a battleship or air over a missile.

However, the war interrupted his investigations, and he went to work on guided missiles. And after the war he left for the USA to do some research for the Navy. While he was crossing the Atlantic, he saw dolphins for the first time, and became fascinated by their speed and grace. He read up all he could on them and became convinced that they had solved the problem he had been grappling with before the war.

In California in 1955 he was able to examine a sample of dolphin's skin under the microscope for the first time. He discovered that the outer skin was not waterproof, in fact the opposite. It was a soft, waterlogged coating on a fatty, hard inner skin. This coating – one-sixteenth of an inch thick – is itself composed of a surface diaphragm supported on thousands of tiny pillars with waterlogged spongy material between them. This meant that any minute oscillation in the water on any single micrometre of the dolphin's surface would be adjusted to automatically. Kramer had discovered 'a highly refined realization of the basic idea' he had expressed in his 1938 patent.

As a final test he set out to simulate the dolphin's skin, using a sandwich of rubber sheeting, supported by rubber stubs, and filled with various viscous fluids, then mounted on rigid models. In air flows of up to 40 mph, the drag was reduced by as much as 60 per cent. Dr Kramer said: 'After the tests the dolphin's secret ceased to exist. Their astonishing performance had found its technical explanation.'

Green Polar Bears

After shrimps with sand in their ears, and the hydrodynamics of dolphins, almost anything could be true . . . but green polar bears? The world's largest carnivore is a remarkable animal, but green ones sound too much like an Eskimo version of pink elephants to be believable.

Zoologists were equally sceptical, but the stories accumulated over the years, and every so often reports would come in from trappers that they had seen such creatures. They were definitely polar bears, and definitely green.

Eventually, a few years ago, Canadian scientists surprised themselves and everyone else by verifying the tale. A bear had been found whose hair was unquestionably green, and when it was examined under a microscope it was discovered that the hollow tube in the centre of each follicle had been invaded by a form of parasitic green algae.

How and why this happens is still a mystery. It must, after all, put the animal at a considerable disadvantage in its white environment. But green polar bears must now be accepted as a zoological fact.

At this point, if you know anything about the animals of South America, you will shrug your shoulders and say So what? What about the sloths? And it is true that the sloths of the tropical rain forest are another example (the only other one) of an animal whose coat turns green from algae. But it happens in very different circumstances.

The sloths have a symbiotic relationship with the algae, and encourage its growth as a form of camouflage. In their case it grows outside the hair, in special grooves that have evolved on the surface for this purpose.

Unlike the polar bear, which is constantly on the move, hunting and swimming, the conditions for the sloth's growth are ideal. Suspended in the humid air, as static as the tree it is hanging from, it is surprising that moss does not grow on it too.

The detailed analysis of the polar bear's hair revealed other surprises, including the fact that they are not really white. The hairs contain no pigment at all. When they are not filled with green parasites, each of the hollow tubes is transparent. The hairs only appear white because their inner surfaces are rough and reflect visible light, in the same way as transparent snowflakes. The hollow cores also serve to improve the bear's insulation and – perhaps the most astonishing discovery of all – they are the exact diameter, and arranged in precisely the right way, to 'funnel' ultra-violet light down to the skin. An example of evolution pre-empting 'fibre optics'.

The structure of the hairs also explains a curious phenomenon first noticed during aerial surveys: neither the bears (nor baby harp seals, whose fur is similarly composed) show up on infra-red film! Their insulation is so good that the outer layers of the coat can be soaking wet and the same temperature as the ice around them, while their bodies remain warm inside.

Research is now under way in industrial laboratories to produce a synthetic version for truly efficient cold-weather clothing.

Grotto of Stars

In the Waitomo cavern on New Zealand's North Island there is a large grotto fed by the warm still waters of an underground river, which is the unique home of *Arachnocampa luminosa*, a luminous fly about twice the size of a mosquito.

On the grotto roof hang huge numbers of the flies' transparent larvae, enclosed in silken sheaths two inches (5cm) long. From each sheath, the larva suspends a cluster of twenty threads covered with sticky globules of mucus, and four to five feet long.

Under its tail the larva has a light-emitting organ which works by chemical action. The light shines downwards, illuminating the sticky globules so that they shimmer like a diamond necklace. They are the larva's bait – any flying insect which sticks to the line is hauled up, and the larva eats both thread and catch.

Visitors to the grotto are propelled by oarsmen skilled in completely silent rowing, and are warned to not even whisper. The threads also act as the ears of the larvae. The least untoward sound causes all the stars to immediately switch off, plunging the grotto into darkness.

Growth Rate

One of the most remarkable things about biological engineering is the speed at which the structures are built, especially at the beginning of an animal's life. For instance, the giraffe grows from a single cell to an independent animal, 6 feet high and weighing 120 lb, in less than a year.

A human embryo increases 240 times in length and over a million times in weight while it is in the womb. And the growth rate continues outside, because a new-born baby doubles its weight every six months. If we continued growing like this for the rest of our life, a thirty-year-old adult would weigh 3,000 million tons.

Yet this growth rate is relatively slow compared to other plants and animals. There is a form of giant kelp that can grow as much as 18 inches (45cm) a day (to a length of about 130 feet). The record for the fastest growth rate of any animal belongs to the baby whale, which can put on weight at the astonishing rate of ten pounds an hour!

H

The Short and Hectic History of Hamsters

There is nothing new about hamsters, of course. They have been hunted as pests in Russia and the Middle East for centuries. Large, unpleasant rodents, about half the size of rabbits, which do enormous damage to crops – they have always been around.

The animals we are talking about here is the gentle, furry little creatures you find running round treadmills and being fed on lettuce by adoring six-year-olds all over the world. Those are very new, so new in fact that as late as 1930 only one person in the world knew they even existed. The story of how they were discovered – or rather, rediscovered – is one of the legends of zoology.

The unlikely hero was neither an explorer nor a scientist, but a Palestinian scholar who specialized in archaic Hebrew and Aramaic texts, and the story began in the late 1920s when he came across a passage in one of the ancient documents he was studying which set him thinking.

The passage said that there had once been 'in the district of Chaleb, a special kind of Syrian mouse, which was brought to Assyria and into the land of the Hittites', and it went on to describe how tame these animals were, and how the children in ancient Assyria and Anatolia used to keep them in cages.

Now this was puzzling, because the text made it clear they were not ordinary mice, but a different kind of animal, yet he could find no record of any living animal that fitted the description. His curiosity was aroused, and in 1930 he arranged to visit the site of Chaleb (now largely occupied by the modern city of Aleppo), to see if he could find any trace of his 'Syrian mice'. He searched the countryside around, questioning everyone he met, and suddenly, much to his surprise, he stumbled on what he was looking for. In a small earth burrow, he discovered thirteen tiny hamsters, reddish-brown in colour and much smaller than any known species.

It was a unique event, because, in spite of intensive field research, no other golden hamster has ever been found in the wild. Although he did not know it at the time, he may have chanced upon the last surviving members of the species, and those thirteen animals became the ancestors of every one of the millions of golden hamsters alive today.

By 1931 they were already grandparents, and Professor Aharoni found himself the owner and foster-father of a new species. They were just as docile as the ancient texts had said, and they multiplied faster than he could give them away. Scientists discovered that they made ideal research animals, and he was soon supplying them to universities and laboratories all over America. Within the next few years they had virtually replaced the guinea-pig both in laboratories and as a domestic pet.

American scientists introduced them to their English colleagues during World War II, and in 1946 the Allied army took a few pairs with them to Germany. They were still reproducing enthusiastically, and children took them to their hearts as they had done in America. The pet shops flourished and, in just over ten years, their European population had grown to more than ten million.

The history of hamsters, ancient and modern, had come full circle: they were even exported to Aleppo.

TERRY OAKES

The Hanuman

A blood-red statue dominates one of the holiest of Hindu shrines, the Pashupati Temple at Katmandu, in Nepal. The temple is dedicated to Shiva, Lord of the Beasts, and the sculpture represents a monkey, a species of langur called the hanuman which is one of the few animals named after a god and still regarded as sacred by devout Hindus.

Hanuman was the son of the wind and a monkey nymph (an odd concept to Western minds) and his role in Hindu mythology was as the chief minister of the monkey people who befriended the legendary hero, Rama (one of the incarnations of Vishnu) when he was banished to the forest, and helped him in the conquest of what is now Sri-Lanka.

Troops of temple monkeys are a familiar sight in Nepal – the Pashupati monks support a colony of three hundred – and the animals are generally respected throughout India. They are allowed to wander at will and, like sacred cows, it is considered sacrilege to kill one. The cult even reaches as far as Bali where they worship another species, the crab-eating macaque.

In the same way that Ganesh, the elephant god, symbolizes prosperity, Hanuman represents a quick wit and ingenuity.

The Eyes of the Hatchet

Hatchets are a form of deep-sea fish that inhabit the weightless, twilight world at a depth of 1,000 to 1,500 feet. They do resemble a small hatchet, with their head and body flattened into a crinkly silver shape like the head of an axe attached to a tubular white tail. The illusion would be complete except for the fact that they are only a couple of inches long.

It was once thought that life of any kind was rare at such depths, but it has been discovered that hatchet fish gather in such large shoals that they can interfere with sonar mapping of the ocean bed.

1,500 feet is the greatest depth at which the human eye can detect any light from the surface (although special cameras can pick up a faint glimmer at 3,000 feet). It is a frontier zone, on the edge of the total dark where animals must provide their own illumination; and creatures that inhabit such places tend to develop multiple systems.

The hatchet fish is equipped with bioluminescence – in the form of red and blue lights underneath, along the 'edge' of the axe – but these are mainly for identification. They mostly rely on what light there is and have evolved an extremely sophisticated visual system to make the most of it.

Their eyes hang like large milky globes in front of their faces, and are so sensitive they would be blinded in daylight. Most nocturnal animals are colour-blind, because it is easier to see a slight movement in the dark in black-and-white (in fact, our colour-vision switches off in poor lighting conditions). But the hatchet fish are colour-sensitive. Since green and blue light penetrate best to these depths, the retina of their eyes is entirely composed of colour cells, tuned to these particular frequencies.

What intrigues biologists is that some species have *tubular* eyeballs that are compressed into a cylindrical shape running back into the head. This suggests that they may actually be telescopic. The increased focal length between the lens and the retina would certainly have the effect of magnifying things – though it is difficult to imagine what use this is to the fish.

On the other hand, they may work on the same principle as night glasses or an image intensifier – gathering the maximum amount of light from the smallest area of the visual field in order to see more detail. It has even been suggested that they might provide a variable system, like a zoom lens, which the animal can control.

The Hemigale Diamonds

The hemigale is a Malayan civet cat with distinctive and unusual markings – five diamond-shaped saddles down its back, which form a series of triangles along the side. There is nothing unusual about these markings in themselves, except that there is only one other animal in the world with anything like them – a water opossum called the yapok, which lives in South America.

These animals have no geographical or evolutionary connection, and what makes the coincidence more remarkable is that the markings are not just similar, but identical down to the smallest detail.

The hoatzin

The Hoatzin – or How to Fly

It is difficult not to feel sorry for the hoatzin, because it must be one of the oddest creatures in the world. A clumsy bird from the swamps of Venezuela which can barely fly, runs up trees, croaks like a frog, and smells of musk like certain crocodiles and turtles. Body odour is rare in birds, and it seems unfair that the hoatzin, struggling to build its untidy nest in the overhanging branches without falling into the swamp, should be smelly on top of everything else.

But it has one remarkable feature – its unique ancestry – which sets it apart. The hoatzin is the last descendant of the feathered dinosaur, *Archaeopteryx*, which makes it the only living model of how birds first learnt to fly.

The life of a bird is dominated by the simple and obvious fact that it is a flying machine. Inside and out, its body has been shaped by the unforgiving laws of aerodynamics. A bird's skull is a miracle of lightweight engineering; its bones are hollow, its skeleton is a highly efficient airframe, reinforced to withstand the stresses of flight, and its brain is programmed with elaborate navigation systems.

In order to get off the ground, two things are necessary: a light enough body (like an insect) and a powerful enough engine (like an airplane).

RAY WINDER

Everything else must be sacrificed to the discipline of flight.

It is no accident that birds are the only class of vertebrates in which none of the species gives birth to its young. The complicated plumbing evolved by placental mammals – not to mention the additional weight of an embryo passenger – are an unnecessary payload which would impair a bird's efficiency. Laying eggs in the branches of trees may seem a risky method of reproduction, but at least the parents remain airworthy.

Many of the organs found in other animals are missing or have been replaced with miniaturized versions. They have even dispensed with sexual organs. In most birds these consist of no more than an opening in the side of the cloaca, and mating is reduced to the rubbing of bottoms. The only birds to possess a penis are ducks, geese and ostriches – species which spend most of their life on the ground, or for whom flight is not important.

Birds are not the only creatures to take to the air, of course. Insects were flying long before birds evolved, and some of the early insect species were giants. Over 300 million years ago, there were dragonflies among the tree-ferns and primeval swamps with wingspans of more than a yard. Their descendants are smaller, but, according to the entomologist Walter Linsenmaier, they may still be the best flying machines on the planet.

'The centre of gravity lies between and below the base of the wings which, in contrast with those of nearly all other insects, are connected directly with very strong flight muscles. Consequently, dragonflies and damselflies are masters of every type of flight, even when the position of the body makes flight almost impossible. They can fly backwards, move vertically like helicopters or even like rockets, or stop and turn in the midst of the most rapid progression, as if they had been rammed into. So violent are these manoeuvres that it is surprising the wing membrane is not torn to shreds. Yet it withstands these strains, for it is not smoothly stretched out, but is ribbed with a bountiful system of veins that make it elastic.'

A large dragonfly can move at up to 60 mph in silent flight, its wings beating too slowly to produce a hum; and some species spend their whole life in flight, except for brief nocturnal pauses or when forced down by bad weather.

Several of the dinosaurs learned how to glide, in the same way that flying foxes do today, by jumping from tree to tree. They developed wings of skin, and some of them grew to the size of airplanes. The pterodons, for instance, which laid two-gallon eggs and had 40-foot wingspans, must have been the most terrifying things that ever took to the air. But they were gliders, not airplanes, and so heavy that they probably had to launch themselves from cliffs in order to get airborne. If they had been smaller, they might have survived, because their basic structure was later adopted by little mammals such as bats.

However one species of dinosaur, the Wright brothers of the animal world, did manage to stay aloft under its own power. The archaeopteryx, like many of the smaller dinosaurs, was warm-blooded – a new development that was to have a curious side-effect.

On one hand, the new metabolism provided a lot more power, but it also required a much higher running temperature, which raised the problem of insulation. A reptile does not need insulation because it simply adjusts to the outside temperature, whatever it may be. But if the temperature of a warm-blooded animal varies by more than a few degrees, it will die.

This is why, at a certain point in evolution, there is a marked change in the appearance of animals, as the leathery skins of reptiles were suddenly supplemented by the hair, fur, wool and subcutaneous fat of mammals. In the case of the archaeopteryx, the reptilian scales evolved into lightweight, complex and delicate structures called feathers.

Feathers were not only good insulation, they also meant that a large aerofoil surface could now be carried by a small body. So powered flight became possible for the first time.

Only five examples of archaeopteryx have been found (they are probably the most valuable fossils in the world) but they provide clear evidence that it could fly. The feathers of flightless birds, like the ostrich and moa, are symmetrical on either side of the spine. The fossilized feathers of archaeopteryx, like those of the hoatzin, are lopsided, with the aerodynamic shape typical of all flying birds.

However, the archaeopteryx was probably not very good at it. Like the hoatzin it still had too many bones in its wing, including a hook-like thumb on the leading edge. The clumsy flight of the hoatzin, with short glide paths and a great deal of struggling through branches, probably gives a good idea of its technique.

Clumsy it may be, but for the late Mesozoic, 65 million years ago, that was a revolution; and from those first birds have developed creatures that can fly at over 100 mph, sleep in mid-air, breathe through their bones, navigate around the world, and spend most of their lives on the wing.

Honey Ants

If you ever happen to be stranded in a desert, one of the hidden resources worth knowing about is the honey ant.

These insects are well adapted to drought conditions, and have evolved a way of storing quantities of their concentrated liquid diet underground. Some of the colony's worker ants, called *repletes*, have elastic bodies, and when they are fed nectar and the secretions of other insects, their abdomens swell up into grossly distorted spheres.

The repletes are dwarfed by these inflated sacs of honey-dew, which are about the size of large grapes, and since they cannot possibly drag them around they hang from the roofs of their tunnels like translucent red globes, regurgitating food on request.

The Honey Guide

Another useful tip for the would-be explorer, in central and southern Africa this time, is to look out for the honey guide – a bird with a distinctive call and a curious but useful obsession with wax.

The black-throated honey guide (*indicator indicator*) is a small, relatively inconspicuous bird, related to the woodpecker, and it gets its name from the way it will guide human beings, baboons and honey badgers to the hives of wild honey-bees.

There is no need to search for it, because the bird will come looking for you. When the honey guide has found a hive, it will seek out a human being, or one of its other partners, and perch on a tree nearby emitting a 'churr-churr' sound. The noise has been compared to 'the sound made by shaking a partly full matchbox rapidly sidewise', and it is repeated again and again until the bird has caught your attention.

It then flies off, with a conspicuous downward dip, to another tree, still churring loudly, and waits for you to follow. When you catch up with it, it flies to the next tree, and so on until it reaches the vicinity of the hive.

It then hands over to you, and waits nearby while you break into the hive and make off with the plundered honey. When you have gone, the bird will swoop down to feed off the broken remnants of honeycomb, which inspires the whole complex sequence of behaviour in the first place.

For it is not the honey that attracts the honey guide, but the wax from which the comb is made. The bird has bacteria in its intestines which extract nutritious fatty acids from the wax. The smell of wax is probably what draws the honey guide to the beehive in the first place. The birds are known to be attracted to wax candles, something noted as early as the sixteenth century when a Portuguese missionary to Africa observed them flying into his church to nibble at the altar candles.

Hoppers

These grotesque carnival floats – surely the oddest looking creatures in the world – are tree-hoppers.

They belong to a wide and eccentric family of insects which includes leaf-hoppers, known as 'sharpshooters' because they spit drops of honey-dew, and the triangular thornbugs which cluster together like bright green darts.

Their best known relatives are probably the frog-hoppers, which are responsible for 'cuckoo spit'. The nymph stage, sometimes called the 'spittlebug', gives off a soapy liquid which it works into the foamy bubbles found on the stems of plants.

Plant-hoppers, like the Chinese candle fly, are

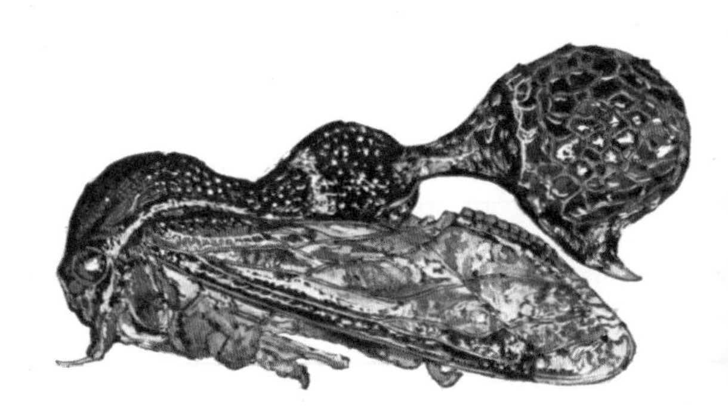

CATHERINE BRADBURY

often brightly coloured and one species even exudes a white wax that hangs on its body like wool. Tree-hoppers are less colourful but make up for it with the baroque architecture they carry on their backs.

These extraordinary shapes are caused by an enlargement of the front part of their thorax, but what is their purpose? To imitate the gnarled texture of a tree trunk? To disguise which way they are going? Or is it the ultimate form of camouflage – to look as unlike an animal (or any other living thing) as possible?

An Orgy of Hornbills

Some of the strangest (and most valuable) horns are those which have been evolved by birds. Since the Middle Ages, large quantities of so-called 'bird ivory' have been exported to China, where it used to cost twice as much as real ivory, and was used both for sculpture and medical potions.

Most of this came from the fifty-five species of hornbills that live in the tropical rain forests of Africa, Asia and the East Indies.

The birds are distinguished by their unusually large, brightly-coloured beaks, surmounted by an extraordinary variety of horny ridges. The great Indian hornbill, for instance, looks as if it had a pair of opera glasses clamped on its beak; and the black casqued species sports a ridge almost as large as its beak, shaped like the shell of a mussel.

Most of the structures are made of a hollow, bony network, and are comparatively light, but the helmeted hornbill of Indonesia (from which most of the 'bird ivory' came) is an exception. Its helmet-shaped prominence consists of solid horn, which makes the head so heavy it would be continually toppling forwards if it was not counterbalanced by two immensely long tail feathers. From beak to tail the bird is five and a half feet (1.7m) long, and its skull weighs over 11 ounces – the heaviest of any bird in the world.

Its long tail feathers are white, the body plumage black, and the beak and neck blood-red, giving it an altogether striking appearance.

One of its more endearing characteristics is a tendency to get drunk by eating too much fruit. The explorer Gustav Schneider, came across one of these hornbill orgies while following an elephant herd in the Sumatran jungle at the turn of the century.

'I heard a strange hammering', he wrote, 'and followed the sound until I came below a waringin tree. Above me I saw a number of hornbills fluttering in the air, violently flying at one another, and striking one another with their foreheads, thereby causing the mysterious hammer beats. After each strike the birds fell completely to the ground or a short distance above it, depending on the intensity of the impact. Some came so close to me that I could have grasped them, and I noticed that those which fell to the ground had the greatest difficulty in getting up again. It was comical to see the long, misshapen birds rising slowly like paper dragons, and then attacking one another.'

A few years later, Schneider encountered a similar situation where hornbills had become intoxicated by gorging themselves on figs.

Horns

Whatever their geometry, whether they are used as battering rams, digging tools or sexual organs, horns basically consist of the same thing: a core of bone covered with either skin (as in the case of deer and giraffes) or horn (as with prongbucks and cattle).

Deer antlers begin to form on two knobs of bone, or pedicles, which are set into the top of the skull. They take three months to grow, and are covered with a velvety skin so sensitive that the animal becomes sexually aroused if it is stroked. At the end of each season, a ring of bone forms around the base, cutting off the blood supply so that the velvet dies, and special blood cells eat away at the antlers themselves until they fall off.

This process repeats itself each year, with the antlers growing bigger and more complex every time. A large set of red deer antlers can weigh up to 70 lb of solid bone.

In most species, only the male grows horns. The one exception is the reindeer, where both sexes have them – a phenomenon that is still not adequately explained.

Giraffe horns, known as ossicones, last a lifetime, and grow beneath the skin as separate bones that later fuse with the skull.

The horn of the rhinoceros is not bone at all, but a matted clump of fibres akin to human fingernails, which does not fuse with the skull. The Javanese and Indian species have one horn, while the Sumatran and the two African species have two. Because of its alleged properties as an aphrodisiac, rhino horn is in great demand, and their survival as a species is now in doubt.

Hot and Cold

The upper limit for the existence of life on earth is the temperature at which albumen emulsifies (i.e. when the 'white' of an egg turns white), and the lowest is when it crystallizes (to be more precise when the fluid contents of our cells freeze solid). Provided the precious contents of its cells and eggs remain fluid, an animal can survive almost any temperature. Certain fish, for instance, can survive being frozen into a block of ice because they saturate their body with glycol antifreeze.

But surviving is not enough. Unless the animals can eat and grow, communicate with each other, mate and reproduce, they will die out in a single generation. What we are really talking about are the limits in which they can *function* – in other words, the running temperature of their biological engines.

This depends on how complicated the engine is. For most micro-organs the limits are still from just above freezing to just below boiling. Much the same applies to reptiles and cold-blooded animals, whose engines are designed to run in such low gear that they are barely ticking over, and work more and more efficiently as they heat up. But when it comes to mammals like ourselves, the limits are critical. Our engines are so powerful that they burn up fuel at an incredible rate, and only work at high temperatures. In some cases the running temperature is only just below the lethal limit. For instance, birds can only fly if their body temperature is a degree or so on either side of 104°F. In human terms, they spend their lives in a high fever. The bird's brain would seize up at this temperature, so it has evolved a sophisticated network of cooling systems around its skull to keep it at a lower temperature than the rest of its body.

Every species has its own problems, and amazing variety of heating and cooling systems, thermocouples, radiators, emergency fuel cells, condensers, ventilation systems and insulation techniques have been evolved.

Our own optimum temperature is 98.6°F – not as high as for birds, but still dangerously close to the lethal limit. So we have tended to concentrate on cooling systems, and our bodies are able to cope with heat much better than they can with cold.

In 1775 the Secretary of the Royal Society, Dr Charles Blagden, tested the human capacity to withstand extreme heat by placing himself and some friends in a room heated to 260°F for three-quarters of an hour. A steak he took along was cooked right through by the time he emerged, while a pot of water covered with oil to prevent evaporation was heated to boiling point.

On the other hand we are very vulnerable to cold. We are the only primate without fur, the 'naked ape', and our body heat radiates away so quickly that a naked human being will die of hypothermia at temperatures that most animals would consider pleasantly mild. Our ability to live in 'heroic' environments depends on the creation of our own micro-climates, by means of clothing, fire and shelters. They are not so much a part of our lives that we are relatively indifferent to changes in the outside temperature. For most creatures these are still a matter of life and death. They govern the whole rhythm of a reptile's life, and some insects are so sensitive to changes of temperature that they can be used as thermometers.

For instance, there is a species of moth in New Zealand, that can detect the approach of weather systems hundreds of miles out in the Pacific (by counting the ions in the atmosphere) long before they register on meteorological instruments.

Another remarkable insect in that part of the world is a grasshopper that lives near the summit of Mount Kosciusco, Australia's highest peak, which changes colour from jet-black to sky-blue at sunrise, and reverses the colours again at sunset.

While many animals can alter their colour to match the environment, this grasshopper is unique in that every cell on the exterior of its body is a colour cell which automatically and independently, with no nervous control, reacts to the change of temperature at dawn and dusk.

Each colour cell consists of granules of black pigment and granules of blue. The blue granules rise to the surface when the ambient temperature reaches approximately 77°F (25°C), the black granules when it falls below 59°F (15°C). The advantage to the insect is that at night its high-altitude home becomes extremely cold and its black colouring absorbs and retains all the heat available. During the day, in contrast, it can become very hot, and the grasshopper might die of heatstroke if it kept its black coat. Changing to light blue serves to reflect much of the heat away.

It is interesting that the colour change occurs in dead grasshoppers as well as live ones, and that it is possible to make one of the creatures half blue and half black by heating one end and cooling the other.

Such delicate refinements would be no use to animals who have to exist in the violent, sub-zero weather conditions in the polar regions. One of their main survival techniques is the ability to control their blood circulation, so that they can cut off the supply to their limbs and other 'unessential' parts of their body, in order to concentrate it around their vital organs. Some of them have several different circulations. For instance, wolves spend much of their time travelling across ice and snow at temperatures that drop to forty degrees below zero, and their giant footpads – five inches (13cm) long and four inches (10cm) wide – are kept just above freezing point by a circulatory system that is independent of the rest of the body.

Emperor penguins, which grow up to 4 feet 8 inches (1.4m) tall and almost as much around the chest, inhabit the bleak wastes of the Antarctic, where the temperature ranges from minus 10 to minus 33 degrees Centigrade, and where blizzards rage at 160 mph. The complete adaptation of the birds to so inhospitable an environment is illustrated by the way in which they deal with blizzards. The colony forms itself into one or more 'tortoises', with 500–600 birds pressing themselves together into an absolutely regular circle which very slowly revolves around its centre. The blizzard may last for two days, and only then do the birds disperse. The 'tortoise' allows them to keep their body temperature 2–3 degrees lower than if they were isolated, so that they do not burn up as much body fat. A penguin in the 'tortoise' loses only 100 or so grammes (3½oz) per day, compared to 200 grammes if isolated.

Most animals favour certain specific temperatures above all others. Humans feel best with a skin temperature of 91.4°F (33°C). Snow flies, which live on glaciers in Austria, prefer 39.2°F, rainbow trout 50.72°F, and ant lions in the Libyan desert 120.38°F. Such exact preferences are discovered by placing the animal in a 'temperature-choice apparatus', a long narrow enclosed space in which there is a continuous temperature gradient from one end to the other.

Temperature preference amongst certain insects is used in ethnic African medicine as a means of diagnosis. Headlice, for instance, are extremely sensitive to their host's temperature; if it rises or falls by only a few degrees, the louse will desert its host for a more healthy one, and the doctor knows his patient is running an abnormal temperature.

People who live by nature learn to seek out these patterns and associations – a lesson that modern scientists now take to heart. For centuries, their approach has been to narrow down their field of study to such fine detail, that no two experts can even understand each other. Fortunately things are changing. Many important discoveries are being made by simply standing back and seeing the wood for the trees. Zoologists, for instance, have realized that noting the similarities between animals is just as important as analysing their differences.

One example, where the evidence has been staring us in the face without anyone noticing the pattern, is Allen's Law, which states that subspecies in colder climates have small protuberances, such as noses.

It is obvious, of course, once it has been pointed out. Cold weather animals also have rounder, stockier bodies, and are generally larger than the equivalent species in warmer climates. The reason is qute simple: if you want to conserve your heat, you reduce the size of the 'radiator'. In other words you need the smallest possible surface area of skin in proportion to your volume. This is why so many of the large land animals, such as bison, mammoths, bears and even our own Neanderthal predecessors, happened to evolve during the ice ages. Like all cold-weather species, the Neanderthals were shorter, fatter and heavier than us – and had much smaller noses.

The best way to illustrate this is by the exceptions. Large tropical animals which are forced to cope with the heat are obsessive bathers, which spend hours wallowing in it (like elephants and tigers), or spend the whole day submerged and only coming out at night (like hippos). And in almost every case they have developed 'radiators' to increase their surface area (like the camel's spindly legs, the giraffe's legs and neck, and the elephant's enormous ears).

The small mice and shrews have a terrible business surviving anywhere north of the Mediterranean. In cold weather they have the ultimate defence of hibernating, but their waking lives are a desperate race against the thermometer.

Their hearts can beat at the incredible rate of 615 times a minute, to pump enough life-giving warmth through their bodies; and the organ itself is as large as it physically can be. Our own hearts represent about 0.42 per cent of our total body weight, but in some shrews it is 2.37 per cent, or *five times* larger. The shrew cannot afford to stop its hectic search for food for a moment. Rest is out of the question, and it is only possible to sleep for a few seconds at a time. Animals like mice, which appear to go to sleep at night, are actually hibernating, so that their body temperature can fall to that of their environment, and their oxygen requirements are reduced accordingly. If they did not do this, they could literally starve to death while they slept.

Another discovery about the cold ecologies came

to light when oceanographers discovered that the Arctic was one of the richest oceans in the world. Why was it that these freezing, inhospitable waters were teeming with life when the warmer seas were relatively deserted?

The answer to this question turned out to be one of the fundamental, most basic laws of life on earth. One of the scientists working on marine organisms was Jacques Loeb of the University of California, who, in 1908, discovered that animals actually live *longer* in the cold. After a series of careful experiments on sea urchins, he was able to prove that a 50°F (10°C) reduction in temperature increased the animal's lifespan as much as a thousand times! In other words, the colder the climate, the more generations of a particular species can be alive at the same time. The Arctic Ocean was not crowded because there were more species there (in fact, there are fewer than in the tropics), but because the population of each one was so enormous.

The same rule explains the dazzling variety of life in the tropics. With only one generation alive at a time, there is more food, and space, for other species to share.

The Howlers

The call of the howler monkeys of South America is reputed to be the loudest sound produced by any animal on earth. One zoologist described it as 'a combination of the bark of a dog and the bray of a mule magnified a thousandfold'.

It is said that in the morning and evening, when the howlers call out from the treetops of the forest, the sound can be distinguished up to ten miles away. When three howler monkeys were kept in a pet shop in London, they could be heard above the noise of traffic two miles downwind.

The power of the howl results from the monkeys' specially developed throat structure. They have unusually large larynxes covered by long hair like a beard, and their throats swell out into resonating balloons so that the sound reverberates. When the howler makes a call, it opens its jaws and extends its lips into a funnel shape. Most animals can produce a loud sound only when breathing out, but the howler uses both inhalation and exhalation. The sound is a rapid repetition of 'a-hü, a-hü, a-hü' – the 'a' being produced when the animal breathes in, the 'hü' as it breathes out.

Howlers live in troops of 10–20 animals, each occupying about 250–500 acres of treetops, and their call has a territorial function. When two howler troops meet on the border between territories, they howl at each other aggressively and continuously until one side backs down. This production of decibels seems to satisfy them, however, as they have never been observed to attack one another.

The Hyrax

The Biblical animal described as a 'coney', which is often assumed to be a rabbit, was actually the Syrian hyrax, otherwise known as the dagon, daman or dassie.

In fact, neither rabbits nor, strangely enough, cats are referred to in the Bible, and the Old Testament scribes seem to have been poor observers of nature, because many of the animals which do appear are wrongly described. For instance, in Hebrew law it is forbidden to eat the coney (or dagon) on the grounds that it does not have cloven feet like other animals which chew the cud. If they had looked a bit closer, they would have found the complete reverse: the animal does not chew the cud, but it does have doubly-cloven hooves.

A more likely explanation for the ban was that Dagon was the name of the national god of the Philistines, a mythical, and therefore heathen, creature, half-man, half-fish.

The hyrax was once common throughout the Middle East, but is now limited to isolated species in Africa. There is a large, grey-brown hyrax in South Africa; a yellowish, rock-dwelling variety south of the Sahara, and an Abyssinian species with dark, silky hair.

There are also a number of smaller, tree-climbing hyraxes, including one with a bright yellow belly which lives between 7,000 feet and 10,000 feet on the slopes of Mount Kilimanjaro.

I

Iguanas

A large number of animals, including the basilisk and the horned toad, are described generally as iguanas, but the term is most usually applied to a group of lively lizards that inhabit Central and South America.

The desert iguana can run at high speed on its hind legs; while the green iguana is a tree-climbing species that hurls itself from branch to branch and can leap 50 feet (15m) to the ground without hurting itself.

They are easily tamed, and still hunted for food in many places. The technique for catching them is to imitate the scream of a hawk, because when they hear that noise they instinctively freeze, and then can be easily netted or simply picked up.

The largest species is the giant 5-foot (1.5m) land iguana which Charles Darwin discovered living in large numbers on the Galapagos Islands. 'I cannot give more forcible proof of their numbers,' he wrote, 'than by stating that when we were left on James Island, we could not find a spot free from their burrows to pitch our single tent.'

The strangest of the Galapagos species is the 4-foot-long (1.2m) marine iguana, the only modern lizard that uses the sea as a source of food. These live exclusively on seaweed and algae, and spend their days huddled in large colonies, basking on the black volcanic rocks; while red crabs clamber over them grooming their coarse skin for ticks.

Darwin was not impressed by the animal's appearance, describing it in his journal as 'a hideous looking creature of dirty black colour, stupid and sluggish in their movements'.

Marine iguanas

TERRY OAKES

One fact that surprised him was that, although they were excellent swimmers and could stay underwater for up to twenty minutes, he found it impossible to drive them into the sea. This is most unusual since most marine animals take to the safety of the water when they are threatened, and he assumed that they were afraid of underwater predators such as sharks. However, it is now thought that it is the temperature of the water which puts them off.

While basking on the shore, iguanas maintain a body temperature of about 95°F, but the sea around the Galapagos is an icy 45°F which slows down their reflexes and makes them even more 'stupid and sluggish'. So they stubbornly cling to the rocks for as long as possible.

The Incubator Bird

The Australian brush-turkey or incubator bird is one of the most temperature-sensitive animals on earth. The bird is one of the megapodes or mound-builders, and in her mound the female constructs an egg-chamber in which she maintains, with the precision of an incubator, a permanent and precise temperature of 91.4°F (33°C) for the six months that it takes the eggs to hatch.

She accomplishes this feat by unceasing activity. As the temperature outside in the bush, and inside the mound, changes according to whether it is day or night, sunny or cloudy, hot or only warm, the bird rushes about digging air vents or closing them, covering the eggs with sand for insulation or removing it, and bringing in sand cooled in the shade or baked in the sun.

When a mean Australian zoologist, Dr H. J. Frith, built three electric heaters into an incubator bird's mound and switched them on and off at random, she became terribly agitated, but nonetheless maintained the precise temperature she required as fast as the zoologist changed it.

The bird has a 'thermometer' organ in its tongue or the roof of its mouth, and every few minutes sticks its beak into different parts of the mound and withdraws it full of sand which it 'temperature-tastes', so to speak. The bird's sensitivity is so highly developed that it is aware of the temperature inside the mound to within a tenth of a degree.

JOHN WOODCOCK

The Interpreters

The Possibilities of Inter-Species Communication

'To be able to break through to understand the thinking, the feeling, the doing, the talking of another species is a grand and noble achievement that will change man's view of himself and his planet.'

– John C. Lilly.

Dolphins

The idea that the Cetacea (whales and dolphins) are intelligent animals is a very modern concept, an unsettling one, which is far from being accepted as established science. Yet there is a growing body of evidence based both on personal observation and hard experimentation to support this fact. There may be life on other planets but it is time we entertained the idea that communication with 'alien' life may be closer at hand than we think.

One scientist, more than any other, has pursued this fascinating possibility the furthest. John Lilly, who began research with the bottle-nosed dolphin in 1958, now readily entertains some futuristic ideas about dolphin intelligence and is working to achieve a communication breakthrough which he believes is not only increasingly likely but also increasingly important.

His first published paper on the subject, in 1958, was a summary of his work up to that time on the positive and negative reinforcing systems within the brain of both the macaque monkey and the bottle-nosed dolphin. Electrodes were inserted into the skull of the dolphin under local anaesthesia, and a punishment area within the brain was stimulated by electric current. The dolphin was trained to operate a switch with its beak, which would shut it off when the pain reached a certain level of intensity.

The dolphin could also operate another switch to stimulate the positive zones in its brain. After initial experiments with one dolphin, events proceeded as follows:

'With a bit of luck with our next animal we found a positive, rewarding starting zone. The next luck was in obtaining an animal who vocalized vociferously: as soon as we stimulated the positive zone, he told us about it by covering a large repertory of assorted complex whistles, bronx cheers, and impolite noises. Giving him a switch at this point was quite an experience – he sized up what I was doing so rapidly that by the time I had set up his switch he took only five 'trials' to figure out the proper way to push it with his beak. From that point on, as long as he could obtain his stimulation, for every push he made with his beak, he quietly worked for the stimuli. But if we cut off his current, he immediately stopped working and vocalized – apparently scolding at times, and mimicking us at others. One time he mimicked my speaking voice so well that my wife laughed out loud and he copied her laughter. Eventually, he pushed too rapidly, caused a seizure, became unconscious, respiration failed and he died. Apparently unconsciousness because of any factor, anesthesia, or brain stimulation, or others, causes death in these animals.'

Lilly was not slow to realize the potential he had stumbled on here. In the same paper he concluded: 'If we are ever to communicate with a non-human species of this planet, the dolphin is probably our best present gamble. In a sense, it is a joke when I fantasize that it may be best to hurry and finish our work on their brains before one of them learns to speak our language – else he will demand equal rights with men for their brains and lives under our ethical and legal codes.'

From these experiments and many others Lilly became fascinated with the subject. Further study of the brains of the cetacea revealed that they ranged in size from that of an ape to six times human size – in the case of the sperm whale.

On closer examination, researchers found that not only were the brains of dolphins extremely complex, but also that they were as advanced as the human brain on a microscopic structural level. There were as many cells per cubic millimetre as in the human brain; the number of cells connected to each other was the same, as was the number of layers in the cortex.

This raised many intriguing questions. After all, the thing that distinguishes our brains from those of the apes is the growth areas in the frontal and parietal lobes – the so-called 'silent areas' – which deal with speed, vision, hearing and other sensory and thought apparatus. It is supposedly these areas of the brain which separate us from the animals and make us special or superior.

Examinations of cetacean brains revealed that they too have enormously enlarged brains in these self-same silent areas. Lilly now believes that these parts of the brain store the whole history of their culture as, of course, they cannot write it down.

It is worth remembering that humans in their present form have only existed for 1/150th of the time that the cetaceans have. As Lilly puts it: 'They went through the dangerous acquisition of the large brain and of the resulting large internal reality millions of years ago. 'They may not only be as intelligent as we are; they have been that way for much longer.'

So disorientating were these findings that Lilly abandoned his research on dolphins for many years, having changed completely his scientific ideas. These, he believed, were not animals *upon which* one performs experiments but rather animals *with whom* one collaborates. It was also clear to him that his findings threw into question the whole concept of an uninvolved scientific observer, and for eight years from 1968 he concentrated his research on himself and other humans, examining his own motives and ideas and seeking inner enlightenment.

Ever since the late 1940s, Lilly along with many other researchers had been studying dolphins from another perspective, exploring the fascinating properties of their sonic and acoustic systems. These operate at ten times the speed of ours and they absorb as much information through their ears as we do with our eyes – and at the same speed. They 'see' with sound (see **Echo-Location**).

Observations at Marineland and other dolphinariums had confirmed that dolphins used these systems to communicate with each other and to hold conversations, but the argument raged then and now as to whether their beeps, clicks and whirrs amount to a proper language as we understand it (dubbed 'dolphinese') or whether it was some completely alien system beyond our imaginings.

These speculations in turn led many researchers to consider the possibility of human communication with dolphins. After all both humans and dolphins, unlike apes, can communicate with sounds, and dolphins have even been taught to mimic human sounds by opening their blowholes in the air.

Lilly returned to his dolphins studies to investigate this question and is currently running a sophisticated human/dolphin communication experiment in California. Called JANUS (Joint-Anolog-Numerical-Understanding-System) this is how it works.

On the human side is a keyboard and a video screen; on the dolphin side is a loudspeaker, a microphone and a TV screen – all underwater. The brain of the system is a computer linking the two. When a human types a letter on the keyboard, JANUS changes this into a sound tone which comes out of the underwater loudspeaker. At the same time, an image of the letter appears on both screens. The dolphin can then reply, either by making the same tone, or another one corresponding to another letter.

There are 48 tones in all, which stand for the alphabet, numbers and other symbols (+ – / !), all within the sound range that the dolphin can hear. By gradually learning these sounds and symbols, it is hoped that the dolphins can communicate their thoughts and ideas to us and we to them.

In the future, Lilly foresees other communications technology aimed at achieving the same results. He has plans for an 'interspecies vocoder' which would allow a human to speak to a dolphin underwater, thus breaking the air/water interface. It would need thirty critical frequency bands – the number involved in human speech and hearing – and a further sixty bands to encompass the much wider range of frequencies used by the dolphin.

A more sophisticated version of this would involve a system linking sonar and video by means of a high-speed minicomputer.

The best description of the unsettling implications of this research is contained in a paper Lilly wrote in 1963:

'This opening of our minds was a subtle and yet painful process. We began to have feelings which I believe are best described by the word "weirdness". The feeling was that we were up against the edge of a vast uncharted region in which we were about to embark with a good deal of mistrust in the appropriateness of our own equipment. The feeling of weirdness came on us as the sounds of this small whale seemed more and more to be forming words in our own language. We felt we were in the presence of Something, or Someone who was on the other side of a transparent barrier which up to this point we hadn't even seen. The dim outlines of a Someone began to appear. We began to look at this whale's body with newly opened eyes and began to think in terms of its possible "mental processes", rather than in terms of the classical view of a conditionable, instinctually functioning "animal". We began to apologize to one another for slips of the tongue in which we would call dolphins "persons" and in which we began to use their names as if they *were* persons. This seemed to be as much of a way of grasping at straws of security in a rough sea of the unknown, as of committing the sin of Science of Anthropomorphizing. If these "animals" have "higher mental processes", then they in turn must be thinking of us as very peculiar (even stupid) beings indeed.'

Conversations with Apes

Communicating with whales is like the space-age discovery of an alien civilization. We know they are talking to us and we can record every detail of their language. But we cannot understand it because their minds are so different from ours that we do not even know what they are talking about. Communicating with apes is exactly the opposite. They look and behave so like us it should be easy to *understand* one another, but the problem has been to find a *language*.

When Samuel Pepys first saw a chimpanzee, in 1666, he wrote: 'It is a great baboon, but so much like man in most things, that though they say there is a species of them, yet I cannot believe but that it is a monster got of a man and a she-baboon. I do believe that it already understands much English, and I am of the mind it might be taught to speak or make signs.'

The fertile possibilities of his last statement have fascinated humans ever since, and, particularly in this century, have led to much scientific investigation.

In 1900, Richard Garner, an amateur zoologist, claimed to have taught a chimp named Moses to say four words. Nine years later, an American psychologist reported on his studies of a trained chimpanzee who could say 'mama'. In 1916 Dr William Furness reported to the American Philosophical Society that he had taught an orangutan in Borneo to say 'papa' and 'cup'.

These pioneering tests were not followed up until, in the 1940s, an American couple, Keith and Cathy Hayes, raised a chimp named Viki in their home for six and a half years, during which time they taught it to say four words, which were recorded on sound film.

However, the real breakthrough came in the mid sixties through the work of Allen and Beatrice Gardner at the University of Nevada. The Gardners realized that the chimp's vocal apparatus was limited but that they were extremely adept at using their hands to communicate. The Gardners acquired a chimp called Washoe, who was trapped in Africa when she was one year old. They installed her in their home in Reno and, in June 1966 (exactly 300 years after Pepys had first speculated on the possibility), they began to teach her the American sign language, Ameslan.

By the time she was three, Washoe had already learnt some 30 signs and, by the time she was sent to the Institute for Primate Studies at Norman, Oklahoma, along with the Gardners' trained assistant, Professor Roger Fouts, her vocabulary had increased to 150 signs and her learning capacity was accelerating.

In 1967 Washoe became the first non-human animal to learn to converse in a human language. She showed remarkable ingenuity in making up her own words – describing swans as 'water birds' for instance – and eventually managed a full sentence structure of noun-verb-object.

Then in the summer of 1976, Washoe gave birth to a baby. Unfortunately it died within a few hours. Washoe reportedly set it down carefully, signed 'baby' to it and started to cry. After its death, she was depressed for months and when asked why, she would just sign 'cry'.

But in January 1979 Washoe gave birth again, to a male chimp called Sequoyah. Researchers are now waiting to see whether Washoe will pass on her new system of communication to her son, which would represent a new breakthrough.

The Gardners' initial success with Washoe led to a boom in research, but also attracted criticism from academic authorities. Many people questioned the objectivity of the results. To what extent were the researchers adding their own interpretations to the chimps' signs? Did they really know what they were saying, or were they simply mimicking the humans?

The experiments were certainly unusual in that they encouraged (and even demanded) an emotional commitment, which is anathema to most scientists. But it is impossible to communicate with animals without forming a relationship with them. As Roger Fouts said: 'Most scientists think of chimps as large white rats to be experimented on. We look on them more as colleagues. We are not so enthralled with our uniqueness that we don't listen to chimpanzees.'

So the research went on. David and Anne Premack taught chimps to write sentences by arranging different shapes and coloured pieces of plastic, each representing a word, on a magnetized board. In December 1978, David Premack reported that he had designed written tests for Sarah, the chimp, using coloured shapes. Sarah had to say whether they were the 'same' or 'different', both concepts which she understood. Sarah got 189 correct out of 237.

At the Yerkes Primate Center in Georgia, a chimp named Lana has been taught to send and receive messages by hitting computer keys labelled with abstract shapes that stand for words. This research by Duanna Rumbaugh took a step forward when, in August 1978, Rumbaugh announced that attempts to communicate with another chimp called Oscar using these artificial symbols had been successful.

The Gardners are now working with other chimps, and caused a stir at an international conference in 1976, when they exhibited a drawing of a bird by Moja, a 3½-year-old chimp, which they claimed as the first self-conscious representational art by an animal.

Chimpanzees had shown little capacity for language, but it came as a complete surprise when Francine 'Penny' Patterson published the results of her work with a female gorilla called Koko. It was widely thought that gorillas would be incapable of learning sign language, but Koko proved a brilliant pupil and rapidly overtook the chimpanzees to become the first truly bilingual animal.

Since Penny Patterson began her experiments in 1971, Koko has learned or invented over 700 signs, and uses about 400 of them fluently. It is the nearest that any other species has come to human speech, and the feelings and ideas she has expressed are uncannily like our own.

Many of the discoveries Penny Patterson has made in conversations with Koko – that she makes up her own words, using combinations of signs, apologizes for things she has done (often days later), has invented swear-words and nicknames for people, frequently asks questions, has strong opinions, cleanliness, fair play and other 'moral' attitudes, and even makes jokes – are amazing enough. But there is one story about Koko that takes one's breath away.

It happened when she was giving one of her rare 'interviews' to a French journalist. Penny Patterson was interpreting, as usual, and Koko was on her best behaviour. He was so amazed at her replies that he felt he had to ask one last question – the ultimate one. He asked Penny to sign to Koko: 'Do you think of yourself as an animal or a human being?'

Without any hesitation Koko replied: 'Me gorilla. Me damn fine animal.

The Gift from the Gods

It is only fair to add that not everyone accepts Penny Patterson's claims. By its very nature, the evidence breaks all the rules of scientific experiments. The investigator is not an objective observer, but actually part of the experiment: there is no control situation to compare it with, and no way of repeating the experiments. Above all, the evidence is second-hand. Penny Patterson and her helpers have to *interpret* Koko's language, and we only have their word for it that she meant it to be

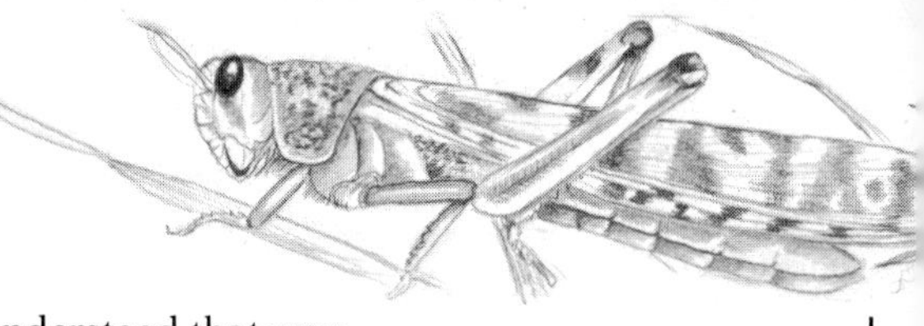

understood that way.

But, then, it is not an 'experiment' in the usual sense. Like a human baby, Koko could only learn what 'a language' was (let alone speak it) within the context of a personal relationship. Emotional empathy and intuition were essential to bridge the gap between human and animal; and the nature of sign language makes it impossible to draw a line between personal 'interpretation' and objective 'translation'.

The whole question may soon be irrelevant, anyway. It took a long time to achieve the initial communication between species, but that was only the first stage. It is what comes next that matters. In the same way that, according to human legend, the gods once gave us fire, we have given the animals language. The really interesting question is what they will do with it.

This has been impossible to find out so far, because it needs a number of 'signing' apes living together, and no other animal has yet achieved Koko's fluency. But the prospects are exciting because, on her own initiative, Koko has started teaching other gorillas, including her own child, how to sign.

There would be no reason for her to do this unless she considered it necessary (in fact, it is so important to her that she even talks to herself when no one else is there); and if she succeeds, there may eventually be a whole family group using sign language amongst themselves.

How will it affect their lives? Will the language skill of, say, a young gorilla give it superiority over older, but dumber, animals? Will they change the language for non-human purposes? Their hands are clumsier than ours, so it might be easier to add facial expressions and grimaces, at which they are very good.

Without a language it is impossible to discuss abstractions, so it will be interesting to see whether they start to coordinate their actions by planning ahead or agreeing on rules. Will they tell each other stories and pass them on to their children, the way that human history must have begun? Maybe, one day, Washoe and Koko will be revered as the ancestral founders of their people, a new Adam and Eve who were given speech by the gods.

More immediately, there is (let us admit it) the most fascinating question of all: what will they have to say, between themselves, about us?

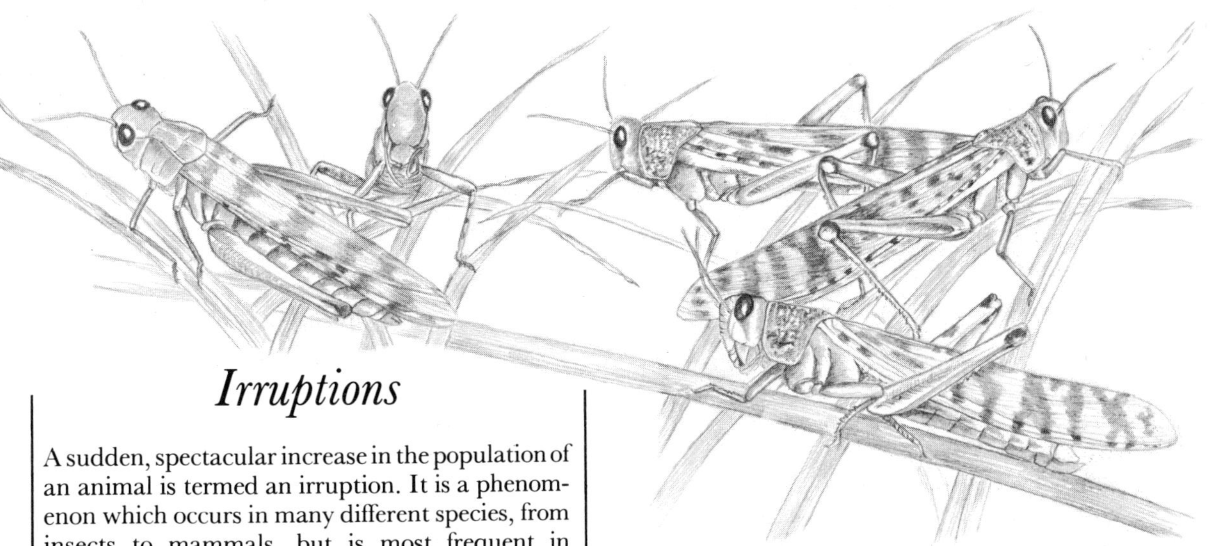

Irruptions

A sudden, spectacular increase in the population of an animal is termed an irruption. It is a phenomenon which occurs in many different species, from insects to mammals, but is most frequent in animals which specialize in one particular food. If for any reason this becomes abundant, it triggers a massive population explosion which, in turn, leads to a shortage of food. The irrupting species may then migrate well beyond its normal range until gradually the population dwindles and returns to its normal level.

The Norwegian lemmings are one of the best-known examples of an irruptive species. They are tied to a four-year cycle of food abundance. But while it is true that many of them do drown while attempting to migrate across rivers or when they reach the sea, the popular notion that lemmings commit 'mass suicide' is pure myth (see **Lemmings**).

Locusts are equally famous for their irruptions, and considerably more destructive. Today, as in Biblical times, they can cause crop damage in tropical parts of the world on a catastrophic scale. A single swarm can consist of 20,000 million insects weighing a total of 40,000 tons. Moving at 10 mph for up to twenty hours a day, they devour everything edible in their path. In 1978 a swarm was spotted in Ethiopia which covered 160 square miles.

Locusts spend most of the time, however, as ordinary and harmless grasshoppers. It is only when particular conditions of temperature and humidity coincide that they begin to breed explosively. The first symptoms consist of subtle behavioural changes. Newly-hatched 'hoppers' start to assemble in groups, stimulating each other into jumping. Once such groups reach a certain critical mass, they remain together and search for food collectively instead of individually. Over a period of time separate groups merge until they form a single, gigantic swarm.

Close examination of the phenomenon has led scientists to the discovery that during the initial period the locusts produce an extra excretory product, dubbed 'locustine', which is deposited as a dark pigment in the body wall. The blood of the adults becomes saturated with it and they pass it on to their young, producing a new breed of hoppers which have darker markings and are also more active. Once the process is started, the insects' breeding cycle accelerates so that a swarm can be produced with explosive rapidity. In addition, some of the males produce a particular pheromone which hastens the maturation process and synchronizes the swarm so that all the locusts are ready to mate and lay their eggs at the same time.

ELIZABETH GOSS

Desert locusts are liable to swarm in a belt extending from Bangladesh to Spain, and can directly affect more than 10 per cent of the world's human population. In Ethiopia, swarms once ate in one year enough food for a million people. 'I have seen people dying of hunger in previous locust plagues during the Second World War and in the 1950s,' one of the world's experts on locust control, M. Jean Roy, told a journalist recently. 'You never forget that, once you have seen it.'

Other irrupting insects include many species of ants and of springtails. In western Canada, swarms of the golden snow flea sometimes completely carpet the snow with their golden bodies. In Switzerland the ecologist Charles Elton once observed trains being held up when swarms covered the rails and made them too slippery for the engines' wheels to get a grip. Amongst springtails, the irruptions end when the insects, under the stress of population pressure, begin eating each other. Since their blood is toxic, their numbers dwindle rapidly.

ELIZABETH GOSS

Many species of birds also undergo irruptions. One classic example occurred in 1969 when the town of Scotland Neck, in North Carolina, suffered from a massive population increase of blackbirds and starlings. An estimated 3 million birds threatened to make the town uninhabitable. Their droppings fouled the water and the streets, and at sunrise they produced an incredibly loud and continuous noise. Various measures were tried to kill the birds, from chemicals to scaring devices, but by the following year their numbers had increased to 12 million. It was only in 1974 that the populations began to diminish.

Some scientists have claimed that swarms of starlings have become increasingly common in recent years because of the trend towards creating larger farms. The destruction of hedgerows and copses, they argue, has eliminated animals like the weasel and marten which prey on the starling's eggs.

In other cases, irrupting birds will make unusual migrations. In 1863, 1888 and 1908 western Europe was invaded by hundreds of millions of sand-grouse from Asia Minor. In this century, Germany has been invaded by massive flocks of Siberian nutcrackers, and New York by waves of purple finches and Boreal chickadees.

Although they are understood in principle, the precise mechanisms that trigger and later end many of these irruptions remain unclear. We are often unaware also of their cyclical nature.

A typical example of this was the irruption of the Crown of Thorns starfish, an ugly, sixteen-armed creature which can grow up to two feet (61cm) wide. One adult starfish can eat an area of coral of its own size in less than twenty-four hours; after its attack, the coral just crumbles and is washed away by the current.

These starfish appeared in numbers in 1963. Over the next few years the population increased alarmingly, spreading from Hawaii in the east to Ceylon in the west. On Guam they exploded in three years from a mere handful to over 20,000, and twenty-four miles of coral reef were destroyed. Scientists grew more and more concerned as to the effects that large-scale destruction of the coral reefs might have on global ecology. One marine biologist said at the time: 'If the starfish explosion continues unchecked, the result could be a disaster unparalleled in the history of mankind.'

Such predictions, however, remained unfulfilled. The starfish irruption ended as spontaneously and inexplicably as it had begun, and as their numbers diminished they ceased to be a threat. The biologists now believe it may be a cyclical phenomenon that we have yet to understand.

There is another irruption which the textbooks rarely mention – that of our own species. In the space of ten thousand years the human population has grown from a few millions at the most to over 4,000 million, and the rate of increase is still growing. The effects on the biosphere have been devastating, with forests destroyed, landscapes 'tamed', rivers dammed and rerouted, and thousands of plant and animal species extinguished.

Will we multiply until we can no longer feed ourselves? Or will we, like the Crown of Thorns, spontaneously and inexplicably begin to dwindle?

The Island Parables

Islands are microcosms – like isolated planets where the plants and animals are free to pursue their own independent line of evolution. Each has its own unique ecology, and no two islands are the same.

It was when Darwin noticed that the finches on each of the Galapagos Islands had developed different kinds of beaks, and the giant tortoises, although they were all the same species, had subtle variations in their shells, that he first began to think about the theory of evolution.

'I never dreamed', he wrote, 'that islands about 50 or 60 miles apart, and most of them within sight of each other, would have been so differently tenanted.'

But this independence is an illusion. Each island ecology is a fragile experiment, protected only by its isolation and governed by rigid (and strangely precise) laws. For instance, the number of species on an island is directly proportional to its size and distance from the mainland. A neighbouring island with ten times the area will support twice as many species, while an island the same size, but twice as far from the mainland will have half the number.

The area of an island also affects the *size* of its inhabitants. There has to be enough food to support a breeding colony, so the dominant species on a small island, like those off the Australian coast, tend to be small mammals, like kangaroo rats. If the food supply increases, there is a temporary increase in kangaroo rats, but there is now room for a larger animal to survive, and sooner or later they will be replaced. On the other hand, if the food supply *diminishes*, something rather odd happens. The little kangaroo rats, which eat less than the others, suddenly find themselves at an advantage. Small is now beautiful and, since they survive longer than larger animals, they have a better chance of breeding. So the species as a whole will *tend to shrink*.

A variety of pygmy breeds have evolved in this way, including sheep, horses (Shetland ponies are a classic example) and even elephants. Pygmy pygmies evolved in much the same way when human tribes found themselves isolated for long enough in similar circumstances. (The only requirements are an isolated community, limited food supply, and too many mouths to feed – a situation which can occur in tropical jungles as well as on islands.)

The first of the following stories show that, under certain circumstances, if the island is remote enough, the most exotic and unlikely species can evolve. But the ecology is so finely balanced that there is no room for mistakes; and the other examples are dramatic illustrations of how the slightest change can produce a disastrous chain-reaction.

JOHN CHESTERMAN

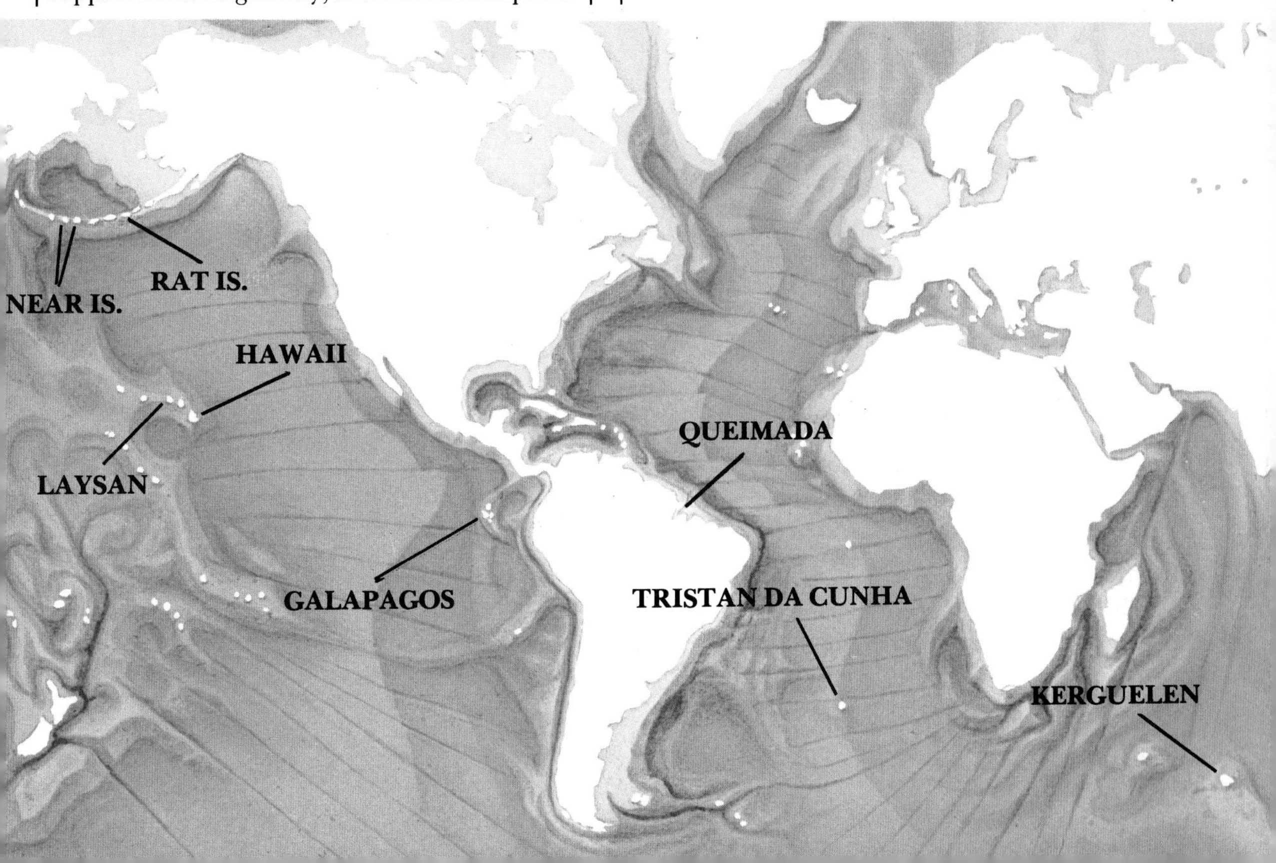

The Rabbits of Laysan

They may look sweet, but no other animal apart from man has laid waste more of the natural environment than the humble European rabbit.

What they did (and are still doing) to Australia is well known. Originally introduced in the 1880s, with the optimistic idea that they would provide a cheap source of food, they rapidly took over the country, reducing wide areas of farmland to a dustbowl and driving the native fauna, such as kangaroos, to the remote corners of their natural range.

But in order to appreciate the full extent of the rabbit's destructive power, one must imagine their effect on a small tropical island with no natural predators. For instance, what the rabbits did to Australia was nothing compared to what they did to Laysan.

Laysan was a coral atoll north of Hawaii. Although it was small it had a comparatively rich ecology, with palm trees, groves of sandalwood, and an undergrowth of bushes and shrubs. Among the fauna were three species of birds unique to the island: a type of honey-eater (*Himatione sanguinea freethii*), a warbler (*Acrocephalus familiaris*) and a species of flightless rail (*Parzanula palmeri*).

In 1903 a group of European rabbits (*Oryctolagus cuniculus*) were deliberately introduced to the island and immediately made themselves at home in what must have seemed to them a tropical paradise. With plenty of food and no natural enemies, there was nothing for them to do but multiply.

By 1912 the population was over 5,000 and growing fast, and the vegetation was seriously depleted. Attempts were made to reduce their numbers by systematic shooting, but the rabbits were already out of control and unstoppable.

The vegetation gradually died off and the topsoil began to blow away. The Acrocephalus warbler disappeared, and two years later the flightless rails were extinct. The last three honey-eaters died in a sandstorm while an expedition was on the island studying them. By 1927 Laysan was reduced to a barren strip of sand, with a few dead tree trunks.

All that was left were the rabbits, which eventually died of starvation.

Laysan was a classic example of how a badly-adapted species can destroy itself and take a whole ecosystem with it. Success is not the same thing as winning; in evolutionary terms, a successful rabbit is one that (occasionally) gets eaten.

The Queimada Vipers

A common problem of island communities is the risk of inbreeding. If the same genes are mixed again and again, they lose their individual characteristics and the gene pool is homogenized like milk. The results of this can be bizarre and horrifying, and, as the story of the Queimada vipers shows, the species eventually destroys itself.

The vipers were a species of lance-headed snakes which were only found on the tiny island of Queimada Grande, off the Brazilian coast. The island is little more than a mile square, but in the early part of this century the vipers lived there by the thousand, feeding off birds, which they paralysed with fast-acting venom.

They were so dangerous that the lighthouse there had to be replaced by an automatic beacon, after three lighthouse operators in a row had died from island viper bites.

It is not known how or when they began to interbreed, but the first signs were noticed during a survey of the snakes made in 1930. The population was then estimated at between three and four thousand, but whereas 50 per cent of them were males, only 10 per cent were females! The other 40 per cent of the population consisted of strange mutants, including female snakes with male copulatory organs, which are known as 'intersexes'.

A few exceptional intersexes can reproduce successfully, but the majority are infertile – and the population of mutants steadily increased. By 1955 the intersexes made up 70 per cent of the population, while the proportion of females was down to only 3 per cent.

It was the final catastrophic result of generations of inbreeding, and the species was doomed. When the last survey was carried out, in 1966, a snake expert was able to find only seven of them. No one has had the heart to go back since. It is possible that one or two are still alive, but they are the last of their species on earth.

The Riddle of Near and Rat

Some of the more bizarre effects of returning species to the wild have been brought out recently by the case of the Pacific sea otter.

Over the past four to five years, attempts have been made to reintroduce the otter to the west coast of America, where it used to flourish before the species was almost wiped out by Russian fur traders. Unfortunately, the animal is what is known as a 'keystone' species, and if it takes up residence again it could trigger off a chain of events that involve the fertilizer business, bald-headed eagles, abalone farming, harbour seals and a whole food web along the shore line.

The evidence for this comes from an ecological survey carried out by Dr James Estes of Arizona University and Dr John Palmisano of Washington University, in 1974, on two almost identical islands in the Aleutians, improbably called Rat and Near. The sea otters have survived on Rat Island, but not on Near, so they give a clear 'before and after' of the animal's effects.

The most obvious difference between the two places is that Rat Island is surrounded by vast beds of a brown seaweed called kelp, whilst the shores of Near Island are carpeted with sea urchins. The reason for this is that the otters eat the sea urchins, and the sea urchins, in turn, eat the kelp. So far, so good?

But the otters also eat other marine invertebrates and fish, including abalone. These are one of the most delicious seafoods in the world, and big business on the West Coast. But the abalone farmers are not worried about the otters so much as the kelp they encourage to grow on the sea bed. Abalone will not grow in kelp, and neither will other filter-feeding sedentary creatures such as barnacles and mussels, so these will also be threatened if the otters return.

On the other hand, the kelp beds support their own ecological system which includes rock greenling and other fish, which in turn are eaten by harbour seals and bald-headed eagles – both of which are common on Rat island.

So, on one side of the argument are the sea urchins, the abalone business and conservationists, and on the other are the otters, the fertilizer business and rival conservationists. What should one do? Try to repair the damage of previous generations, or leave well alone?

Wingless on Kerguelen

Most insects produce wingless mutations from time to time, but genetic mistakes of this sort are at such a disadvantage that they do not last long. However, there are some eccentric environments where losing one's wings can be a positive advantage! One of these places (where commonsense is apparently stood on its head) is a tiny speck in the Indian Ocean called Kerguelen Island.

There are plenty of insects on the island, but every one of them is wingless. There are flies on Kerguelen, but they do not fly. The moths crawl and the butterflies have to climb the plants to reach the flowers. Not one of the native species of insects is capable of flight.

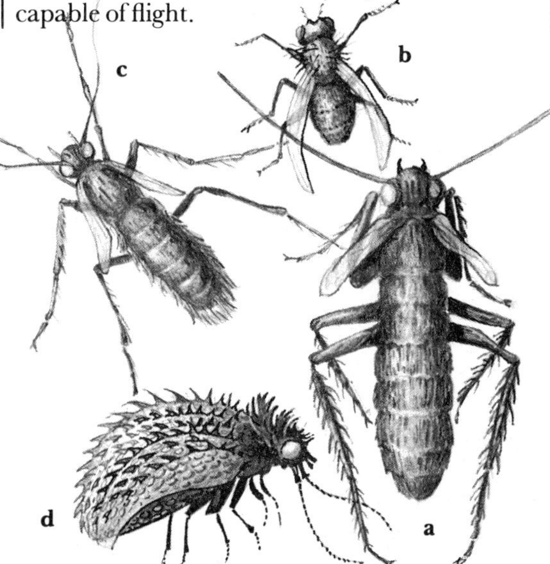

a. *Flightless moth (Kerguelen)* **b.** *Fly (Tristan da Cunha)* **c.** *Moth (Tristan da Cunha)* **d.** *Lacewing (Hawaii)*

The reason for this extraordinary state of affairs can be summed up in one word – the wind. The winged ancestors of today's species found that their main problem on Kerguelen was to avoid being blown out to sea. The island is in the vast emptiness of the 'roaring forties', south of South Africa, where the wind never stops blowing, and the next landfall they would encounter is two-thirds of the way round the world.

So when the first wingless mutant appeared, it turned out to be a triumphant adaptation rather than a pathetic failure. The grounded freaks it gave rise to lived longer, bred more often, and eventually replaced the winged varieties.

In the course of evolution, the ugly duckling often survives the swans, and a successful species will always have a few alternative models on hand in the event of a crisis.

JOHN CHESTERMAN

J

The Days of the Jackal

The jackal's reputation has gone steadily downhill since the days of ancient Egypt when Anubis, the jackal-headed ruler of the underworld, Lord of the Mummy Wrappings, was regarded as the main link between this world and the next. Nowadays most people assume that they are cowardly, somehow 'dirty' animals, little more than packs of scavengers who live off the scraps left by others. The Egyptians knew better.

Like many animals in this book, their reputation is an ill-founded insult. Far from being pack animals, they are among the rare 2 per cent of all mammals (a group which includes the dik-dik and the elephant shrew) that form a pair-bond for life. In fact they are model parents, and within the family there is complete equality between the male and female, with their roles being interchangeable.

The least deserved of the epithets is that jackals are scavengers. Like most carnivorous predators, they will take carrion if they get the chance, but there are many other animals, including lions, ahead of them in the queue. Recent studies on African game reserves show that hyenas scavenge for about a third of what they eat, lions depend on carrion for 15 per cent of their food, but it represents less than 6 per cent of a jackal's diet. It is the vultures who turned out to be the main scavengers, and consume 80 per cent of all the carcases on the Serengeti plains.

Jackals live mainly on lizards, beetles and small birds, but they also go after bigger game. In spite of the fact that they live independently, the families come together in small groups for hunting, and are capable of bringing down deer or antelope with ruthless efficiency.

Unlike the lions, they go to great lengths to ensure that their young get a fair share of food. They can range over a wide area when hunting, and the kill often takes place several miles from their burrow. So they eat as much as they can for the return journey, and regurgitate it when they get back.

Finally, and it almost goes without saying, they are not 'dirty'. They are sleek, beautiful animals, with an alert intelligence seldom found in domestic dogs, and their lairs are immaculately clean.

Jaguarundis

The jaguarundis are a group of cat-like American animals whose classification (as *Herpailurus*) provokes endless debate among zoologists. Are they really cats? Are they related to the jaguar? Or even to each other? Who knows.

They are mainly found in the south-western United States and Central America, though there is a rare species with silver markings, called the colocollo, on the western slopes of the Andes.

The Jaguarundis are said to have been domesticated by the Indians before the arrival of Europeans.

The Giant Jellies

In the cold, green depths of the Arctic Ocean there lurks an animal which is 200-feet (60-m) long and almost entirely composed of water.

As there is only about 5 per cent of organic material in its entire body, it has nothing resembling nerves or a brain. If it was accidentally washed ashore on a beach, it would simply evaporate, leaving nothing behind but a damp stain on the sand. It consists of immensely long tentacles attached to a bloated body 6–7 feet (2m) in diameter and though it is not very intelligent, it can swim, catch and eat its food, and live its simple life to the full. It is called the Cyanea, and it is the largest jellyfish in the world.

Jellyfish is a general term used to describe a variety of cnidarians, hydras and coelenterates, ranging from a blob the size of a grape, through the beautiful Aurelia found in European waters, to the vicious sea-wasp, or Chironex, whose sting kills in seconds and is responsible for mounting fatalities on Australian beaches every year.

Stings and jellyfish are synonomous for most of us, especially if you have been stung by one, and the name that springs most readily to mind is the Portuguese Man-of-War. That is a pity, because this well-known threat to the tourist trade in coastal resorts is a fascinating creature in its own right.

The Portuguese Man-of-War is one of the most beautiful and intricate examples of symbiosis in nature. It looks like an untidy jellyfish and behaves like a predatory animal, whose sting has been compared to 'being struck by a bolt of lightning'. It even protects other creatures, such as the Nomeus fish, which is allowed to swim through its spiral tentacles in order to attract their prey within reach.

Yet the Man-of-War is what zoologists call a semi-colonial coelenterate. It behaves like a single organism but it is actually a cooperative venture between four kinds of animals, involving nearly one thousand individuals.

They each have a specialized role to play: providing buoyancy, digesting food, reproducing or manufacturing poison. They probably began as parasites which became dependent on each other and worked together so well that they could not survive on their own.

The surprising thing about such a colony is that, in theory, it need never die. Coelenterates are known for their powers of regeneration and can regrow any part of their body. The one exception is a region at the base of the animal, where old or inefficient body cells migrate, like old people to a retirement home, and eventually die off. With breeding colonies to produce new individuals to crew the Man-of-War, there is no reason why it should ever get any older.

In reality, the creatures do die – from storms, starvation or accident – and must therefore reproduce themselves, by a simple system of budding. But under ideal conditions they could, in theory, be immortal.

Portuguese Man-of-War

PETER BOMAN

John Dory

When an animal has stalked its prey, it usually takes it with a snap of its jaws or by lashing out with its tongue. In some cases the predator is moving so fast that the prey is forced down its throat. In the case of the John Dory, however, this creature throws its whole face at the intended victim.

The Dory (*Zeus faber*) is a golden-yellow member of the mackerel family, with elaborately hinged jaw-bones. These are normally folded flat, giving the fish a downturned mouth and rather unhappy expression. But when it approaches its prey, the whole apparatus folds outwards, like an old-fashioned bellows camera (or one of the new Polaroids). The pram-like hood engulfs the victim and, without either of them moving, it finds itself swimming inside, rather than outside, the mouth.

The Dory's name has a fine, swashbuckling sound, but its origins are more prosaic. It probably derives from the French *jaune dorée* and refers to its golden-yellow colour.

Jumbo

We have already referred to elephants in general, but it is fitting that Jumbo should have an entry to himself. After all, he was once the best known animal in the world, and the only one whose name has been adopted as an affectionate nickname for his whole species.

His story began at the Jardin des Plantes, in Paris – because Jumbo was originally French. But his career in show business began in 1865 when, as the result of an animal exchange with the Regent's Park Zoo, he crossed the Channel and soon became one of the most popular attractions in London. They called him Jumbo after *jambo*, an African word of greeting which also means 'big packet' – a suitable name for a 9-ton African bull elephant.

For fifteen years he used to give rides to children at the zoo, and eventually became the most famous and best loved animal in England. But, like many elephants, he grew bad-tempered and unpredictable in middle-age. On one occasion he became so aggressive he made a frenzied attack on an iron door and broke both his tusks. This only added to his misery because the jagged ends grew upwards and curved back so that they irritated the insides of his cheeks. This eventually caused painful abscesses, which had to be lanced. By then, Jumbo was kept apart from the public and the zoo's superintendent even bought a gun, in case he got out of control.

Then, in 1882, to everyone's surprise (and relief), the zoo received a bid for him from the showman, Barnum, owner and founder of The Greatest Show on Earth. They were only too glad to sell him and, on 18 February, a banker's draft for £2,000 was handed over.

A huge crate was constructed and Barnum's agent, William Newman, or 'Elephant Bill' as he was known in the ring, tried to chain Jumbo in so

that he could not move. Jumbo refused to co-operate, and pictures of Jumbo in chains stirred a wave of sentiment, and Jumbomania broke out. Even Queen Victoria was reported to have become concerned.

Jumbo still refused to be crated. It was suspected that the keeper had something to do with his disobedience, so he was given leave of absence to accompany the elephant to America. Finally, on 21 March, Jumbo entered his crate and was pulled by six horses to the docks where the *Assyrian Monarch* was waiting to take him to the United States.

The newspapers on both sides of the Atlantic had been full of the story, and huge crowds were waiting to greet the ship in New York. Jumbo was no longer a national phenomenon, but an international star.

He toured America with Barnum's Circus, moving from town to town by train, like a royal progress.

The life suited him better than the daily chore of giving rides at London Zoo, but unfortunately his days of stardom were short-lived. Three years later, while being unloaded in a freight yard in Western Ontario, he was hit by Special Locomotive 151, and died on the trackside within minutes.

Jumping Jerboas

In World War II, the British Army in North Africa adopted the jerboa as its symbol. The silhouette of their mascot was painted on the sides of military vehicles, and the troops themselves became known as the Desert Rats.

It was not the first time that the jerboa's speed and agility had been recognized, because the Pharaohs had adopted it for similar reasons three thousand years before, and added the same silhouette to their language as the hieroglyph for 'swiftness'.

The animal is certainly a fast mover, capable of taking off in flying leaps, and able to run backwards almost as fast as it can forwards.

The most recognizable feature of the African species (*Scarturus*) is its Mickey Mouse ears. Large ears are characteristic of most desert animals (as radiators to keep down body heat), but in this case they are something of a nuisance, as they increase the drag on its tiny, streamlined body. So the jerboa has solved the problem with collapsible structures that can be opened up, like dish aerials, or folded flat alongside its shoulders when moving at speed.

The most remarkable thing about these little animals is that they come closer than any other desert species to being independent of water. Jerboas have lived quite happily for up to fifty-five days in arid surroundings on a diet of nothing but dried seeds, without a fluid intake of any kind. The reason they can do this appears to be that their bodies can make their own water internally. The chemical reaction is not fully understood, but they seem to be able to metabolize fluids directly from nothing but carbohydrates and oxygen!

ELIZABETH GOSS

K

PHILIP HOOD

Kangaroos

Just how a baby kangaroo gets into its mother's pouch was disputed for more than a century, and the argument was not finally settled until 1959, when the whole process was filmed for the first time, at Adelaide University. It is still difficult to believe what happens.

The task facing the partly-formed embryo, in its hectic sprint from womb to pouch, is a cross between a steeplechase and assault course, with a lethal time limit and all the odds stacked against it.

The baby is born after only thirty-three days growth. It is deaf and blind, few of the senses are developed, and the limbs are no more than rudimentary stumps. However, the olfactory centre is working and the nostrils are wide open, so presumably it smells its way. It weighs about ¾ gramme and is so small that you could pick up a litter of baby kangaroos in a teaspoon.

Yet this vulnerable organism is suddenly propelled down the birth canal, ejected into the outside world and, from the moment it is born, has less than five minutes to find safety. If it takes any longer, it will die of hypothermia or exhaustion.

The mother makes it as easy as possible, lying on her back with her tail stretched out between her legs, and licking a pathway in her fur for the baby to follow. But she does not touch it or help in any way. It is up to the baby to decide where it is and what it has to do.

Hand over fist, it slowly climbs through the forest of hairs. The slightest delay or slip could be fatal, but somehow it always makes it to the pouch – usually within 3–4 minutes. Once there, it can relax in the warmth and comfort, with a ready supply of milk, for the next 235 days, till it weighs 5–10 lb and is ready for its second birth.

This represents such an emotional refuge that adolescent kangaroos will nuzzle up to their mother and stick their heads in her pouch whenever they can, even when it contains another youngster.

The whole process is so risky it is a wonder that any animal adopted it, let alone the entire marsupial population of Australia, but we will return to that curious subject later. It is enough to say that the whole sprawling family of kangaroo-like animals come into the world this way.

There are fifty-five species of kangaroos and wallabies alone. The big reds and greys are the best known, but there are numerous smaller species such as mountain wallabies and tree kangaroos (which behave like overgrown squirrels).

The kangaroos' famous leap is not as spectacular as some people imagine. It normally carries them about 3 feet (1m) off the ground and allows them to travel at about 25 mph. However, they can keep it up for long distances and, at full stretch, with the wind in their ears and their tails stretched out behind as a balance, they can do much better. They are known to clear 9-foot-high boundary fences, can jump 30 feet (the record is 45 feet) and have been timed at up to 88 mph.

The red kangaroo is so called because of the unique colouring matter it exudes. This is a pink, powdery substance which is secreted on the chest, and the animal rubs it all over its body, including its back, with its hands. The grey produces a similar, colourless substance.

It may be that their alarming birth process hardens a kangaroo for life, because they are remarkably resilient animals. Although they are grass-eating ungulates – like deer, zebra and bison – they are far tougher and more adaptable.

The reason they have been able to survive their exile in the Australian outback is that they are prepared to eat the coarse spinnifex grass that even sheep leave alone. In a good year, when the sheep population can be expected to double, the kangaroos quadruple.

They pant like a dog when it is hot, and lick their armpits to cool down. At the same time, they can go for weeks, or even months, without water, provided they eat vegetation. They are the only Australian animals that know how to dig for water, and wild pigeons, cockatoos and emus have been seen drinking at kangaroo water-holes. In other words they are ideally equipped for the outback.

What comes as more of a surprise is that they are equally at home in water. Kangaroos are excellent swimmers, and it has been observed that when they are attacked by, say, dingos, they sometimes retreat to water and hold their enemies under till they drown. There is even a small species of kangaroo that can live off sea-water.

Over the years, the kangaroo's virtues have attracted the attention of entrepreneurs, and there have been many attempts to transplant them to other countries. In the nineteenth century, herds of kangaroos and wallabies could be seen grazing in the meadows of the Rhineland and Silesia (it is said that the red-necked wallabies did best). Wild wallabies can still be seen in parts of the English countryside, and there was once a herd on Guernsey, which was eaten in World War II.

Kihikihi

The Moorish Idol fish (*Zanclus canescens*) is an example of how an animal can be both immensely popular and virtually unknown at the same time.

Its Hawaiian name, Kihikihi, is preferable, as the other one makes no sense (the Moors never had idols, and the fish has never been near North Africa). Either way, you would certainly recognize it, because it is one of the most famous of all tropical fish that inhabit the coral reefs of the Pacific and Indian Oceans.

Its white and yellow body, with dark brown bands and huge tail fin, have appeared on a thousand wallpaper and fabric designs, and it features in every aquarium.

Yet, paradoxically, almost nothing is known

RICHARD SPARKS

about it. Its behaviour has never been studied. The details of its mating habits and spawning are still a mystery. It probably eats small crustaceans, but even this is not known for sure, and its anatomical oddities (such as the spines which grow from the corners of its mouth) have never been explained.

This fish has simply been adopted as a popular image, like a toy or decoration, without eliciting the slightest scientific curiosity.

King Snakes

King snakes are a group of reptiles which are harmless to human beings but are a terror to other snakes. Some are green with white speckles, some brown with yellow rings, some black and red, and some – like the false coral snake – imitate others' markings, but they all have one thing in common. They are anarchists who short-circuit the natural system by breaking one of its fundamental rules. They eat other snakes.

Snakes accidentally swallow each other from time to time, especially when they have grabbed either end of the same piece of food. Once they have started swallowing something it is difficult to stop, regardless of what is attached to the other side. However, the king snakes are specialists. They hunt other snakes, any snakes, even their own relatives. Cannibalism has nothing to do with it; as far as they are concerned a snake is a snake is a snake.

Their technique is to grab the other snake by the neck, wrap themselves around its body and crush it to death. They are immune to all venoms, and have no hesitation in tackling even the most poisonous varieties, including rattlesnakes and copperheads. This is most unusual. The cobra, for instance, which also eats snakes occasionally, has no such immunity and will only eat non-poisonous varieties.

Though king snakes, strictly speaking, are confined to North America, there are species in other parts of the world, such as the African file snake, with very similar habits.

The extraordinary thing is that they have no difficulty in swallowing a snake larger than themselves. A file snake is on record as swallowing two fully-grown night adders, together with the frog they had both got hold of. When a king snake meets another king snake, the matter is decided not by length but by whose jaws open widest.

The ultimate example of this was a double-headed king snake at San Diego Zoo, called Dudly-Duplex. This freak of nature survived fairly well until one day one head tried to swallow the other. They were separated just in time, by the keeper. But that sort of thing rankles, and the other head had its revenge shortly afterwards, swallowing its twin's head and killing them both.

The Kiwi

The waddling little creature that symbolizes New Zealand and has appeared on millions of stamps, coins, textiles and tins of shoe polish, is the smallest flightless bird in the Southern Hemisphere. Its anatomy is so different from the others – the ostrich, rhea, cassowary and emu – that it is probably more closely related to the prehistoric moas.

Highly prized by the Maoris, who wove its hair-like plumage into robes, it is a modest nocturnal animal that spends the day in burrows under large trees. At night it waddles out, on stubby legs set unusually far apart, in search of food – and this is where its one unique talent comes into play. For the kiwi is the only bird known to detect its food by *smell*.

Most birds have no sense of smell, and the idea of the kiwi hunting by smell seemed so unlikely that at first no one believed it. But in 1968, Dr Bernice M. Wenzel of the University of California decided to put the story to the test.

Kiwis eat worms and larvae which they dig out of the ground with their thin, curved beaks. So a number of tapering aluminium tubes were set into the ground of two kiwi aviaries. Some were flavoured with strong smells, some contained food, and others just earth. By changing around the tubes and masking the smells with various scents, it was proved beyond doubt that the kiwis could detect the smell of food several inches down.

A Stomach for Koalas

It is an undeniable zoological fact that when a baby koala bear misbehaves, the mother bear puts it over her knees and spanks its bottom, while it screams and cries like a human child. If the cuteness of this stops you in your tracks, you are not alone. But that is unavoidable when talking about koalas, because these prototype teddy-bears live up to their cuddly appearance in every cloying detail (except for one, which is so repulsive it might sink their reputation overnight). They *are* cute and gentle. They *do* make loving parents, and provided you do not get too close they even manage to keep their vicious claws to themselves. And they do all this against the most fearful odds.

The first disadvantage the koala has imposed on itself is that its marsupial pouch points backwards. This is an absurd handicap for a tree-climbing animal because most of the time, in the nature of things, it opens *downwards*. The baby koala gets itself out of this hazardous pouch as soon as possible (after about six months) and spends the rest of its infancy clinging to its mother's back in the pose familiar from countless travel brochures.

A more serious handicap is its extreme fussiness about food. To describe the koala as particular would be an understatement. To start with, it will only eat eucalyptus leaves (which is why these animals smell strongly of throat lozenges), but that is only the beginning. Koalas in different areas will only feed on certain *types* of gum tree. In New South Wales they refuse to eat anything but spotted eucalyptus. In Victoria they will only touch red gum. Then, to make life really difficult, the bears will only eat *certain* leaves of these *certain* trees at *certain* times of year. The reason for this complication is that the food they are so obsessed about can actually be poisonous to them. At some times of year the older leaves, and the young shoots at the tip of the branches, can release prussic acid when chewed!

The causes of their strange addiction is not properly understood, but there seems to be some ingredient of eucalyptus oil that is essential for their metabolism. Koala bears that have been raised in captivity are prepared to eat other foods, including bread, milk and mistletoe, but they die unless they also have eucalyptus leaves.

Whatever the reason, as the trees are increasingly felled the Australian koalas have become prisoners of their diet and are literally starving to death.

The Komodo Dragons

Naturalists had heard rumours of them for years, but they were deeply sceptical of their existence. South-east Asia abounds with stories of legendary dragons and monsters, and this one had all the classic ingredients: ferocious prehistoric beasts marooned on remote uninhabited islands, which no white man had seen before (and for which there was no tangible evidence), and which the natives regarded as primeval spirits. It was too good to be true.

So it was not until 1912 that the myth became reality, when Major P. A. Ouwens captured four of the animals and brought them back to the Buitenzorg Botanical Gardens in Java; and then zoologists reluctantly agreed that the descriptions had been correct in every detail.

The Komodo Dragon is, indeed, the last of the giant reptiles, a dinosaur in all but name, which has survived for millions of years in the jungles of three tiny islands (Rintja, Padar and Komodo Island itself, which are part of the Sunda Island group in Indonesia).

They turned out to be 10-foot-long (3m) monitor lizards, 300 lb of prehistoric bad temper with supple scales wrinkling over their muscles, and claws that can rip a deer or wild boar to pieces. They stalk their prey by scent alone, with their tongues flicking over the ground ahead of them like snakes, until they are close enough to strike or stun victims with their tails.

Like most reptiles, they are at their most vulnerable during the laying and hatching of their eggs, and the Komodo Dragon has evolved extraordinary behaviour patterns to protect them. The eggs are buried as deep as 30 feet underground, in huge trenches which they laboriously excavate and refill. And when the young eventually hatch, and manage to tunnel their way out, they spend their early years living in trees! So they have managed to combine, in this one species, two of the least likely characteristics attributed to 'mythical' dragons: their reputation for living underground, and their ability to fly.

They cannot spit fire, of course, but no one who has seen a Komodo Dragon can be in any doubt that such legendary beasts (or something very like them) could once have existed. And, for all we know, still do.

TERRY OAKES

L

Ladybird, Ladybird

Ladybird, ladybug, ladybeetle – call them what you like, hardly anyone has a word to say against them. There are four thousand enchanting species, with more dots than a set of dominoes, and they all look as if they were designed by Walt Disney. But do not be deceived; like many brightly coloured insects, they are ruthless (and poisonous) predators. What endears them to us is that their instincts happen to coincide, to a remarkable degree, with our own requirements. The ladybird happens to eat what we want eaten.

The reddish ones have a voracious appetite for aphids (a single ladybird larva was recorded as eating ninety insects and three thousand of their larvae), while the blackish ones conveniently go for a range of other pests, including mealy bugs and scale insects. Fortunately for us, nothing seems to eat ladybirds, because they have a battery of defences including warning colours and a vile taste of histamine, which they also manage to exude through their knee joints. In other words, they are perfect allies in our war against other insects.

They won their finest battle honours in 1889 when they saved the entire Californian citrus crop from a plague of scale insects. It was one of the first experiments in biological control as an alternative to insecticides. Australian ladybirds were imported for the job, and they proved so successful that the species was later introduced into South Africa.

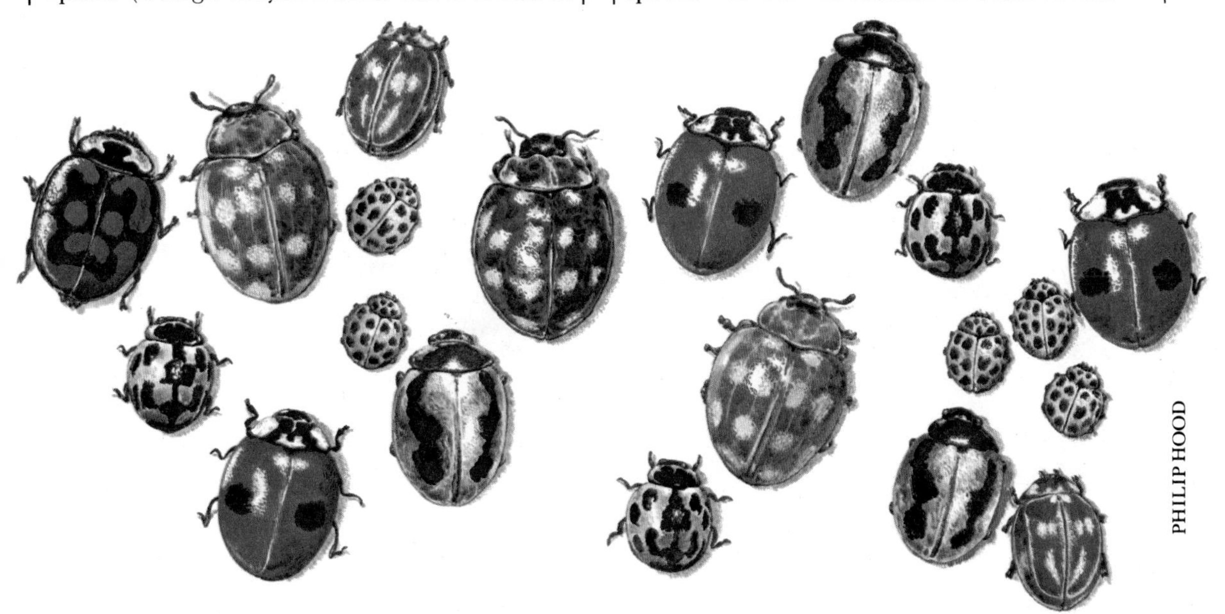

PHILIP HOOD

Enterprising collectors soon discovered a native species which was almost as effective, a thriving trade grew up, and for many years the Californian farmers used to buy them by the litre (there are 10,000 ladybirds to the litre).

In 1928 alone, an estimated 48 million beetles were released into West Coast orchards – evidence of how effective they were, or at least of people's faith in them.

There is nothing new in this, however, because farmers have recognized and encouraged them for centuries. Their name dates back to their association with the Virgin Mary in the Middle Ages, when they used to be called 'the beetles of our Lady'.

There is a reason why children used to chant the old rhyme:

Ladybird, ladybird, fly away home!
Your house is on fire and your children all gone.

The verse comes from the south of England, where the hop vines were traditionally burnt at the end of the season, and it was a warning to an old friend. Incidentally, the second verse runs:

Except little Nan, who sits in a pan,
Weaving gold laces as fast as she can.

This is a reference to the way the ladybird larva weaves a chrysalis-like case for the pupal stage.

The Law Breakers

'Let him go for a scapegoat into the wilderness.'
– Leviticus XVI

The Old Testament urged the Jews to catch a wild animal to which their sins could be ceremoniously transferred, and which could then be driven away. It was a neat solution to the problem of sin, but proved to be an uneasy compromise between the old, tribal beliefs (that we should obey the law of animals) and the later, Christian ideal (that they should obey ours). St Bernard, for instance, had no hesitation in excommunicating a swarm of bees that interrupted his sermon, and by the Middle Ages it was common for animals to be tried for human crimes.

As late as the seventeenth century, wolves were solemnly being exiled to Siberia, and in 1659 an Italian judge issued a summons to the local caterpillars to appear before him on a charge of trespass and wilful damage – and had the summons nailed to the trees in five districts.

Over the centuries many animals, from pests such as moles, locusts, snails and horseflies to household pets, have been put on trial for their misdemeanours. The first recorded example was the hive of bees condemned to death by suffocation in 864 AD, and even today a newspaper editor is never short of filler items about whimsical traffic cops booking escaped kangaroos for speeding.

A cockerel charged with unnatural practices, for laying an egg, at Basle, Switzerland, in 1471, was sentenced to death and burnt by the executioner. Animals have often been tried for murder, the earliest known case being that of a pig alleged to have eaten a baby at Fontenai, France, in 1268. A century later the French were executing bulls for 'unruly behaviour', and a horse which threw and killed its rider at Dijon in 1639 also suffered the ultimate sanction. A pig stood trial for murder in Yugoslavia in 1864, and a dog was charged with murder, along with two men, in a Swiss court as recently as 1906. The men received life imprisonment, the dog was executed.

In medieval times it was common for pigs to be flogged in public (often as stand-ins for human villains) and dogs were hung for the mildest offence (presumably because it was easier than sending them to prison). The sentence is likely to be more merciful today. In the latest case we have been able to track down, a dog received a month's imprisonment, with a diet of bread and water, for biting someone's hand in Libya in 1974.

Then, as now, the legal rituals were observed to the letter. When the Franciscan monks of Maranhao, in Brazil, put their local termites on trial in 1709, they appointed a lawyer to defend them and were so swayed by his eloquence that they gave the insects a conditional discharge and bound them over to keep the peace. A sow was executed for murder in 1547, but her piglets were released because of their mother's bad influence; and in 1499 the trial of a bear in Germany was delayed for over a week because of legal submissions that it had a right to be tried by a jury of its peers, i.e. other bears.

The animal trials of the Middle Ages produced their own Perry Mason – a French lawyer, Bartholomé Chassenée, who established a reputation for the ingenious defence of his 'clients'. In 1521 he was appointed to defend the rats which had destroyed a crop of barley. When they failed to show up for the trial (which must have been a fairly common occurrence), he successfully pleaded that the summons was invalid because it had not been served on *all* the rats in the district.

When further summonses were issued, Chassenée accused the court of prejudice. His clients, he said, were being intimidated by the 'evilly-disposed cats' of the prosecutor, and believed that their lives would be in danger if they surrendered. With a perfectly straight face, he demanded an undertaking from the prosecution, under penalty of a severe fine, that the cats would not attempt to molest the rats on the way to court. The prosecution, however, refused to guarantee their safety and the case was dismissed.

Animals are no longer held legally responsible, but attorneys can still find themselves representing a four-legged client.

In 1979 a Pharaoh hound called Kinky made British legal history when a high court judge in London granted the dog's owner an injunction against his neighbour, to stop her enticing Kinky's affections.

More recently, the plight of a five-year-old collie bitch called Sido led to two trials in Californian state courts, and a new law being passed by the state legislature. Before committing suicide in December 1979, Mrs Mary Murphy, an elderly San Francisco widow, added a clause to her will specifying that Sido should be put down, since the animal could not be protected from neglect and mistreatment in someone else's home.

The will's executrix, Rebecca Smith, submitted a three-page petition to the probate court pleading that she be excused from this provision if she could find Sido a good home. The judge ruled, however, that the law considered pets to be property to be disposed of as the owner wished. A massive outcry ensued. Sido was taken into care by the Society for Prevention of Cruelty to Animals (SPCA). Thousands wrote in offering support. A group called Attorneys for Animals' Rights filed a friend-of-the-court brief. And the California state senate passed a unanimous motion demanding that the court hold another hearing.

The motion led to a new law being passed which prevents malicious or unnecessary destruction of animals. It was signed by Jerry Brown, the California governor, just hours before the start of the second trial. As a result, Judge Jay Pfotenhauer overturned the provision of Mrs Murphy's will. 'The will,' he announced, 'seeks to have carried out an act I find to be illegal and a violation of public policy. Even stray and abandoned dogs have rights. While Sido can't be deemed to be a stray or abandoned dog, she is entitled to no less protection.' The ruling was greeted with whoops of joy from spectators crowding the courtroom.

The Problem of Leaking Fish

The idea that fish might leak is difficult to credit at first – but they do. And in some cases the problem is so severe that a major part of their metabolism is devoted to preventing them from drowning.

The problem is that fish have very thin skins, and water is drawn through them by osmosis – a process that occurs when liquids of different density are separated by a semi-permeable membrane. Freshwater fish have more salts inside their bodies than there are in the water surrounding them, so the water floods in and they have to constantly bail themselves out.

Fish in the sea, on the other hand, live in surroundings which are more salty than their body fluids. So they are forever being drained and have to drink a lot of water to make up for it.

The problem of salt water affects many terrestrial animals that live off the sea. Many marine birds, for instance, have evolved nasal 'salt glands' to regulate the saline intake of their bodies. A gull, given one-tenth of its weight in sea water, excreted 90 per cent of the salt within three hours. Some sea birds, however, have become so adapted to drinking salt water that they will die if denied access to it.

Marine iguanas, on the Galapagos Islands, which dive into the sea for their seaweed diet, also have nasal glands which accumulate the salt from their bloodstream, and have been seen to sneeze every so often, ejecting a gob of briny mucus.

Leeches

Take a lesson from the leech,
He's a feller who can teach.
– English popular song of the 1930s

Doctors were once called leeches, and there was a time when no self-respecting medical practitioner would go on a call without a jar of *Hirudo medicinalis medicinalis* in his bag. They were as necessary as a stethoscope.

The leech was first introduced into European medicine in 50 BC by a quack called Themison of Laodicea, and remained in use up to the beginning of the twentieth century. Quite recently, the rugby-playing students of St Bartholomew's Hospital in London used leeches to treat their minor bruises and swellings.

Leeches found favour in the Middle Ages amongst the monastic orders because bleeding, like flagellation, gained them special privileges.

In the early nineteenth century there was an absolute craze for them, as a result of the theories of Francoise Broussais, head of the French Military Hospital in Paris. Broussais believed that all diseases were caused by a single pathogenic agent – 'excitation' – which manifested itself in two forms. If it was too weak, it produced debility; if it was too strong, it resulted in irritation. Both problems were centred in the stomach, and there was only one cure – leeching.

For the sixteen years that Broussais' theories held sway, it was estimated that leeches sucked about a million pints (or 1,680,000 litres) of blood from the French people every year.

When they ran out of French leeches, they imported them from Bohemia, Hungary and the Baltic, in staggering numbers. In 1827 the figure was 33 million; by 1833 it had risen to 45 million. When governments began to impose tariffs, the trade went underground, and at one point there was a busy leech-smuggling organization operating across the borders of Russia.

According to Roy Sawyer of the University of California, the medicinal leech has still not recovered from these depredations, and he wants it to be declared an endangered species.

The medicinal leech is grey-brown in colour, a few centimetres long and slimy to the touch. It has a sucker at each end of its body. When feeding, it will suck up about a fiftieth of a pint (10–15 millilitres) of blood, dropping off when satiated. The blood is then dehydrated and thickened in the leech's intestine before being stored in special pockets in its mid-gut, where it is prevented from decomposing by bacteria. Because of this system, the leech can survive for six months on just one meal. Even then, if no further food appears, it can survive a while longer by breaking down its own body tissues. One scientist was so impressed by the leech's imperviousness to hunger that he suggested it would make the best astronaut on long-duration spaceflights.

When a leech bites, it makes a Y-shaped incision with its needle-sharp teeth, anaesthetizes the wound, and then injects from its salivary glands an anticoagulant called hirudin. Modern researchers use hirudin in research on blood-clotting, but its chemical structure is unknown and so it cannot be synthesized.

The medicinal leech is not the only member of this family. The duck leech, for instance, penetrates the mouth and nasal passages of waterfowl, and can sometimes kill the birds by suffocation. The European variety are said to do the same thing to horses and cattle. There is one leech that will only feed off the basking shark, and another which clings to the lips of crocodiles.

The fiercest are the south-east Asian leeches, familiar to Vietnam veterans and so often seen attached to movie heroes as they trek through jungles. If you are ever unfortunate enough to encounter one, a pinch of salt is more effective than the traditional cigarette end.

Lemmings

How to make room for your neighbours

Lemmings do not commit mass suicide by jumping over cliffs. This may come as a disappointment, but they happen to be Scandinavian rodents and, as any Norwegian can tell you, the mystery is not where they go, but where they come *from* in such large numbers. According to traditional folklore they fall from the sky when it rains.

It is odd how myths can develop, for the seaside suicide notion is a recent addition to lemming lore. The idea of lemming showers, on the other hand, is part of a very old tradition.

The truth is that very rapid changes can occur in the population of small rodents like lemmings, voles and field-mice, and these are often accompanied by sudden migrations. But lemmings do not leap off cliffs, and their story is more complex, and surprising, than mass hysteria.

To start with, the cycle of populations is astonishingly regular. The peak populations of Norwegian lemmings occurred in 1862, 1866, 1868, 1871, 1875, 1879, 1883, 1887, 1890, 1894, 1897, 1902, 1906, and 1909. Boom–bust–boom–bust, at average intervals of 3.8 years. Wherever they occur, from Canada to Russia, the same 3–4 year cycle holds good. In some cases the cycles of different species in different areas are so close in time that they appear to be synchronized; and these even affect the population of animals which prey on them, such as the arctic red fox.

But that is not all, for the numbers do not simply increase and decrease. Within each cycle, they act out an elaborate, fluctuating pattern. None of the obvious explanations – a recurring disease, or changes in the climate, or growth of vegetation – fits all the cases, and until recently the whole phenomenon was a mystery. However, as the result of twenty years of research, the story was finally pieced together in the early 1970s.

The key factor was the discovery that within any population, there are two kinds (or genotypes) of these rodents. One is aggressive by nature and good at withstanding the stress of overcrowded conditions, but does not reproduce very rapidly. The other is fertile, reproduces in large numbers – but cannot stand stress.

For the sake of argument, they could be called the 'breeders' and 'survivors'. Both sets of characteristics are genetically inherited and passed on to their respective young. It is the varying fortunes of these genotypes which produces the cycles.

The story is worth telling in full because it is a fascinating example of how instincts can produce behaviour which alters the environment, which in turn alters the pattern of inheritance – and so changes their instinctive behaviour. It bears an uncanny resemblance to the children's story of the Town Mouse and the Country Mouse.

There is one rule to bear in mind, which sets the whole thing in motion. In any population of animals, the circumstances can only favour one genotype at a time. The 'breeders' cannot breed at times of stress in the colony, and the 'survivors' are not aggressive in times of peace.

The following scenario is based on studies of meadow mice (Microtus pennsylvanicus) carried out at Indiana University, though the same principle applies to lemmings. The animals live for about a year, so each individual is born at a different stage of the cycle and faces a different set of circumstances.

The First Year

The cycle begins in the spring or early summer of the first year, with the population at its lowest ebb and numbers down to as few as one mouse per acre. However, there is plenty of food, survival rates are high, and conditions favour the 'breeders'. So when the breeding season starts, the population rapidly increases. It continues to rise through the summer and autumn, with the 'breeders' producing litter after litter, at such a rate that numbers may increase by as much as 10 or 15 per cent per week!

If they do not reach the maximum limit by the end of the year, they often continue to breed through the winter, which makes up for natural losses through cold and hunger.

The Second Year

With such a large population surviving the winter, the first generation produced in the New Year pushes their numbers over the top. When the population reaches its peak the colony faces a major crisis.

There may now be several hundred animals per acre and like in an overcrowded city, the competition is fierce. Conditions no longer favour the 'breeders', and the 'survivors' now come into their own. There is considerable aggression, especially between males. Food supplies dwindle and the birth-rate slows down, and then stops.

Some of the 'breeders', especially the young females, disperse into neighbouring areas, but many of them literally die from the stress. One way or another, by death or desertion, the population may be halved in a few weeks.

The remaining mice, however, find a sudden improvement in their conditions. The 'breeders' no longer have to compete with the 'survivors', and, as their self-confidence returns, they start reproducing again. The numbers rise again during the summer, and by the autumn they are usually back at their springtime peak. But this time there is a difference. Before their second crisis can develop, the winter is upon them, and brings their activities to a halt.

There is no breeding in the second winter. No young are added, and the population slowly decreases through natural causes, with the old or infirm being weeded out.

The Third Year

In the spring the crisis is upon them, and this time it is a major disaster. Weakened by the winter, the mortality rates are high, and there are massive dispersals by the 'breeder' genotype which go on throughout the summer.

It is these migrations during the third year of the cycle which gave rise to the lemming myth. It is obvious that if a small rodent falls into a river or the sea it will drown, but the lemmings are not heading for the sea. They are just trying to get away from it all.

The 'survivors' who remain behind suddenly find themselves the dominant genotype of the colony. But unfortunately they only have the advantage in conditions of stress. On their own in the open, as they are now, they have two major disadvantages. Firstly, their reproductive rate is low, so they cannot easily make up the numbers. Secondly, they are more susceptible to the ordinary causes of mortality, such as disease.

Their shorter life-expectancy only adds to the

colony's problems. The numbers continue to decline through the autumn, and winter takes a terrible toll of those that are left.

The Fourth Year

The fourth spring finds the animals back at the start of the cycle again and one of three things can happen.

They can begin to reproduce again and, if there are a few 'breeders' left in the colony, the cycle will repeat itself. If there are no 'breeders', the 'survivors' will remain the dominant genotype and keep a sparse but steady population going. Finally, it is always possible that if the weather, predators and luck are against them, they will simply die out.

No one had suspected the importance of dispersal tactics before, and their role in regulating the cycle came as a complete surprise. In the classic tradition of such discoveries, it was the failure of early experiments that provided the clue.

In order to study the rodents at all, the researchers felt it would be necessary to keep them in some sort of enclosure. But as soon as the colony was enclosed (i.e. it could no longer disperse) the whole cycle stopped! The population rocketed to between four and twenty times that of similar groups in the wild. The 3–4 year cycle was suppressed and from then on the numbers rose and fell on a seasonal basis, depending on how much food there was.

The Lion's Share

The lion's role as the King of the Beasts is challenged by a number of other animals, but in one respect its reputation is justified – the animal copulates with astonishing frequency.

Lions are lazy animals that spend days on end lying around, and since it is a matriarchy, where most of the work is done by the females, the males have a lot of spare time. Their inclination is to spend as much of it as possible in copulating, and when there is an available lioness on heat, they perform remarkable feats.

One animal was watched for two and a half days. In the first 24 hours he had copulated 86 times with two lionesses. In the following 24 hours he copulated a further 62 times, and at the end of 55 hours' observation he had brought his score up to 157. The average time for each session was twenty minutes.

But even this is not a record, for there is an animal which makes the lion seem almost celibate. This is Shaw's jird, a kind of desert rodent which on one occasion thc naturalist Bouliere recorded as copulating 224 times in two hours!

Locomotion

Would You Rather Run on Wheels?

One way or another nature has already evolved the lever, the crank, the piston, the hinge, the ball-and-socket joint, the pendulum, siphons, pumps, valves, jet propulsion and almost every other device known to human engineering – with the exception of the wheel.

This is unfortunate, as it rules out such useful additions as pulleys and caterpillar tracks, and is a severe drawback when it comes to locomotion. Several animals have learned to roll (which is certainly the quickest way to go downhill), but there is no substitute for the wheel as the fastest and most economic way of getting about. If caterpillars did have tracks, there would be no stopping them.

If nature can produce circles, why not wheels? The problem is that a living organism must be in touch with every part of its body, through nerves and blood vessels. Now a wheel is certainly *in contact* with an axle and it is even possible to pass a message from one to the other (the way electricity passes through the brushes of an electric motor, for instance), but they are not *connected*. So it would be impossible for living tissue or, say, an artery to cross the gap.

Only one biological organism has been discovered that uses anything like a wheel. It is one of the microscopic marine organisms, a tiny rotifer which has evolved a unique fringe of cilia, or hairs. The creature is shaped like a flat disc with a hairy fringe around the edge. At first it was thought the hairs were merely waving, but they proved to be attached to a band that revolved around the edge. The junction was formed of two interlocking gutters (one inside the other) which acted as a duct all round it, through which body fluids could pass. The friction of this junction must have been enormous and it would be impossible to reproduce at a larger scale, so it is not surprising that evolution gave it a miss.

Back at the drawing board, the search for an alternative began. There were several options open. An animal could simply float or drift, or flow (if it was fluid enough). It could suck or puff itself along. It could throw the front half ahead, and then pull in the tail (as most snakes do); or just wriggle its body against whatever resistance it could find (like a fish).

All these methods had their limitations, but a solution arrived with the articulated skeleton. This provided the animal with its own resistance, the grip of muscle on bone, and opened the way to a whole new range of mechanical systems. It enormously improved the other methods, and was adopted – in the form of wings, fins and legs – by all the larger animals.

The animal world may be wheel-less, but almost every other means of locomotion has been exploited, including such ingenious variations as the Slide, the Squeeze and the Hop.

The octopus has a highly developed form of jet propulsion, which is its preferred form of travel. It sucks water in through its gills and expels it forcefully through a tubular, siphon-like exhaust port located below its head. Octopuses can also squeeze their bodies through very small cracks and holes; one large specimen at the Miami Seaquarium repeatedly passed from its own tank to the one next-door by way of the half-inch openings in the glass partitions between the tanks.

Animals love sliding around on mud when they get the chance, but penguins take it seriously. An Emperor penguin usually waddles across the Antarctic ice at a stately 2–3 miles an hour. However, the animals have discovered that they can move more rapidly by adopting a 'tobogganing' position, lying on their stomachs and propelling themselves over the ice with their hind limbs. It takes a lot of energy, and they only do it when they are frightened; but, according to the French authority Prevost, 'their speed is so great that even a man on horseback takes a good many metres to catch up with them'.

Contrary to popular opinion, snakes cannot move rapidly. Racers are amongst the fastest snakes in the world but they can only achieve a speed of three and a half miles per hour. The deadly eastern green mamba is supposed to outrun humans, but in experiments it moved at a maximum of only 7 mph.

The clam worm (*Cerebratus lactus*) burrows along several inches below the sea-bed by a unique form of drilling. Its head is usually broad and rounded but, by a muscular contraction, it can form it into a point which it thrusts forward into the mud. The head then becomes round again, so as to pull the body along behind it. Then the worm makes another contraction, and another thrust forward. The process occurs so rapidly that, like the individual frames of a film, it blurs into a continuous drilling motion.

The largest frog in the world, the goliath frog of West Africa, can leap nine feet (2.75m). Smaller frogs, however, can leap further in relation to their body size. *Litoria microbelus*, which was recently discovered in a tropical jungle at the northern tip of Western Australia, is the world's smallest frog, measuring no more than half an inch in length. It can, however, jump one hundred times its own length, or over four feet.

The leaping abilities of frogs cannot compare, however, with those of fleas. Measuring a mere 1–10 millimetres, fleas can leap 13 inches (33cm), or up to 350 times their own length. This is equivalent to a 6-foot human making a 2,000-foot-long jump, or about seven soccer pitches. The flea's acceleration has been compared to that of a moon rocket escaping earth's gravity. Yet the flea jumps off its knees.

The one animal which is useless at ground level is the South American sloth. Its claws, or fingernails, are so long that it cannot walk. When forced, reluctantly, to move from one tree to another, it sprawls on its stomach, legs splayed out at ungainly angles, and painfully claws itself along, as if swimming.

One of the most unusual forms of locomotion is the way certain species of ribbonworms get around. Each worm is equipped with a harpoon-like spear that nestles between the two lobes of its brain, and which it can shoot out (attached to a hollow string) with considerable force. It is normally used as a weapon, but in some species it also serves as a means of locomotion. Lined with minute hooks the string is shot out like a grappling line and used to haul the worm over beach or sea-floor. The string is sometimes as long as the worm's body, and occasionally is fired off with such force that it snaps – in which case the worm grows a new one.

Some moths have evolved an emergency escape system rather like the ejector seat of a jet fighter. If dangers threatens them in flight, the safest place is usually at ground level. So they stop dead, in mid-air, and hurl themselves into a parabolic trajectory, like a rocket, and fall to earth.

Big animals are supposed to be clumsy, but they often move with great care and delicacy. Elephants, for instance, do not crash through the jungle; they move quietly and with such a light tread that they hardly leave any tracks. Their feet have a combined surface area of about 3½ square feet, so that the pressure per square inch of sole, even with a bull weighing several tons, it not very great. It is less, for instance, than the pressure on a woman's stiletto heel. They normally amble at a human pace, but can keep up a fast walk of 6–7 mph for hours at a time. When charging or fleeing, they have been timed at 24 mph, but only for about a hundred yards. Elephants always run. They cannot gallop or jump. Though they can easily climb steep slopes, they are brought to a dead stop by even quite a small vertical wall.

Among the faster animals, a greyhound can manage about 40 mph, and a racehorse has been timed at a top speed of 48 mph. But they would both be left standing by a Mongolian antelope or American pronghorn, which are capable of speeds up to 60 mph. Fastest of all, of course, is the cheetah. The most phenomenal speeds have been claimed for this animal, of 80, or even 90 mph, but this has not been substantiated. Many attempts have been made to run cheetahs on racecourses and dog-tracks, but the animals refuse to exert themselves under artificial conditions. They have no competitive instinct and tend to lose interest in a race, even when they are winning.

The cheetahs' maximum velocity over level ground is probably 65–75 mph, but their bodies are adapted for sudden bursts of energy, and their real talent lies in a phenomenal acceleration. Their lungs are unusually large and they can burn up oxygen and fuel so fast that they can accelerate from a standing start to 45 mph in two seconds!

We ourselves do not begin to compare with these natural athletes for speed or energy. The world records for track events may sound spectacular when they are timed in hundredths of a second, but the fastest speed yet achieved by any human being amounts to just under 23 mph over 100 yards.

In spite of this, we do have one unique advantage. We may be slow, but human beings are the only mammals capable of a fully bipedal gait, which uses up so little energy we can keep it up almost indefinitely. In other words, we can *walk* – and walking is the most efficient form of locomotion yet evolved.

A human can run for about 100 miles at, say, 5 mph, but it is possible to *walk* at 2½ mph for three times that distance, and keep it up day after day. In fact, the record for the 6,800-mile Trans-Asia Walk is 238 days, or nearly eight months.

Another advantage is that our joints are so flexible we can use a greater variety of locomotion. A horse, for instance, can move in four ways – walking, trotting, cantering, or at a gallop. But Desmond Morris has identified no less than twenty forms of human locomotion, from slithering to swimming, and about half of them – walking, strolling, hurrying, jogging, sprinting, tiptoeing, marching, goose-stepping and hopping – depend on being able to walk. This facility had far-reaching effects on our evolution, and is probably the reason why humans are the only species to adopt migration as a *permanent* way of life.

The Loud Silence

The sound of life on this planet may turn out to be a deep diapason: a low, continuous rumble, which we cannot hear but which pervades the world around us. It may even be louder than the familiar noise we take so much for granted.

This extraordinary possibility is raised by the discovery of the first land animal which communicates with 'inaudible' ulta-low frequencies (ULF). Many animals produce high-frequency noises, and it has long been suspected that creatures like whales and dolphins may also use very low frequencies. However, the unlikely subject of these experiments was the capercaillie bird, or common grouse.

The call of the grouse has been described as 'the sound of two sticks being knocked together followed, without a break, by a champagne cork being drawn, and ending with a sound like the grinding of a knife'. The audible range is no more than 650 feet, and it is a remarkably soft noise for such a large bird (especially one that is polygamous and has to attract the attention of females over a wide area).

However, Scottish scientists have now discovered that the audible noise conceals ULF signals at frequencies below 16 Hz, which we cannot hear, but come through loud and strong to other grouse. To make doubly sure, the grouse emits them at a volume of 60 decibels – considerably louder than the audible sound!

This is not just a quirk of nature. Scientists believe they have stumbled on a new and quite remarkable communication system common to many animals. Recent research by M. L. Kreithen and D. B. Quine at Cornell University has shown that pigeons even respond to extraordinary noise called *infra-sound*. This consists of frequencies below 10 Hz which can travel hundreds of miles without attenuation, at intensities of over 100 decibels!

Our modern cities generate a considerable volume of infra-sound, which means that a pigeon in Washington DC could clearly hear the noise of New York. Kreithen and Quine even go so far as to suggest that birds might use the massive rumble of cities as navigation beacons for long-distance flights!

M

The Amazing Macaques

It is natural that we should be more interested in the great apes than any other kind of monkey, because they are the most 'advanced' and 'intelligent' species. In fact, we hardly think of them as monkeys at all. But we make this judgement entirely from our point of view. How close are they to us? Can they do the things we do (like speak, or use tools)? We ask how 'intelligent' they are, when what we really mean is how 'human'.

But there is another way of looking at it, by asking how un-animal they are. What can they do that other monkeys cannot? Is there a threshold of 'intelligence', a frontier you cross with a sudden leap of evolution? Or is it a gradual process?

The only way to find out is to compare the super-primates with other monkeys. The macaques are an interesting example, because they are still unambiguously *animals* – a species with comparatively small brains and none of the higher attributes of gorillas, chimps and baboons. Yet they have become one of the largest and most successful species in the world (while their 'wiser' cousins are facing extinction, in the wild) – and their achievements raise some fascinating questions about where intelligence begins and ends.

Their curiosity, inventiveness and greed have allowed them to adapt to almost any climate, from the deserts of north Africa to the Arctic, and they now occupy the widest range of any primate other than ourselves: sixty species and sub-species spanning half the world, from Gibraltar to the Pacific.

They are the only non-human primates in Europe, and the only monkeys which swim. Some tropical species actually dive for crabs in mangrove swamps. Malaysian macaques have been trained to climb palm trees and pick coconuts; and the troops of rhesus macaques which can be seen in Indian bazaars and temples are the largest wild animals ever to adapt to an urban environment.

Their versatility was always well known, but it was not until the first scientific studies were carried out, in Japan in 1952, that the full extent of their talents was appreciated. A series of remarkable discoveries showed that the Japanese macaques were not simply opportunists living on their wits. They were inventing and learning, devising their own technology and, what is even more surprising for such a 'primitive' species, passing on their skills to other members of the group.

A Taste for Saunas

Japanese macaques are the most northerly species of monkeys and have developed thick, shaggy coats to protect them from the winter snows. Some even inhabit the harsh environment of the mountains in northern Japan, and scientists were keeping watch on a group of these when they witnessed an extraordinary adaptation.

The monkeys were exploring new territory when they came across some volcanic springs. In spite of their long hair, they plunged in, and the whole troop was soon sitting up to their necks in steaming pools of water.

Although it was a radical departure from their usual pattern of behaviour, the animals soon developed a taste for this natural sauna. They hung around the same place for weeks, and then months, though there was better food elsewhere, spending day after day immersed in the pools.

The message somehow spread to other troops, as more macaques began to adopt the new lifestyle, and it now affects others for miles around. Within a few years the behaviour of the species has totally changed, and every winter the pools are crowded with snow-covered Afros bobbing on the surface, and shivering animals trying to dry off in the freezing air.

There is, there can be, no evolutionary advantage to this. They are vulnerable, do not get enough to eat, and suffer from lack of exercise; but they would rather starve than leave the tranquillizing warmth of the water. But it certainly has an evolutionary effect. Their social structures break down in the passive proximity of the pool, ritual displays and aggression are forgotten, and young are brought up differently. In time there may even be physical changes. They might lose their hair, for instance, or develop a layer of subcutaneous fat such as we have. Who knows? In due course, natural selection might favour a form of bald water-monkey.

Imo and the Koshima Beach

The research programme run by scientists from Kyoto University now covers thirty groups of macaques, with a total of more than 4,300 individuals. The most interesting of these are found where the monkeys live in isolation in the wild; and the most interesting of these is this troop on Koshima, a small island off the coast of Japan and separated from the mainland by treacherous currents and tidal races. They were an ideal group for primatologists to study, but the scientists were quite unprepared for the effect their arrival would have.

CATHERINE BRADBURY

When detailed studies began in 1952, the animals were very shy and had to be coaxed out of hiding by offerings of sweet potatoes left on the beach. Eventually the whole troop would come down to the shore every day for their free meal, and the scientists were able to observe their behaviour closely.

The shoreline was not part of their normal range, and the monkeys made short, nervous forays into the open. It was only the older and slower ones who lingered. The leaders and more aggressive males went to extraordinary lengths to get as much as they could, clutching an armful of roots to their chests, stuffing another in their mouths and hobbling away as fast as they could on three legs. It is difficult for macaques to run on two legs, but many of them tried, and it is easy to see how such a trait might evolve.

One of the liveliest members was a 3½-year-old female called Imo (the names used here are those chosen by the scientists). About a year after the study began, Imo made a remarkable discovery. Instead of picking up the potato and scampering away to eat it, she carried it over to a pool of water and carefully washed the mud and sand off it. Whether she had worked this out, or it was a random experiment, she proceeded to wash her food every day from then on.

A few weeks later the scientists were amazed to see the younger monkeys following her example. Their instinct warned them not to expose themselves in the open for any longer than necessary, so they must have calculated that the risks were worth it. Four months later, Imo's mother was doing the same, and by the end of the year the whole troop, with the exception of the older monkeys, had adopted this new, and wholly unnatural, practice.

Imo experimented with several pools for washing her food, and eventually tried it in the sea. The waves made it rather difficult, but the salt water obviously improved the flavour, so she changed her tactics accordingly.

To encourage the monkeys to spend more time on the beach, the food supply was changed from potatoes to rice. The idea was that it would take longer for them to pick up the grains from the sand, but it only served as a fresh incentive to Imo, and her inventive mind soon solved the problem. She scooped up handfuls of mud, sand and rice and threw them into her pool. She watched the mud dissolve and the sand settle to the bottom, and then simply skimmed off the grains that were left floating on the surface.

Imo now had a special role in the troop. She was not the leader – in fact her eccentric behaviour made her something of an outsider – but she was clearly regarded as an innovator, and the others watched her closely. So, in the same way that they had learned to wash and salt their food, they now learned to winnow grain.

Babies, clinging to their mothers' backs, watched them at work and copied them when they grew up. The information was thus passed from generation to generation, and descendants of the original macaques still do the same today.

The Mantis

The praying mantis is notorious for devouring her mates, once they have completed their necessary function in life. As one author elegantly put it: 'Many a male suitor finds himself first in the arms and then in the stomach of his intended.' She may not even wait that long, and begins to eat the male during mating, starting with the head, while his hind end staunchly continues to copulate. However, this gruesome climax may not be inevitable. Some authorities claim that the male is seldom a passive victim, but often fights back and manages to escape.

The prayer-like attitude of the mantis, which is due to its unusual front limbs, has given the insect a reputation for magical properties. The name *mantis* was given by Linneaus, and comes from the Greek word meaning 'soothsayer' or 'prophet'. In Africa, the insects still play a considerable role in tribal religions.

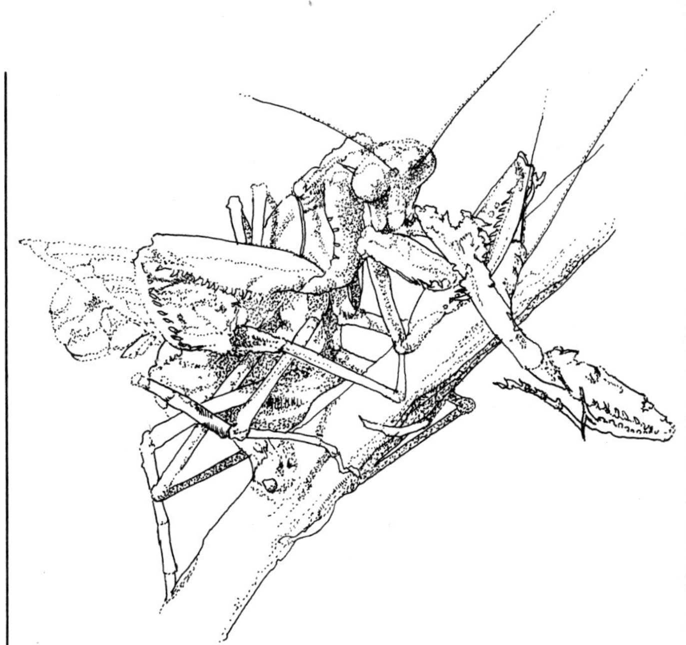

There are some 1,500 species throughout the world, most of them tropical, and they are fearsome predators. The larger ones, which can grow to six and a half inches in length (16.5cm), have even been observed attacking and overcoming small lizards and frogs.

Their curiously hinged front legs can be extended with lightning rapidity to catch their prey. The whole movement of extension, prey-catching and retraction has been timed at about one twentieth of a second – and their appetite is prodigious. An adult praying mantis was once seen to eat ten cockroaches (which happen to be close relatives) in less than three hours.

The Marsupial Experiment

Kangaroos and certain other animals which make brief appearances in this book, such as quokkas and thylacines, are all marsupials – a group of animals that parted company with the rest of evolution when their continent parted company with the rest of the world.

Their story began at a time when Australia was joined to South America, and so they evolved on both continents. Their only surviving descendant in the New World is the yapok; but the Australian species found they had a previously barren continent to themselves as it slowly drifted north into warmer climes – and they thrived.

In complete isolation, a gigantic evolutionary experiment took place. An alternative form of mammalian evolution was played out, down to the smallest detail, over millions of years. In a classic example of convergent evolution, the marsupials moved into the same ecological niches as their counterparts in the outside world.

Apart from the usual herbivores, there are marsupial versions of weasels, wolves, anteaters, lemurs, squirrels (and flying squirrels), badgers, moles, rats, shrews, mice, martens, bears and tigers. There was even a marsupial lion. In fact, there is only one 'normal' mammal on the continent – the dingo or wild dog – and that is descended from the domestic animals brought in by the first settlers.

The marsupial lion was one of the many giant ice-age fauna, including giant kangaroos and koalas, which have since died out. Of all the giant animals featured in science fiction, from ants and bees to gorillas (and even rabbits, in a hilarious film called *The Night of the Lupus*), no one has yet come up with giant koala bears.

What all these marsupials have in common is a reproductive system which stopped halfway between the reptiles (which get rid of their young as soon as possible, as eggs) and the mammals (who hang on to them as long as possible, so they will be better able to survive on their own).

The marsupials realized that by getting rid of the embryo as soon as possible, they could combine the advantages of both systems. By storing it in what amounted to a second womb, they could conceive again immediately, and with one baby in the pouch and another on the way, they doubled the chances of survival.

There are other curious variations in their anatomy. For instance, the male's penis is behind the testicles (which are carried on the stomach), and the larynx, instead of being halfway down the throat, is in the mouth (so the digestive system and respiration are separate). But these are minor variations on the theme. It was the double womb that dictated their evolution.

The pouches were an obvious problem, especially for an animal which walks on all fours, and a number of experimental models evolved. The koalas developed backward-facing ones like observation cars and some species just relied on the embryo's blind instinct to find a teat and hang on. But evolution favoured an animal which sat upright, so the babies would not fall out.

Sitting is one thing, but remaining upright while on the move is extremely difficult (we are the only animals with a true bipedal gait). Animals legs are hinged in such a way that they cannot stand upright without toppling over; and even if they do, they will find that they face upwards, towards the sky (because the spine joins the skull at the back, not underneath like ours.

The problems were solved by a new neck joint and a tail, and that, dear friend (as Kipling wrote in his animal stories), is How the Kangaroo Learned to Hop.

RAY WINDER

The superb Golden Lion marmoset, one of the rarest and most beautiful South American mammals. It is intensely shy of civilization, and the few remaining animals have retreated high into the mountains south of Rio de Janeiro.

The Eggs of Mhorr – and other Medicines

An extract from the sex glands of the rare green-lipped mussel found off New Zealand is now used routinely in Australian hospitals to stop arthritic pain. Squalene from shark liver oil is an ingredient in skin lubricants, suppositories and fat-soluble drugs. And ara-A, a substance produced by the Caribbean sponge, has led to a breakthrough in the treatment of virus diseases such as herpes encephalitis. These are just a few recent additions to the long list of animal products which have been used as medicines over the years.

From tribal remedies down to the recent discovery that salmine (from salmon sperm) and clupine (from herring sperm) act as anti-coagulants to stop haemorrhaging – there are numerous examples.

The Wart Biter, a brilliant green European cricket, if caught in the hand, will bite quite sharply while simultaneously vomiting up a small glob of brown stomach juice. This juice was believed to have the power to remove warts from the skin, and was used for that purpose in various parts of Europe as late as the 1940s.

The Eggs of Mhorr, or Baid-al-Mhorr as they are known in Arabic, are a form of kidney stones found in the stomach of the Mhorr gazelle (*Gazella dama mhorr*) from southern Morocco. Many ruminants have such concretions, or bezoars, in their intestines, but these particular ones are especially prized in oriental medicine as an antidote to poison. As a result the Mhorr gazelle, an elegant little animal about 30 inches (76cm) high and with curved horns, now survives only in the rocky deserts of the Sahara, and is rapidly being hunted to extinction.

Snake venoms are widely used. Cobra venom, for instance, is employed as a pain-killer, rattlesnake venom to treat epilepsy, and sand viper venom in a variety of preparations including injections for rheumatism and sciatica. In certain cases, large numbers of deadly snakes are kept in snake farms and regularly 'milked' for their venom. When a snake is milked, its head is held firmly over a Petri dish and its venom glands gently rubbed against the edge of the dish or massaged with the fingers. This releases about half the venom in its glands.

Finally, a Heidelberg chemist has discovered that the glands of an obscure water beetle contain as much cortexone as can be extracted from the adrenal glands of 1,300 cattle. Cortexone is vital in the synthesis of certain medicines, and currently sells for $65 a gramme. Commenting on the discovery, one scientist said that 'insects have become the new frontier for natural products chemistry'.

The Voyage of the Medina

The medina worm (*Dracunculus medinensis*) is a parasite which divides its time between crustaceans and human beings; and the life-cycle which connects these two improbable hosts is a mystery tour that depends on a chain of blind coincidence.

The female medina grows up to three feet long (91cm), though only 1.7 millimetres in diameter, and infects humans in tropical and subtropical regions, causing painful swellings of the skin, especially on the legs. When the leg is immersed in water, during swimming or bathing, the worm pushes her head out through the swollen blister and releases thousands of larvae. The larvae curl up and simply float in the water, for days or weeks, until they happen to meet a crustacean of the *Cyclops* family.

If they do not, they die; but if they are lucky and one comes along, they are suddenly activated by its presence and attach themselves to it. They then bore through the skin, lodge themselves in its interior, and pass through two larval stages before returning to the water.

Once more they float for days or weeks, this time in the unlikely hope that they will be swallowed by a human being. Simply bumping into them is not enough, they must actually be swallowed if the cycle is to be completed. Oddly enough, it does happen, because a few of them will inevitably get into drinking water.

Once inside their second host, they settle in the gut, where they develop into sexually mature adults over a period of about a year. They eventually mate, and the female then makes her way through the host's tissue to a suitable spot beneath the skin, where she lays her eggs and starts the whole cycle over again.

Migrations

The migration of animals is one of the great mysteries. The length of the journeys, the uncanny timing and the extraordinary accuracy of their navigation are almost supernatural.

The sooty tern is an attractive seabird which

inhabits a wide area off the coast of West Africa, and every year 10,000 of them cross the Atlantic to a tiny island off the tip of Florida called Bush Key. They build their nests there, and when the young are fully fledged, they make the return journey to Africa.

There is a race of golden plovers which make an even longer sea crossing, from Alaska to Hawaii and the Marquesas Islands. There seems no limit to the distance they are prepared to tackle. There is another kind of plover, for instance, which makes the incredible journey across two continents, from the north of Canada to the south of South America, and back, each year.

There is no doubt that they know the way. One particular Manx shearwater was taken from England to America by plane, released in Boston, and had no difficulty finding its way back to its nest in England twelve days later.

And it is not only birds which migrate, of course. Canadian biologists studying the homing instincts of fish, once marked half a million sockeye salmon in a tributary of the Frazer River. The following year, 11,000 of them were recovered from the same stream; although not one was found in any of the neighbouring streams or rivers.

How do they make these extraordinary journeys? For most migrating animals it is a matter of walking, flying, swimming, keeping their eyes open and following their leader, much as we would do. But some species are equipped with far more sophisticated guidance systems than we possess. The following are some of the optional extras that have recently been discovered.

The Black Rainbow

Many insects and birds, including pigeons, have polarized vision, and this has a curious but useful side-effect. If each eye is sensitive to light at a different angle, the polarity of the two images will interfere with each other when they are superimposed. (It is what you see when you look through two pairs of polarized sunglasses.) For a pigeon, the interference pattern looks like a dark 'rainbow' across the sky, that stretches from horizon to horizon and moves like the hands of a clock according to the angle of the sun. In fact, even when the sky is overcast, a pigeon can tell where the sun is, and therefore what time of day it is, by this slowly revolving band of shadow in the sky.

The Taste of Home

Visual systems, whether or not they are polarized, are not much use under water. Salmon and eels crossing the deep oceans have no use for clocks either. They live in a continuum, where the 'geography' is constant movement. They recognize where they are by how buoyant they feel (i.e. how salty the water is), how warm it is, how many micro-organisms are floating around them, how hard they have to swim against the current and, above all, what the water tastes like.

Their sense of taste (which is often misleadingly referred to as 'smell') is so acute that they can tell the slightest change in its chemical composition.

The salmon needed no map to find their way back to the Frazer River. All they had to remember was a simple code, such as 'Swim back up the current until you can taste your river'. From then on they followed the flavour, and when they were faced with a choice of rivers or a branch in the stream, they simply chose the one with the strongest taste. A thousand miles later, without having to think about it, they were back in their home creek.

Star Maps

It is now known that night-flying birds can navigate by the stars. In a classic series of experiments S. T. Emlen, of Cornell University, released a number of indigo buntings under the artificial night sky of a planetarium. The birds altered the flight in accordance with the position of the constellations even when they bore no relation to the sky outside.

As part of the experiments, the buntings were exposed to shortened and lengthened periods of daylight, so that one group thought it was time for the spring migration and another thought it was the autumn. When they were released in the planetarium, the spring group flew north and the autumn group flew south.

By progressively blacking out the constellations, Emlen discovered that the birds tended to steer by those around the Pole Star.

The Sixth Sense

If you were taken blindfold to an unfamiliar place and handed a compass, you could head north or south – or any other direction you chose – but you could not head for home. For that you would need both a compass *and* a map.

For homing pigeons to navigate six hundred miles back to their lofts in a single day, they must somehow acquire a map of the route, and a means of following it, which do not depend on sight, sound, smell, taste or touch.

In another series of experiments at Cornell University, this time by William T. Keeton, it was shown that pigeons do indeed possess this 'sixth' sense – a sense of magnetism.

Somewhere in their bodies is a highly accurate compass which can detect small variations in the earth's magnetism. The picture they get of it is a series of stripes or bands, rather like the rock strata on a geologist's map, which represent different strengths in the magnetic field. Although the signals are incredibly weak, they appear to be able to detect them even when they are travelling in a train or airplane.

In his experiments, Keeton eliminated all the other sensory signals, one by one. But even when they were blindfolded, the birds flew in the right direction. It was only when he attached tiny magnets around their necks that they lost their way and became confused.

It has since been established that many other animals possess this sense, from bacteria to fish, and that the 'internal compass' is exactly what the name implies – small flecks of magnetized material imbedded in nervous tissue.

The big question, of course, is whether we also possess it. Some people claim to have a 'bump of direction', and recent experiments with blindfolded subjects seem to bear this out. There is no hard evidence as yet, but the search is now on to find traces of magnetite in the human body.

Military Aid

'Cry Havoc! and let loose the dogs of war'
– Shakespeare

From Hannibal's elephants to biological warfare, an amazing variety of animals have been used as weapons on human battlefields – cats, bats, pigs and even beetles – but the most common has been 'man's best friend' (or, of course, enemy), the dog. They even award them medals.

The dogs of war were probably first let loose in the tribal battles between our hominid ancestors. At least four thousand years ago, according to bas-reliefs in the British Museum, Babylonian troops were accompanied by companies of mastiff-like dogs who harassed or attacked the enemy. When Julius Caesar invaded Britain in 55 BC, he was so impressed by the swiftness and ferocity of the war dogs of the Britons that he later had a number shipped back to Rome, where they caused a sensation in the arena.

The Spartans trained dogs fitted with spiked collars to charge into a mass of cavalry and stab and tear the horses' bellies. Dogs were used for the same purpose in Europe in the Middle Ages, and were often fitted with a complete coat of armour for their own protection. Alternatively, the dogs had pots of burning resin strapped to their backs and were sent against the cavalry belching fire, smoke and toxic fumes.

In his war against France, the Emperor Charles V employed several hundred war dogs sent to him by England's King Henry VIII. They fought so courageously that he urged his human soldiers to display the same kind of valour in combat.

In more recent times, military dogs have been relegated to auxiliary roles – as sentries, ammunition-carriers, messengers and ambulance dogs. In World War I both the Germans and the French used large numbers of dogs. The Germans set dogs to hauling heavy machine-guns, light artillery and one-man or two-man 'ambulances'. The French developed a particularly efficient messenger system using dogs to link forward patrols with base. Casualties on both sides were heavy; the French had five thousand highly trained military dogs killed or wounded.

Bat bombs, pigeon missiles and exploding pigs

In World War II many bizarre plans were developed to use animals as offensive weapons. The Russians carried out experiments in which trained dogs loaded with explosives ran under enemy tanks; an antenna activated a detonator, blowing up both tank and dog. They also trained sea lions to cut mine cables; while the Swedes toyed with the idea of using kamikaze seals to blow up submarines.

Allied proposals included an unlikely US Air Force scheme which involved rounding up some 30 million bats in 1943, with the intention of building a bat bomb. The idea was to attach to each bat an incendiary device weighing one ounce, and triggered by a delay fuse. The bats would be released over enemy cities where, it was hoped, they would fly into attics and under the eaves of houses and await ignition.

Following an investment of $2 million, the bats were declared operational in 1945, but were never used. When some of the bats were accidentally released, they destroyed a hangar and a general's car.

During early experiments on surface-to-air guided missiles in 1940, pigeons were installed in the nose of the Pelican missile to guide it on to its target by continuously pecking at its own image, projected through a lens system. Temporarily abandoned, the idea was renewed after the war at the Naval Research Laboratory in Washington as Project Orcon (standing for Organic Control), and later as Project Pigeon. Experiments in which pigeons were confronted with film simulating the dive of a 660 mph missile on to a target ship demonstrated that the bird's brain could be an effective control system, but the idea was never put into operation.

According to author David Rorvik in *As Man Becomes Machine*, 'The Russians . . . are experimenting with disembodied cats' brains . . . creating bio-cybernetic packages for implantation in air-to-air missiles. The cybernized cats' brains will, if all goes as planned, be able to recognize optical impulses emanating from their targets and to transmit guidance signals accordingly, so that the missiles always stay on target.' Rorvik's information came from the RAND Corporation's *Soviet Cybernetic Review*.

During the Middle East conflicts in the 1960s there were reports that the Israeli air-force had recruited pigeons as reconnaissance animals. One breed, the white carnaux, was trained to recognize up to eighty different ground features, including highways, rivers, buildings, and aircraft runways. Specific targets could then be located by training the birds to land on them while their flight was tracked via built-in electronic sensing devices.

Much of the early research with whales and dolphins was financed by the military. Dr Rehman of the US Navy's Ordnance Experimental Station at China Lake, California, wrote: 'If communication between dolphin and man could be established and the animal proved trustworthy, then they could be employed as guides to divers or to carry mechanical devices up to interesting submerged objects, to place mines in American and foreign harbours or on shipping lanes, or even to report by radio the presence and bearing of submarines on the high seas.'

Communication with dolphins was certainly established at some level. Michael Greenwood is a former Navy and CIA scientist who worked on biological weapon systems involving dolphins. In 1979 he testified for the defence at the trial of two men, Le Vasseur and Sipman, who were accused of stealing (or liberating, according to one's viewpoint) two experimental dolphins in Hawaii. Greenwood told the court that dolphins had been used to kill enemy frogmen during the Vietnam War by butting them with syringes loaded with a high-pressure gas that caused the lungs and stomach cavities to explode.

Vietnam provided the Americans with a testing ground for several animal systems. Dogs were trained as long-range sensors at the Land Warfare Laboratory north of Washington DC. Dr E. Carr-Harris showed, in experiments sponsored by the US Air Force, that dogs can be trained not only to sniff out mines, trip-wires, and dead or wounded bodies, but also to respond in different ways to each find. Dogs were used in Vietnam with electronic trackers fixed to their bellies which indicated where the animals stopped and whether they were sitting (which meant a mine) or lying down (indicating a body).

A species of large, oriental, cone-nosed bug was field-tested by the US Army in 'Vietnam-like' conditions as a device for tracking down enemy troops in the jungle. Dubbed 'combat bedbugs', they were carried in capsules and could sniff out a human at some considerable distance. When they sensed 'the nearness of human flesh', they emitted a 'yowl' which, when amplified, could be heard by the human ear.

Pigs have been trained in the past to sniff out mines and carry small loads in battle conditions, but recent experiments carried out at Animal Enterprises, Arkansas, were designed to establish whether they could carry loads *internally* as well.

Animal Enterprises is a curious establishment which specializes in 'brain-washing' animals – they have taught pigs, for instance, to dance and take showers. In this case, they cut open a number of wild boars and implanted such bizarre objects as wooden blocks, aluminium cylinders and ball-bearings in their abdominal cavities. The objects were coated with beeswax so that the boar's body would tolerate them more easily. The experiments proved that the animals could carry up to 25 lb internally.

Whether those 25 lb eventually turn out to be an electronic package or a bomb, the idea of an 'exploding pig' seems a fitting successor to the incendiary bats and the pigeon-guided missiles.

Missing, Believed Extinct

There is no frontier of extinction. It is not a matter of 'now you see them, now you don't', but a slow process that moves from concern to apprehension to growing certainty. After all, that prehistoric fish, the coelocanth, was thought to have been dead for

The crested shelduck

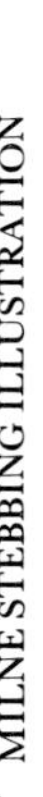

70 million years when a specimen was fished up off Madagascar in 1938.

The last specimens of the James Island rice rat were collected in the Galapagos in 1906, and it, too, was thought to be extinct until the skull of a recently dead animal was found in 1966. The magenta petrel, last recorded by an Italian ornithologist visiting the Pacific one hundred and ten years ago, was photographed at Whangerei in New Zealand in 1978.

The white-winged Guan was a rare Peruvian flower-eating bird last sighted in 1877, and known only through three museum specimens. Then an American ornithologist rediscovered it on a remote farm in Peru in October 1977. When questioned, the local residents told him: 'What's all the fuss about? The birds have been here all along.'

Another missing bird was the crested shelduck, which was to Chinese art what the scarab had been to the ancient Egyptians – a natural shape of such beauty that they adopted it as a symbol. With its dark, metallic green markings on a pearl-grey background, the shelduck appears over and over again in classical Chinese jade and porcelain, on screens and fans, in tapestries and books. It must once have been fairly common, but in this century it had been spotted only three times, in Korea, in 1913, 1916 and 1924.

But forty years later, in 1964, two experienced Russian bird-watchers saw what they thought were three of them, two ducks and a drake, mixed in with a flock of harlequin ducks south-west of Vladivostok. The sighting was confirmed when another pair, or possibly two of the original trio, were seen again in the same area. By sheltering with another species like the harlequins, the crested shelducks may yet cheat extinction.

But perhaps the strangest case of a creature being thought extinct and then rediscovered is that of the Socorro isopod. This little crustacean, about 10mm long, managed to maintain its place in evolution for 130 million years. But its numbers gradually declined until, by the middle of this century, its only known habitat was a small spring at Sedillo, in Mexico. Finally, in 1949, the spring was capped over and the isopod's long history seemed to have come to an end.

'They developed when New Mexico was covered

by the sea,' explained Mike Hatch, whose job is to save rare water creatures for the New Mexico Fish and Game Department (and whose interest in isopods is boundless). 'Then, as the sea receded, they made the change from saline to fresh water and began living in thermal springs. Man has now wiped out their native habitat. There's not a square inch that hasn't been interfered with.'

The isopods made a dramatic reappearance in 1978, when Hatch was glancing through some technical papers and came across a reference to an area of hot springs inhabited by 'bug-like' creatures. He went out hunting them with a partner, and discovered an entire population of the isopods living in 90 feet of drainpipe under an abandoned bath-house in New Mexico!

He told *New York Times* reporter Molly Ivins: 'The day we found the isopods, it was like we'd just made touchdown in a big game. We screamed and hugged each other – we clowned around a lot. But, you know, I really felt like handing out cigars. There are about 2,500 of them left in this one place. The thermal springs are a stable ecosystem – there are three of these springs right around here and two of them are linked up with this drainage ditch, where the last colony of isopods lives.'

Hatch had quite a battle to achieve official recognition. A spokesman from Washington eventually called and said no action had been taken because everyone thought the nomination was a joke. Hatch recalls: 'He said whenever they needed a good laugh, they'd take out my nomination of the isopod and read it over.'

This kind of attitude is nothing new to Hatch. 'I have a hard time getting people interested in saving them. You know how game wardens are. If I told them there was a rogue isopod loose down there, throwing boulders on the highway, they'd come in a flash. I'm always surprised by the limits of man's affection for the lower life forms. Everyone likes puppies and kittens and baby deer, but that's about as far as it goes.' After all, Hatch speculates, God may look like an amoeba. 'Man is so presumptuous. We weren't the first species on Earth and we won't be the last. These little guys have been here for 130 million years. I think they deserve some respect.'

Fortunately, the story has a happy ending, because the Socorro isopod has recently had the distinction of becoming the first crustacean to be included in the US Government's list of endangered species.

Mistaken Identity

The story goes that when Captain Cook first landed in Australia, he was intrigued by the strange animals he saw hopping about and asked a group of natives what they were called. The natives, who did not understand him, politely replied: 'Kangaroo' – a term which, it later transpired, meant 'I beg your pardon?' in their language.

True or not, it shows how easily an animal can acquire a misleading or totally inappropriate name. For instance:

— The king or horseshoe crab is not a crab but a primitive arthropod, measuring up to two feet (61cm) in length, which is more closely allied to scorpions and spiders than crabs. It is unique in possessing sky-blue blood.

— The Bombay duck is not a duck but a streamlined, salmon-like fish that occurs in the Indian ocean and irrupts in large numbers during the monsoon season. Dried and salted, the 12–16 inch (30–40cm) fish is an indispensable ingredient of a good Indian curry. But it has never been caught or seen near Bombay and the source of its popular name remains a mystery.

— The Spanish fly is not a fly but a beetle which causes an intense burning pain and a blister if touched – hence its alternate name, the blister beetle. Its redoubtable qualities, produced by a chemical called cantharidin, have also led to its use as an aphrodisiac (presumably on the principle that if it hurts, it must be effective), in diluted form. In the days when blistering was a popular technique in medicine, cantharidin was frequently used; Spanish fly ointments were prepared by drying the beetle in the sun, after immobilizing it with vinegar vapours. It was also taken internally for bladder problems, because of its diuretic qualities.

The larvae of the Spanish fly hatch on the ground and then crawl up flower stalks. When a honeybee settles on the flower, the larvae seize some of its hairs in their jaws and are transported back to the hive, where they feed on bees' eggs. In fact, when the beetle larvae were first observed on bees, they were dubbed 'bee-lice' – a further case of mistaken identity.

There are even occasions when animals and plants become confused. The aweto, or 'vegetable' caterpillar, is actually the discarded outer skin of the insect, filled with a kind of fungus.

The Horrible Moloch

The moloch is one of the weirdest of all lizards – a kind of reptilian porcupine whose body, legs and tail are covered with spines, including two especially large ones on its head. Its whole body is patterned in yellow, red, brown and black, which it can vary to some extent to match its background. There is only one species, which lives in central and southern Australia, and its official name is the *Moloch horridus*.

In spite of its ferocious appearance, the moloch is sluggish and entirely harmless. It feeds almost exclusively on black ants, for which it has a voracious appetite. Sitting beside an ant trail it licks up 20–30 of them a minute. According to one estimate, the average moloch meal consists of 1,800 black ants.

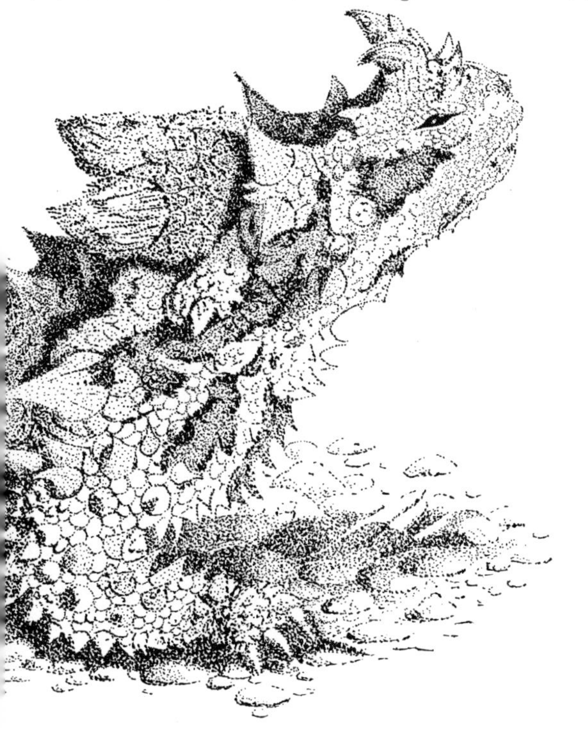

The animal has a bulge of fat on its neck which, in times of drought, it can use to produce water. Another curious adaptation to its desert environment is that when the moloch does come across water, its whole skin sucks it up in seconds. The water, however, is not drawn through the skin but into hundreds of tiny canals between its scales. All these canals converge on the corners of the moloch's mouth, so that it can drink just by chomping its jaws.

Mouth Breeding

There are many ways of incubating your eggs apart from sitting on them. The kurtus fish, for instance, keeps them in a special cavity in its forehead; and the Pipa toad carries them under the skin of her back. One of the most unusual techniques is that of the mouth-breeding frog (*Rhinoderma darwinii*), which was discovered by Charles Darwin in Argentina.

After the female frog lays her twenty-five or so eggs, the male stands guard over them for a couple of weeks and then, when they are about to hatch, picks them up with his tongue and allows them to slide down his throat so that they settle on his vocal sac. The male can carry up to seventeen tadpoles in this manner. A short time after they have developed into complete froglets, the father opens his mouth and they jump out.

Several species of fish are also mouth-breeders. Male cardinal fish, which are brilliant red and only about three-quarters of an inch long (2cm), can carry up to four hundred eggs in the mouth until they hatch. The gaff-topsail catfish carries this even further. The male carries up to fifty eggs for sixty-five days – during which time he does not eat – but even after they have hatched, he carefully guards them as they feed, and just as carefully draws them back into his mouth, settling on the ocean bed to sleep away the day. Only when the fry reach three inches (7.5cm) in length does the father finally relinquish his brood.

The same kind of mothercare is provided, most unexpectedly, by crocodiles. The female buries her eggs on land, but after they have hatched, she takes the babies into her mouth, providing a refuge until they have grown large enough to fend for themselves. The female Nile crocodile has a special pouch in the floor of her mouth in which she can accommodate six young at once.

N

The Horn of the Narwhal

The narwhal, known for centuries as the sea-unicorn, is one of the most mysterious species of whales. They acquired their name from the Norse *Na-r*, meaning a corpse, because their mottled appearance resembles a body that has been floating in sea water. But the most recognizable feature is their long, spiral horn which has been the source of legend and scientific speculation for centuries.

Narwhals are shy inhabitants of Arctic waters. They usually travel in groups of from three to ten, except for about four times in the summer, when they congregate in herds of hundreds or even thousands.

The adults are 12–15 feet (3.75–4.5m) long, and each of the males sports a 6–8 foot long tusk or spear made of brittle ivory. It is twisted like a corkscrew and always spirals from right to left, even in the rare case of a double-tusked animal.

There are many theories about the use of this horn: as an ice piercer, a defensive or offensive weapon, as a secondary sexual characteristic like a man's beard, or as a visual stimulus for the opposite sex. Herman Melvilles's jovial theory in *Moby Dick* was that the whale used it as a page-turner, to help it wade through pamphlets.

One unusual theory is suggested by Dr Peter Beamish, a bio-acoustician who believes the males use it for what he calls 'acoustic jousting', radiating sounds from the tip of their horns in order to repel rival males from their harem. Obviously a long tusk is an advantage in this, as it can be placed closer to a rival's ear and produce a louder sound!

The only analysis of the narwhal's underwater sounds, carried out by cetologists at the Woods Hole Oceanographic Institute, suggests that the regular clicks it produces are used for communication rather than echo-location.

Unfortunately, the narwhal's horn has made it a valuable prey for hunters. Medieval monks believed that powder made from them was 'a very powerful and almost universally applicable medicine' which could be used for curing sore eyes, heartburn, and corns, as well as overcoming feminine modesty. European monarchs believed that horn goblets were a foolproof way of detecting poisons.

The Eskimos still hunt the narwhal and sell the tusks to the Hudson Bay Company for $30–$35 each. They also eat the inch-thick skin, which they call *muktuk* and which contains as much vitamin C as melons, raspberries or potatoes.

The Shell of the Nautilus

When the giant sea-shells of the Pacific and Caribbean first arrived in Europe, no one thought of them as animals. They were a form of treasure. The original inhabitants were no more than dried shreds which had to be scraped out to reveal the pearly nacre underneath. The pale pink spiral of the nautilus shell, in particular, was so beautiful it was mounted in gold or set with jewels and used for an exotic drinking cup.

Aristotle believed that they were blown along by the wind, using their arms as sails, but no one really knew what they looked like until the Dutch naturalist, Rumphius, working in Indonesia in 1705, described them properly for the first time. It is only in the last century that their life story has been pieced together.

The nautilus is of special interest to zoologists because it is the 'missing link' between the humble shellfish and advanced, free-swimming creatures like the squid and the octopus. These animals are so different that it is difficult to see the connection, but they are all molluscs, and there is a direct line of descent.

The nautilus still has a snail-like shell of its ancestors, but it evolved a revolutionary new use for it – as a buoyancy chamber. Instead of using it as a protective canopy anchored to the sea bed, it pumped it full of gas so that it acted like an underwater balloon and allowed the creature to float.

By adjusting the pressure in the various chambers, it could spend the day resting on the bottom, and rise to the surface at night in search of food. But to make the most of this new three-dimensional environment, it has to learn how to swim.

The single, muscular foot of its predecessors was no longer needed for crawling along the bottom, so it expanded outwards as flaps and tentacles. It developed gills, and a gentle form of jet propulsion, and so became the first mollusc to take command of its own destiny.

The pressures of its new lifestyle encouraged the development of better eyesight, balance organs, a more efficient metabolism, and a host of other features. It became a predator that hunted for its food rather than waiting for it to come along. This, in turn, needed sharper reflexes, and as its instincts and behaviour pattern became more elaborate, it developed a larger brain.

In fact it was far more than just a pretty shell. By changing the rules of the game, the nautilus opened up a whole new pathway of evolution.

RAY WINDER

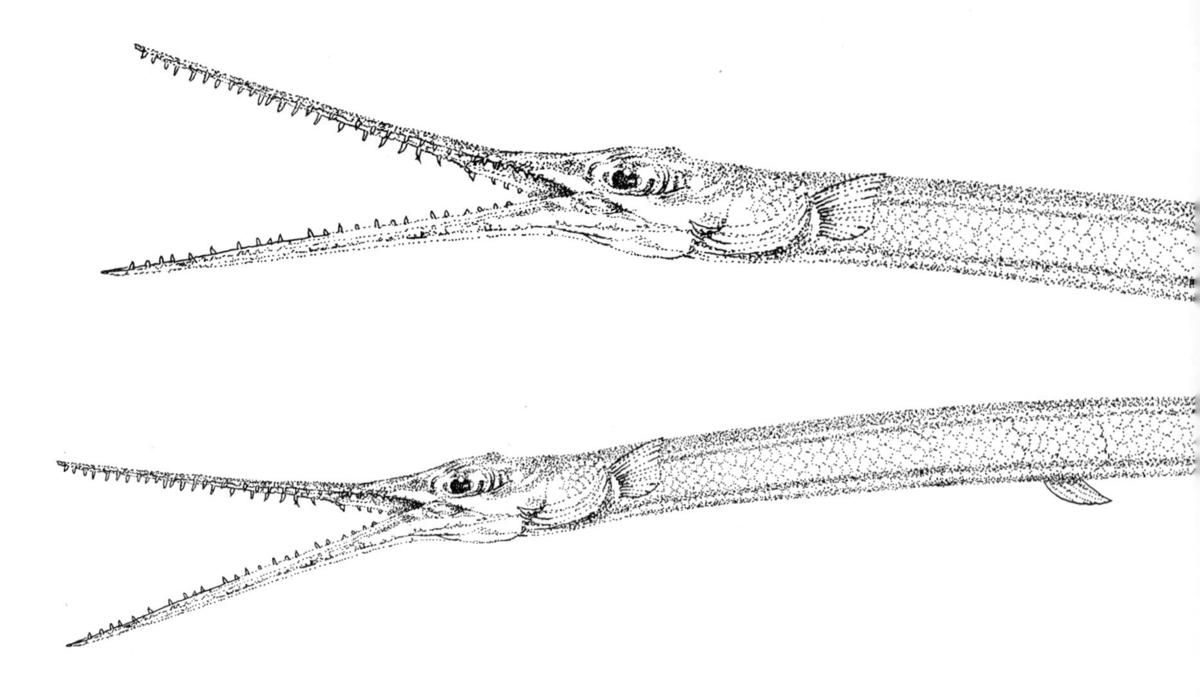

Needlefish

Narwhals and creatures like swordfish occasionally use their protuberances to impale other fish. But the sharpest of marine creatures are probably the needlefish or houndfish, which are nearly five feet (1.5m) long, weigh 10–12 lb, and swim frantically about, leaping out of the water when excited or confused.

There are several documented cases of people being injured on such occasions. Twenty-year-old Lorelei Sullivan, for instance, recently had to have a piece of the fish's beak surgically removed from the side of her nose after such an incident.

The Nematodes

Most people have never heard of the nematodes or threadworms, and only a handful of the species – like the Medina worm – have common names. Yet they are the most abundant multicellular organisms on earth. Relatively immune to heat and cold, flood and drought, they have invaded almost every place where life can be maintained, from the Antarctic ice to the human gut.

It has been estimated that an average cubic foot of soil contains six million of them. The American zoologist N. A. Cobb once said that if the entire material of the world disappeared, the Earth would still be recognizable as a ghostly hollow ball consisting of nematodes. Mountains, rivers, oceans, valleys, deserts and forests, even towns and animals, would still be outlined by the worms they contained.

About 15,000 species of threadworms have been identified, and new ones are discovered at a rate of 250 a year. One source estimates that there may be as many as 500,000 species in existence.

The majority of them resemble pale, semi-transparent threads, although the marine species often have a pink or blue shimmer. The smallest, at one-tenth of a millimetre, is the plant parasite *Sphaeronema minutissimus*. The largest, *Placentonema gigantissimus*, inhabits the placenta of sperm whales and can reach a length of 25 feet (7.5m).

A large number of them are parasites which cause diseases in plants and animals, including human beings. One intestinal inhabitant, *Ascaris lumbricoides*, causes stomach problems and diarrhoea in children. Another is responsible for elephantiasis. Hookworms, guinea worms, whipworms and kidney worms are all the cause of illness and even death, especially in the Third World. It was recently estimated that 644 million people were infected with ascarids alone, 356 million with whipworms and 457 million with hookworms.

Threadworms have sensory structures that respond to light, touch and chemical stimulus. They can move by whip-like motions of their bodies, but

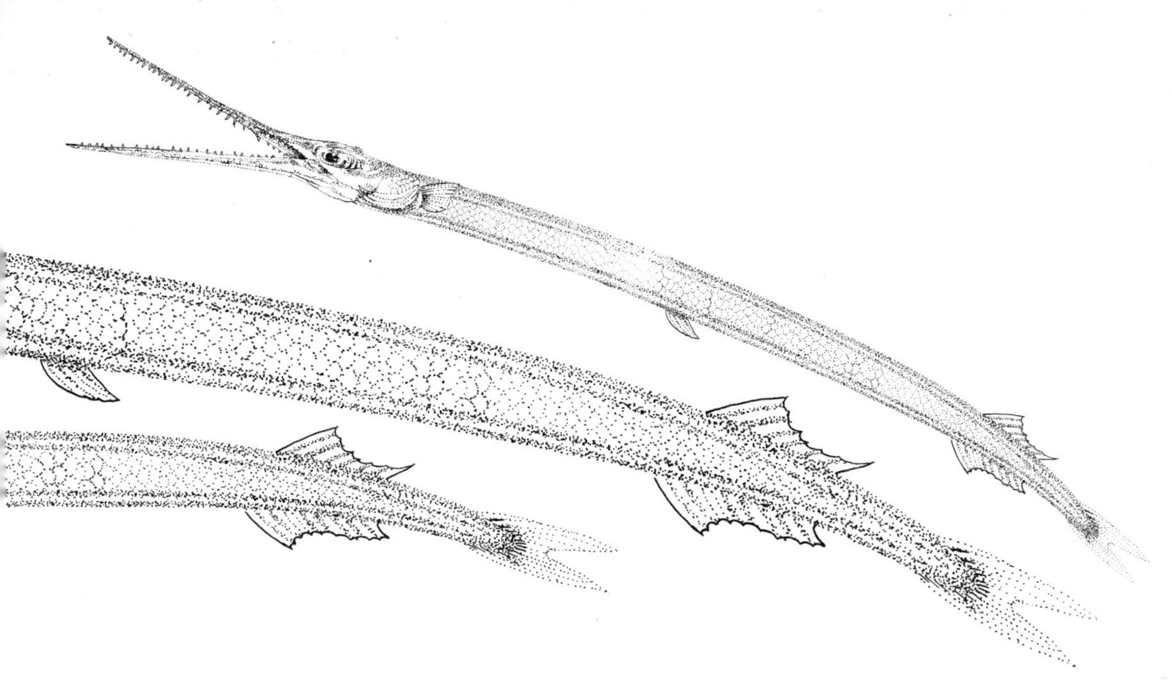
CATHERINE BRADBURY

Needlefish

their spread around the world is largely due to passive travel. Plant parasites, for instance, may be carried from one field to another on the hooves of cattle or the tyres of a tractor; and encapsulated nematodes can simply be blown from one place to another on the wind.

Animal parasites, on the other hand, usually wait for their host to come along and then hitch a ride. This may involve clinging to a blade of grass for weeks or months until the smell of a passing animal triggers their dormant instincts and they make a wild leap for it. Others enter their host by pure chance, through its food or drinking water; and some species, like the Medina worm (see earlier), go through regular cycles, inhabiting one animal after another and making long migrations through their hosts' bodies to get in and out.

The secret of this haphazard lifestyle is their profligate numbers. Countless billions of them never make it, but it only needs one or two chance encounters to produce the next generation of the species.

Newts

Newts have jaws with minute teeth and a muscular tongue which, when shot out, carries the whole floor of the mouth with it. Having no appreciation of size, newts sometimes choke on prey too large for them. Snails are often swallowed whole, the body digested and the shell passed unbroken.

The only sound newts make is a faint squeak like someone drawing a wet finger quickly over glass.

Pond-dwelling amphibians that grow three to four inches (7.5–10cm) long, they can change colour from light to dark over a period of days, and regularly shed their skin. It comes away complete with fingers and toes, the only holes being for the mouth and eyes. It is often eaten by its ex-owner.

How newts fertilize each other was discovered in 1880 when Gasco, an Italian naturalist, mounted a clear glass aquarium on his ceiling to study the whole process. The male newt displays his crest, packed with sense organs, to prepare the female. He then drops a packet of sperm (a spermatophore) which the female collects by pressing her cloaca against it, a trick she carries out with startling accuracy. The sperm is then stored inside a special receptacle until ready for fertilization.

Young newts are quite often found in the state of *neoteny* – instead of maturing from the larval stage, they remain larvae but grow in size. Neotenous newts are garish creatures, lemon yellow on top, white underneath, with pink or scarlet gills.

Warty newts, a large European species, live for up to twenty-seven years. They secrete a white, gummy fluid in defence. It smells of horse-radish, is extremely bitter, and irritates and burns the skin.

The Octopus

The octopus is a mollusc with emotions – the most highly evolved creature in the world that is not a mammal, with a nervous system as complex as ours, and possessed of what Jacques Cousteau described as 'the soft intelligence'.

Unlike the manic activity of squids, it has returned to a quiet life at the bottom of the ocean, an intensely shy and nervous animal which leads a solitary existence in the deepest cave or crevice it can find.

However, it can move with lightning speed and coordination to escape from enemies or to snatch in any passing prey. Its preferred diet is crabs, which it eats by pecking a hole in their shells and injecting a poisonous saliva that first paralyses and then liquefies the victim so that the octopus can suck it out.

Victor Hugo was the first to popularize the octopus as a horrible monster in his novel *The Toilers of the Sea*, where a sailor is consumed by an eight-tentacled 'devilfish'. 'The tiger can only devour you,' he wrote, 'but the devilfish *inhales* you. To be eaten alive is more than terrible, but to be *drunk alive* is inexpressible.'

The truth is that octopuses have never been known to attack, let alone bite, a human being. There are a few reports of them grabbing divers for a 'feel'. but they have always released them after the examination. The only injuries or deaths attributable to the creatures have resulted from people accidentally stepping on the blue-ringed octopus, which happens to be poisonous.

Far from being monsters, most of the 150 species are less than 3 feet across. One species is full grown at half an inch while the giant of the family, *Octopus hongkongensis*, grows to a maximum of 30 feet.

Their brains are larger and more complex than a squid's, with a distinct frontal lobe – the area which, in the human brain, is associated with the higher thought processes. It is an alien intelligence that evolved in very different circumstances from ours, but thanks to the pioneering work of the biologist J. Z. Young, at the Stazione Zoologica in Naples, we have some idea of what the octopus 'thinks' about.

For instance, it is the only higher animal that has two separate visual systems. Unlike our own, its eyes are not stereoscopic, but point in different directions, and each is connected to its own half of the brain. In other words it sees, and can act on, different events simultaneously. Gravity plays an important but mysterious part in this. The octopus places such importance on which way up it is, that each eye is controlled by a separate gravity-sensing device to keep it level.

However, most of its information about the world comes from the incredibly sensitive skin of its tentacles. This is something quite beyond our experience because, when an octopus touches something, it not only feels it, but tastes and smells it at the same time. It can carry out a complex chemical analysis by the tip of one tentacle. Its taste-buds can discriminate between different species of crabs through their shells, and it can tell the difference between, say, glass and metal from their surface texture alone.

This information is not simply acted on by blind instinct, but passed on to the conscious area of the frontal lobe, so that the octopus can actually think about it. Within the undifferentiated nervous tissue of its 'upper' brain, the creature can remember what happened to it before, brood on it, associate ideas, learn from its experience, and plan for the future. The result may be very different from what we think about, but there is no other word for it but intelligence.

The tiny blanket octopus (*Tremoctopus*) is even a tool user, collecting the tentacles of the Portuguese man-of-war, a type of stinging jellyfish, cutting them to the right length, and using them defensively in battle or offensively to shock and kill the shrimps it eats.

At a New Jersey aquarium one octopus was observed to kill a cockroach and place it outside its lair; it then hid until an unsuspecting crab came along to investigate, when it pounced on its real prey.

It is tempting to speculate on what would have happened if the octopus had left the sea, in the way that simpler molluscs like slugs and snails have done, and continued its evolution on dry land. Unfortunately, there are now overriding reasons why it will never make the transition. No land animal of that size could move without a skeleton, and its skin is far too thin and sensitive, but the main reason is the sheer inefficiency of its metabolism.

The essential prerequisite of surviving in freshwater, let alone fresh air, is the ability to regulate the osmotic pressure (i.e. the salt content) of the blood. This, in turn, is a function of the molluscan kidneys, which are adequate for small, simple creatures like snails, but hopelessly inadequate for the complex metabolism of the octopus.

At the same time, the octopus's bloodstream carries oxygen in the form of a copper-based pigment called haemocyanin, which is not nearly as efficient as our iron-based haemoglobin. Within its buoyant, balanced saltwater environment, none of this matters. On land, without the energy to move, suffocating and poisoned by its own bloodstream, its situation would be fatal.

The octopus decided on these evolutionary patterns a long time ago, and developed them to an astonishing degree. But they were the wrong choice, and paradoxically it is now too sophisticated and too specialized – and too successful – to change.

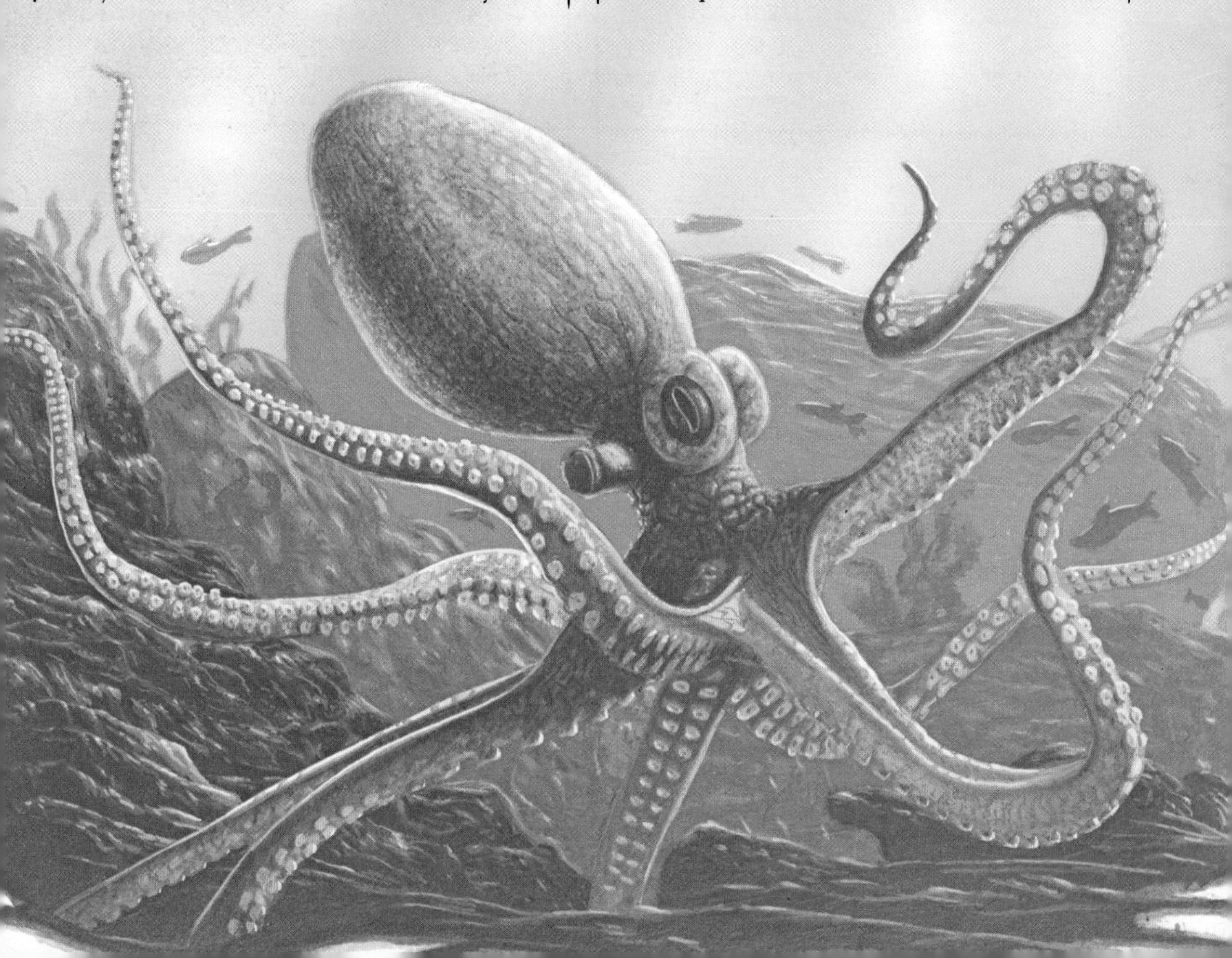

Oil-Birds

Oil-birds are a nocturnal species from tropical America which are closely related to nightjars, but have a lifestyle all their own. They are one of the very few birds that are equipped with sonar, and the only night-flying species in the world that eats fruit.

They spend the daylight hours in deep caves where they find their way about, like bats, by echo-location. They use a frequency range of about 6–10 kilocycles, which is much lower than the 70 kilocycles used by bats, but still well beyond the limit of human hearing.

At night they fly out in search of the oily fruit of palm trees, which is how they acquired their name. They do not use sonar in the open air, but rely on their very sensitive night vision, keeping in touch with each other with harsh, rather discordant cries. The palm fruit has a pungent aroma and it is thought that oil-birds may be the only birds apart from kiwis with a sense of smell.

The Ojam

The ojam, or *Galago*, is the attractive bundle of fur with saucer-like eyes commonly known as the bush-baby. It is a tree-climbing animal from equatorial Africa, and its huge liquid brown eyes are the obvious sign of a nocturnal species. But what merits its inclusion here are its other, lesser known characteristics such as a revolving head and (believe it or not) a mouth organ.

MILNE STEBBING ILLUSTRATION

The ojams spend the day in hollow trees or dense foliage, clinging together in groups of three or four with their limbs so entwined it is impossible to tell them apart. At night, however, they come alive and scamper about in search of fruit or birds' eggs, uttering the plaintive, almost human, cries which acquired them their name.

Their remarkable climbing skills are largely due to long, slender toes equipped with suction pads that enable them to run up and down trees without using their claws. Oddly enough for such an agile animal, their eyes are fixed in their sockets and cannot be moved around like ours. To compensate for this, they have evolved unusually flexible neck joints which enable them to swivel their heads through 180 degrees. They can even face directly backwards over their own shoulders!

But this is not their only peculiarity. Together with a few other lemur-like animals, such as the aye-aye, they have evolved a most unusual mouth organ (or rather, organ in their mouth). It consists of a strip of cartilage with a row of sharp spikes, like a comb, which fits under their tongue. The analogy with a comb is appropriate because this appears to be its purpose. The animals have been seen using it to free the fine hairs that get caught between their teeth, and to remove burrs and twigs from their fur. The only other phenomenon remotely like this (and it is wild comparison) are the enormous plates of cartilage in the mouth of baleen whales that are used for sieving krill.

The ojams may look like soft toys, but it is wise to remember those claws which, in one species, end in needle-sharp points. Although they are said to make docile pets, like many 'cuddly' animals they can be most aggressive, and in the wild they often engage in vicious fights to the death.

The Olm

In the underground lakes of certain deep caves in Yugoslavia, there lives a kind of salamander called the olm. Not that it matters what you call it, because the species which inhabit these black, silent, anonymous worlds tend to lose their identity as they adapt to a minimal lifestyle. There is no need for ritual colours or behaviour in a world without sight; and there is no need for sight (and very few of the other senses) in a changeless environment where nothing ever happens and even the biological clocks slow down.

In the olm's case, the water is cold enough to inhibit the activity of its thyroid gland (which controls growth) and prevents it ever growing beyond the larval stage. The blind, white, shapeless creature lives out its whole life as a child.

However, unlike the other ghost-species, the olm still shows some signs of its original identity. Though no one will ever see them, it retains a pair of flamboyant, bright red gills, and when it is removed from the timeless dark, and exposed to the light of day, its skin darkens like a developing photograph, and its life processes resume.

Opossums

Small and defenceless, it is a wonder that the opossums have survived at all, yet today they can boast of a rapidly expanding population and the conquest of territories far from their original home in South America. The seventy-six species of opossum are the only marsupials existing outside Australia. X million years ago, when South and North America became linked, the more efficient placental mammals migrated down over the land bridge at Panama and quickly killed off all marsupials except the opossums. Yet these small creatures, which range from the size of a mouse to that of a cat, have no special armour or other means of protection. They have brains that are small for their body weight, and are relatively slow-moving. But they have a few strategic assets: extremely acute hearing, the ability to feign death, an unpleasant taste which most carnivores avoid, and the ability to endure pain or injury which would kill animals of comparable size.

Opossums have faces like rats, with hairless ears reminiscent of bats. Their tails, which are frequently longer than their bodies, tend to be partially or completely bare, and are prehensile like those of certain monkeys; though opossums only use them as a kind of anchor when climbing, and never wrap them around a branch or use them as a true 'fifth hand'.

Most species live in forests and parklands. The yellow woolly opossum has adapted to urban life and can be observed in the trees lining the traffic-jammed streets of South American cities. The common North American opossum has extended its range into Canada, but during a hard winter may lose its naked ears and tail as a result of frostbite. They are flexible animals who will use any dark hole as a den, from a cavity in the trunk of a jungle tree to the space beneath the floor-boards of a modern house.

Opossums have the rare and curious ability to open their mouths by more than 90 degrees. They can retain this threatening appearance for fifteen minutes, displaying rows of fearsome tiny teeth and hissing furiously at an intruder.

Opossums were the first marsupials to be discovered by Europeans, and were thought to be unique until the discovery of Australia. The Spanish explorer Pinzon brought an opossum with young in her pouch home from the New World in the late sixteenth century and presented it to King Ferdinand and Queen Isabel. They slipped their fingers inside the pouch and 'were astounded that such a peculiarity should occur in nature'.

The yapoks or water opossums have adapted to an aquatic existence and live near creeks, ponds and rivers. They have webs between the toes of their hind feet, and long bristles on their faces like otters and seals. For a long time zoologists puzzled over what the female yapok did with her young while hunting underwater for shellfish and fish spawn. How did she prevent them from drowning? Finally it was found that her marsupial pouch opens towards her rear and can be closed completely watertight by her well-developed sphincter muscles – thus creating 'a small air-filled nursery' with a temporary supply of oxygen.

TIM HAYWARD

Most opossum species have forward-opening pouches, of course, though a few do not have pouches at all. Their gestation period is extremely short. In the North American opossum it is only thirteen days. The twenty-five or so young are born, all within the space of five minutes, as minute, barely-formed creatures weighing only a sixth of a gramme. The whole litter will fit into a teaspoon. These worm-like babies then have to make a three-inch journey from the vaginal opening to the entrance to the marsupial pouch, all by their own efforts. In other words, the moment they are born they are faced with an epic migration through their mother's fur. Usually only half of them survive, which is perhaps a good thing since there are only thirteen teats inside the mother's pouch; if more than thirteen newborn reach the pouch, the latecomers die of starvation.

The young climb out of the pouch after about ten weeks and are completely independent at 3–4 months. In pouchless species, the newborn simply hang on to the mother's teats by their teeth. 'My heart beat faster,' wrote Wolfgang Gewalt, 'whenever I observed the mouse opossum mother swinging recklessly through the twigs with her eleven appendages. As a result of her hasty movement, the youngsters dangled in all directions. Some would bounce against twigs, become caught in a forked twig, or even fall to the ground. A lost baby would immediately scream piercingly, a sound well within the ultrasonic region and not audible to human ears. The mother responded quickly to the cries of her lost young.'

In the human sound range, the hearing of opossums is so acute that they will flinch, and even jerk as if in pain, at a noise as slight as the rustling of paper. This auditory sensitivity is no doubt a major advantage in detecting potential predators.

North American descriptions of the opossum have traditionally emphasized its terrible odour. This was said to be so noxious that it could penetrate wood or stone, and even make Indians topple over dead. In fact, opossums smell no worse than other animals, but it does seem that most carnivores regard them as distinctly unappetizing. Foxes never eat them, and a dog that pounces on an opossum will shake it a few times but then leave its carcass alone. In some rural parts of the United States, however, the animals are considered a delicacy when eaten with sweet potatoes – though the gourmet is recommended to 'concentrate on the potatoes'. There are even photographs of President Franklin D. Roosevelt eating roast opossum.

During periods of cold, drought and hunger, opossums are able to sink into a condition of 'lethargy' similar to hibernation. All their body systems slow down and they live off deposits of fat under the skin. In one case, a group of opossums were found in the cold-storage hold of a banana boat from Latin America. Since green bananas are not palatable to them, they had spent the weeks of the journey to Hamburg in the state of lethargy, waiting for more favourable circumstances to arise. In fact, they ended up in zoos.

This lethargic state is quite distinct from the opossum's ability to voluntarily enter a condition of paralysis approximating death. Playing possum is a common technique amongst insects, reptiles and birds, but is rare in mammals. In this state, the opossum lies on its side, with its eyes closed and its tongue hanging out of its mouth. It can be carried around by its tail for some time, completely unmoving until it suddenly comes alive again.

Some years ago Dr J. D. Black of the University of Kansas examined the skeletons of ninety-five opossums in the university museum. To his astonishment he found that over a third had recovered from broken bones – injuries which would have killed other animals of the same size. The opossum has been described as 'the great pain endurer, which lives by submitting and gritting its teeth' and this remarkable ability to recover from injuries may have a lot to do with its survival as a species.

Opossums colonized the North American continent millions of years ago, but in recent times they have also been introduced into New Zealand, the West Indies and Madagascar. The population in New Zealand is today estimated at over 30 million, and is increasing at the incredible rate of 6–7 million per year.

The Latin name for the opossum family is *Didelphidae*. Like most marsupials, opossums have paired uteri with two separate exits. *Didelphis* means 'two vaginas'.

The Ostrich Trick

Human beings are the only species who 'bury their heads in the sand'. The old story that ostriches react in this way at the approach of danger says more about our stupidity than theirs. No animal can afford to ignore a danger; however apprehensive or frightened it may be, it will always react.

The fable was first invented by the ancient Arabs, and later taken up by the Greeks and Romans, who had a taste for bizarre animal stories, and so it was passed down to us.

It is not true, of course, and an insult to one of the most sharp-witted – and aggressive – of creatures. But there is an ingenious strategy ostriches sometimes use to escape from pursuers in open country, which might be mistaken for it.

The metabolism of an ostrich, especially its heart, is so efficient that it can run at 50 mph for up to half an hour at a time – a feat unequalled by any other animal. With a head start, an adult ostrich can easily out-distance a predator but this is not enough, on its own, to ensure all their safety. Young birds cannot keep up with the pace, which slows down the rest of the herd, and because of their shape the birds are conspicuous targets, which can be seen, and followed from a distance.

The African species stands more than 9 feet (2.75m) high, and when they are running, their bounding strides add another 4 feet to their height. To overcome this handicap they have developed a 'disappearing act', whereby they suddenly throw themselves full-length flat on the ground. To a predator, say, half a mile away, the birds simply vanish from the horizon, and there is no way to distinguish them from the background of bushes and scrub.

The ostriches lie perfectly still until the danger is past, but if the pursuers catch up with them the birds will leap to their feet again and run off.

Incidentally, if you are trapped in a group of hysterical ostriches, you should fall flat on your face. Even in extreme panic, the birds will not tread on you.

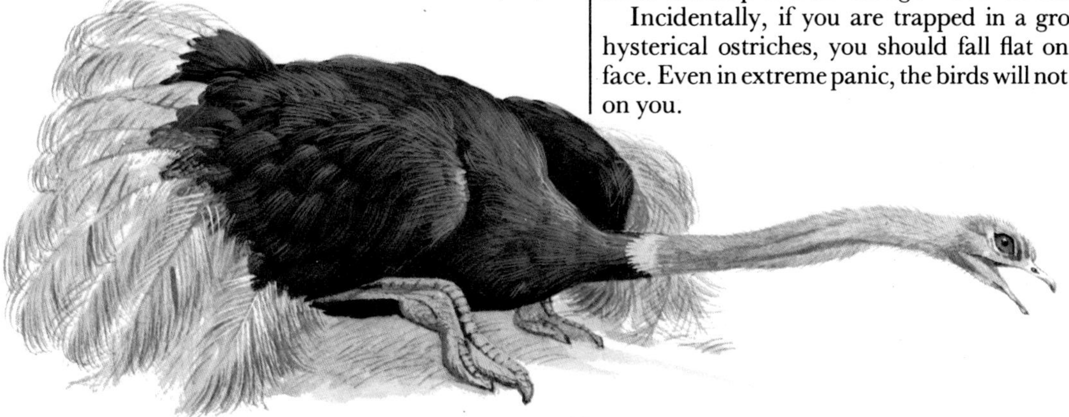

The Passenger Pigeons

'It was proverbial with our fathers that, if the Great Father in his wisdom could have created a more elegant bird in plumage, form and movement, he never did.'
– Chief Pokagon of the Michigan Indians.

The passenger pigeon was once so numerous that at the beginning of the nineteenth century it constituted one half of the *entire* bird population of North America, and its mass migration were one of the greatest spectacles of the natural world.

John James Audubon, the great American naturalist, once witnessed such a phenomenon. He described how they came low out of the north-east like a gigantic pink cloud driven by a hurricane. As predatory hawks circled above them, the pigeons suddenly split, with almost military precision, into great coiling, snake-like formations. Then, as the hawks began to strike, these snakes rushed together into a single, compact mass with a noise like thunder. They dived and swept close above the ground at incredible speed, and then soared straight up into a vast column, before wheeling and twisting in a continuous line like the coils of a giant serpent.

When the birds reformed after their evasive action, Audubon estimated that they formed a single column, over a mile wide, which passed overhead at a rate of about a mile a minute. They obscured the sun and turned day into an unnerving twilight over an area of nearly 80 square miles, and he calculated that the flock must have contained about a billion birds!

The passenger pigeon's usual habitat was in the endless forests of Quebec and Ontario, where it fed mainly on acorns. The birds tended to concentrate in certain areas. One of these northern nesting sites covered an area 3 miles wide and 30 miles long, containing between 30 and 50 million birds. In the winter they usually migrated southwards in smaller groups, but once every ten years or so, when the acorn crop failed, the birds assembled in their countless millions and migrated as a single, enormous body.

Their roosting places along the way would occupy vast areas of forest. After their departure, the ground would be covered several inches deep with their dung, the grass and bushes destroyed, the surface strewn with branches that had collapsed under their weight, and the trees themselves 'killed as if girdled with an axe', over thousands of acres.

The naturalist Alexander Wilson wrote: 'The marks of this desolation remain for many years on the spot. Numerous places could be pointed to where, for several years after, scarcely a vegetable made its appearance.' Wilson also described one of the pigeons' mass breeding places near Shelbyville, Kentucky. It stretched through the woods for forty miles. 'In this tract almost every tree was furnished with nests wherever the branches would accommodate them . . . The noise was so great as to terrify the horses of people coming to have a look and it was difficult for one person to hear another speak . . . The view through the wood presented a perpetual tumult of crowding and falling multitudes of pigeons, their wings roaring like thunder, mingled with the frequent crash of falling timber.'

The last mass nesting occurred at Petosky, Michigan, in 1878. By that time, the birds were commercially hunted on a systematic basis, and an average of ten million were being killed every year. They fetched 50 cents a dozen on the Chicago market, and a pigeon hunter could expect to make $10–$40 a day.

Last-minute attempts to rescue the species failed, because they were unable to breed in captivity; and in 1914 (the same year that another American bird, the Carolina parakeet, became extinct) the very last passenger pigeon, called Martha, died in the Cincinnati zoological gardens.

Pets

Whether you regard them as friends, toys, status symbols, substitute children – or just a form of psychotherapy – pets have been with us since the beginning. The earliest record of animals being treated as companions, rather than food, comes from one of the first human settlements in the Levant, about 15,000 years ago.

The Natufian people were hunter-gatherers who had put down roots, and their culture had advanced enough to make tools, build houses and organize burial grounds (usually the first sign of religious belief). In 1978, two Israeli archaeologists were working on a Natufian site when they uncovered a grave containing the skeleton of a man. He lay on his side, with his knees drawn up in the huddled position of most primitive burials, and his hand was resting with an obvious gesture of affection on the skeleton of a 4 or 5 month old puppy, which lay by his head.

Jewelled Eels and the President's Alligator

In later times the history of pets tends to be the history of their famous owners.

Some took them seriously – like Nero with his pet tigress, Phoebe; or the Emperor Charlemagne with his elephant, Abul Abba, which was presented to him by the Caliph of Baghdad and accompanied him everywhere – but the choice of animal often depended on a whim of fashion.

For instance, the Romans used to breed domestic fish, including the murena eel (*Muraena muraena*), which was especially popular at banquets. But it was also considered chic to adopt them as pets, and gossip at the time recorded that Antonia, the daughter of Drusus, fitted hers with golden earrings; and Marcus Crassus went one better, with earrings and a jewelled necklace.

The French monarchy was obsessed with animals and, apart from building zoos, their permanent successes include the introduction of canaries to Europe (by Louis XI) and the invention of the goldfish bowl (by Louis XV, who was an ardent fish-fancier).

By Victorian times pets were a part of the furniture, and the tradition is kept up by modern heads of state, from the Queen of England's corgis to the extraordinary variety of animals kept by American presidents.

John Quincy Adams, for instance, kept an alligator in the East Room of the White House, and his staff would amuse themselves by showing guests into the room, and watching their hurried departure. Calvin Coolidge had a pet racoon which he took for walks on a leash; and Teddy Roosevelt kept a whole menagerie, including bears, zebras and a hyena, at his summer White House on Long Island. But the most eccentric presidential pet was probably Warren Harding's Airedale terrier, Laddie Boy, which was provided with its own valet and had a special chair at cabinet meetings.

Many pets have been immortalized in literature, often in fictional disguise. For instance, the character of the Dormouse in *Alice in Wonderland* is supposed to be based on a pet wombat owned by Dante Gabriel Rossetti, which had a habit of falling asleep at table.

Some of the oddest animals make the best pets. Pigs, for instance, are noble animals, about whom we will have more to say later, but it is worth mentioning in passing that both Sir Walter Raleigh and the rock singer James Taylor have kept them as pets. Waterhole Ike, the pet of Mark Cowley of Golconda, Nevada, is the only pig in the world with a savings account registered in its name – and its own social security number, a condition insisted on by the bank.

TIM HAYWARD

In Florida, in 1977, a posse of police were savaged by a pig. The owner of an illicit crop of marijuana had trained a large sow to guard it. When the police raided the patch, the watch-pig bit two of the sheriff's deputies before it was subdued.

The size of the present pet population is staggering. There are 5 million pet dogs licensed in Britain, 8 million in Germany, and 16 million in France – but this is nothing compared to the United States, where there are an estimated 40 million dogs, 40 million cats, 15 million caged birds, and 10 million other pets.

The range of animals kept by people in their homes is just as astonishing. Robert Lehman recently made a film called *Manimals* about the pets he had discovered in New York. This is how the review in *Variety* summed it up:

'Lehman settles down to enumerating what is going on behind closed doors. Namely: gila monsters, pink poodles, lion cubs, racoons, doves, possums, sheepdogs that hate the country, bees, rabbits, seals, geese, mice, hamsters, frogs, owls, tarantulas, cows, goats, a parrot in a New York city cop car, another parrot in a New York Yankees uniform complete with mitt and cap, a turtle whose owner puts him in the tub and gives him a simulated thunderstorm by turning on the shower and flicking on and off the light, leopards, weasels, a toothbrush-wielding monkey, crayfish, porcupines, gorillas, crocodiles, coyotes, and other assorted bugs, rats, fuzzy-wuzzies, creepy-crawlies and monsters that defy description.'

The Psychology of Pets

The word 'cosset' was originally an eighteenth-century expression meaning a lamb which had been reared by hand. The fact that it came to be used as a verb for the affectionate treatment of any animal illustrates the emotional (and, according to psychologists, highly significant) relationship that can develop between pets and their owners.

Freud, in a letter, described the relationship between dogs and people as an opportunity to give affection without ambivalence, and a chance to admire a life free from the almost unbearable conflicts of civilization.

Professor Aaron Katcher, who teaches a course entitled 'The Nature of the Bond between Humans and Animals' has come up with some interesting observations after considerable study. For instance, men fondle their pets in exactly the same way that women do, so the idea that women used dogs as a substitute for maternal care is an invidious sexist stereotype.

When people stroke their pets, their heartbeat and blood pressure both diminish. Ninety per cent of owners talk to their pets, a relaxing habit which is less stressful than human conversation. Katcher has also discovered that when dogs and humans sleep together, their sleep and dreaming cycles are synchronized.

And it is not only our mental health which is affected. Studies by Dr Erika Friedmann of the University of Pennsylvania showed that eleven out of thirty-nine petless coronary patients died within a year of their heart attacks, compared with only three out of fifty-three patients who owned pets. Friedmann suggests that 'pets are a form of social contact that . . . keep you from being totally preoccupied with yourself'.

Other academic research has raised different questions about the pet-human relationship. For instance, Dr Michael Ostrowski of Harper College, Illinois, has argued that the choice of pet betrays the owner's innermost personality (no less). If you own a dog, according to his theory, you have an affectionate and generous nature. Birds mean you are possessive, while cat owners are cool and aloof. People with tanks of tropical fish are unwilling to become emotionally involved, but mouse and hamster owners are innocent and totally trusting.

Just where that leaves the owners of gila monsters, coyotes, tarantulas or geese remains uncertain.

Piddock Tunnels and the Underground Submarine

It is difficult to imagine an animal which could tunnel through solid metal, but there is a kind of mollusc, called the piddock, which is known to have bored holes right through the cast-iron supports of piers and bridges.

These spectacular demonstrations of its drilling technique are largely accidental, though, because the piddock prefers to spend its life grinding through rocks. It does so by anchoring itself with its muscular foot and rocking and twisting its whole shell, so that the surface is gradually scoured away by rows of minute teeth.

The technique is slow, but it produces a perfectly smooth rounded tunnel. Once its course is set, the piddock continues in a straight line, often boring through other piddocks' tunnels, and even the piddocks themselves. Which animal bores through which presumably depends on the angle at which they happen to meet.

Curiously enough, for a creature that spends its whole life entombed in rock, the piddock is strongly phosphorescent and glows with a powerful bluish-green light. But, then, their whole existence is extraordinary.

Unlike the creatures which burrow through earth, they are not making a 'home' for themselves in the rock. They do not excavate chambers, or move in and out, and since they cannot turn round, they are not even aware of the tunnel behind them. They live in solitary confinement, hemmed in on every side in a space no larger than their own bodies, without day or night, purpose or choice or direction – nothing but the single, obsessive instinct that drives them onwards.

Yet the piddocks are not alone in this behaviour, because there is a whole range of tunnelling molluscs which have evolved a similar lifestyle.

The best known – and most notorious – of these is the shipworm, which, despite its name, is another bivalve. Its chosen medium is not rock, but wood that is immersed in seawater, and since its tunnels are a quarter inch wide and up to a foot long, so can easily penetrate the hull of a boat, it has long been regarded as a menace to shipping and harbour installations.

This problem attracted the attention of the Victorian engineer, Isambard Kingdom Brunel, and though he failed to solve it, his studies had an unexpected but useful result. It was by observing the way that the creature 'screwed' itself into the wood, scraping away with the serrated edges of its shell as it revolved (so that the diameter of the tunnel was wider than the shell itself), that he hit upon the idea for the rotary shield still used in tunnelling operations today.

As shipworms seldom meet one another, it is rather difficult for them to reproduce; and they cannot even escape from the wood, because just before the tunnel reaches the surface, it narrows to a pinhole effectively trapping the creature in its burrow. So, in order to maintain the species, both male and female pass their reproductive products out to sea with the current, where the eggs are fertilized and the next generation of larvae develop.

The sort of damage that shipworms can do was dramatically demonstrated in San Francisco in 1920, when they were responsible for the collapse of 20 million dollars' worth of wharves and docks.

It was the collapse of another engineering project, the Bell Rock lighthouse in the Firth of Forth, a century earlier, which led to the discovery of another tunneller. When the lighthouse builder, Robert Stephenson, examined the wreckage, he found that the timbers had been eaten away by a tiny creature, about one-fifth of an inch long, called the gribble.

Unlike the others, it is not a mollusc but an insect similar to a woodlouse, which chews its way into the wood with a powerful set of jaws.

However, the strangest of all tunnelling techniques has been evolved by a curious little animal the size, shape and colour of a ripe date, and called (not unnaturally) the date mussel. Scratching, screwing and chewing have their advantages, but the date mussel literally *melts* its way through rock.

This strange creature has a special gland which produces acid capable of dissolving chalk and limestone, and surrounded by a fizzing bath of this substance it actually 'swims' through the rock.

On the face of it, this seems a hazardous method for any mollusc to adopt, because its own shell is made of calcium and just as likely to dissolve as the rock around it. But nature has an answer to everything, and the date mussel has evolved a layer of horny material to protect it from its own corrosive fluid. And so, sealed in its plastic coating like a small underground submarine, it moves through a totally hostile environment, as isolated from the rest of nature as it is possible to be.

Pigeon Post and the Yak Express

In an emergency you can put your message in a bottle, or tie it to a balloon, or rely on runners with cleft sticks. But the safest door-to-door delivery is still by carrier pigeon.

The pigeon post is thought to have originated in China around 500 BC. Pigeon lofts were set up in all the major towns, and government officials travelled with baskets of carrier pigeons.

By the thirteenth century Kublai Khan had linked the entire Chinese empire with a network of pigeon-post relays, a system that survived until the end of the nineteenth century when there was an Imperial Pigeon Post still working at the court of the last Empress of China.

The Greeks learnt about carrier pigeons from the Persians, and the crusaders brought them back to Europe.

One of the most famous uses of carrier pigeons was by Nathan Rothschild in 1814, when he received word of Napoleon's defeat at Waterloo twenty-four hours before the general public. As a result he made a killing on the Stock Exchange and consolidated an already massive banking empire.

Pigeons were employed to carry messages when Paris was surrounded by German troops in 1870, and over 15,000 government telegrams and a million airmail messages were delivered in this fashion.

In 1886 the first airmail connection between London and the United States was established by pigeons. In 1890 the German Army set up a 'military pigeon post'. During World War II, some 20,000 carrier pigeons were released from British planes over occupied France.

The famous Reuter's news agency used to employ carrier pigeons, and Japanese newspaper publishers still do. It is still the cheapest way of transmitting lengthy reports – and often the fastest.

The birds have proved just as useful in transporting other things than mail. The first-ever aerial photographs were taken by camera-carrying pigeons in the nineteenth century, and they have even been used to transport blood samples and drugs between various London hospitals.

More recently, pigeons strapped to the undersides of helicopters have been tested at the US Naval Oceans Systems Centre in Hawaii as a means of detecting people lost at sea. Human helicopter crews only detect some 40 per cent of such people, but the pigeons scored 90 per cent every time. The birds are trained to peck at a switch whenever they spot the colour orange (life vests), yellow (most life rafts) or red (distress flares). The switch connects to a light in the cockpit which tells the pilot when and where to search ('and which bird to reward with food'.) Douglas Conley, who conceived the programme, said of the pigeons: 'They're cheap, docile and very light. They find the target long before the pilots do. They can't be too dumb.'

However, to return to postal animals, one has only to think of the Pony Express to realize that four legs can be as effective as a pair of wings. Their famous slogan that 'The mails must get through' still applies, but there are places where ponies must give way to more appropriate forms of transport. Even the rough riders of the Wild West would have found it hard going across the Sahara or the Himalayas.

Herman Dembeck has compiled this catalogue of postal quadrupeds which are still in use in the more inaccessible parts of the world:

— Dromedaries carrying a mounted postal messenger and 90–110 lb of mail, covering 40–50 miles a day, in Arabia and north Africa.
— Teams of 9–18 Laika dogs hauling a covered sled with one mailman, one passenger and 200 lb of mail, in Kamchatka, Siberia; the teams cover 20 miles a day in rough terrain, 50 miles a day on the plains. Eskimo dogs are used in Alaska and northern Canada.
— Llamas with mounted mailman and 50–60 lb of mail, in the Andes of Bolivia, Peru, Chile and Argentina.
— Elephants with mounted mailman and 400–600 lb of mail, or in teams of two elephants hauling a stagecoach with driver, four passengers and 400 lb of mail. They cover 35-45 miles a day in India and south-east Asia.
— Two reindeer pulling a sled with mailman and 125–150 lb of mail, covering 50–60 miles a day in Canada and Siberia. Express service using relays of reindeers can cover up to 100 miles daily.
— Yaks with mounted mailman and 65 lb of mail, sometimes accompanied by additional pack yak with a further 170–200 lb, covering 15–20 miles a day in central Asia. In the same part of the world a mule-mounted mailman sometimes leads a string of postal sheep carrying 25–30 lb of mail each.
— Single Altai wapiti (a large type of elk) with mounted mailman, or two wapiti drawing a sled with mailman and passenger, in Siberia.

In Praise of Pigs

'No man should be allowed to be president who doesn't understand hogs.'

– Harry S. Truman

Condemned by two world religions, ignored by Western culture, and insulted in everyday speech, the pig is the most maligned and misunderstood of all domestic animals.

'Stop hogging it all' – 'You eat like a pig' – 'You live like a pig' – 'This place is a pigsty' – 'You stupid pig' – 'You swine' – the hurtful catalogue runs right through our language.

We talk about hogwash, roadhog, ham, swine, to be high on the hog, or to go the whole hog. Pigs are the epitome of greed, and synonymous with dirt. Lazy pig, pig-in-the-middle, pig-in-a-poke, the fall-guy of every cliché and the butt of every joke. If ever an animal was entitled to sue the human race for slander, it is the pig.

Walt Disney made them the pink little victims of

the Big Bad Wolf – although pigs in their once-wild state would have seen the wolf off the premises before it could huff its first puff. George Orwell made them the greedy dictators of *Animal Farm*, which was a slight improvement, because at least he gave them credit for being shrewd. But all these conceptions are wrong.

Contrary to its public image, the pig is a paragon of intelligence, with an enquiring mind and a capacity for sustained wonder. 'It is not suspicious or shrinkingly submissive like cattle and sheep,' wrote the naturalist W. H. Hudson, 'nor an impudent devil-may-care like the goat; nor hostile like the goose; nor condescending like the cat; nor a flattering parasite like the dog. He views us as fellow-citizens and brothers, and takes it for granted, or grunted, that we understand his language.

If we all lived like pigs, the world would be a cleaner place. Pigs only wallow in mud through force of circumstance. Their skin lacks major sweat glands, and they need to keep it cool in order to regulate their body heat. Given the choice, and access to water, they are immaculately clean animals, and bathe as often as they can. They love swimming because their fat makes them buoyant, and they show a marked preference for clean water.

Trapped in a pigsty, they have little choice in the matter, but the pig is such a meticulous animal that it will always dung in the corner furthest away from where it sleeps.

'As for greed,' wrote the English novelist John Beresford, 'not even the most sincere apologist of pigs or lover of bacon can deny that they enjoy their victuals.' Pigs eat a lot, it is true, but they are most discriminating and, unlike humans and horses, they never over-eat. For instance, they are not very fond of fruit, and in common with many other animals have a strong dislike of onions. In one classic experiment, a pig was presented with a choice of 243 vegetables. It refused to touch 171 of them and partook of the others with varying degrees of enthusiasm.

Pigs are immune to snake venom and will eat most varieties of poisonous snake. It is not known why they are immune, but it is possible that their thick layer of fat neutralizes the venom in some way. 'A pig'll slurp a snake down just like a piece of spaghetti,' a Kansas farmer was quoted as saying. 'They just love 'em. I keep a couple of hogs down at the cattle pond, just for insurance; that's where a lot of cows get snake bite. You see, a snake can't hurt a pig, not even a poisonous one.'

Swine first evolved about 39 million years ago, which makes them older than man; and along with goats and sheep they were the first animals to be domesticated when humans began establishing permanent settlements. Pigs are reluctant to be herded anywhere and would have been useless to nomadic tribes – which may be one of the reasons they were considered 'unclean'. However, over the centuries they were gradually domesticated throughout Europe, and selective breeding eventually produced the benign porker we know today.

The pig's chubby pink stereotype gives no idea of their variety. The voluptuous Poland China, with its swollen thighs and spiral tail, comes closest to the 'piggy bank' image; but colours range from the glossy black coat of the Hampshire to the vivid orange hair of the Bush Pig. And pigs vary in size from this fierce little animal, with the body of a drag-racer and a long tapering snout, to domestic species like the great Yorkshire White – a slab-sided container of an animal, four or five times its size.

There is no doubt about their usefulness. Pigs consume half the corn supply of the United States each year, and 75 million of them are slaughtered to provide an annual supply of 65 lb of pork per head of the population. But that is only the beginning.

Although a pig is 65 per cent food, the rest of it is used in the manufacture of more than five hundred products, including glues, disinfectants, a high-quality leather (which 'breathes' better, because the bristle holes go right through the skin) and medical products.

Sterilized pigskin is used in hospitals for treating burns, and a bioplasticized form is used for artificial heart-valves; and because their metabolism is remarkably similar to our own, pigs supply us with insulin for diabetics, thyroxine to treat underactive thyroids, and a compound from their pituitary gland called ACTH, which is used to relieve rheumatic fever and arthritis.

Because their bodies and internal organs are so like ours, they are increasingly used as experimental subjects. There is even a 'mini-pig', bred specially for the purpose, with the same average weight and body surface as a human being. A 'guinea-pig', in fact, which can be used to test the toxicity of new chemicals, experimental surgical techniques (like organ transplants), and the effects of auto crashes.

But pigs have advantages in their own right, including an acute sense of smell, which are put to less gruesome (and some would say better) use – in the hunting of truffles. This delicacy of French cuisine, which fetches up to £100 a pound, is a kind of fungus that grows from two to twelve inches

(5–30cm) underground. The truffles take some finding, and the pig demonstrates an effortless superiority over dogs in this task. Dogs need to cover the ground each day because they can only detect truffles when they are really ripe. Pigs, however, only have to sniff out the ground once a week.

Pigs may be fat, but to the discerning eye of G. K. Chesterton there was no doubt about their beauty. 'The actual lines of a pig (I mean a really fat pig) are among the loveliest and most luxuriant in nature; the pig has the same great curves, swift and yet heavy, which we see in rushing water or in a rolling cloud.'

But Chesterton was a convert (and a fairly stout one at that) and such praise is rare. Although there is a whole genre of painting devoted to horses, artists have not been moved by the pig. There are no great statues of pigs, and one has to go back as far as ancient Greece to find a serious school of pig-painting. Literature has passed them by and, with the exception of nursery rhymes, the poets have remained uninspired. To put it bluntly, the pig has been written out of history.

Fortunately, however, there are signs that things are changing. One notable champion of the beast was the English humorist, P. G. Wodehouse, who wrote a whole series of novels celebrating pigs in general, and one animal in particular – the legendary Empress of Blandings, a sow of vast proportions and impeccable pedigree, who was doted on by her equally blue-blooded owner.

Wodehouse imbued his creation with such dignity she became The Pig incarnate, the grande-dame of all her kind – as noble an archetype, in her way, as King Kong is for gorillas, or Kermit for frogs. Except that, as anyone who has seen the Muppets knows, the real star of their show happens to be the only pig ever nominated for a Hollywood Oscar.

If it takes the sex-appeal of a pink felt puppet to change our attitude, at least it is a step in the right direction. For it is we who are the losers in not recognizing what a remarkable animal we have been living with – for being so 'pig ignorant'.

Play

The idea of animals playing games may sound rather whimsical, but one has only to watch puppies and kittens to realize that they have a deadly serious purpose. For most young animals these games are a way of practising the skills of hunting and fighting they will need in later life. However, there are exceptions – activities that animals seem to indulge in for no other purpose than sheer enjoyment.

Wolves, for instance, have been seen playing games of tag with ravens. Pairs of ghost and fiddler crabs have been observed running along beaches at high speed, apparently for no better reason than the excitement of the race. Even the tiny Socorro isopods seem to have invented a game whereby they climb on a leaf until it sinks to the bottom, and then let it rise to the surface again for another ride.

The young sea lions in the waters around the Galapagos Islands sometimes team up to play a particular game with the marine iguanas that live on the rocky island shores and feed off the underwater seaweed. 'Pushing each other like elbowing children, the sea lions compete to grab the reptile by the tail and drag it through the water like a toy,' writes naturalist Tui De Roy Moore. 'Or they follow it to the shore, only to flip it back in the water at the last possible moment.'

There are even some birds which seem to possess a sense of fun, especially toucans, who are the jokers of the South American forests. They often beat their huge beaks against a branch, apparently because they enjoy the noise. Sometimes one toucan will seize another by its beak and push it backwards until it falls off its perch. Alternatively one will toss up berries which a bird on a higher perch tries to catch. Their most distinctive sport is fencing with their beaks, which was described by an ornithologist who observed this behaviour in Panama:

'I saw fourteen toucans scattered about in a big leafless tree in the centre of the jungle. Two appeared to be fencing. They stood in one spot and fenced with their bills for half a minute or so, rested, and were at it again. Presently they flew off into the forest, and then I noticed two others that had now begun to fence . . . They did not move about much while fencing, although sometimes one climbed above the other as though to gain an advantage. They fenced against each other's beak and never seemed to strike at the body. There was a fairly rapid give and take, the bills clattering loudly against each other.'

Monkeys, of course, are notoriously playful. The red-backed squirrel monkey, or saimari, which lives in the Amazon jungle, is reputed to ambush wild pigs just for the fun of it, leaping down on them from trees and riding them – literally piggyback – for as long as they can hold on.

Gorillas, as one would expect, are even more inventive, and the young ones, those under about six years, have been seen playing a whole variety of games including 'king of the castle', where one of them defends a tree stump or hillock against the others; and 'catch', where they throw round fruit or gourds from one to another.

There is no doubt that whales, dolphins and the higher primates, like chimpanzees, play games for fun in exactly the same way that we do. There are far too many examples to go into here, but one remarkable fact is worth mentioning: dolphins in marine circuses are known to invent their own new tricks. For instance, without any prompting from their human attendants, they will discuss some variation in their performance in a lengthy conversation (in both sound and sonar) and then carry out a new display of leaps or twists with split-second timing.

The Poison Paradox

Animals have evolved a lethal range of poisons to kill, maim or simply digest each other, but they are surprisingly selective. For every dote there seems to be an antidote, and a substance that reduces one animal to instant purée may have no effect on another.

A porcupine, for instance, can eat as much opium in one go as a human addict smokes in two weeks, and wash it down with enough prussic acid to poison a regiment, without so much as a burp.

Common parsley is poison to parrots, while datura and henbane, which are deadly to human beings, are common foods for a snail.

When penicillin was discovered, fortunately no one tried it out on guinea-pigs, because it kills them outright. On the other hand, they can happily eat strychnine.

The birdwing butterfly will only feed on a plant called Dutchman's Pipe, which is extremely dangerous to humans and many other animals because it contains an abortive substance called prostglandis.

And so it goes on . . . sheep can swallow arsenic, owls can eat potassium cyanide, and rabbits thrive on belladonna. Morphine, which calms and anaesthetizes human beings, produces manic excitement in cats and mice; while tuberkulin, which cures TB in guinea-pigs, actually causes it in humans.

Some animals have an unbelievable resistance to toxins. An Australian scientist, who was trying to find a way to kill sharks, injected them with thirty different poisons without effect. Eventually, with some relief, he discovered that they succumbed to strychnine nitrate, though it took more than eight minutes for them to keel over.

The Potto

The potto has the unique distinction of being the only mammal with part of its backbone *outside* its body.

It is a small, slow, tree-climbing animal from Africa, which looks like a loris and hangs upside-down from branches like a sloth. The spinal column itself is internal, but each of its vertebrae has a bony spike projecting through a hole in its skin to form a row of sharp teeth down its back.

These are usually concealed in a coat of thick yellow fur, but when the animal is threatened it flattens the hairs on either side to expose its armoury, and then doubles up, with its head between its hind legs, so that the spikes form a gleaming white circle around its body.

Normally this is enough to put off any predator, but if the encounter escalates to open conflict, the potto has several options. It can charge forward like a battering ram, or stand its ground like a hedgehog and let the other animal damage itself, or hurl itself forward in a series of rolling cartwheels so that the spikes rip into its enemy's flesh like a bandsaw.

It is surprising that the potto should have evolved this strange weaponry, because it is a gentle animal (in West Africa it is known as the 'softly-softly') which spends most of its time in the trees and has few natural enemies. And it already possesses a means of defence in the form of its powerful hands, with large thumbs and toes, and a grip so strong that it is impossible to break its hold on a branch, even when it is dead. But it lacks the claws of a sloth, and its reactions are probably too slow for it to get involved in hand-to-hand combat.

The Pudu

The pudu is officially classified as a species of deer, but one would hardly recognize it as such. The fully-grown adult 'stag' is about the size of a fox terrier, the female is even smaller, and a baby pudu looks like nothing so much as a hamster with hooves.

Although they bear little resemblance to the elegant horned animals we think of as deer, they belong to the same order, the Cervines, and they just happen to be the smallest breed.

They live on the slopes of the Andes, from Colombia to the tip of Chile, and are sometimes found on the offshore islands. Their horns are almost invisible, and because of their thick reddish brown hair and rather canine heads, they are often mistaken for dogs. They have even been adopted, with some success, as domestic pets.

Q

LINDA GARLAND

The Quagga

The quagga may, or may not, be the rarest zebra. It definitely is (or was) a zebra, *Equus quagga*, a beautiful animal with an unusual three-colour coat consisting of black and cream stripes on a brown background. Whether it still exists is another matter, because it is thought to have been hunted to death in South Africa during the last century, and must now be listed as another species that is 'missing, believed extinct'.

Quaggas were relatively slow animals, an easier shot than antelope, for instance, and for several decades they provided the main source of food for the native labourers in the colony. The last wild quagga was shot near Kingwilliamstown, in the Orange Free State, in 1861. They survived a few more years in captivity, but the last known specimen eventually died in the Berlin zoo in 1875.

However, it is still not certain that they are extinct. There may still be a breeding colony at large, because occasional sightings of the animals are still reported from remote areas of south-west Africa.

Queen Victoria's Butterfly

Queen Victoria gave her name to so many cities, states, styles of architecture, and even a period of history, that it is surprising how few animals are named after her. However, there is one species that commemorates her and, appropriately enough, it is one of the largest and most beautiful insects on earth – the giant birdwing butterfly.

With its enormous 10-inch (25-cm) wing-span of brilliantly iridescent colours and its slow majestic flight, the birdwings are truly noble creatures. So a tradition grew up of dedicating each new species to the royalty of the time. Apart from Queen Victoria, Queen Adelaide also had one named after her, and so did one of the famous 'White Rajahs' of Sarawak, Rajah Brooke. By general consent, his species (*Troides brookiana*) is the most beautiful, but a magnificent variety with long swallow-tail wings (*Ornithoptera paradisea*) comes a close second.

They were originally called birdwings (*Ornithoptera*) because of their size, but they also have some curiously bird-like characteristics. For instance, it is the male who wears the plumage, while the female birdwing makes do with dowdy colours, speckled evenly all over with white. They also share the same environment as birds.

Butterfly collectors had great difficulty in finding them at first, until they realized that they spent their lives in the tree-top canopy and seldom came down to ground level. This made them just as difficult to catch as birds, and collectors eventually had to resort to the same solution. Incredible as it sounds, they actually shot them down with guns, using a charge of 'dust shot'. Would you believe butterfly guns? But, then, almost everything about the birdwings is a little larger than life.

The Quetzal

The quetzal, whose plumes were once as precious as jade or gold, was sacred to the ancient civilizations of Central America, and the Aztecs regarded it as the living spirit of Quetzalcoatl – the Plumed Serpent.

The long tail feathers were so valuable that only noblemen could wear them. Fortunately, it was not necessary to kill the bird to obtain them, because the quetzal belongs to a family of birds called *trogons* whose skin is so fragile that the feathers fall out easily. So their captors learned to pluck them, and set the quetzals free to grow more.

The bird is still honoured in Guatemala, where it is the national symbol. The country's second largest city is called Quetzaltenango, its highest honour is the Order of the Quetzal, and even the Guatemalan currency is named after it (a quarter quetzal piece shows the bird perched incongruously on an Ionic column).

The reason for its fame is that the quetzal is, quite simply, one of the rarest and most beautiful birds on earth. It is found only in remote rain forests – an inaccessibility that probably saved it from extinction at the hands of Europeans.

Its underside is scarlet, the back a deep blue-green, and everything else – from its crested head and neck to the wings and immensely long tail coverts – is an iridescent golden-green. And, as if this dazzling plumage was not enough, it gives itself away as it swoops through the jungle by flashes of white underfeathers.

It is a relatively small bird. From beak to tail it measures about 14 inches (35.5cm), but the tail coverts trail another 2–3 feet behind it. This shimmering train is so long that it is impossible for the quetzal to take off from a branch in the usual way without ripping it to shreds. Instead it launches itself backwards into space, like a parachutist leaving an aircraft.

Its nesting habits make life even more difficult. Instead of constructing a nest in the open, which it could comfortably sit on, it takes up residence in hollow trees, like an owl. The local Indians were convinced that its nest had two holes, one to go in by (leaving the tail outside) and the other to use as an exit. In fact, there is only one small entrance, which the quetzal backs into. When the bird is safely tucked up inside, the tail goes up the rear wall, bends over its head, and hangs out through the hole in front of it.

When it takes to the air, the tail becomes a positive advantage. It acts like the tail of a kite, giving extra stability in flight, and the bird is so skilful at aerobatics that it can eat fruit and berries on the wing, like a flycatcher.

However, beauty is only skin-deep – or, in the case of the quetzal, an optical illusion — because the feathers do not actually glitter, and it has recently been discovered that they are not even green. When examined under a scanning electron microscope to a magnification of one thousand times, the pigment in the feathers was found to consist of tiny brown granules spaced about 5,400 angstroms apart. The wavelength of green light is in this range, and it is the interference pattern set up by the granules that gives off the greenish hues.

ROGER GARLAND

The Quill Pig

Erethizon dorsatum possesses one of the most famous and formidable defence systems in nature. A member of the rodent family, its common name derives from the Latin *porcus* (swine) and *spina* (thorn), and for centuries it – the porcupine – was known as the quill pig.

When the animal is relaxed, its armoury of 30,000 sharply pointed spears lie along its body, protected by long guard hairs so that it does not prick itself. But when it is threatened or attacked, the porcupine rattles them menacingly; and if its growls and stamping are ignored, it braces its stubby legs and tucks its head under its bulging stomach, so that the quills stand fiercely erect.

Each of them is under complete muscular control, and in the case of the crested porcupine they may be 28 inches (70cm) long, so they make a formidable array.

The animal then turns around and backs into its opponent, lashing its tail back and forth. It has no wish to get stuck to the other animal, so the quills are designed to break off easily. They are so loosely attached that they occasionally fly off, which gave rise to the story that porcupines can shoot them like arrows.

In fact, as a ramming machine, porcupines are not very efficient, and a predator will only come to grief if it tries to embrace one. If, for example, a desperate bobcat leaps on top of a porcupine, its paws and face will be riddled with quills, and it will roll off howling in pain.

The tip of each quill is as sharp as a needle, and just behind the point are rows of minute barbs, like fish-hooks, which make it impossible to extract without tearing the victim's flesh. On the other hand, if the quills are not removed, muscular action will draw them deeper and deeper into the victim.

Although they look ungainly, porcupines are one of the fastest animals on four legs. When alarmed they are inclined to rush hysterically through the undergrowth with complete disregard for obstacles, and the smaller species will sometimes knock themselves out by running into logs, or shoot out into ponds and streams, and have to swim back. Fortunately they are quite good swimmers.

Porcupines turn up everywhere, from the tropics to the Arctic, and there is even a quill-less species (*Trichys lipura*) in Borneo. In northern Canada, you are likely to find them looking down from the branches of trees, where they often spend the winter to avoid the snow on the ground.

This tree-climbing species (*Coendou prehensilis*), as its name implies, has a prehensile tail which it coils around branches like a giant two-foot-long chameleon. Porcupines are very fond of salt, but the tree-climber has positive obsession for it. It has been known to gnaw the handles of farm implements that have been moistened with human sweat, and it will even chew bottles discarded by campers because of the salt in the glass.

North American tree porcupine

The Quokka

The quokka's main claim to fame, apart from its delightful name, is that it solved the mystery of the kangaroo's stomach.

The quokka, or Rottnest Island wallaby, has been more extensively studied than any other small Australian marsupial. It is small and docile, which made study easier, but what most attracted scientists was what it revealed about the marsupial digestion.

Many species of kangaroos and wallabies are browsing herbivores, like cows, but they are not true ruminants. That is to say they do not chew cud or regurgitate it from one stomach to another. Their internal organs are much simpler and, in the case of the smaller animals, there is not enough room in their bodies for multiple stomachs. Which raises the problem of how they manage to cope with something as indigestible as grass.

As it happened, the analogy with cows turned out to be misleading, because their digestive system is more like a sheep's. Instead of using its own enzymes to digest the food, it was found that a part of its stomach, called the caecum, contained a strain of cellulose-dissolving bacteria, similar to those in a sheep's rumen.

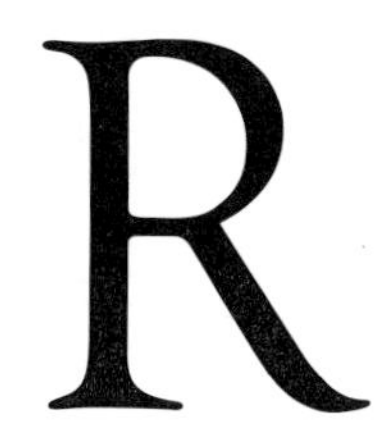

Rats!

It is difficult to look at the rat objectively. The sight of a rat means just one thing to most of us – a gut response of revulsion and hostility.

Consider this tragic account of how a responsible, adult citizen was reduced to a gibbering wreck by a single rodent. It is the report filed in October 1977, by Police Officer Steve Briggs of Fort Lauderdale, Florida, after he was called out to deal with a rat in a woman's bathroom.

'The undersigned, while equipped with a nightstick, entered the bathroom. At this time, the rodent was observed and the undersigned proceeded to attempt to destroy it.

'However, during the course of this officer's action, the animal, due to its size, was able to outmanoeuvre the undersigned. At one point, the rodent approached this officer in a very quick manner, and therefore in an attempt to avoid the possibility of being bitten, the undersigned quickly jumped on to the bathroom sink cabinet.

'Meanwhile, the rat managed to jump across the undersigned, during which time this officer struck at the animal, and as a result broke his nightstick.

'At that point, the rodent made a spectacular leap across the bathroom and landed on the mirror, which was directly attached to the wall, directly next to the undersigned's face.

'Then, in an attempt to escape the possibility of the rat then leaping on to this officer's face or shoulders, the undersigned quickly leaned away from the animal, while at the same time attempting to strike it with what remained of his nightstick.

'Unfortunately, this officer lost his balance and fell off the cabinet and landed against the opposite wall of the bathroom. As a result of the fall, the undersigned struck the wall with both his elbows and his head, thus receiving bruises to both the elbows, and as a result of the blow to the head the undersigned's front tooth broke.

'At that point, the undersigned requested back-up contact to come to the scene, in order to supply the undersigned with an additional nightstick, in order to continue the battle.

'Shortly thereafter, [another officer] *arrived and the rat was destroyed.'*

Dirty rats, low-down rats, corn-eaters and plague-bringers, the case against them is overwhelming – but they do have their defenders. In the face of almost universal animosity, there are still a few people prepared to take a stand on their behalf.

'We humans like to classify wild animals as "good" or "bad," writes Victor B. Scheffer. 'By labelling them, we fit them neatly into an arrangement; we bring a degree of order to a natural world that seems at times unorganized and frightening. We pass quick judgement on the rat; we call him "vicious, filthy, sly" and we avoid the burden of understanding his life.'

One person who has taken up the burden is a Frenchman, Michel Dansel, the founder of an extraordinary organization called the Académie Internationale du Rat, whose aim is to restore the rat to its 'rightful place in society', and whose motto is: '*Liberté, Egalité, Fraternité*'.

Paris is a hotbed of anti-rat feeling. What other city has a special police squad for killing rats, the *Brigade de Lutte contre les Ronguers* (Brigade for the Struggle against Rodents). But now Dansel, from his attic apartment known to the Académie's two hundred members as The Ratothèque, is fighting back for rat rights.

Dansel, who studied the rat in nineteenth- and twentieth-century literature for his Sorbonne doctoral dissertation, explains why: 'Rats are worth studying if only because people fear them so. They have been symbols of death and destruction for centuries, so naturally people are afraid ... They're threatening, too, because they are rodents, nibblers. That's why they're often used to represent time nibbling away at our lives.

'Rats are the lower depths,' he says, 'not just of the sewers, but of our psyche. The part we have to make friends with if it is not to conquer us.'

Dansel got an enthusiastic response when the Académie received coverage in *Le Monde*, and he now receives so much mail he has had to hire a secretary. In recent years he has met his share of rat cranks. He could not dissuade one woman from visiting him in person to show him a picture of her husband with rats squatting on his arm.

Dansel's scholarly study of rats has led him to admire their clever strategies. 'Guess how rats steal eggs?' he asks. 'One rat enfolds the egg with its body to protect it, and the other drops him off by the tail! We must stop destroying them. There is so much we can learn!'

The Rat Race

The US government estimates that there are more than 30 million rats on American farms, 30 million in towns and a further 20 million in large cities. They cause an estimated $1 billion in damages, or more than $10 per rat per year. Corn is contaminated with rat faeces, sugar with rat urine, canned foods with rat hairs.

In Chicago, the city supports a rodent control programme that employs 26 four-man teams armed with cyanide gas and other poisons. In 1976 there were 230 reports of people being bitten by rats in Chicago. When an alderman of a West Side ward offered a bounty of a dollar a rat, he shelled out $550 in just two weeks.

In Washington DC, the city council spreads 50 tons of poison bait around the city each year, but to little avail.

In San Antonio, rats broke into the courthouse cellar where marijuana was being stored, developed a taste for it and, according to one report, 'grew as big as cats' on their hallucinogenic diet.

But rats are a worldwide problem. Madrid experienced a plague of rats in 1974 – an estimated 7 million of them, or more than two for every human citizen.

In Hong Kong in 1977 the urban council received 3,888 rodent infestation complaints. Grace Ho, chairwoman of the environmental hygiene committee, commented at the time: 'The situation in Hong Kong is that food and shelter are freely available to rodents in all parts of the urban areas. No amount of effort by way of direct control measures – for example the use of poison and traps – will ever have more than a transitory effect on the population.'

In July 1978 more than 50,000 Tokyo commuters were trapped inside their trains for an hour after rats gnawed through a main signal cable.

In India rat skins are now used to make purses, vanity bags, gloves, babies' shoes and watch straps.

In October 1977, rats measuring up to a foot long poured down from the hills near the border between Burma and Bangladesh, and proceeded to terrorize villages and devour crops. Most of the villagers bemoaned their fate as a scourge sent by Buddha. But not everyone regards the rat as a pest. The Pankho tribespeople positively welcomed the invasion – because they eat them.

A fundamental question is, what do rats eat? The popular supposition that rats and mice have a special craving for cheese is mistaken – they have no such preference. US pest exterminator Edward Batzner baits his traps with sticky, lemon-flavoured sweets because he claims rats and mice prefer them.

According to New Jersey chemist Dr Gerson Ram, on the other hand, the best way to kill rats is to use his special, quick-setting biscuits. The recipe is simple. Prepare a stiff biscuit dough with 0.45 kilograms of white corn meal, one tablespoon of peanut butter and 0.9 kilograms of barium sulphate. Cut into the required shape and bake for twenty minutes. Rats love them, and the barium sulphate sets like concrete in their intestines shortly afterwards.

But rodents rapidly learn to tolerate poisons and avoid traps, so it is probably best of all to leave pest control to cats. There is no need to worry about what *they* like.

The Regent's Bower

From the simplest form of reproduction to one of Byzantine complexity, because no other animal could possibly require such demanding foreplay as the bower birds of Australia.

They are known as 'avenue builders' because their courtship revolves around the construction, by the male, of a kind of temple or pavilion in which the act of mating will eventually take place.

The plans for this elaborate structure are buried deep in his instincts but, when the time is ripe, the blueprints somehow rise to the surface of his mind and he goes to work with obsessive enthusiasm. The details are always the same.

He selects his site and starts by clearing away all the leaves and debris until he has a circle of bare earth, about 4 feet across. He then collects his building materials, and begins with the floor, which is composed of small twigs laid side by side. Along either side he plants a row of larger, upright twigs by pushing them into the ground with his beak, and then binds them together with strips of vine and plant fibres.

These form the walls of a passage wide enough for the male to walk through with his wings outstretched. The exact dimensions are important and he repeatedly tries it for size, making adjustments where necessary. He then decorates the floor with a bright mosaic of pebbles, flowers, shells, bones and fruit.

In the case of the regent bower bird, the decorations are taken a stage further and he actually *paints* the structure. He grinds and mixes the paint himself, using saliva, charcoal and plant pigments, then dips a piece of bark or wadded leaf into the mixture and paints the walls so that they are a glowing green or grey-blue.

It is not until this extraordinary edifice is complete that the female starts to take an interest in the proceedings. She inspects the nuptial bed from all angles, suspicious at first but with growing excitement. Eventually, if the details are right and she finds the architecture sufficiently erotic, she works herself up to a pitch of receptivity, crouches between the walls, and allows the male with his wings outstretched to mount her.

ELIZABETH GOSS

Remora – the Retriever Fish

Bird-dogs can be taught to retrieve game, but it is most unusual to find a fish used for the same purpose. The remora is the only example of what might be called a retriever fish that we have come across.

Remoras are parasites which attach themselves to whales, sharks, turtles, marlins – and even boats – by means of a suction pad that covers most of their head. Although they are born free-swimming, they soon feel the urge for a symbiotic relationship and attach themselves to the host whose life they will share. If it happens to be a shark, they will feed on scraps of its prey or any other parasites. The sharks, though generally accommodating, occasionally eat them in turn.

The pad on the remora's head, which can grow to about 8 square inches, develops a suction power of up to 100 lb. With a fishing-line tied to their tail, there is no need for a hook or bait. You just throw them in the water and they will go looking for something to catch.

Remoras are still used like this to catch fish and turtles in many parts of the world. 'The suckerfish is reported to be treated with extreme respect by the native fishermen', writes James J. Parsons in *The Green Turtle and Man*. 'Their relationship is somewhat similar to that between a hunter and his retriever dog. It is stroked, spoken to with soft words of encouragement and thanks, and fed special food. When it fails to perform, it is verbally scolded, given the lash, or even bitten. The natives seem to believe that this remarkable fish will understand human speech.'

Roadrunners

In the dry and dusty heat of the American southwest, there is a bird, a member of the cuckoo family, which has a passion for streaking across the desert, trailing a distinctive cloud of dust and sand. It has been immortalized in Hollywood cartoons, biologists know it as *Geococcyx californianus*, but its popular name is the 'roadrunner'.

These birds cannot fly in the conventional sense, but roadrunners have no need for wings. With their skinny legs taking 22-inch (56-cm) strides at a rate of twelve steps a second, they have been clocked at over 15 miles an hour. This is quite fast enough for their needs, and, by using their long tail as a rudder, they can execute perfect 90 degree turns at high speed, and easily overtake the lizards and low-flying insects they prey on.

Water can be a problem in the desert, especially after a fierce pursuit over the hot sands, so the roadrunner tends to hunt large, juicy animals for their water content – and this includes snakes. To catch a snake, the roadrunner first ruffles its feathers to prevent penetration of the reptile's fangs, and then runs circles around the coiled snake, often coming to a screeching halt, kicking up blinding clouds of dust, then reversing direction. It continues with this frenzy of circles until, suddenly, it clouts the bewildered snake on the head with its long, sharp beak. After a few more pecks to the brain, the snake usually collapses.

Snakes, of course, are well known for eating their victims whole. Which makes the roadrunner's method of devouring its prey one of nature's ironies. It swallows its victim head first, eats as much as its belly will hold and then just waits (tail-end of the snake hanging out of its mouth) until its digestive juices make room for more. There is no waste: the entire snake is usually eaten by the next day, and the roadrunner is off again, although perhaps not moving quite as fast as it did on an empty stomach.

CATHERINE BRADBURY

S

Safety in Numbers

Flocks, shoals and herds of animals all work on the same principle – by confusing a predator they force it to pick off the animals on the edge of the crowd.

This is to the advantage of the others, because those on the periphery are either the fastest (and best able to escape) or the stragglers, usually the old or infirm (least important to the group). In the long run, a predator may take just as many of them, whether or not they stick together, but by this means the victims ensure that more of the healthy, breeding individuals survive.

Whether they are starlings, mackerel or dik-dik, the same principles apply, but for very small organisms, like insects, it is the exact opposite.

Insects are more vulnerable *en masse* than they are on their own, and a large swarm is nearly always a sign of disastrous overpopulation (as with locusts) or a desperate once-in-a-lifetime activity (like the mating of bees or ants). However, insects too have discovered that in certain circumstances there is safety in numbers.

Many species, including butterflies, have learned the trick of clustering together so that they resemble a single, large animal, in order to frighten off predators. As they are so small, they cannot actually *do* anything – such as fight back or run away – so they have to put as much effort as possible into *looking* dangerous, by vigorously waving appendages, bobbing up and down and displaying their most brilliant colours.

The owl-fly larvae (*Ascaloptynx funiger*) bunch together when a predator, such as an ant, starts to climb the stem they are on. Turning to face the intruder, they raise their heads and present it with a forest of snapping jaws. The ant, which could easily overcome a larva on its own, will usually be forced to retreat from this concerted defence.

'When spiders' webs unite,' runs an old Ethiopian proverb, 'they can halt a lion.'

The Searchlight Squid

Animals which have evolved bioluminescence use it in different ways, but the luminous squid is well ahead of the others. The organic 'searchlight' it uses to illuminate its prey and dazzle its enemies is an amazing piece of technology.

The biologists Lorus Milne and Fritz Bolle have described the organ as having lenses, concave mirrors, diaphragms, and shutters which act as natural blinds. Some are retractable, and the squid controls them so accurately that it can direct a beam of light, of any width, in any direction it chooses.

Two types or models have been evolved. The light source used by shallow-water squids is a colony of luminous bacteria stored in nutrient solution in small sacs or tubes under its skin. The deep-water version depends on a luminous fluid secreted by the squid itself, which is actually capable of changing colour.

According to Hans-Eckhard Gruner, another scientist who has studied these creatures, 'by different devices like coloured filters (such as changes in skin pigments) and glittering mirrors, all sorts of colour shades may appear in one particular creature. It may produce red, blue, green or white light. Its luminous organs, when active, will then sparkle in these colours like precious stones.'

The description of the searchlight is strangely reminiscent of another highly sophisticated organ – the eye. In a sense, that is exactly what it is, except that it has the opposite function. Instead of receiving light, it emits it, and the two organs share the same similarities (and differences) as a radio receiver and a transmitter.

See-through Animals

There are several animals, like the Namibian gecko and the glass frog, which have transparent skins that allow you to see the workings of their internal organs; but some species have gone a stage further and adopted invisibility as the ultimate form of camouflage.

The Indian glass fish (*Chanda ranga*), when you can see it at all, looks like a 3-in (7.5-cm) splinter of crystal, reflecting the colours of the water around it, with nothing but its eyes and a pale violet stripe down its side to indicate its presence.

The aptly named X-ray fish, of the Amazon and Orinoco, is even less substantial. It is a relative of the notorious piranha, but even its fierce, saw-like teeth are transparent. If you look at it closely, it is possible to make out the spun-glass outline of the skeleton and swimbladder, but it is only when the fish has food in its stomach that it takes on any solid visibility.

There are thirty known species of tropical American moths and butterflies which have almost completely transparent wings. Curiously enough, they have all achieved this effect by different methods. In some the scales on their wings are tilted on their edges so that light passes through them; in others the scales have been reduced to fine hairs, or have become transparent themselves.

Glass fish

Even more impressive are some damselflies, whose bodies are also transparent. The great entomologist, Linsenmaier, wrote: 'South American damselflies of the family *Pseudostigmatidae* sail almost invisibly through dark parts of the forest in spite of their size. These are ghostly creatures, venerated by the natives more or less as the souls of the departed. In the deep shadows of a luxuriant vegetation, where the smell of mould holds sway, one sees transparent, iridescent wings like a quivering veil. Occasionally, perhaps, one can imagine he sees a long slender body floating horizontally behind, like a magic wand. And one involuntarily doubts that all this belongs to a single being.'

Sex Changes

Many animals, especially those at the lower end of the evolutionary scale, are hermaphrodites (both male and female); while other species have adopted a different method of enjoying the best of both worlds – they reverse their roles.

Oysters, for example, change sex several times during their lives. Indeed, one sex change apparently makes an oyster more likely to experience another. These creatures are also extremely prolific. According to one source, 'A single Pacific coast oyster produces approximately 10,000,000,000 descendants a year. If all survived, in five generations they would constitute a mass eight times the size of the world.'

The female swordtail has good reason to change her sex, which she does when she travels to the breeding grounds to deposit sperm on the eggs of younger females. The male of the species has a penis which is a modified anal fin, and which is covered with hook-like projections that would undoubtedly injure any female unfortunate enough to copulate with it. So the female swordtail, it seems, has abandoned sexual intercourse in favour of a gentler method for fertilizing the species' eggs.

Other role reversals also occur in the animal world. Amongst European flower crickets, for instance, it is the female who mounts the male during copulation. The male has a tiny pit on his back which is filled with a combination of sex smell and edible protein. This attracts the female, who climbs on his back and begins to lick out the contents of the pit, during which time the male attaches a small tube full of his sperm, the 'spermatophore', to her genital opening.

Amongst sea-horses, role reversal goes even further. The male and female meet in the water and perform a slow courtship dance before embracing – 'belly to belly, cheek to cheek, tails intertwined'. The male has a pocket on his belly which he opens as they embrace, so that the female can pass her eggs into it – instead of the male passing his sperm to her. So it is the male sea-horse who carries the now fertilized eggs and who, two months later, gives birth to the young.

Sharks

The golden age of sharks was one hundred million years ago, when many hundreds of exotic species thronged the carboniferous seas. Excavations in the rocky ravines of Bear Gulch, Montana, have revealed a shark with a horn protruding from behind and bending over its head, nicknamed the 'unicorn fish'; also a shark version of flying fish which could glide above the surface for several hundred yards; and a 4-foot-long (1.2m) shark with a hinged dorsal fin, like a rudder. So well preserved were these fossils that in some cases minute shrimps could be seen in their stomachs.

There are still more varieties around than is generally realized. Neither of the two largest species, for instance, are carnivorous. Both the basking shark and the gigantic whale shark will not eat anything but krill. And the smallest shark is only 6 inches (15cm) long. This is the *Squaliolus laticaudus*, a jet black cigar-shaped animal with white fins, which was first discovered in 1908. The Japanese call it *tsuranagakobitozame*, which means 'the dwarf with a long face'.

Then there is the thresher shark, which churns the water with its scythe-shaped tail to round up shoals of herring and mackerel; and the swell sharks which inflate their stomachs as a means of defence, and which are known as 'shy-eyes' because, like cats, they cover their heads with their tails when they sleep.

The oddest sharks are probably the hammerheads, which have wing-like planes on either side of their skulls. Their eyes are on the leading edge, like the headlights of a car; and they may have the equivalent of stereoscopic smell, because their nostrils are placed as far apart as possible, on the outer corners. It is not known for certain why they evolved this way, but they are born with their embryo hammer folded neatly against their body.

Sharks have no bones in their bodies, and their skeletons are composed entirely of cartilage. Their skin is covered with thousands of tiny teeth, which can blunt a knife (and it was used for soldiers' helmets in Roman times). Their main teeth are so loosely set in their gums that they are often lost during feeding, and are regularly replaced by an

Great White shark

NORMAN WEAVER

endless supply of fresh teeth, with an average turn-over of only seven or eight days.

Sharks are heavier than water, so they either sink or swim. They have to swim, anyway, to pass enough water through their gills to breathe, and as a result they spend their whole lives on the move, even when they are asleep. They have very large livers which act as a food store (and were the main source of vitamin A before it was synthesized).

They are reputed to be insensitive to pain, and one source quotes the story of a shark that was gutted, thrown back over the side of the ship, and then caught again with a hook baited with its own intestines.

Whether or not this is true, the shark's other senses are acute. Their hearing operates between 100–1500 cycles per second and is sensitive over thousands of yards; while nearly two-thirds of their brain is given over to smell, and they can sense one part of human blood in 10,000,000 parts of water. Frightened animals give off a particular odour which stimulates them. However, experiments have shown that human sweat, which has a different odour, actually repels them.

So it is sound rather than smell which first attracts them to human bathers, and if you are ever unfortunate enough to find yourself in shark-infested waters, the best thing to do is to force yourself to keep still and, if possible, float on the surface. Sharks are comparatively short-sighted and they may not even notice you.

But they can detect the vibrations of someone struggling in the water from about 200 yards away, through a row of sensory nerve endings called the lateral line, along their bodies. If they stray within 50 yards, they will begin to pick up your smaller muscular movements. At 50 feet, they will be able to hear your breathing and heart beat, and by that time they should be able to see you, so they will probably come over for a look.

The first thing they do is to make a close pass at your body, so that they can bring their most accurate sense organ into play. This is a device called the 'ampullae of Lorenzini', which can register a curious mixture of pressure, temperature and alternating current fields. It only works at close range, but it is extremely sensitive, and gives the shark a vivid picture of you (though we can only guess at what it 'sees').

If it is not satisfied, it may come back for a second look. Then it bites.

It is commonly supposed that sharks have to turn belly-up when they attack, but their jaws can open almost vertically, and they can come at you from any angle. The force exerted by the jaws of an average eight-foot shark has been measured at three metric tonnes, or 6,613.8 pounds per square inch (using a whimsical instrument called the Snodgrass Gnathodynamometer).

The shark's senses are so delicate that when they are overloaded, it suffers a nervous breakdown. If there is a lot of blood in the water, and they are buffeted by pressure waves and deafened by the thrashing of other sharks around them, the animals lose control and a 'feeding frenzy' can take place, in which they eat anything in sight, including themselves.

In fact attacks by man-eating sharks are comparatively rare, even in tropical waters. On a worldwide basis, the fatalities amount to about one thousand deaths a year – roughly equivalent to the number of those struck by lightning or stung to death by bees.

Very few of these attacks are by 'Jaws' himself, the Great White Shark, because that is one of the rarest species. But the legend lives up to reality in one sense, because the Great White is certainly the most powerful and aggressive of all sharks. The largest recorded specimen was 21 feet (6.45m) long and weighed over 7,000 pounds. It is a ruthless predator, as vicious as its reputation – and very frightening.

Silverfish

Silverfish are wingless Australian insects usually found in ants' nests, termite mounds, or living out in the open. Some species, however, have adapted to life in human buildings, where they are particularly partial to wallpaper, especially the embossed kind. They will also happily eat other kinds of paper, chewing around areas where unpalatable ink has contaminated their meal; and they obtain protein for the growth and development of their eggs by eating the glue in book covers.

Silverfish are able to live on this unusual diet because they are one of the few insects that can digest the cellulose in paper. Some of these insects rely on bacteria in their gut, but silverfish have a special enzyme called *cellulase*, which is even more effective.

Immature silverfish can live for two years on a purely paper diet. They can also fast for a whole year, though they are liable to turn to cannibalism under such conditions. Invariably the males get eaten first.

Of Sleep . . . and Dreams

Sleep is one of the last great mysteries of nature. Despite years of research, no one yet has any idea why it happens, what good it does us, or even if it is necessary. All one can say with certainty is that some animals asleep, some do not, and their requirements vary in every conceivable way, not only between species but even between individuals.

In general terms, sleeping seems to be related to the size of the brain. Animals with a simple nervous system, like insects, may rest for periods but they do not 'sleep' in the accepted sense. Ants, for instance, remain on the go for six months of the year, working non-stop, night and day. The other six months they simply turn themselves off, and show as much sign of life as a car parked in a garage.

Reptiles and cold-blooded animals speed up or slow down according to changes in the environment, but this daily pattern is not really 'sleep' either. However, they do have dormant phases (rather like hibernation) when their brain-wave pattern resembles what, in humans, is called 'deep sleep'. The electrical traces from their senses flatten out, muscular movement ceases, and only the automatic processes, like breathing, are active. This seems to be the oldest and most fundamental form of sleep, and occurs in most of the higher forms of life. It seems to have evolved to protect the animal at dangerous times of day, by putting it out of action in a safe place. By slowing down its body functions, not only is energy saved, but while it remains still and unobtrusive the creature avoids the attention of predators.

There is no question of it *needing a rest*, because, in physiological terms an animal is much better off awake and eating, and most sleep like this for only an hour or two a day. In some species even this length of time is dangerous, and smaller mice and shrews can only afford to drop off for a few seconds at a time.

The environment can be an important factor, too. In the case of the blind Indus dolphin, which lives in rough, disturbed water with strong currents, sleep is a positive hazard. It has to keep swimming the whole time to avoid injury, and as a result it has learned to sleep in short bursts of 90 seconds or less.

The giraffe has another kind of problem. Whereas most animals can spring into action the moment they wake up, if a giraffe is caught napping, it takes the poor animal 10 to 15 seconds merely to stand up. Therefore it keeps its periods of deep sleep to the minimum.

The neatest solution to the problem of sleeping comes from another dolphin. Like all mammals, dolphins' brains are divided into two halves. Each hemisphere has a different job to do, but they keep in constant touch through a massive network of nerves called the *corpus callosum*. What the bottle-nosed dolphin can do (and we, unfortunately, cannot) is to put each hemisphere to sleep *independently*. Thus while one half of its brain is sound asleep, the other is wide awake and keeping watch.

The Dreams of Dolphins

In addition to this *deep sleep*, there are two other kinds. One is a light sleep, analogous to 'dozing' or 'hypnosis', when the body is relaxed but the brain is on stand-by, just below the threshold of consciousness. The other is the fascinating and mysterious condition known as REM, named after the rapid eye movements which were the first symptom to be identified. The sleep of dreams.

It is unlikely that reptiles, fish or birds can dream, because REM sleep only occurs in animals with a neocortex – the upper level of the brain with which we 'think'. It is here that memories are compared, words translated, and we make decisions. It is only this ego (the 'I' that makes decisions) which takes a rest during REM sleep. All the other brains are awake. Our muscles move and all our body functions, including the sexual ones, are active; our limbs thrash around and our bodies can even perform simple tasks (sleep-walking takes place during periods of REM), we can talk and, above all, we dream.

Our senses are still reporting to the brain, but there is no one there to sort out the information. Fragments of memory drift up from the busy cortex, jostling together like an ill-fitting jigsaw, coloured by the emotional chemistry from our hormone centres and instincts from deep in the base brain. Everyone knows what this feels like: we all dream for periods of 15–20 minutes five or six times a night, though we seldom remember more than the last few minutes before we wake.

Some people can even control dreams (i.e. they know *at the time* that it is a dream and can decide what to dream next). This phenomenon has only recently been recognized, but it raises an intriguing possibility. Could it be that, like the bottle-nose dolphin, one half of our brain can 'watch' the other half sleeping, and tune in to its dreams?

All mammals probably dream in some way or other, and dolphins certainly do. But what do they dream about? Even if we could communicate with them, it is doubtful if they could tell us. We cannot even find the language to describe it to ourselves.

. . . and Snoring

The noise of a snore is usually made on the intake of breath, and is nearly always associated with animals that have a soft palate that can flutter and vibrate.

Humans are among the noisiest snorers, along with dogs – especially those breeds like the bulldog and pekinese which have been selectively bred to have flat faces and large soft palates. In some cases this whimsical redesigning of animals has gone so far that they can hardly breathe at all, let alone snore.

The same basic process occurred during our own evolution, except that it had one unexpected advantage. In fact, the odd snore is a small price to pay for it, because the flattening of the primate skull was the modification which enabled us to speak, and led to the development of human language.

A loud human snore may well rival the noisiest dog, but neither can be compared with the sound heard one evening by an Alaskan trapper sitting quietly in his cabin. He thought at first it was a low-flying aircraft, but when he ran outside with his lantern, he discovered that the noise was coming from a big bull walrus, asleep on a passing ice-flow.

Birds have hard palates, so they do not snore in the usual sense, although recordings of sleeping owls show that they make a distinct noise as they exhale each breath.

Fish do not snore, of course, but surprisingly enough, whales do. Silvia A. Earle, who has studied whales in Alaskan waters (where they spend much of the time sleeping), describes them as producing 'burbling, mumbling, whale-sized snores'.

Spiders' Webs

A spider's web is a welded structure with the strength of high-tensile steel, finer than anything human technology has yet achieved (the thinnest man-made thread is a gold filament about 4 microns in diameter, but the spider's go down to 1 micron). And it is much more than a device for catching insects.

The web is an extension of the spider's own senses. A dish aerial that keeps it up to date on the temperature, wind speed, humidity and other information about the environment – a territorial marker, alarm system, a shelter, and more besides. The spider is programmed to build it to exacting specifications, and it is as much a part of the insect's life as a shell for a tortoise or the antennae for a moth. The size of the spider is, literally, the size of its web.

It is such a total expression of the creature's behaviour that Dr Peter Witt, a researcher studying hallucination and mental illness, decided to try the effects of certain mood-altering drugs on its web-spinning behaviour.

He found that amphetamine caused the spider to build a smaller web, with a grossly distorted pattern. Under the influence of mescalin, it produced shorter lengths of thread, so the size of the web and the regularity of its angles was affected. Strychnine had the effect of cutting down the frequency of web building; but the drug that had the most dramatic effect was a high dose of caffeine, which produced a structure so distorted that it could not even be called a web.

The only chemical which improved the spider's performance was LSD. With small doses of hallucinogen, it spun a larger and more 'perfect' web each time!

Spiders weave their thread into cocoons, funnels and webs of all shapes and sizes. There is even one species that makes a tiny web, about the size of a postage stamp, which it holds between its front legs like a butterfly net, to catch insects.

But the oddest of them all must be the bolas, or lasso spider, which dispenses with a web altogether. It spins one long strand of silk covered with sticky droplets which it combs down to the end to form a large, viscous globule. The creatures have poor eyesight, but they emit a special odour which attracts moths, and when they feel the vibration of the insect's wings, they hurl their line towards it (like a bolas or lasso). If the globule sticks to the insect, they haul the victim in, grab it with their exceptionally long front legs, and kill it with a poison bite.

The globule loses its stickiness after a time, so if nothing has been caught within half an hour, the spider winds in the bolas, eats it, and makes a fresh one.

An African species has developed a variation of this technique by whirling it round above its head like a helicopter blade. Instead of waiting for the prey to arrive, it keeps the line spinning (with a change of bolas every fifteen minutes or so) until an insect flies into it.

The spider's thread is so versatile that it is surprising we have not thought more of spinning and weaving it – though that was tried during the eighteenth century. For centuries, the axis of the east-west trade had been the Silk Route between Europe and China. Silk was as important to the Chinese as oil now is to the Arabs, and their production methods were a closely guarded secret. So they were deeply disturbed at rumours that Europeans were experimenting with a substitute, and by the publication in 1709 of *A Dissertation on the Usefulness of Spider's Silk* by a Frenchman, Francois Xavier Bon de Saint Hilare. At the Chinese emperor's own command, the book was immediately translated into Manchu. Although it was difficult to weave, Saint Hilaire had a pair of mittens and some stockings made from spider silk, and he suggested it could be produced commercially by running spider farms.

However, the Chinese were able to relax when it became obvious that he had taken no account of the problems of mass production. The technique involved unwinding the thread from spiders' cocoons, as with those of silk worms; but they were so much smaller, and the thread so fine, that later investigation showed it would require 27,648 cocoons to produce one pound of silk!

Which explains why spider silk is not only the finest and strongest but still one of the rarest materials in the world.

The Skink

It is common enough for lizards to lose their tails, as already mentioned, but none of them do it with such flamboyant style as the skink.

The young of the Polynesian species, *Eumeces shiltonianus*, has a vividly bright, sky-blue tail. A tail as glaringly odd as the nose of a proboscis monkey or the rear end of a baboon. The rest of the animal is patterned in the usual earthy colours, but the tail looks as if it has been dipped in a can of paint.

In the normal course of events, it would ruin the animal's camouflage, but its purpose becomes apparent in moments of crisis. When danger threatens and the skink is forced to shed its tail, the extraordinary object continues to bounce around of its own accord. Its movement is sustained by automatic spasms of muscles, and since a predator finds it impossible to ignore this bright blue object leaping around on the ground, it is distracted from the pursuit, and the skink has more time to escape.

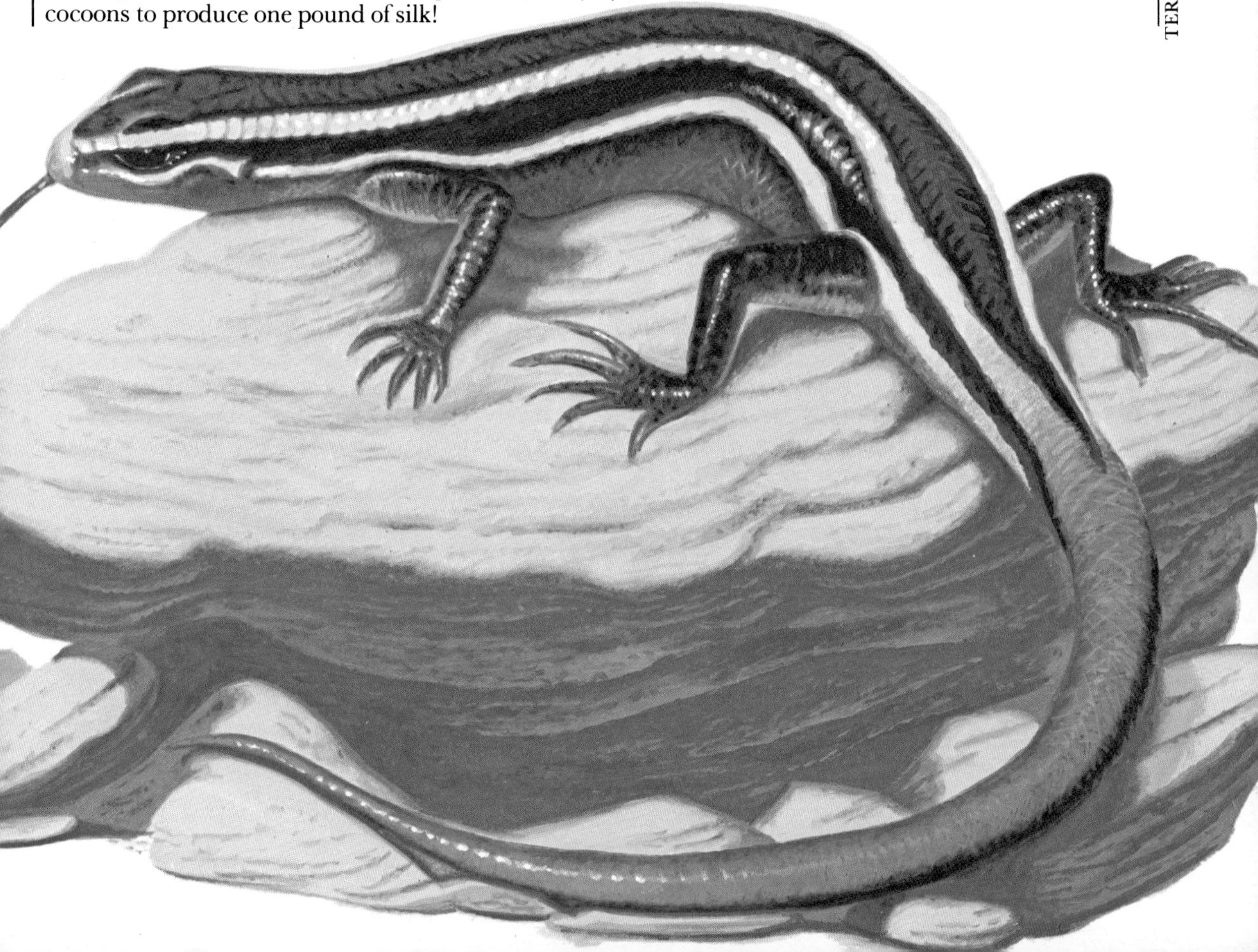

The Squeaking Competition

Shrews are the smallest mammals. They can starve to death in three hours, have red teeth, and are so nervous they can literally die of fright; but there is nothing in their tiny, highly-strung lives quite as odd as their ritual squeaking competitions.

They used to be described as vicious, quarrelsome animals because naturalists had observed them locked in mortal combat, biting and screaming at each other. At least, that is what it would look like to someone 50,000 times their size. It was actually a miniaturized, if high-pitched, version of encounters between howler monkeys – a meticulously organized ritual designed to ensure that neither animal was hurt.

Shrews are forced to lead a solitary life because they need every scrap of food in their vicinity, simply to stay alive. So the discovery of another shrew in one's territory is a serious matter, and the intruder must be seen off as quickly as possible. Fighting is out of the question because even a small wound, or nervous exhaustion, could put a shrew in shock, so they repel intruders by throwing a tantrum.

The animals approach each other until their whiskers touch, and then start squealing as loudly as possible. This is usually enough to send the intruder packing, because animals are well aware when they are trespassing, and have what one could almost call a guilt complex about it. If the intruder stands its ground, the defender rears up on its haunches, and if that does not work, it rolls over on its back with its paws in the air, and the squealing rises to a crescendo.

If the intruder can match this performance, the two animals wriggle around on their backs, beside each other, until one of them catches the other's tail in its mouth. It clamps on to the tail and eventually the other manages to do the same, so that they are clasped in a tight embrace, still shivering with indignation and squealing their heads off.

This amounts to a deadlock, but it does not go on for long. Sooner or later, hunger intervenes, and one or the other will break off hostilities to get on with the serious business of finding the next meal. Neither animal is hurt, and nature has ensured that the shrew population in the area is distributed a little more evenly.

CATHERINE BRADBURY

The Stormy Petrel

The stormy petrel is another scrap of life which somehow survives in a huge and hostile environment. If shrews are the smallest land mammals, the genus *Procellaria* is the smallest sea-bird, and the smallest bird of any kind with webbed feet. It is also one of the least known, because it is so well adapted to marine conditions it spends its whole life at sea, where birdwatching is a rather haphazard activity.

Ironically, in spite of the difficulty of making an accurate count, most ornithologists agree that it is the most numerous type of bird in the world. Their population is spread out across millions of square miles of empty ocean, able to ride out the worst storms, eating, sleeping and mating at sea, and only coming in sight of land when it is time to lay their eggs.

Petrels are part of an ill-assorted group of birds including the albatross and the skua, and their name comes from an association with St Peter (*Petrus*). This is quite appropriate for the stormy petrels, because they can almost literally 'walk on water', skipping along with their legs just breaking the surface, in search of food.

In fact, their legs are not much use at sea, and they appear to be evolving into the first legless bird. Their limbs are already so weak that when the birds eventually come ashore, they have to use their wings as crutches.

Stormy petrels are out of their element on land, and they usually nest in Antarctica, where they find themselves in competition with other teeming hordes of wildlife along the shores of the continent. So they wisely come ashore at night, and immediately burrow into the ground. There are so many predators around that they need to stay under cover to survive. So, apart from a few nocturnal expeditions to find food, they remain in their burrows until the fledglings are hatched – and they can head back to the safety of the open sea and wider skies.

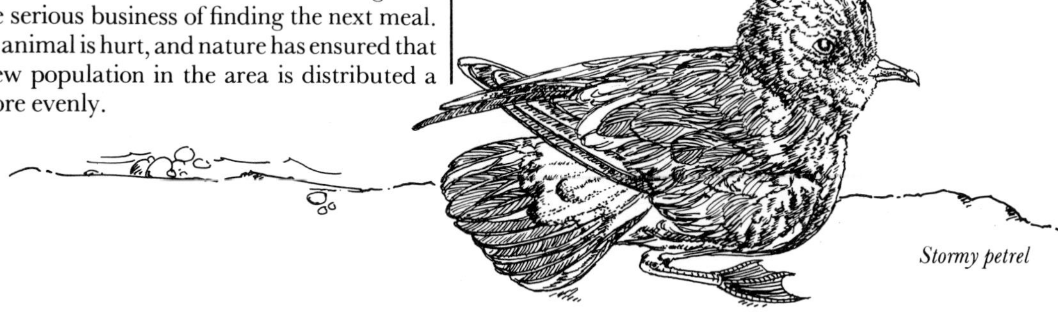

Stormy petrel

Pyrenean desman, the swimming mole

The Swimmers

The Pacific salmon, with names that roll off the tongue – chinook and sockeye, chum and cherry, coho and pinks – are tireless natural athletes.

The unofficial world altitude record for a fish is held by a sockeye which scientists persuaded to climb up an artificial waterway for five days, reaching the equivalent of an altitude of 6,648 feet, or more than a mile. The salmon in fact exhausted the scientists, and was still going strong when the test was halted.

Swimming is the most efficient form of locomotion. The buoyancy improves the power to weight ratio to such an extent that a salmon is capable of sustained effort for weeks on end.

Charles H. Gilbert of the US Bureau of Commercial Fisheries recorded the passage of the chinook up 2,000 miles of the Yukon River in Alaska. From the mouth of the river to Whiskey Creek, 622 miles upstream, they averaged an incredible 50 miles a day. Over the next 230 miles to Fish Creek they actually increased their speed to 70 miles a day. Swimming non-stop through some of the roughest white water in the world, they were still making 50 miles a day when they passed Dawson City, 650 miles further upstream!

Some very curious animals take to swimming. There is, for instance, a swimming mole called the Pyrenean desman. Sloths, which are hopeless on land, are quite at home in water. Many species of snakes are natural swimmers, and the sea snakes of the Indian and Pacific Oceans are fully adapted to a marine environment.

Several species of diving birds have learned to use their wings to 'fly' underwater. Like the stormy petrel, they find that legs can be a drag; and there are four species of loons which have solved the problem with a retractable undercarriage. They are the only birds whose legs are encased in their bodies right down to the ankle joint. With their feet working like propellers at the back of their body, they are superb swimmers, and there is even a record of one being caught by a fisherman at a depth of 240 feet!

Apart from the Japanese macaques already mentioned, there is only one species of primate – the proboscis monkey – that has taken to water. It lives in the swamps of south-east Asia, and its huge nose seems to have evolved to prevent water going up its nose when it's diving for crabs and shellfish. Gorillas, chimpanzees and macaques all have open noses, and the only other primates with hooded nostrils are human beings – which raises the intriguing possibility that our ancestors may also once have been water apes.

Symbiosis

The Greek historian Herodotus is said to have observed a crocodile having leeches removed from inside its mouth by the small bird we now call the courser, or crocodile bird, and was so impressed by this unlikely partnership that he coined a new word for it, from *syn*, 'together', and *bios*, 'livelihood'.

Relationships in which one partner keeps the other free of parasites are relatively common. Barber fish, for instance, eat fungi and lice from the bodies of other fish, and the ox-pecker bird performs the same service for buffalo and cattle.

It is thought that the ox-pecker can only live on blood that has been passed through a tick's body. The bird also serves its partner as an alarm system, alerting it if a human is approaching. It only calls out if perched on a wild animal, not a domestic one, and can distinguish between humans and other animals.

Bee-eaters ride around on the backs of ostriches, eating the insects that they kick up. And there is a gecko in the Seychelles, *Phelsuma abotti*, which lives on the back of the giant tortoise, feeding on the insects attracted by its droppings, and hiding under its shell at night.

Another curious example is the symbiosis between the clown fish and poisonous sea anenomes on Australia's Great Barrier Reef. This brilliantly coloured fish, with red and white stripes, darts about in front of the anenome's poisonous tentacles until it attracts the attention of a larger fish. Then, just as the predator is about to lunge, it disappears among the tentacles, and before the predator realizes the trick, it is stung and killed by the anenome.

A curious twist to the story is that the clown fish is not *naturally* immune to the anenome's poison. It gradually builds up an immunity by hanging around the vicinity of a particular anenome. Unfortunately, the protection wears off when the fish grows old, or is injured, and it is eventually devoured by its guardian.

Two special forms of symbiosis are commensionalism (literally, 'one who eats at the same table as others'), as with pilot fish and sharks, and inquilism (where the animals share not only the same food but the same home).

A classic example of commensionalism are the sea anenomes carried around by hermit crabs. The crabs gain protection from the stinging tentacles, while the anenome shares the crab's meals and gets free transport to new feeding grounds.

The most famous example of inquilism is a species of marine worm that lives on the west coast of America and has so many residents in its burrow, including goby fish, scale worms, pea crabs and small clams, that it is known as the innkeeper worm.

Termite nests provide a home for more than three hundred species of beetles and numerous mites, who help to keep the nest clean. There is also an African species of ant which lives in termite nests and rides around on the heads of the termite soldiers, picking up scraps of food when they are fed by the workers.

Ants are themselves hospitable creatures. It has been calculated that over one thousand different types of creatures have been found living in the nests of the twenty-seven species of British ants.

One of the most unusual examples of this is the total dependence of the Large Blue butterfly on red ants. The caterpillar of the Large Blue hatches on wild thyme, and feeds on the plant until it reaches about 1 centimetre in length. It then falls to the ground, turns carnivorous, and begins searching for insects. However, it is not very good at this, and will starve to death unless it is discovered by a red ant who takes it back to its nest.

There the caterpillar crawls down into the brood chamber and begins devouring the larvae. The ants do not seem to mind this, but in return they milk the caterpillar of a sweet secretion, like honeydew. Eventually the caterpillar spins its cocoon, and when it emerges, it flies out from the ant's nest as an adult butterfly.

Love affairs between animals and vegetables seem doomed from the start. Yet the extraordinary symbiosis of insects and flowers has led to several instances of a direct sexual relationship. It can even bear fruit, of a kind.

The igneumon wasp, for instance, regularly 'copulates' with a certain orchid which looks exactly like the female of his own species. The shape and colour are such an exact replica of the female igneumon that the male finds it impossible to distinguish between the flower and the real thing. The orchid, in turn, is totally dependent on the wasp's sexual attentions for pollination, and it may even reproduce the female wasp's sex pheromones to arouse the male.

A similar case is a species of beetle in South Africa which spends its winters in burrows underground. In the spring, the male disinters itself a few weeks before the female, but quite fails to notice the absence of a mate, since a local species of orchid emits exactly the same sex smell as the female beetle. For a few weeks the male beetles enjoy an orgy of sex with the flowers, until the females finally emerge and they turn to the business of perpetuating the species.

Another example is the moth which only lays its eggs in the flower of the yucca plant. It injects them directly into the plant's ovaries and then 'rewards' the plant with a deposit of pollen on the head of the ovary. As the baby caterpillars grow inside the plant (safe from predators), they feed on the seeds which their mother has thoughtfully fertilized in advance.

The Synchronized Cicadas

There are species of cicadas that sing only once every seventeen years. Yet their lives are so synchronized that the larvae emerge from their long underground existence in the same week, on the same day, and even at the same hour.

The reason for this remarkable timing is to give them a fighting chance of survival. As the parents may well be dead by the time the young hatch out, they have to rely entirely on their instincts. But the surroundings they find themselves in must match their genetic memory in order to trigger the right responses. In other words, they need to be controlled by a built-in timing device, like an alarm clock, which is linked to the environment outside.

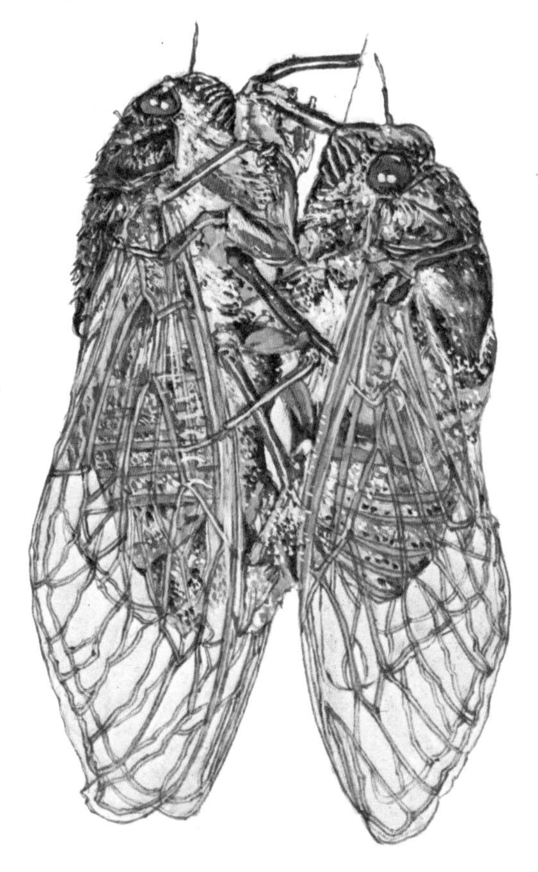

Cicadas mating

Plants, which have the same problem with their seeds, have evolved some sophisticated natural clocks (like the species of bamboo which is programmed to flower every 120 years), but the cicadas are just as efficient.

The species known as *Magicicada* spends most of the time underground in the form of a larval nymph, but at precise intervals of either 13 or 17 years the grubs come to the surface and are metamorphosed into flying insects. Their timing is designed to minimize the chance of them appearing at the same time as their predators, most of which work on a 5-year cycle. If *Magicicada* reproduced according to a 15-year cycle, the cicadas would meet their predators each time they bred. But 17 and 13 are prime numbers, so they only bump into each other every 65 (5 × 13) or 85 (5 × 17) years!

The accuracy with which the cicada grubs emerge is uncanny. Not only do all the grubs in a certain area respond to the same invisible signal, but each group is synchronized with its neighbours so that they all hatch out within hours of each other, years after the eggs were laid.

Two entomologists, Moore and Alexander, watched one of these multiple births in Clinton County, Ohio.

'In some years practically all the population in a given forest emerges on the same night, or two or three different nights. There is always one night of maximum emergence.

'In the woods that during the afternoon had contained only scattered nymphal skins and no singing individuals, in which no live adults had been found during a two-hour search, nymphs began to emerge in such tremendous numbers just past dusk that the noise of their progress through the oak-leaf litter was the dominant sound of the forest.

'Thousands of individuals simultaneously ascended the trunk of each large tree in the area, and the next morning foliage everywhere was covered with newly moulted adults.'

The cicada's strategy breaks all the rules (like perpetual motion or the perfect crime) but it is extraordinarily effective.

'No ordinary predator,' writes E. O. Wilson, 'can hope to adapt specifically to a prey that gluts it for a few days or weeks and then disappears for years. The only way to solve the problem is to track the cicadas through time, by entering dormancy for the next 13 or 17 years!'

No species is known to have adopted this trick, although, as Wilson cautiously adds, 'the possibility has not been excluded'.

CATHERINE BRADBURY

T

Condor

Tardigrades

The tardigrade is one of an extraordinary group of animals which are capable of 'suspended animation'. Like any other organism, it needs water to survive, but if its surroundings become dehydrated, it switches off all its systems and literally ceases to be a living creature. Its body, which is 85 per cent water, dries out almost completely and shrinks to a small, resistant husk known as a 'barrel'. The tiny amount of water retained in the barrel is kept under such high pressure that it can neither freeze nor evaporate, but the animal itself is dead, and remains so until conditions improve.

It may look like an endearing soft toy, a kind of crumpled caterpillar on four pairs of stumpy legs, but the tardigrade (which is also known as the 'water bear') is amongst the hardiest organisms on earth. When German researchers subjected tardigrades to the 'torture chamber' experiment, they stood up to the most heroic environments.

'For an hour bear animalcules were exposed to a stream of hot air of 197.6°F (92°C). When they were moistened afterwards at room temperature, they were lively again half an hour later. They were fused into glasses lacking any oxygen; they were kept for months in pure hydrogen gas, pure nitrogen, pure helium; in carbonic acid, hydrogen sulphide, coal gas – it did not do them any harm. The shrunken mummies woke up again every time as long as they received water, which is their livelihood. For twenty months the little barrels lay in liquid air at about minus 392°F (−200°C), and afterwards for eight and a half hours in liquid helium at an outer space temperature of minus 519.8°F (−271°C). Yet they thawed out again and became as lively as before.'

Tardigrades have about twelve months of active life but, by switching on and off in this way, they can survive for as long as 60 years. Some have been found in museum specimens of dried moss, and briefly revived after 120 years!

The reason they are capable of suspended animation is that they are very small and very simple organisms. In fact they are no larger than a pinhead, although they possess all the attributes of animal life.

Under a microscope, one can see that the body is divided into five segments, including a recognizable head equipped with two eyes (though they consist of just a single visual cell each) and a piercing apparatus which the creature injects into plant cells to suck out their contents. In addition to this vegetarian diet, they have been observed eating other microscopic creatures, including each other.

The four rear segments of the tardigrade's body each has a pair of legs, ending in small claws which it uses in climbing or scrambling around. However, its progress is relatively slow, hence its Latin name of *tardigrada*, or 'slow walker'.

Tardigrade

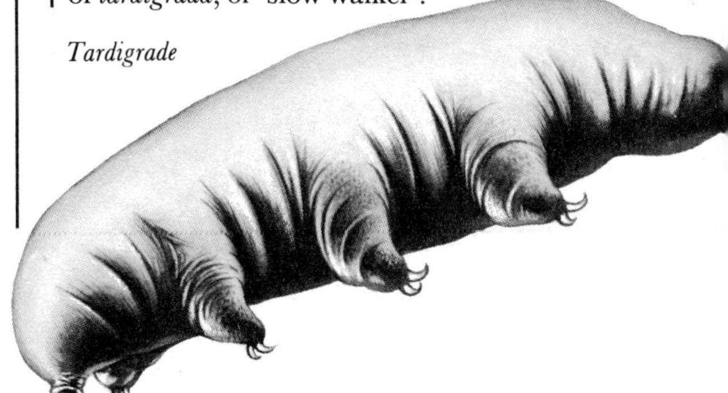

The Thunderbirds

The Indians called them 'thunderbirds' because of the noise they make when flapping their wings. We know them better as a big, black, coarsely feathered scavenger with a bald yellow and red head, puffy jowls and a crooked neck – called the condor. On the ground, it must run and hop up and down to gain enough speed to take off, but once aloft it is transformed into a creature of beauty.

The condors are legendary fliers, often ranging 50 to 60 miles a day. They can soar to heights of 15,000 feet, cruise at 35 mph, and reach speeds of up to 100 mph when diving. They are expert gliders, and have been observed to fly for over an hour without once flapping their wings, in order to conserve their energy in the long patient search for food.

The Indians once used their feathers in religious ceremonies, and regarded them as a link between the living and the dead. In a sense they are, because they have lived beyond their time. The heyday of the condors was about a million years ago – and, like the dinosaur (or the tuatara) they seem doomed to pass away.

The Californian condors were amongst the most tragic victims of the Great Bird Kill. In 1900, at a time when the average mill-worker could expect to earn $8 a week, a blown condor egg fetched $300 on the New York market. A female condor only lays a single egg every two years, so the birds did not stand a chance against egg hunters.

The remaining condors have been steadily eradicated by the ravages of DDT or by eating the carcases of cattle which have been poisoned with strychnine put out for wolves or coyotes.

Today there are only 15–30 Californian condors left alive. No chicks have been seen for several years and, unless the birds breed, the species could be extinct within twenty years. Their final refuge, California's Big Sespe Canyon, is now threatened with oil-drilling operations. The only Californian condor in captivity was found abandoned as a chick and is now in Los Angeles Zoo. Although it is a comparatively young bird (they live for about thirty-five years), it never learned to cope with conditions in the wild, so it cannot be released.

On the other hand, the Andean Condor has been successfully bred in captivity (by the Bronx Zoo) and returned to its wild relatives by careful stages.

Thylacine

The Thylacine

The thylacine, or pouched wolf (*Thylacinus cynocephalus*) is the largest living carnivorous marsupial. The last captive specimen died in the Hobart Zoo in 1933, but a few of these strange animals still survive in the mountains of Tasmania.

They look rather like hyenas, with distinctive chocolate-brown stripes across their back, and the muzzle and tail of a dog. But they live and hunt like wolves.

These animals lead a nocturnal existence in pairs or small groups, inactive by day but hunting at night – like wolves – by padding relentlessly after their prey until it is worn down by exhaustion. They usually track down wallabies or other small marsupials, but they occasionally kill sheep (which does not improve their chances of survival, as the farmers are inclined to shoot them on sight).

In other respects they are fully marsupial. Their young are born in a typically semi-embryonic form, and carried by the mother in a shallow backward-facing pouch, equipped with teats. Like many marsupials, their jaws can open to 180 degrees, revealing what one authority has described as 'the most vicious set of teeth known among land mammals'. Surprisingly enough for a four-legged animal, they can even hop.

They normally run on their toes, again like a wolf, though not as fast. However, when they are closing in for a kill, or need to make a rapid escape, they go up on their hind legs and bound along at high speed, like a kangaroo.

Torrent Ducks

Ducks are not usually associated with surf-riding, or the salmon leaps of rushing mountain streams, but there are certain breeds for whom white water is a permanent home.

The harlequins (*Histrionicus histrionicus*) spend their breeding season in mountain streams and then head for the coast, where they seek out the roughest surf they can find. Sea ducks like the surf scoter (*Melanitta perspicillata*) also prefer the rough and tumble of broken water, but the real masters of this unlikely environment are the 'torrents'.

The torrent ducks (*Merganetta armata*) live in the streams of the High Andes at altitudes of 11,500 feet, and have adopted these rushing, turbulent waters as their natural habitat. Their grey and white colouring makes them almost invisible in the spray, and they use their specially stiffened tail feathers as an oar or counter-balance for their acrobatics.

'By far the most impressive and unforgettable spectacle in the behaviour of torrent ducks,' writes Paul A. Johnsgard, 'is their ability to master the most impossible rapids, fighting up-river against an overpowering current or turning, rolling over bottoms up, and shooting down the rushing rapids, unconcerned about rocks and almost disappearing among the spray and foam. I have observed adult torrent ducks falling down falls of several metres, mainly when they tried to escape from danger.'

Tortoise and Turtle

The tortoise may be slow, at least in comparison with the hare, but it can be remarkably aggressive. Male tortoises will often fight strenuously with each other until one of the combatants retreats or is flipped on to its back. A 'back-down' is far more serious than a 'back-off', because an inverted tortoise is in mortal peril. If unable to right itself, it is in danger from predators, and will almost certainly overheat and die from exhaustion in the sun.

However, nature has an answer to everything, and there is a particular species in the south-western United States (*Gopherus agassizi*) in which the loser of such a fight is allowed to surrender. When it is on its back, it emits a distinctive cry, or bleat, which induces the winner to turn it the right way up again.

Such altruistic behaviour on the part of the victor is extremely rare in animal combat, and it certainly does not apply to snapping turtles, a primitive freshwater species which is probably the most aggressive organism between two shells.

The snapper and its cousin the alligator snapping turtle have a definitely crocodilian air about them. Their tails are almost as long as their shells, and serrated like a crocodile's. They have sharp, hooked beaks like birds of prey, and a readiness to bite which has given them their name. Both species devour fish and water birds, and have been known to bite the toes off swimmers.

The alligator snapping turtle usually lurks near a river or lake bottom, lying in wait and 'fishing' with its wide-open mouth. The bait is a bright red, forked protuberance on its tongue, which it wriggles about in imitation of a worm. If an unwary fish is tempted to investigate, the waiting jaws snap tight around it and the turtle gulps it down.

Snapping turtles have also been called the 'dog of the American inland lakes' because of their renowned ability to track down underwater scents. In a murder case in the USA in the 1920s, detectives were at a loss to find the bodies they suspected had been dumped in a deep lake. An old Indian promised to find the bodies, so long as no one else watched. And find them he did, one every few hours. The puzzled detectives then spied on the old man and found he was using a snapping turtle on the end of a long line. The turtle would dive to feed on the bodies, and the Indian just followed the line to find where they were.

Although tortoises live on land, and turtles in water, it is reasonable to bracket them together. They both belong to the order of *Testudines*, and zoologists refer to them collectively as chelonians. And, apart from a few marine adaptations like salt glands and flippers (and the snapper's tongue), they are anatomically similar.

It is true that there are a few eccentric species, like the pancake tortoise, whose shell is as flat as a table top, and soft to the touch; and the hinged African tortoise, the rear of whose shell can be lifted up or snapped down like a visor – but they are the exceptions.

The chelonians live so long, and have evolved so slowly, that whether they are a 3-inch (7.5-cm) 'stinkpot' (the young musk turtle), the pet at the end of your garden, or a giant from the Indian Ocean, they all follow the same design. The ancestral tortoise seems to have originally come ashore and evolved on land, and the turtles represent a few of the larger and more intelligent species which later returned to the sea – in the same way that certain mammals did.

To pursue the analogy a bit further, if one can think of the great leatherbacks and green turtles as the chelonian equivalent of whales and dolphins, then the gorilla of the tortoise world must be the noble giant of the Galapagos.

The Galapagos Islands are the only place in the world where a tortoise has become the dominant species. These majestic animals, which can grow to over 5 feet (1.5m) long, were once so numerous that when Charles Darwin first saw them he described how one could walk across their backs for a considerable distance without touching ground.

The depredations of the last hundred years have reduced their numbers, but, according to zoologists who have recently visited the islands, they still go about their immemorial rituals. For instance,

Galapagos tortoises

TIM HAYWARD

M. Mlynarski and H. Wermuth have described their remarkable adaptation to the lack of water.

'They live chiefly on the warm, but completely dry, lava soils in the lowlands of the islands, and wander at regular intervals over long paths, beaten smooth by countless generations, to the volcanic highlands where they find drinking water and an abundance of plant growth. There they wallow for hours at a time in the pools, drinking their fill and eating, eventually returning down the same paths to their own habitat. Millions of giant tortoises, over innumerable ages, have polished the stones on these tracks with their shells; a man can now use them to find the way to drinking water.'

It is not known how old these creatures are, but there is a tortoise still alive on Tonga which is supposed to have been presented to the island by Captain Cook in 1774. The longest authentic record, however, belongs to one known as Marion's Tortoise. This animal was brought to Mauritius by Marion de Fresne in 1776, when it was a fully-grown adult; it outlived George Washington, Napoleon, and Queen Victoria, survived the First World War, and eventually passed away 152 years later, in 1918. So it is perfectly possible that the tortoises still climbing the slopes of the Galapagos are the same ones which bore Darwin on their backs.

The Third Eye of the Tuatara

In its own way, the tuatara – a beak-headed dinosaur which lives on a few rocky islands off the coast of New Zealand – is as much a survivor as the tardigrade. It looks like a 2-foot-long lizard, but its ancient anatomy contains the ribs of a bird and the skull of a crocodile, and it is the slowest, coldest and oldest of all living reptiles.

It can remain active when its body temperature drops as low as 45°F because its whole metabolism works in such low gear. It only has to breathe once an hour (or once every seven or eight seconds when it really exerts itself), and its gestation period is so long that it does not lay its egg until a year after mating, and the eggs do not hatch out until a year after that! Captured specimens have lived for about fifty years in zoos, but its natural lifespan may be a century or two. Like the tardigrade, the tuatara takes life easy and makes it last.

It lives in the burrows made by petrels, and is so

dependent on these birds that it is only found on islands where they have manured and burrowed the topsoil into a loose mulch, several feet deep. However, it is an uneasy symbiosis, and when the tuatara shares a burrow with nesting birds, it often eats their eggs.

But the strangest aspect of the tuatara is its optical equipment, because on top of its head, beneath the skin, there is a circular opening in its skull, and just below that, nestling on top of its brain, is an eye.

It has a lens and retina, like a human eye, but it is connected to a different part of the brain. The nerves run directly to a gland at the base of the brain which, in higher animals, is known as the pineal, and is one of the organs that control the hormone system (and therefore the behaviour) of the animal.

The function of this third eye is an intriguing zoological mystery. It has no iris, so it cannot focus an image; it can only register light and dark in the most general terms through the skin; and, as far as we know, the pineal gland has nothing to do with vision. Yet it obviously plays an important part in the creature's life.

There are one or two other reptiles, including the horned toad lizard, which have a similar organ, but it is most developed in the tuatara, and seems to be a mark of prehistoric ancestry because many species of dinosaurs have been found to have the same tell-tale opening in their skulls.

A possible clue to its purpose has emerged as the result of some ingenious 'zoogeography' carried out by a group of scientists in 1975. They started with the assumption that, since only a few lizards had inherited this feature, it must be of more use to some species than to others, and therefore their geographical distribution might indicate what it was used for.

It turned out that this third eye runs in families. Of the four great lizard families, the iguanas and agamids had it, but the geckos and teiids did not. This is interesting, because the geckos and teiids nearly all live in the tropics, within about 9 degrees of the equator, while the three-eyed species (including the tuatara) live further north or south.

Lizards are generally more abundant in warmer regions, as one would expect of a cold-blooded species; and those in temperate climates are particularly vulnerable to seasonal changes. So it is reasonable to suppose that the third eye is a way of getting the seasonal timing right for the birth of their young.

The organ must have a very slow response (if you can talk about an eye in terms of speed) or else the animal could be taken in by a sudden spell of sunshine or warm weather. So it probably measures the length of daylight hours and then averages them out in some way, so that the animal can be certain when spring has really arrived.

The behaviour of the tuatara seems to bear this out, because its eggs are fertilized, laid, and eventually hatch out, at exactly the same time each year, in November or December – at the beginning of the New Zealand summer.

The Turtle Snatch

Perhaps the only record in the annals of crime of a turtlenapping occurred in October 1978, when Little Rock, a 75 lb show-business turtle, was kidnapped from his owner's room in a Brooklyn motel. The owner, Mark Ruggles, was extremely concerned because Little Rock suffered from a sinus condition and was accustomed to spending most of his time in the bathroom under the hot shower, to keep his nasal passages clear.

The snatch occurred on a Wednesday. On Thursday, Ruggles received the expected telephone call demanding a ransom, and he informed the police. Two detectives were assigned to the case, and, after several further phone-calls, a ransom figure of $650 was agreed and a meeting arranged.

The detectives concealed themselves in the back of Ruggles's menagerie van – with the windows open to alleviate the smell of his monkeys and goats – and when they reached the place of assignation, in a nearby parking lot, they arrested the woman who was waiting to meet them.

She immediately broke down and led them to the back-yard of a house, where Little Rock was discovered, suffering a severe sinus attack. Four members of the woman's family were arrested, and while they were being booked, Little Rock was put in the police station bathroom, with the hot shower on to relieve his distress.

Tyger, Tyger

Tyger, tyger, burning bright
In the forests of the night,
What immortal hand or eye
Could frame thy fearful symmetry?

—William Blake

How else could one describe nine feet of fearfully striped symmetry, burning in tawny golds and bronze and rufous red from its massive head to the tip of its tail? Blake's fierce vision sums it up.

But this largest of the feline carnivores is burning in another sense, because the tiger originally came from the wastes of Siberia and suffers terribly from the heat of the tropics where it now lives. These animals always make for the densest cover – the *forest of the night*, indeed – and will often spend hours swimming or just lying in water to cool off.

Their brilliant colours are one of the adaptations they made to life in the jungle, because the original snow-lions of central Asia were probably black and white. They still retain a creamy coat on their chest and stomach, like that of the Himalayan snow-leopard.

One wonders what Blake would have made of a 'snow-lion'. The idea has a bizarre beauty, and it is not as paradoxical as it sounds. Lions and tigers may look superficially different, but if their skins are placed side by side it is difficult to tell them apart. There are tigers with manes, and lions without them. They move with the same grace, hunt the same kind of prey, and are two of the laziest animals in the world.

Their hunting techniques are slightly different: lions usually kill with a blow from the paw, while tigers cling to the victim and bite its neck. They also make a curious bell-like noise when hunting, called 'titting'. But the main difference is in their social life.

Tigers, unlike lions, are solitary animals. The only time they see one another is to mate, and they hunt for themselves (usually hiding the kill so they

can return to it several times). For this reason, quite apart from their natural laziness, they kill less often than most predators. In fact, they are such placid animals that when the ancient Romans imported them for the arena, they were a complete flop because they simply slunk away from the opposition.

So it is surprising that they should have such a ferocious reputation, especially for attacking humans. In the days of the British Empire in India, man-eating tigers became something of a legend. Tales were told and books written about them, until they almost came to be regarded as a separate species. But this reputation was highly exaggerated. The tigers which attack humans are invariably infirm or disabled in some way, and only do so out of hunger and desperation.

However, there is a strange exception to this rule. In the marshy delta of the Ganges called the Sundarbans, near Calcutta, there is a long history of man-eaters, and more than 275 people have been killed by them in the last ten years. The fact that so many attacks were concentrated in this one area seemed worth investigating, and scientists have now come up with a possible explanation. It is that the tigers have been drinking the highly saline water of the Sundarbans for generations, but their metabolism has not adapted to it, so the salt steadily accumulates in their bodies and eventually damages their liver and kidneys. This, in turn, causes pathological changes in their behaviour, which turns them into killers.

On the whole, tigers have more to fear from humans than we have from them. In 1914 there were at least 500,000 tigers in Asia; today there are less than 5,000 of all species. Of the eight races, the Bali tiger is now extinct, six others have virtually disappeared, and the Indian tiger was only saved by a huge effort mounted by the World Wildlife Fund.

In Java, despite the fact that they are revered as the souls of the departed, they have been reduced to a population of less than ten animals. The Russians systematically butchered the Caspian tiger in the name of agricultural efficiency, and the Royal Bengal tiger was wiped out by 'sportsmen'. In 1965 one maharaja proudly boasted that he had killed 1,150 tigers during his life.

The Underground City

Animals are capable of some remarkable feats of engineering, from massive construction projects like termite mounds and coral reefs, to the intricate architecture of beavers, weavers and bower birds. But there is a small, furry creature called *Cynomys parvidens* that puts them all to shame.

It is a form of ground squirrel, a plump rodent about a foot long, with a flattened head, coarse brown hair, and a white tail. For many years it was hunted as a pest, and is now on the verge of extinction, but the homes that it builds – or rather excavates – are on an astonishing scale.

In case you are wondering why you have not heard of this 'underground squirrel' before, it is more usually known as the prairie dog.

Before the coming of the white man to America, the prairie dogs lived in communal burrows that stretched for miles under the western plains. Their tunnels were complex, beautifully constructed systems. They had special embankments to prevent them from flooding, and were even equipped with their own air-conditioning, for the animals had discovered that if they piled earth around some of the entrance holes to form 'chimneys', a forced draught was created and air was drawn through the system. (The same technique is used in the traditional architecture of Arab countries, and is based on the fact that the wind-speed is always less at ground level than it is a few feet above the surface.)

During the nineteenth century, before the campaign to eradicate prairie dogs got under way, one of their systems was discovered in the Midwest that involved a continuous network of tunnels 100 miles wide and 250 miles long – a 2,500-square-mile underground city with 400 *million* inhabitants!

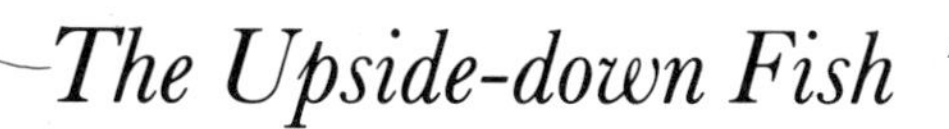

CATHERINE BRADBURY

The Upside-down Fish

If you had to name the villain of the seas, there is no doubt which name would spring to mind, because the shark is now accepted as public enemy No. 1, the leading anti-hero of the animal world. But if you had asked the same question a century ago, the answer would probably have been the whale or the giant squid. If you went back still further, to the fifteenth or sixteenth century, the answer would have been more ambiguous – beginning with sea serpents and all manner of mythical leviathans. But if you pinned the medievals down to a real flesh-and-blood animal, they would probably have settled for the 'silurus'.

That is the Latin name they would have used for a type of freshwater fish which has since acquired a variety of common names – the wels, the waller, and the sheathfish – and which we now call the catfish.

It hardly seems in the same league as the shark, but *Silurus glanis* can grow to a length of more than nine feet (2.75m), and it was the largest fish seen in European lakes and rivers. It was an aggressive predator with a reputation for attacking anything it encountered, including small animals like lambs, and even children. A sixteenth-century writer called Gesner reported that on one occasion a human head and a hand, with gold rings still on the fingers, were found in the stomach of a large catfish.

Most species of catfish are much smaller than this old-time European giant, but they can be just as dangerous. Some varieties, like the madtoms, are poisonous, and many of the smaller ones are parasites. Perhaps the most nightmarish member of the whole family is a tiny catfish called the candiru (*Vandellia cirrhosa*), which is obsessively attracted by the scent of human urine and can make its way into the urethra of naked bathers. It is difficult to write about catfish without being side-tracked by their bizarre activities, but it is time to introduce the oddest of them all – an African species we have chosen to call the upside-down fish.

Now, animals can live at any angle they like. There is a whole order of insects, for instance, called the *Notonectals*, which are designed to live upside-down (like the water-boatman). Most fish swim upright, but the manta ray lives sideways, and the flatfish – like plaice – change from one side to the other as they grow up. But they are all *designed* to operate like this. If you turned a water-boatman upside down it would sink, and a plaice could not swim on its back without getting sand in its eyes.

The Indian catfish, however, does have a choice – and seems to exercise it in a quite arbitrary fashion whenever it chooses. It may be swimming along in the usual way, with the sky above and the ground beneath, and then suddenly reverse its whole perspective, so that the bright surface becomes its floor and it is gazing upwards into the murky depths. The clues it uses for judging distance, like the angle of shadows, are all subtly altered (like the experience of a tourist having to drive on the 'wrong' side of the road), and there must be other, more drastic, changes in the way it perceives the world. For instance, its sense of buoyancy must also go into reverse (which, in human terms, would be like gravity starting to push us upwards, off the ground, instead of holding us down!).

But none of this bothers the catfish. Some change sides from day to day, others stay the same way for most of their lives, but at any given moment about half the population is up, and half is down. This produces a problem in traffic control, but these fish actually seem to enjoy colliding with each other. They also seem to find such clashes sexually stimulating, because an 'up' fish nearly always chooses a 'down' fish as its mate.

Their courtship consists of a ritual head-banging, in which the male and female swim straight at each other and collide head-on, repeating the process over and over, at half-minute intervals, until the female is sufficiently concussed to lay her eggs, and the male is stunned into fertilizing them.

This curious lifestyle is so deeply embedded in their instincts that they have developed a strange genetic defect. Appropriately enough in their mirror-image world, they have a tendency to produce Siamese twins, and one hardly need add that the young are born as a perfect reflection of each other, joined at the stomach, one looking upwards and the other down.

Venom

Animals of many kinds produce venom, both as a means of attack or defence and to aid digestion. Venomous mammals include several species of shrews and the duck-billed platypus (see 'duck-mole') whose sharp, inch-long spurs on its hind legs are connected to venom glands in the thigh. It is recorded that a zoo warden spurred by a platypus fell to the ground in intense pain, his hand and arm became swollen, and it took several months for the poison to be fully eliminated from his system.

Stonefish are warty, covered with slime, and have thirteen poisonous spines down their backs. Humans who step on them suffer extreme agony, with legs swelling up to elephantine proportions, and fingers and toes turning black and finally dropping off.

Stingrays cause more injuries to humans each year than all other species of fish combined. Estimates for the USA alone range from 750–1,500 victims per year.

The most venomous creature in the oceans, however, is the blue-ringed octopus (*Octopus maculosus*), which lives in the surf and shallows of Australia. The slightest graze of its beak will kill a human within minutes.

Many species of frogs and toads secrete poisons from their skin. Several European toads secrete bufotalin and bufogin which, like digitalis, slow the heart and act on the central nervous system. But it is the tropical frogs that are most venomous of all. The kokoa frog of Columbia secretes batrachotoxin, which can cause paralysis, convulsions and death in humans. The Indians of the region claim that each 1½-inch-long frog can supply enough venom to make fifty lethal darts, which they use to paralyse prey such as birds and monkeys.

Another tiny green frog which lives in Panama is reported to exude a potent nerve and respiratory toxin – but only after it has been roasted over a slow fire.

The best known venomous insect is the black widow spider, whose venom has been shown experimentally (on rats) to be fifteen times more potent than that of a rattlesnake. Less well known are the three thousand species of assassin bugs, whose name and lifestyle are based on the speed and ferocity with which they grab and poison their victims.

As with other carnivorous insects, the assassins digest their meal externally before eating it. They have a powerful, hollow beak with which they first puncture their prey, then inject a toxic saliva that works on the victim's nerves and muscles. The saliva goes on to break down the flesh into its constituent amino-acids, which the assassin sucks up through its beak and into its stomach.

The speed of this digestive venom is fast. In a caterpillar, for instance, which is over four hundred times the assassin's weight, all signs of life terminate within 10 seconds. When it is lucky enough to find such a large prey, the assassin will feed off it for days or weeks, often doubling its own weight.

Snake venom is also a modified form of saliva which acts first as a killing and digestive substance, and only secondly as a means of defence. Chemicals in the venom immediately begin to decompose the victim, which is why some snakes inject still more venom even after the prey is dead, and others, such as vipers, leave the prey, immediately after poisoning it and then track it down later. It has been estimated that the venom of the jaracucu, a South American lance-head snake, allows it to digest in 4–5 days what would otherwise require 12–14 days.

Injecting the prey with venom thus begins the process of digestion before the snake has even swallowed the meal. It is the reverse of the human practice of putting preservatives into food, and can even be said to have a similar function to cooking – which helps prepare food for our digestion. So essential is the snake's venom that many poisonous species cannot survive if surgically deprived of it.

In mambas the venom is white; in rattlesnakes and cobras it is yellow. Most snakes use only a part of the venom stored in their venom glands each time they strike. The poison contains either nerve toxins (e.g. cobras and sea snakes) which cause death by respiratory arrest; or blood toxins (vipers and pit vipers) which destroy red corpuscles or cause the blood to coagulate.

If the fer-de-lance of Central America strikes a large blood vessel, a person's entire blood supply will coagulate within twenty minutes. Symptoms of a viper bite have been described as: 'Prominent local irritation and symptoms of severe blood poisoning, with burning pain, inflamed swellings, pronounced discoloration, sudden drop in blood pressure, internal bleeding, degeneration of the tissues, and the formation of an abscess. Death ensues because the heart stops.' The few snakes whose venom is both neurotoxic and hemotoxic are amongst the deadliest in the world.

There are some snakes, including the banded krait of Indochina and certain sea snakes, which are deadly at night and docile by day. The reasons for this are still a mystery. Children often play with these snakes and suffer no harm. The herpetologist R. Mell has written of the Indian krait, *Bungarus fasciatus*: 'During the day one can hit it, torture it, stick it, beat it on its head, and even nail it to a board, and still the krait remains phlegmatic even to the point of being killed; to my knowledge no one has ever managed to get a sexually mature *Bungarus* to bite during the day.' After dusk, of course, it's a very different matter.

The fangs of most venomous snakes are backward-pointing and equipped with grooves down which the poison is channelled into the victim. In vipers and pit vipers, the most highly evolved snakes, the venom runs down a tube inside the fang, so that the action is just like that of a hypodermic needle. These snakes are also distinguished by having hinged upper jaw-bones, so that the fangs attached to them can be rotated through 90 degrees. When the snake's mouth is closed, the fangs lie back and are covered by a fold in the mucous membrane; when the mouth is opened, a kind of spring action causes the fangs to jut forward, ready to bite.

Snake fangs are subject to a lot of use, and are worn out rapidly, but venomous snakes have up to six replacements continually growing on each jaw behind the functioning ones, like the cartridge clip of a pistol. When a functioning fang is worn out, the snake swallows it rather than spitting it out, and it can later be found in the creature's faeces. Most venomous snakes replace their fangs every few weeks.

Finally, there is one extraordinary case in the animal republic where creatures not only eat venomous prey without suffering any harm but then go on to use the prey's venom for their own defence. They are certain species of small, shell-less snails or *nudibranchs* who thrive on a diet of poisonous sea anemones. These anemones are equipped with thousands of stinging organs, known as nematocysts, which are quite potent enough to injure humans. The anemone fires off nematocysts as soon as it is attacked, but the sea snail is unaffected by them and proceeds to swallow the anemone. While digesting it, the remaining, unfired nematocysts are somehow separated out and passed through the snail's tissues to organs on its exterior. There they perform the same function for the snail as they did for the anemone.

There are two species of these nudibranchs, *Glaucus atlanticus* and *Glaucilla marginata*, which can even selectively retain only the especially potent nematocysts of one kind of anemone, ignoring those of others.

Vestigial Organs

The atrophied remains of organs that are no longer used – such as the wings of flightless birds or the minute teeth of baleen whales which never emerge from their gums – can provide interesting evidence of a creature's ancestry.

Snakes such as the python and the boa constrictor bear traces in their skeleton of the hip-girdle and hind limb bones which were fully developed in their lizard-like ancestors 70 million years before.

The egg-cells of marsupial mammals like the kangaroos still contain vestigial traces of yolk, albumen and shell membrane, even though these animals gave up laying eggs some 100 million years ago; and marsupial embryos still have rudiments of the egg-tooth used by their ancestors to break out of their shells.

In most cases vestigial organs prove no handicap to an animal. In some instances they have evolved to fill a new function. The hind wings of flies, for instance, now serve as gyroscopic organs, while the feeding organ of primitive vertebrates has been transformed into the thyroid gland.

One of the most remarkable examples is found in the jaw-bones of very early marine creatures, which can be traced through the first land animals, the reptiles, and our own ancestral mammals, right down to us, where they now provide the structure of our inner ear.

The Vogue for Vicuña

The vicuna was regarded as a god by the Incas, a profitable investment in the commodities market by Spanish businessmen, and a status symbol by Chicago gangsters – and its fortunes have waxed and waned over the years as it has been variously worshipped, ignored, and hunted to the verge of extinction.

It had good luck to begin with, because the Incas of the Andes were one of the most advanced civilizations there has ever been in terms of game conservation and management of the environment. They recognized the value of their mountain forests, and protected every wooded valley by law. They built extensive irrigation systems and terraced their cultivated hillsides to prevent erosion. They cropped fur-bearing animals selectively, so that populations were never endangered. But it was in their treatment of the vicuña that their conservationist attitudes could be seen most clearly.

The vicuña is a small, tawny-coated relative of the llama, with silky white hair growing around its neck. Its wool is light-weight yet incomparably soft, and has been shorn and worn by man since 5000 BC. The Incas considered the vicuña sacred – daughter of Pachamama, goddess of fertility. Only the Virgins of the Sun were allowed to weave its fleece, and only members of the Inca royal family could wear it. Killing a vicuña carried the death penalty.

ELIZABETH GOSS

Our knowledge of the Incas' attitude towards the vicuña comes from *The Royal Commentaries* by Garcilesco de la Vega (1529–1616), the son of an Inca princess and a Spanish conquistador. The *Commentaries* described how Inca hunts were strictly organized.

'When the Lord-Inca decreed that a *chaco*, or royal hunt, should take place,' summarized Guy Mountfort in *Back From The Brink*, 'tens of thousands of beaters surrounded the chosen area and in the course of a week or more all the animals were driven slowly to the centre, where the deer and other species required for food were speared or clubbed and their meat dried or distributed. Vicuña, however, were never killed, but captured with nets; after being carefully shorn of their wool, they were released unharmed. In order that wildlife should maintain its numbers by undisturbed breeding and to give vicuñas time to grow fresh wool, hunting sites were rotated on a four-year basis. Had the Incas themselves not been exterminated completely by the *conquistadores* in the eighteenth century, we would not have found ourselves, at this late stage, having to learn how best to look after wild life.'

Ignoring Inca wisdom, the Spaniards proceeded to kill some 80,000 vicuñas a year, until the species retreated to the relatively inaccessible high Andes. There they were left more or less in peace until the 1920s, when the wearing of fur coats became fashionable. For the rich it meant mink and silver fox, for college students it meant racoon skins, but the real status symbol of success, especially to the bootleg barons and mobsters, was a $1,000 full-length vicuña overcoat.

This style soon spread to Europe, the demand increased, and the slaughter began again. Between 1950 and 1970 some 400,000 vicuñas were killed, until only an estimated 10,700 were left in Bolivia, Chile and Peru. Over the next few years, the export of vicuña wool was banned, and reserves were set up and guarded against poachers who, in 1976, could make £450 per square metre of vicuña wool.

However, the efforts of the conservationists eventually paid off, and by 1977 the population was estimated to have grown to almost 50,000 animals.

Vision

Like most of the human anatomy, our eyes are the result of a slow evolutionary compromise. On the whole, they provide us with a well-balanced, stereoscopic system which can focus on an object in great detail – but any compromise has its limitations. We cannot compete, for instance, with the telescopic resolution of a hawk, whose eyesight is equivalent to looking through a pair of ×8 binoculars. We have a comparatively narrow field of view, a slow reaction time, and we can only detect 'visible' light (i.e. wavelengths between 0.4 and 0.7 nanometers), which is less than half the spectrum available to other animals.

But the system is suited to our needs, so we tend to forget the limitations. We are so used to the minor drawbacks (that, for instance, your point of focus is being jerked along this line by saccadic eye-movements to give it time to take in the shape of the words, or that there are two blank 'holes' in the text corresponding to the blind spots on your retinas) that we are unaware of them. We just take it for granted that we are looking out, through a kind of window, at the shapes and colours of the 'real' world.

Other animals see things differently, however, and their perception of the world can be so alien to ours that it is difficult to imagine. For instance, what do you 'look' at when you can see in every direction simultaneously? How could you describe the 'colour' of ultra-violet? Or understand what it means to see things 'faster'? These are just some of the difficulties in comparing our visual system with that of insects.

The Ultra-Violet World

The most obvious difference we would notice, if we could see the world through the eyes of insects, would probably be their ability to detect ultra-violet light. This is now known to be common to many species, including bees and butterflies. It gives them an entirely different view of the world, especially with regard to flowers.

'For us,' wrote Karl von Frisch in *The Dancing Bees*, 'the yellow blooms of treacle-mustard, rape and charlock are hardly distinguishable in colour and shape; but the bees know better. To them only the treacle-mustard is yellow. The rape blossoms reflect a little ultra-violet light as well, which gives them a slightly purple tint. The petals of charlock reflect a lot of ultra-violet, so charlock looks deep crimson to the eyes of a bee, which can easily distinguish between the three species. Anyone who could look at the world through a bee's eyes would be surprised to discover more than twice as many kinds of bloom as our ultra-violet-blind eye can see, with ornaments never registered before.'

Do insects use the same colour code as us and, as Frisch suggests, simply stretch it out to include higher frequencies? Or do they see a different colour altogether? Unfortunately, we will never know, because, although we can photograph the patterns in ultra-violet, we can only record the results in black-and-white (or the colours we already know).

The Flicker Factor

Dragonflies have the best vision in the insect kingdom. Each of their large compound eyes has 10,000–30,000 facets (or *ommatidia*) which together cover most of the creature's face. Because they can move their heads sideways 180 degrees, upwards 70 degrees and downwards by 40 degrees, they are able to see in every direction. They can perceive movements 40 yards away and, since their eyes are sensitive to every photon of available light, they can hunt at night.

One might think that 30,000 views of the world would be confusing, but that is not how a compound eye works. Instead of focusing an image on the retina, each of the omnatidia has a direct connection to the brain, where the image is analysed and put together. Whatever the insect 'sees', it has a single, coherent picture of its surroundings.

Because the information is processed along many parallel channels, the insect is aware of its entire visual world at every moment, unlike vertebrate animals who have to build up the picture, a bit at a time, by moving their head and eyes.

The compound eye is especially sensitive to movement, which is why insects can respond so rapidly by taking off or changing direction in flight. The fastest movement the human eye can detect is about 1/24th second. Films, for instance, are run through a projector at 24 frames a second to give the illusion of movement, but when they are slowed down to, say, 16 frames a second (like the old silent movies), our 'continuity of vision' breaks down and they start to flicker.

It has recently been discovered that the flicker factor of insects is much higher, and even if it was run at twice the speed, a film would look like a series of still photographs with long pauses between.

The compound eye can detect movements of hundreds, or thousandths, of a second. A fly buzzing around a light bulb flies from darkness into light and back 50 to 60 times a second, as the AC current reverses. It can track the spot of light on a TV screen – or watch the flight of a bullet.

This high-speed vision is essential to insects' survival, because they inhabit such a hostile world. At that size scale, the air is so dense it feels like fluid, and the delicate precision of their flight is (from their point of view) a clumsy and exhausting struggle to remain airborne. The flicker factor at least enables them to slow the environment down, so they can respond to the air currents and avoid the sluggish movements of creatures like ourselves.

Triple Vision

Compound eyes are not unique to insects. Fish, crustaceans and many other marine organisms have evolved their own version of them. Their sensitivity to dim light is particularly useful to deep-sea fish, some of whom have as many as five layers of receptor cells to back them up (compared with the single layer in human eyes). Even surface species, like anableps, have a bifocal arrangement which enables them to look above and below water at the same time.

One of the strangest of these multi-lens systems is that of the Atlantic flying fish, whose eyes are constructed like a three-sided pyramid. Each lens has a slightly concave surface, and the fish is able to look forward and upwards through one facet, backwards through another, and downwards through the third, giving it an undistorted view in any combination of elements. It also explains how this fish, which inhabits the seaweed-clogged Sargasso Sea, can leap from the water and, during the few seconds it is in the air, select a precise re-entry point.

Eyeballs and Eyewash

The disadvantages of a compound eye soon became apparent when it was scaled up in size. As larger animals evolved, the distance between the eye and the brain increased, and the multiple nerve channels became too complex. At the same time, the number of receptor cells was limited by how many omnatidia they could fit on the surface, so they had to make a choice between improving the definition or improving the lenses.

As many species began to discover, with a hollow eyeball they could do both.

It allowed for a single, large, flexible lens, which could be focused by muscular control, while the retina could be packed with many more receptors to improve the definition. It reduced the number of connections, and allowed the image to be processed before it reached the brain, so that extraneous information could be discarded and the animal could concentrate on the important details. The eyeball had so many advantages over the compound eye that it was eventually adopted, in much the same form, by all the higher animals.

The basic principles were evolved by marine species, but the first animals on dry land found it worked just as well in air – though it took them some time to develop a suitable lid to protect and clean it. It sounds absurd that animals could suffer from dirty eyeballs; but it was a very real problem for intermediate species, like geckos and chameleons, whose eyelids are fused together to form a transparent 'contact lens'. They cannot clean them in the usual way, by blinking, so when a gecko has finished a meal of insects, and cleans its face with its tongue, it has to carefully lick its 'glasses' at the same time.

Movable eyeballs proved to be one of the most versatile organs: there are eyes on stalks, eyes that swivel independently in different directions, and even some that migrate around the creature's body, like those of flat fish. In fact, their only drawback is that they are limited to certain wave-lengths of light. Very long wave-lengths, for instance, cannot be focused through the internal fluid – but the species for whom this kind of radiation is important, have developed another, quite different, kind of 'eye'.

Heat Vision

In the same way that insects have specialized in ultra-high frequencies, there are certain snakes which can detect very *low* frequency radiation, like heat.

The pit viper, for instance, is a species of rattlesnake which has two small dimples, or pits, at either side of its head, between nostril and eye. The exact purpose of these organs remained a mystery until 1952, when an American neurophysiologist, Professor T. H. Bullock, discovered that they were the snake's heat-sensors.

He found that the thick skin lining the pits, was packed with sensory cells similar to those in human skin which enable us to feel warmth. However, we only have about three cells per square centimetre, in our most sensitive areas, whereas the rattlesnake has 150,000 cells in an equivalent area of its pit organs.

This fantastic array of thermal sensors allows the snake to 'see' the frequencies known as *near* infra-red. It can detect differences of temperature of only a few tenths of a degree Centigrade – which could mean the difference between a warm stone and a very still rabbit – and the pit organ is shaped like a reflector which allows it to determine the shape and size of an object by moving its head.

It is not surprising that thermovision was evolved by snakes, which were the only reptiles to become fully adapted to life underground. It enables the pit viper to hunt its prey in total darkness, even when there is no sound or scent, and the animal is motionless. And it is just as useful above ground, because it allows the snake to distinguish creatures like lizards and salamanders which can change their shape and colour to camouflage themselves.

The Volcano Rabbit

No one could describe the rabbit as a noisy animal. Their fictional counterparts chatter away in the pages of Beatrix Potter, Lewis Carroll and *Watership Down*, but in real life, like most small mammals, they find it safer to keep quiet. If one tries to recall the cry of a rabbit (or any other noise they make, apart from a soft sniffling), one's mind goes blank.

However, there is one eccentric species with a garrulous disposition and a very definite voice of its own. It is called the volcano rabbit (*Romerolagus diazi*) and it only exists in one place in the world – a twenty-mile stretch of hillside in the Valley of Mexico, just east of Mexico City. Its English name derives from the volcanic soil of the region, which also supports the variety of aromatic mint, which is its favourite food.

The volcano rabbit is a curious creature with very short legs and no tail, but its most distinctive feature is a high-pitched querulous voice, which it uses to keep in touch with the other rabbits. They are very sociable animals, and on a still day they can be heard calling to each other from the entrance of their burrows in the coarse zacaton grass.

Unfortunately their numbers are dwindling because the Mexicans, who call them *teporingos*, often drive out from the city at weekends to shoot them for sport.

The Walrus

If the sea is not roo rough, the walrus can sleep vertically in the water, keeping itself afloat by inflating air sacs under its throat like life-vests.

The great ivory tusks of the males, which can grow up to three feet, once earned them the name of whale-elephants, and one early chronicler described them as 'monstrous swine, which by means of their teeth climb to the top of cliffs as up a ladder and then roll from the summit down to the sea again.' The Norsemen called them *hvalross* or whale-horses, but their Latin name, *odobenidae*, 'those who walk by their teeth', is rather more accurate, because they use their tusks to haul themselves over the ice and to rake furrows in the sea-bed to dig up the shellfish and seaweed they feed on.

Their tusks also make fearsome weapons of defence. In fact the walrus bears the same relationship to seals and sealions as the prehistoric sabre-toothed tiger did to wild-cats and bears. Even the polar bear, which will attack almost anything, is reluctant to take on an adult male walrus, whose only natural enemy appears to be the killer whale. In 1936 a panic-stricken herd of walruses were driven ashore on St Lawrence Island by a group of killer whales, and they piled on to the beach in such numbers that more than two hundred of them were crushed to death or suffocated.

They are normally peaceful and extremely curious creatures, and often approach outboard skiffs and other low-slung craft, hooking their tusks over the gunwale to examine the boat and its crew. But usually they become stuck and the crew has to unhook them.

Walruses live in family herds of cows, calves and young bulls, numbering up to a hundred individuals per family. The mature bulls, who average 10–11 feet (3–3.5m) in length and weigh 1,500–2,000 lb, form a separate herd and join up with their families only during the spring breeding season. Gestation lasts a year, and the cow usually gives birth to a single pup about 4 feet (1.25m) long and weighing 100 lb. These giant deliveries take place on the eternal ice-floe, and the pups usually ride around on their mothers' backs until they learn to fend for themselves.

The animals have been hunted by Eskimos for centuries to supply their needs for food, oil, clothing and sled harness (their hide was used to make the strongest known form of rope before the invention of artificial fibres). However, such annual killings had little effect on the numbers of the herds until the European hunters began to shoot them as a substitute for whales in the nineteenth century.

Walruses greatly enjoy a communal lifestyle, huddling and piling on top of each other on ice-floes in order to conserve warmth and energy – but this makes them an easy target. During the Alaskan gold rush, in the early years of this century, prospectors and gamblers shot them by the thousands from the decks of steamers. The skippers even claimed this action was necessary to clear a path through the dense swimming herds.

If a walrus is shot before it has accumulated its winter coat of up to 900 lb of blubber, it sinks like a stone – so the slaughter was not only wilful, but pointless.

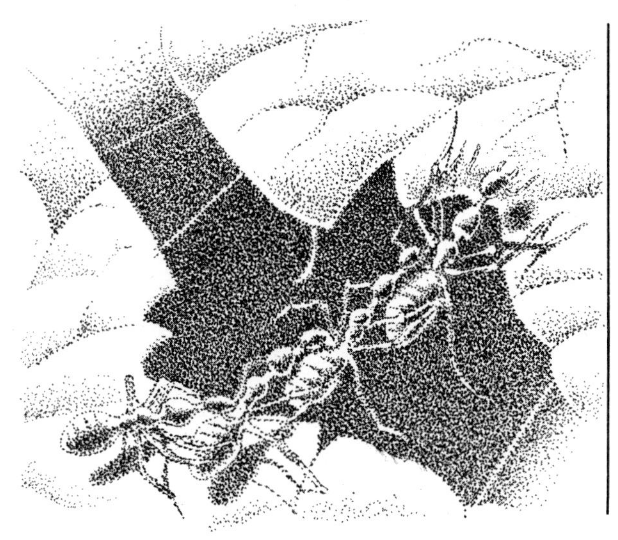

The insects maintain their aerial condominium very efficiently, with a specialized crew of workers and soldiers to take charge of any emergency. If the nest is torn or damaged, they rush to the scene and – having cleared civilians out of the danger area – try to pull the edges together. If the gap is too wide for a single insect, they form a chain, up to five or six long – each ant holding on to the one in front with its mandibles. It may take hours of struggling to close the gap, but the edges need to be properly aligned before the back-up team can start repairs.

This consists of a column of worker ants carrying the tiny larvae on their heads. They move into position with well-drilled precision, biting neat holes through the leaf and passing the larvae back and forth between them, like little shuttles spinning their own thread, until the edges are laced together.

TERRY OAKES

Weavers and Tailors

Ants usually construct elaborate underground colonies, but there is one species, the tailor ant (*Oecophylla smaragdina*), which manages to combine the technique of spiders, the habits of birds, and some extraordinary needle-work – and literally *sew* their nests into trees.

They are able to do this because the tailor ant larvae secrete a silken thread from special glands, like the spinerets of a spider. The adults use the thread to sew the edges of leaves together, with a simple but effective buttonhole stitch, to form the shell of the structure, and attach this to a suitable branch. They then fit it out with internal partitions and chambers until the nest resembles a multi-storey apartment block – and the colony moves in.

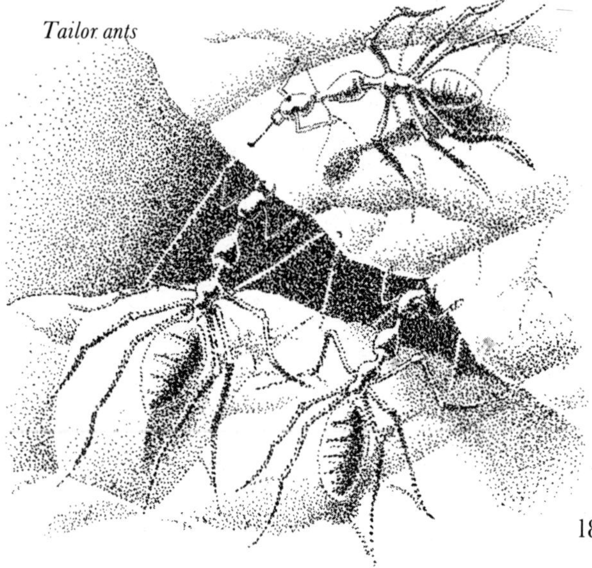

Tailor ants

A quelea weaver bird lays down the structure of its spherical nest

From the ants' point of view, leaves are as strong as sheet steel, but they are rather too weak to support the weight of a bird. Some of the smaller species of bird do stitch their nests together, but most find it safer to rely on a woven structure of some kind, and the most sophisticated exponents of this technique are the African weaver birds.

The village weaver bird (*Ploceus cucullatus*), for instance, has developed a meticulous over-and-under weave of strips torn from palm leaves, which produces some of the most elegant nests in the world. And in terms of mass-production it is difficult to beat *Philetairus socius*, the species which uses an interlocking thatch of twigs to build huge conglomerations of nests in the thorn trees of South West Africa. These sociable colonies can be up to 25

'Sociable' weaver birds

feet across, and contain sixty or more sleeping chambers, each with its own entrance in the nest roof, and occupied by as many as five birds during the winter.

The construction work is full-time occupation for the males, who practise for a year or more on 'dummy' nests before they are allowed to start on the real thing. The idca, as with the bower bird, is for the male to attract a female to share the nest with him and, as usual, she is extremely fussy – though it is the strength of the nest, rather than its colour or design, which interests her in this case. However, the male is now so obsessed with nest-building that he cannot wait to get on with the next one, and he abandons the female as soon as they have mated, leaving her to raise the brood alone.

The Weevil Memorial

Only two civic memorials have ever been erected in honour of an insect – as far as we know. One is the statue of a monarch butterfly in the Californian town of Pacific Grove – the butterfly whose annual migrations have made it a symbol of the area, and which is welcomed by the farming community because it helps to keep down the deadly milkweed plant.

The other is dedicated to one of our worst enemies, a creature that ranks alongside the mosquito and tsetse fly as one of the most virulent and damaging insects in the world. In the town of Enterprise, Alabama, stands a female statue in classical robes holding aloft a silver bowl on which is perched a huge black boll-weevil!

This malignant species originally crossed the Rio Grande from Mexico in 1892, and gradually spread from state to state, laying waste the cotton fields of the deep South. It reproduced at a rate of ten generations a year, and there seemed no way of stopping it. In 1918 and 1919 it destroyed the entire cotton crop of Alabama and many neighbouring states.

The disaster was on such a scale that it changed the whole pattern of agriculture in the area – but it proved to be a blessing in disguise. The boll-weevil still costs the US cotton industry $2 million a year, but in the following season many farmers in Alabama and Georgia abandoned cotton, and planted peanuts instead. The new cash crop was so successful that it restored the economy of the area, and Enterprise now proudly claims it is the Peanut Capital of the world.

The boll-weevil (*Anthonomus grandis*) is the only one of its malignant family to lead to any good. Its other relatives, all 40,000 species of them, are among the oldest and most indestructible of human pests.

The Anglo-Saxon word *wifel*, from which weevil is derived, refers to the most notorious of all, the grain weevil (*Sitophilus granarius*) which has infested stores of grain since prehistoric times. In a curious way, people came to accept them as an inevitable part of life, unpleasant but unavoidable.

In the days of the great sailing ships, weevils were a standard ingredient of the food on long voyages, because they thrived on hard-tack. Some sailors would snap the hard biscuits open and rap them on the table to dislodge the bugs. Others ate them with the weevils inside, either through laziness or the belief that a little extra protein would improve the diet.

STEWART BODEK

XYZ

Z is for Life

'In the days when zoomancy and zoolatry were common, the zoic anthologies had a strongly zoophobic or zootheistic bias. But the zeal of zoologists, zoographers, and the zoonomy and zoometry of zootomistists has changed all that. We now recognize that each of us, every individual of every species – and the whole zeotrope itself – began as a single zooblast. So our definitions are wider and the alphabetical zootaxy of this zoographia runs from the simplest zoochronic zoobiotics to the largest zoophagic zoons, including ourselves, the human zoons.'

The eskimos are supposed to have a million and a half different words for snow and, by the same token, we seem to have an obsession with our relationships to animals. If you turn to the back pages of any large dictionary, somewhere between zonda (a dry wind in the Andes) and zoom (a loud, deep, persistent buzzing) you will find column after column of close-set type dealing with zoo-words. Some have a lunatic charm (zoothapsis, for some reason means premature burial) and most are superfluous, but they are all based on the simple Greek word for an animal, *zoion*. This, in turn, is based on the even simpler word *zoe*, which means life. They knew what they were talking about.

The commonest of all zoo-words is zoo itself. Unlike the others, it is not a scientific term which someone sat down and invented. It was a piece of slang which gradually came into use as a healthy reaction to all this polysyllabic jargon. How and when it happened is part of the story of zoos themselves.

Zoos

The idea of collecting wild animals can be traced back to the beginning of what we call 'history', when 20,000 years of tribal society gave way to modern 'civilization', and hunting became a hobby rather than a matter of life and death.

The ancient kings of Persia set aside areas of wilderness for their sport and called them paradises, in the same way that the Norman kings of England enclosed their private hunting parks and chases. They also began to collect more exotic species of creatures, which usually arrived as gifts from foreign heads of state or as trophies of war. These were regarded as valuable status symbols and were often put on show in special enclosures within their palaces.

King Shalmanazar II is recorded as accepting tributes of dromedaries, buffaloes, elephants and apes; and the Egyptian queen Hatshetsup was particularly proud of her collection of monkeys, leopards and giraffes.

The first person to regard them as something more than exotic toys was Alexander the Great, who collected many rare species on his campaigns, urged his tutor, Aristotle, to make a careful study of them and was later responsible for founding a large zoo at the library of Alexandria. The early Chinese princes adopted a similar approach by establishing 'parks of intelligence', where scholars were encouraged to draw the animals, observe their habits and (being Chinese) write poems about them.

The first major change of attitude came with the Romans, who began to import animals wholesale from all over their empire, and breed them for their games. This international trade in wildlife, which continues to the present day, not only put a commercial price on their heads but launched them on their long career in showbusiness.

The first public menageries seem to have originated in England. Ever since William the Conqueror had been given a bear as a house-warming present by his son William, the English royalty had been enthusiastic collectors. But they became increasingly expensive to maintain, and Henry III eventually demanded that the citizens of London should pay for the upkeep of his collection, which by then included such exotic items as a polar bear and the first elephant to cross the Channel (as a gift from Louis IX).

In order to recoup some of the costs, the Sheriff of London had a 20 by 40 foot elephant-house constructed, and charged visitors a fee to see it. The idea soon caught on, and animal exhibitions became so popular that a royal menagerie was later built in the Tower of London, which was lined with 12-foot-high cages of lions, and featured special attractions such as bear baiting.

The same thing was happening throughout Europe. Popes, princes, the Borgias, the Sforzas, the Medici and the kings of Portugal all had menageries. One of the Medici, Cardinal Ippolito, even had a human zoo full of slaves from Africa and India.

The French lead the way in this. King Louis XI, for instance, had been responsible for introducing canaries to Europe, and it was Louis XIV who raised the status of the animals from sideshow freaks to things of beauty in their own right, which deserved to be displayed in spacious and elegant surroundings.

King Louis had owned his own collection as a child (he had ridden his first camel at the age of five) and retained a deep love of animals all his life. He built his first zoo at Vincennes, which was later moved to a vast complex at Versailles, where the animals were surrounded by gardens full of rare plants and trees – the first example of what we would now call 'zoological gardens'. To be more precise, this was the first example in Europe, because a subtle and sophisticated civilization on the other side of the world was already two centuries ahead of us.

On an autumn day in 1519, a group of exhausted Spanish mercenaries reached the Emperor Montezuma's headquarters at Lake Tezoco in the highlands of Anahuac – and stared in wonder at the vast island city of Tenochtitlan. When they entered the capital and began to explore its temples and palaces, they came across something quite extraordinary.

'Set amid the ancient trees at the back of the Emperor's palace,' writes Herman Dembeck in *Animals and Man*, 'was an animal park which from our modern viewpoint fully deserves to be called a "zoo". They saw jaguars and pumas behind bronze bars in sturdy pens. There were ant bears and curious monkeys, sloths and armadillos. In the bird houses fluttered birds more brilliant and varied than anything in Europe had to show; indeed, not even on the island of Cuba had the Spaniards seen anything like them.

'They looked down into six sunken basins, the Emperor's aquaria, and saw fish of incredible beauty and colour. Shudders went down their spines at the sight of the poisonous snakes, striated with green, red and blue, while the giant serpents slithering in sunken terraria, the boas and anacondas of the country, must have seemed to them creatures of fable. The size of the animal park is indicated by the fact that hundreds of attendants were employed just to take care of the waterfowl, which were distributed among ten ponds. There were specially trained nurses for sick animals. Other attendants had no other task but to gather up the feathers cast by birds; they were used for making ornamental robes. Hordes of workmen cared for the predators and the fish. Several hundred turkeys a day were used solely for feeding the raptorial birds.

'There was even a buffalo kept in an enclosure, a tantalizing fact in the history of pre-Columbian civilizations. The animal had a heavy mane of shaggy hair round its head, and the Spaniards were told that it came from "the land toward night", that is, from the north, far beyond the borders of Montezuma's empire . . .'

Only one thing marred this magnificent spectacle, the fact that alongside the animals was the forerunner of the freak-shows which were to be so common in Europe – a collection of human curiosities: bearded women, dwarfs, and deformities of every kind, who had their food thrown to them in their cages as if they, too, were wild animals.

Up till now, animals had been regarded as pets, trophies, garden decorations, status symbols and sideshow freaks, but no one had yet followed the advice of Alexander the Great, and studied them for their own sake. In fact, it was not until the nineteenth century that zoology was recognized as a serious science, and civic authorities began to think of zoos as an educational facility as well as an entertainment.

The first municipal menagerie was the Blau-Jan (Blue John) in Amsterdam, but the first truly modern establishment was the famous Zoological Gardens in Regent's Park, set up under the charter of the Royal Zoological Society in 1829. They were so popular they almost immediately became known as the 'London Zoo'. The word had not been used before, but the affectionate shortening was instantly adopted. It appeared on posters and in music-hall songs and, by common consent, officially entered the English language in the 1847 edition of the Oxford English Dictionary.

The Zoo of the Future

With a few variations, all modern zoos follow the same pattern, but their function has changed dramatically in recent years. Instead of being merely exhibitions of wildlife, they have become refuges. Species of wild animals are disappearing so rapidly that there is a desperate battle now to preserve what few remain. The traditional zoos are at a disadvantage here, because although they can preserve a particular species, without its natural habitat it is no more than another domestic animal.

On the other hand, it is no use isolating a piece of countryside, building a wall around it and leaving nature to its own devices. When game reserves like this were first tried in Africa, the illegal hunting and poaching actually increased. And what happens if there is a sudden population explosion, or an outbreak of disease? Do we stand by and watch the animals die? And if we intervene, to what extent?

Whether we like it or not, wild animals are now *our* responsibility, and they can only survive under our control. Here are three examples of how a 'zoo' of the future might approach this whole problem.

The Artificial Wilderness

The wildlife in America has increased dramatically since the introduction of game laws in the 1930s. The population of white-tailed deer, for instance, has risen from half a million at the turn of the century to sixteen million now. There are now twenty-four times as many elks as in 1907, and seven times as many antelopes. There are even some ten thousand buffalo. But the success of these game reserves shows that the 'natural' wilderness can only be preserved by ruthless management and control.

'Game control in America,' writes Don Atyeo in his book *Blood and Guts*, 'has developed into a highly technological and sophisticated science. Populations are checked and monitored, licensing is strict, "harvests" are controlled. Limits for ducks and geese are determined by satellite photographs. Large game is fitted with radio-controlled collars to keep track of its movements. The vast reservoir of game is watched over by more than 25,000 state and federal "wildlife conservation" workers and supported by a budget of more than half a billion dollars.'

The Hunting Park

Another solution may be a return to the private hunting parks of the ancient kings and princes. Wealth and status are still the main criteria, but today's version takes the form of the exotic game ranch. There are now about two hundred of these elite killing grounds, organized on a no-game no-pay basis, throughout the USA, and they account for roughly 10 per cent of the country's hunting.

Wayne Preston, the manager of one of these ranches, sells shots at Texan buffalo for $7,000 each, including air travel, wining and dining, accommodation and trophy mounting. You, literally, pay your money and take your choice. The catalogue of his India Creek Ranch offers: Corsican Ram – $250; Mouflon Ram – $300; Sika Buck – $4,000; Blackbuck Antelope – $500; Aoudad Sheep – $750; and a Russian Boar for $400.

This quest for the exotic means that there are now more blackbuck antelope in Texas than on the entire Indian subcontinent, where they originated!

The Animal Archive

If the worst comes to the worst, and all the wild species are either extinct or domesticated, it would still be possible to preserve their genetic code. It would be more like a library than a zoo, an archive where the blueprint of any animal could be stored, so that future generations could bring it to life again by genetic engineering.

This is not so far-fetched as it sounds. Gene banks are already being established at universities around the world. For instance, Dr T. C. Hsu, a cell biologist at the M. D. Anderson Hospital in Houston, Texas, has already built up a 300-animal 'cell zoo' in his laboratory.

'I have everything from aardvark to zebra,' Hsu claims, 'in the form of cells from the animals which are stored in a special liquid-nitrogen freezer maintained at a constant temperature of −240°C.'

'At that temperature,' he adds, 'they are neither dead nor alive. You might say they're sleeping for a while.' And one day, in a hundred or a thousand years, when the techniques of cloning are properly developed, the cells may be awakened, and elephants or rhinos, tigers and whales will appear again on a planet that is beginning to forget them.

Zyzzyx – The Last Word

An entomologist who was determined to have the final word in dictionaries and encyclopedias invented the name 'zyzzyx' for a species of wasp he had discovered. It won him an honoured place in crossword puzzles and games of Scrabble, but the joke is unlikely to be repeated, because anyone wishing to name a species now has to apply to a higher authority.

The people who really do have the last word are the members of the International Commission of Zoological Nomenclature, in Zurich. This august body allowed zyzzyx to stand, but decided that enough was enough when another scientist tried to name a group of bugs Peggichisme ('Peggy kiss me').

If zyzzyx is the last creature in our language, the runners-up (or down, depending how you look at it) appear to be the pocket gopher (*Zygogeomys*) and the hammerhead sharks (*Zygaenidae*). But it seems unfair that any one animal should take the final bow, so we have chosen, instead, to present a whole selection of them.

Some have already appeared elsewhere in the book, but these are not a mere list of alphabetical left-overs. Far from being the dregs of the dictionary they form an intriguing zoological collection: a miniature bestiary which includes one of the oldest and one of the most dangerous creatures on earth – and the world's largest crustacean.

Xenarthra: a term meaning 'strangely-jointed ones', applied (rather loosely) to anteaters and sloths. In the case of the latter there is some truth in it because, whereas nearly all mammals, from mice to giraffes, have seven bones in their necks, the three-toed sloth has nine.

Xenogale: a Congolese mongoose, resembling the civet.

Xenopsylla cheopis: the flea which inhabits both rats and human beings and carries the plague bacteria (*Pasturella pestis*) in its saliva. It is the only organism to seriously threaten the survival of the human race. During the Middle Ages it was responsible for the Black Death which killed off a third of the population of Europe.

Xenurus: a species of armadillo with plates on its tail.

Xenusion: one of the oldest multicellular creatures on earth. Fossilized examples of xenusion have been discovered in 500 million-year-old limestone, which are identical to a living animal called the perpatus – a 3-inch-long, worm-like creature with twenty pairs of baggy legs.

Xylopargus: a West Indian hermit crab that lives in hollow cylinders of wood.

Xiphias: the genus of swordfish.

Xiphosura: the King Crab, the largest crustacean in the world. Specimens have been caught off Japan whose spindly legs span more than ten feet (3m).

Xysticus cristatus: the crab spider, known for its curious 'bondage' tactics while mating. In order to prevent the female eating him, the male ties her legs to the ground with silk threads before attempting to have sex.

Yeast: not usually thought of as an 'animal', but in fact a living organism. At the end of the nineteenth century, one species had the distinction of being the first man-made organism to be registered at the US Patents Office.

Yaffingale: the name invented by the poet Tennyson for the green nightingale.

Yak: a long-haired ox, without horns, that has been domesticated in Tibet, where it is milked, ridden and used as a beast of burden. Yak butter is exceptionally rich, and used to sweeten tea. The Tibetans once used the animal as a means of communication by tying knots in the long hair hanging from its belly – in the same way the Incas did with llama fur.

Yapok: a marsupial South American water-opposum.

Yellow: this word appears in many common names, including the bird known as the yite or yellow-hammer (*Emberiza citrinella*) and the species of American hornets (*Vespa crabro*) known as yellow-jackets.

Yeti: the 'abominable snowman'. A possible survivor of the original species of human beings, the Neanderthals. They were shorter and bulkier than Homo Sapiens, but had considerably larger brains. Footprints found in the Himalayas are identical to Neanderthal footprints preserved in a cave at Basua, in Italy, while the climate of central Asia is remarkably similar to the ice-age conditions in which Neanderthals thrived.

Yoldia: a primitive form of bivalve mollusc found in the Pacific.

Zaedyus: a pygmy armadillo, whose name translates as 'the very pleasant one'.

Zagouti: an extremely rare rodent with a prehensile tail, only found in the tops of trees in a few square miles of remote mountains in the north of Haiti.

Zamous: a short-horned West African buffalo.

Zanclus canescens: the kihikihi, or Moorish Idol fish.

Zalopus: the genus of sea-lions.

Zebra: the familiar striped horse of the African plains. There are four recognizable species, including Mountain Zebras, together with a zebra-horse crossbreed known as zebrorses. Contrary to popular opinion, they are black animals with white stripes, not the other way round.

Zeren: a pale goat-like gazelle from the grass lands of Mongolia, which grows an unusual winter coat of long pinkish-fawn hair.

Zho: a lugubrious form of Himalayan cattle, crossbred from yaks.

Zind: an Ethiopian insect like the tetse-fly.

Zirphea crispata: a form of mollusc known as the boring piddock.

Ziphoid: the genus of beaked whales, a group of very rare species in the Pacific, which include cow-fish and Cuvier's whale.

Zokor: a burrowing mole rat of the Asiatic steppes, reported to be the main food of the upland buzzard.

Zopilote: the American turkey-buzzard, or urubu.

Zorille: the African version of the skunk. Although not related to the American animal, it is identical in size, shape, colour and habits – and smells even worse. In the Sudan it is known as 'the father of stinks', and if one of them appears at the site of a kill, even the lions stand aside. However, like skunks, they are beautiful and strangely dignified animals.

Zorro: a South American dog-like fox, with black face markings (hence 'The Mask of Zorro').

Zygaena: the brightly coloured species of Burnet moths.

Zygaenidae: the genus of hammerhead sharks (from the Greek *zygaina*, or shark).

Zygogeomidae: the thirty species of pocket gophers, one of whose curious characteristics is the ability of the females to dissolve their narrow pelvic bones in order to give birth.

Zyzzyx: an entomological, and etymological, curiosity.

I think I could turn and live with animals, they are so self-contained,
I stand and look at them long and long.
They do not sweat and whine about their condition,
They do not lie awake in the dark and weep for their sins,
They do not make me sick discussing their duty to God,
Not one is dissatisfied, not one is demented with the mania of owning things,
Not one kneels to another, nor to his kind that lived thousands of years ago,
Not one is respectable or unhappy over the whole earth.

– Walt Whitman

INDEX